MID-CONTINENT PUBLIC LIBRARY - BTM
15616 E. 24 HWY.
INDEPENDENCE, MO 64050

3 0003 0...

110647793

"Clever plot. ... ...oice with deeper layers that t... ...the whole package. A delight ...

~Rachel Hauck, awa... ...or of

...e Upon a Prince

"If there is such a thing as a perfect story, Melissa Tagg has written it with this first novel. Laugh-out-loud funny, a delightful premise, hunky heroes, surprising plot twists and poignant, heart-tugging moments, all wound together with beautiful writing. *Made to Last* is a keeper that will charm its way onto your shelf, and into your heart."

~Susan May Warren, RITA Award winner
and bestselling author of *Take a Chance on Me*

"*Made to Last* is a fun romantic comedy that will have you turning the pages. Melissa Tagg is a fresh voice to watch."

~Jenny B. Jones, award-winning author
of *Save the Date* and *There You'll Find Me*

"Melissa Tagg has written a fun, fast-paced romance. Her first novel will certainly not be her last."

~Kristin Billerbeck, author of *The Scent of Rain*

"A must for fans of romantic comedy! Melissa Tagg's endearing characters charmed me and their story line captured my imagination. Reading *Made to Last* was like eating a hot fudge brownie sundae with girlfriends. Fun. Delicious. Completely entertaining."

~Becky Wade, author of *My Stubborn Heart*
and *Undeniably Yours*

"Sweet, fun, and faith-filled, Melissa Tagg's *Made to Last* is a story made to delight lovers of romance and behind-the-scenes reality TV. Pull up an armchair and enjoy!"

~Lisa Wingate, national bestselling author
of *Blue Moon Bay*, one of *Booklist*'s Top 10 of 2012

WITHDRAWN FROM THE RECORDS OF THE MID-CONTINENT PUBLIC LIBRARY

"With witty dialogue, lovable characters, and an entertaining plot, Melissa Tagg is sure to become a new favorite among fans of Christian romance. *Made to Last* reminds us all that we are more than the roles we play. At our core, beneath our failures and hang-ups, we are loved and cherished by a faithful God."

~Katie Ganshert, author of *Wildflowers From Winter*
and *Wishing on Willows*

"Readers are going to fall in love with Melissa Tagg's novels! She writes vivid stories filled with true-to-life characters who wrestle with questions about life, faith and romance. Melissa's writing is equal parts laugh-out-loud humor and moments that touch your heart. I can't wait for others to discover this talented new author!"

~Beth K. Vogt, author of *Wish You Were Here*
and *Catch a Falling Star*

"What happens when a harmless lie you didn't intend to tell takes on a life of its own? When you're Miranda Woodruff, star of a home improvement show, you learn how to let go and become who God called you to be because nothing else is left. A great story with life-impacting truth surrounded by romance to make you swoon."

~Cara Putman, award-winning author
of *A Wedding Transpires on Mackinac Island*

"Reading *Made to Last*, Melissa Tagg's debut novel, was like meeting new friends whom I wanted to continue hanging out with long after the book ended. Melissa's fresh voice and ability to craft a well-written story hooked me with the opening line and held my attention to the very end. Her flawed characters, LOL moments and spiritual truth provided a foundation for a stellar debut novel. I even had to dab my teary eyes a couple of times. Melissa Tagg is an author to watch and one whose books I want to fill my shelves."

~Lisa Jordan, award-winning author
of *Lakeside Reunion* and *Lakeside Family*

Made
to
Last

Made to Last

Melissa Tagg

BETHANYHOUSE

a division of Baker Publishing Group
Minneapolis, Minnesota

© 2013 by Melissa Tagg

Published by Bethany House Publishers
11400 Hampshire Avenue South
Bloomington, Minnesota 55438
www.bethanyhouse.com

Bethany House Publishers is a division of
Baker Publishing Group, Grand Rapids, Michigan

Printed in the United States of America

All rights reserved. No part of this publication may be reproduced, stored in a retrieval system, or transmitted in any form or by any means—for example, electronic, photocopy, recording—without the prior written permission of the publisher. The only exception is brief quotations in printed reviews.

Library of Congress Cataloging-in-Publication Data
Tagg, Melissa.
    Made to last / Melissa Tagg.
      pages cm
    Summary: "TV host Miranda Woodruff has built a perfect life for herself onscreen. But everything could fall apart when she falls in love for real"— Provided by publisher.
      ISBN 978-0-7642-1132-4 (pbk.)
      1. Women television personalities—Fiction. 2. Deception—Fiction. 3. Reporters and reporting—Fiction. I. Title.
    PS3620.A343M33 2013
    813'.6—dc23   2013016849

Scripture quotations are from the Holy Bible, New International Version®. NIV®. Copyright © 1973, 1978, 1984, 2011 by Biblica, Inc.™ Used by permission of Zondervan. All rights reserved worldwide. www.zondervan.com

This is a work of fiction. Names, characters, incidents, and dialogues are products of the author's imagination and are not to be construed as real. Any resemblance to actual events or persons, living or dead, is entirely coincidental.

Cover design by Dan Thornberg, Design Source Creative Services

Author represented by MacGregor Literary Group

13   14   15   16   17   18   19   7   6   5   4   3   2   1

To Mom and Dad:
because more than anyone I know,
you've shown me what
"made to last" love and faith look like.
And because I love you.

Chapter 1

On any other day of the year, in the lull of routine, she could almost forget the lie she lived. But today's would-be anniversary made forgetting about as easy as building a house from cotton sheets.

Miranda Woodruff hooked a thumb under her tool belt and stepped onto the outdoor set, squinting against the familiar glint of studio lights. The light crew usually played off the sun when taping outside, but this evening's canopy of low-lying clouds dimmed the valley already hazed over by the smoky cover of the Appalachians.

Mission: Smile. Access her inner Colgate commercial and convince everybody she meant it. Forget the date on the calendar, and while she was at it, pretend this afternoon's lousy interview never happened. Hey, if anybody could fake it—

"Randi! Where've you been?" Across the set, Whitney's heels clicked over the bluestone patio. How did her assistant walk in those stilts? Especially with a tangle of cords and wiring webbing the set.

Miranda skirted around a camera to meet Whitney, pasting on a grin about as plastic as the lighted Ficus trees hedging the patio. Only one more sequence to shoot, and then they

9

could call this week's taping of her show, *From the Ground Up*, a wrap.

Whitney reached her, disapproval tugging her face into a frown. "What's with the cookie crumbs all over your shirt, girl?"

Busted. "Got a secret stash of Chips Ahoy! in the truck." Along with enough Coca-Cola to de-corrode a few car batteries. The stuff of emotional self-medication.

"Let's see, we've covered your season finale, plans for next season. Now I'd like to get personal for a moment." Hours later, that reporter's nasally voice still played on repeat—accompanied by a feeling so achingly routine it barely stung.

Fine, not true. A dozen raging wasps couldn't do to her what today's interview did.

"What do you have to say regarding the rumors about your marriage?" Miranda's shoulders stiffened all over again at the memory of the reporter's averted eyes as she posed the question—the subtle-as-a-foghorn interest edging her words, the disappointment when Miranda's underwhelming answer fell flat. *"I'm sorry. I don't talk about my personal life to the media."*

"You know everybody's curious about where you disappeared to today." Whitney brushed the crumbs off Miranda's white V-neck tee.

And probably annoyed, too, since her last-minute appointment with the magazine journalist meant taping would run late tonight. "One of those spur-of-the-moment interviews. Brad coerced me."

"We need this, Rand." Why the worry in her manager's voice as they'd spoken over the phone? Surely after their third season finale her homebuilding television show had finally hit its prime. "Is the crew mad?"

Whitney stepped back, glance darting from Miranda's boots and denim up to her signature tee. "Not mad. A tad irked, maybe. No one likes to stay late. Might've helped if you'd hit the catering table with everyone else. You always eat with the gang."

Except on October 4. But none of the studio bunch knew the gut-punching significance of the date. And she'd just as soon keep it that way. Otherwise there'd be no holding it together through tonight's taping. "Needed a little quiet. That's all."

"Well, let's hope the break has you in top form so we can close this in one take. That dark sky won't hold out forever." A spotlight snapped on as the set hummed into post-break activity. Whitney pulled a tube from her pocket. "Now, pucker up."

"Right, because a girl can't build a house without lipstick."

"Correction: lip *gloss*. Now get out there and do the Home Depot thing."

As Whitney pranced away, Miranda turned her eyes to the green ridges peeking through dusk's fog. Those paunchy clouds *did* promise rain, and soon. They just needed to get through this taping. . . . Correction: *she* needed to.

And she would. Always did—on all four October 4ths since *he* left.

Robbie.

But she couldn't let her mind wander there—to Robbie, the anniversary. She needed to ditch thoughts of that prickly interview, too. *C'mon, think favorite things. Real Sound of Music–like. Bubble baths. Bonfires. Ooh, or how about the new Powermatic 2000 3HP table saw?* Now, there was something to put a little spring in a girl's step.

"Oh, please tell me that grin means what I think it means."

Her focus slid to the right. Brad Walsh. Yup, there he stood in all his hair-gelled, leather-shoed, this-century's-William-Holden glory.

"And what do you think it means?" And why in the world did her manager have to pick today of all days to visit the set?

"That you're happy to see me," Brad said, sweeping his arms wide. "That you realize, after years of my devotion, you're finally ready to make the move from client to dinner date." He honed in on her mouth.

Don't even think about it, Walsh.

"Kid, you've got lipstick on your teeth."

She brushed a finger over her front teeth. "Uh-uh, lip *gloss*. And thanks. But no dice on the dinner date. We've had this chat a thousand times."

Brad rolled his chocolate-brown eyes. "I know . . . I'm city, you're country. Hogwash."

Despite the blues she'd lugged around all day, giggles pushed out now. "Hogwash? Is that your way of trying to fit in down here in backwoods-ville? Nice attempt, but you need a debutante, an urbanite. Maybe a ballerina. I'm too . . . flannel and scrambled eggs." Seriously. He should see her at breakfast.

She stepped away from Brad, nodded at the head cameraman as he settled in his perch at the Panasonic, and found her own spot behind a granite-top island.

"You're hardly a lumberjack, Rand." Brad moved beside her. "You're television's tomboy darling. So said *TV Guide* last week."

She surveyed her props for the closing how-to segment: pitcher of water, steam iron, oak slab. "What're you doing here, anyway?"

"Lincoln called, said we needed to talk."

Sure enough, the show's producer strode across the set now. He stopped, exchanged words with the director, and then angled for Miranda and Brad.

"He looks intense," Miranda said.

"Always does."

Lincoln reached them, held out a hand to Brad. "Good to see you, Walsh. Randi, I need a few minutes with the two of you."

Oh, please don't let it be bad news. Anything else today and she'd need a bucket of ice cream to go with the rest of her cookies. "Should we sit?" She gestured to the rattan furniture positioned on one side of the porch set.

Lincoln leaned against the island counter. "Actually, let's make this a standing meeting. I've got to run in a sec. Here's the thing: I've got good news."

Miranda tasted relief, syrupy sweet.

"And some bad."

Good-bye, Aunt Jemima. "I vote for the bad first."

Lincoln folded his arms over his black sweater, which matched his wide-rimmed glasses. "Okay, I'll give it to you straight: Season four of *From the Ground Up* is on shaky ground."

Was it just her, or were those heavy clouds sagging even lower in the sky? "Well, we knew the network was looking at fiddling with our time slot, right?"

Lincoln was shaking his head before she even finished. "I'm not talking a time-slot switch up. We may be on the chopping block."

Which explained the ripples of anxiety in her manager's voice when he'd called about the interview. Brad must have sensed this coming. "Doesn't compute," he said now. "The show's done well for three seasons. Randi's as popular with viewers as ever."

"And we're half done filming season four," Miranda added.

"I know it's unpleasant to hear, but if you look at last season's ratings and future projections, it's not entirely unbelievable. But nothing's certain. We have time to make our case to the network before they settle on the spring lineup. Which brings me to the good news."

Lincoln straightened his glasses and leaned forward. "I've had the best publicity brainstorm of my life. I have a plan to save the show and up your celebrity status by the zillions, Randi, dear."

Why did that sound more foreboding than hope inspiring? "Whatcha gonna do? Parade me in front of every grocery-aisle tabloid?"

Lincoln's smug smile stretched his cheeks. "Not just you."

Brad's sharp intake of breath signaled his realization. She met his eyes, read his "stay calm" expression. What had he just figured out that she hadn't? "Who else?" A niggle of alarm slipped under her skin.

"Drum roll, please. . . . Your husband." Lincoln's words rushed like the breeze now rolling into a steady mountain wind. "You know, the unseen character on your show. The one who taught you all you know."

Oh. Oh no. Disbelief crowded out the elation of only seconds earlier. He couldn't be serious. Lincoln Nash didn't know what he was asking.

Except that he did. And somehow that made it worse. Miranda hugged her arms to her body. "That's impossible. You know I'm not . . . never was." Her voice dropped to a hush. "You know Robbie left before the wedding." The one that would've happened three years ago today.

"What I *know* is you talk about him in every show."

"Because of you, the audition, the pilot. Because while we taped the first season, I naïvely believed I'd be married by the time it aired. Because my contract stipulates . . ." And then there was the little matter of her guilt. She shot Brad a pleading look, swallowing sour desperation. *Say something!*

But Lincoln spoke first. "Don't tell me you haven't seen the fan websites, tabloid headlines—'Who is Randi Woodruff's mystery man?' Not naming the guy was the best decision we ever made. Especially since, well . . ."

He didn't have to finish. They hadn't named her husband because the man who should have filled the role had ducked out early. She'd shielded that truth from her fans, even most of the crew, citing her desire for privacy. Up until now it had worked.

"Anyway," Lincoln went on, "you finally give people the peek they want, and you'll save your show. Be sure of it."

"The only thing I'm sure of is"—pain latched itself to her shell-shocked words—"I don't have a husband." She felt Brad's palm on her arm, the chill of the coming storm.

Lincoln only shrugged. "So we get you one." He checked his watch. "Gotta run. We'll chat more."

And before she could hurl even one of the arguments clogging her throat, Lincoln was off.

"He's dead serious, isn't he." She slumped against the island counter.

"Like Colonel Sanders in a chicken coop." Brad's eyes were pinned on Lincoln's retreating form.

"And I'm the chick with her head on the chopping block." As Brad placed his arm around her shoulder, grumbling clouds drew her gaze. And suddenly all she wanted was escape. She itched for the comfort of the mountains, her workshop. The heady smell of sawdust, the feel of wood underneath her fingers, glass-smooth and waiting for her magic. Home.

Where her lies couldn't find her.

Well, apparently, until today.

MINNEAPOLIS, MINNESOTA

"This is officially the stupidest thing you've ever talked me into."

The click of Matthew Knox's shoes echoed on the heels of his brother's hissed words, the empty, dark hallway stretching before him like a cave. Only a slit of light beckoned from under the closed door at the end of the corridor. On the other side of that door, a journalist's treasure trove.

For real—he'd hit the jackpot this time. Political favors,

special-interest pandering. The evidence was at his fingertips. As long as he didn't get stuck with one leg into this gaping window of opportunity.

Matthew paused. This was the direction he'd seen the former politician walking, right?

Behind him, his brother heaved a sigh. "Dude, did you even hear me? I'm talking epic proportions of stupid."

So his older brother didn't approve. So what was new? "Voice down, camera ready. Is that so much to ask?" The story hovered so close, he could feel it. Surely it completely justified breaking into the zoo's administration building.

No, not breaking in. After all, he and Jase hadn't busted any locks or climbed any fences. They'd only followed ex-Senator McKee in. From a safe distance. When no one was looking.

"What about Margaret McKee?" Jase whisper-shouted. "She's the celebrity. Your article's supposed to be about her. You asked me to come to take pictures of her and the glamour crowd. Instead we're sneaking around an empty building while she's out dazzling the masses. You know Delia Jones is out there, too, right?"

"'Course I do. And Jones is going to throw up when she realizes she spent the night buddying up to the senator's daughter when the senator himself was playing dirty politics right under her nose."

Yes, it was a departure from his assignment—to write a feature on recent acting phenom Margaret McKee, daughter of the former senator—but surely the editor of *Today* would forgive him. And, oh, how spicy the taste of victory when he beat Jones to the story.

It was his nemesis, Delia Jones herself, who'd let it slip that the *real* news of tonight's gala at the zoo was the former senator's plans. *"Rumor is McKee's stepping back into the political boxing ring with a little prompting from Shawn Keegan."*

Keegan was not only the zoo administrator but also an investor with fingers in no less than a dozen corporations and foundations in the Twin Cities . . . and whose underground influence in politics was the stuff of electoral legends. It would make sense the man would want a friend in the State Senate.

And while a local political scoop wouldn't normally be of much interest to a national magazine like *Today*, surely the fact that the ex-senator happened to be the father of celebrity up-and-comer Margaret McKee would help Matthew's case.

Finally a hard news break. Good-bye fluffy human-interest pieces, hello nitty-gritty reporting.

"Come on, Jase, this is my chance. Besides, you should be thanking me. With business slow at the gallery, I'd think you'd appreciate picking up a photo sale to *Today*." Anyway, he hadn't asked Jase to join him for this extracurricular portion of the evening. Jase could've stayed outside with the rest of the Twin Cities' fancy-schmancy types.

He just wants to make sure I don't get into trouble. And considering Matthew's recent history of botched freelance gigs, could he blame him? Still. "Don't mess this up for me, Jase."

Jase sighed. "You're that convinced?"

Matthew squinted in the dark. "Would I have rented a tux, endured this whole hoity-toity fund-raiser, if I wasn't?" He raked his fingers through his short brown hair. He'd sacrificed his shaggy look in favor of a close cut for tonight's gala, had even gotten reacquainted with his razor—no hint of his usual five-o'clock shadow. *Anything for the story.*

And the good senator's daughter seemed to like the change, too. Two days ago, during their initial interview, Margaret McKee had been about as attentive as a narcoleptic. Tonight she'd hovered at his side, claiming his arm at every dance.

Too bad he was out to dig up her father's wrongdoing. Rumors of the senator's up-for-grabs votes—for the right price, of course—had dogged McKee throughout his two terms. Now he was meeting behind closed doors with one of the state's biggest financial tycoons. Oh yeah, there was a story here.

Jase switched his camera bag from one shoulder to the other. "You better be right. How many times have we gotten into scrapes over your hunches? Oh, right, not hunches. Journalistic instinct. I'm just surprised your 'instinct' hasn't landed us in jail."

"Yet." Matthew grinned and continued down the hallway.

"That's not funny." Jase shuffled behind him. "You can James Bond it all you want, but I've got a wife and daughter."

Matthew only waved Jase on. The faint strains of the orchestra's music glided in from where the city's movers and shakers mingled over hors d'oeuvres and champagne. He reached into his coat pocket, clasped his digital recorder.

"What if you're wrong?" Jase's whisper filled the silence.

Polite of Jase not to tack on the obvious: Wouldn't be the first time. "Then we shrug and say we got lost looking for the restroom."

"You always do this, Matt."

Seriously, did Jase have to be so talkative tonight? He clearly didn't get *covert*. "Do what?"

"Dig for something that's not there. What happened to my trusting kid brother?"

Disappeared the same night Dad did. Matthew sucked in a sharp breath. "I'm not wrong this time. I saw the senator and Keegan sneak off. Considering what Delia told me—"

"And that's another thing. Why, of all people, would *she* tip *you* off?"

Fine, so that question had poked at Matthew all night, too. The woman despised him. "Maybe she didn't realize what she was giving me, or maybe she's finally forgiven me."

He could practically hear Jase's eyes roll. Right. Not likely.

But Delia's reasons didn't matter right now. He stopped outside the office door. Recorder on. Hands sweaty.

"Now what?" Jase whispered.

"Um, truthfully? I haven't thought that far ahead." He fingered his collar, loosened the strangling bow tie.

"Perfect. What do you think we're going to find, anyway? Two men smoking cigars, inking a contract with the mafia?"

"Jase, I just need you to trust me." Even as the words left his lips, he gulped for their return.

"Son, I just need you to trust me."

Trust. Yeah. Right.

A laugh boomed from the other side of the door. Matthew pushed his ear to the wood. The senator's muffled voice leaked from the room, words tinged with reluctance. "I don't know about this. But a deal is a deal, I suppose. Perhaps it *is* best I lay low."

"The things we do in the name of elections, eh?" This from Keegan.

Matthew held his breath. *Keep talking, Senator.*

"You think there's really a shot with a write-in campaign this late in the game?" Keegan.

Ah, there it was. "Here's what I'm thinking, Jase," he spoke in a hush. "We wait here until they leave. Soon as they open the door, you snap a photo."

Jase grunted. "Nothing doing. They'll call Security and have us arrested."

"So what do you suggest? Busting in on them?"

"Hey, you're the captain. Lead away. For the record, I still think this is—"

"I know, I know. The stupidest thing we've ever done." But it was possibly the best career move of his life. If he could only land something concrete. Allegations alone did not an ethical article make.

Like trespassing and eavesdropping are ethical?

"All right. New plan." He lifted a fist, knocked.

The voices on the other side of the door silenced. Another knock, and the door swung open. Matthew grinned as the ex-senator's burly form filled the doorframe. He had a few inches on Matthew's six feet three, and his shoulders suggested a past career in the NFL rather than the statehouse.

"Uh, if you're looking for the restrooms—" McKee began.

"Actually, no. The name's Matthew Knox, and I'm here to talk to you and Mr. Keegan."

"Party's outside," Keegan called from inside the room.

"Yes, but—"

"And you're trespassing," the zoo administrator finished.

Matthew would have pushed past McKee if the man didn't look poised for a takedown. Instead, grasping at confidence, he folded his arms. "Look, I'll cut to the chase. I know you've got an announcement to make soon, maybe even tonight. I know you're planning a late entry into the election, and I can write an article hinting at your plans and thus fizzle your big PR splash, or you can let me in on it. What do you say?"

The senator raised an eyebrow as Keegan joined him in the doorway. Jase coughed.

"So you're paparazzi, are ya?" Keegan's eyes pressed into slits.

"We're not paparazzi!" Matthew blurted. "Are you kidding?"

"Dude, I don't think you're the one who should be offended here," Jase muttered.

"I promise, you won't be sorry," Matthew gushed. "Just talk to me." Way too close to begging. Why did his voice sound so tinny? And why were both McKee and Keegan smiling all eerie-like? Not good.

McKee chuckled. "Oh, I know *I* won't be sorry, son."

Matthew angled to see Jase swiping beads of sweat from his forehead.

"You see," McKee continued. "That big announcement you're talking about . . ." He lifted his hand, checked the watch on his wrist. "I'm guessing it's going down right now. And you, my friend, are missing it all."

"So you're not . . ." And just like that, it made sense. Delia's divulging what she knew about McKee's plans. No, what she'd concocted. She'd planted the idea in his head knowing he'd bite, knowing he'd go and do something stupid. And now she was out there with the real story while he faced the fiery amusement in McKee's eyes.

"We should go, Matt," Jase urged.

"Yes, do." Keegan poked a finger at Matthew's chest. "'Else I'll arrange for an escort."

Matthew whirled on his heels after Jase, the back of his neck burning with heat. Jase stalked ahead, spine rigid.

"I can't believe you!" Jase called over his shoulder as they burst outside. "We could've been arrested."

Strings of light decorated the zoo's courtyard, enveloped in late-summer warmth. A server walked past with a tray, trailed by the scent of shrimp. Maybe whatever announcement McKee had alluded to hadn't happened yet. Maybe Matthew hadn't missed it.

Maybe he hadn't royally screwed up just yet. Again.

He scanned the crowd for Delia.

"I'll never be able to bring Celine to the zoo," Jase said, stopping, yanking on Matthew's arm.

"There are other zoos—"

"You just couldn't let it go, like always. You're wasting your talents."

"Hey, I didn't ask you to follow me."

"It's because of Dad and that article, isn't it? You're trying to prove something."

Music, dancing, it all faded as dark hurt snaked through him. "Don't go there, Jase."

His brother trapped him in an angry stare until the blare of his cell phone broke the moment. Jase exhaled and pushed past Matthew, reaching into his pocket for his phone.

Matthew turned, gaze falling to the ground, where his shoes glowed against overhead lights. Alone in a glitzy crowd. Frozen by humiliation.

And the truth of his brother's razored words.

"Matthew?"

And the hits just kept on coming. Not Margaret. Not now, with that pouncing smile.

"Matthew Knox, you missed my announcement." She slithered an arm through his elbow.

And there was Delia. Watching from the crowd, grinning as if she'd nabbed a trophy. Ever the rival, ever a step ahead. The realization thudded through Matthew.

"You mean *you're* the write-in candidate?"

Margaret's confirming nod jabbed the final stake in this failure of a night. "I purposely waited until my father disappeared for a few minutes. I want people to vote for me as me, not just as 'the senator's daughter.' People think I'm only into the acting scene, but I've always intended to make a difference in a bigger way. And since I'm convinced our current pool of candidates don't cut it, I decided to jump in."

And *Today* could've had the story ahead of everyone if he hadn't ignored his assignment. *Done for. So completely done for.*

A yank on his arm jerked his attention from Margaret.

"Whoa, bro, what's the hurry?"

"It's Celine. She's in the hospital. Bike accident." Jase shoved his camera bag at Matthew, his cell phone balanced between his shoulder and his ear. "Honey, I'll be there in twenty minutes."

And in the time it took Jase to clamp his phone shut, all thought of Margaret McKee and his repeat failure fled. In its place, the kind of pulsing dread he hadn't felt since . . .

Since the day everything fell apart.

❧

"Listen, we'll figure this out. I'll talk to Lincoln."

Miranda pulled away from Brad's hold. No amount of her manager's optimism could erase the suffocating truth: When Lincoln Nash made his mind up, he was as immovable as the Smokies.

"I don't have a husband."

"So we get you one."

Like men waited in droves to stake a claim on a woman more comfortable in Levi's than lipstick. Catching her director's impatient glare—right, there was still tonight's taping to finish—she moved into place behind an oak two-by-four balanced over two sawhorses. "Tell Lincoln husbands—pretend or otherwise—don't grow on trees." And that even if they did, it was just too easy for a restless wind to blow them away.

Brad's chuckle defied her morose words. "You know, if you think about it, maybe it's not such a bad idea."

The sounds of the set crew filled the air—voices, footsteps on the patio, cameras rolling into place. "It's a horrible idea. It's bad enough I've gone along with a lie for three seasons straight, all because it supposedly cutes me up." But she had to admit it had worked. She'd protected her privacy, holed away in the mountains, drew a strict line between her public persona and personal life. "Now you want me to bring the lie home by playing house with a pretend husband? And what about Robbie? He's out there somewhere and—"

"That's it, isn't it? You're worried if you do this, Robbie

23

will catch wind of it, maybe think you're really married, and never come back."

With her back to Brad, she ran a hand over the oak slab. Smooth and unmarred, perfection. But why hadn't someone from props dented the wood already? The whole point of this episode's how-to was to highlight her repair techniques. Couldn't do that with a pristine piece of lumber.

Brad stepped closer, spoke over her shoulder. "Robbie's still got a clutch on you."

She pulled out her hammer, poised to do the job herself. "Don't start. Not today."

"Three years and an ocean. And you're still holding on."

Grip tight around the hammer, she faced him. Overhead, cumulus clouds rolled and growled. "*Stop.* Don't you dare come here and Dr. Phil me. You're not my therapist. You're not my friend. So just . . ." She whirled, raised her arm with hammer held high, and pounded into wood, a lightning-like crack echoing over the set. The slab rattled and stilled.

"Rand." Brad's clipped word punctured the now-quiet set as a wave of mountain air scraped over her cheeks.

She couldn't look at him. Not her friend? What was she thinking? He'd found her a wallowing mess three years ago on her bathroom floor. He'd answered every single middle-of-the-night call those first few months. He might be her manager now, but they'd been college pals first. And if *he* wasn't her friend—being one of the few who knew . . . all of it—then who was?

She ran a hand through her curls and turned on her heels, hammer swinging. "Brad—" And hit a wall. A soft, growling wall. And what was that warm . . . ? Oh, swell. Coffee, hot and oh-so-brown against the white of her shirt.

"Good evening to you, too, Randi," Tom Bass, the show's director, spoke in monotone.

"Sorry," she muttered. "And sorry for the holdup." She

peered around Tom to see Brad's retreating form. *I didn't mean it, Brad*. It was just this brutal day.

Eyes back to Tom, her gaze traveled from his gray whiskers to his dusty and now coffee-covered jeans. "I, uh, had an accident with the wood."

He folded his arms. "I see that. It's cracked."

Possibly along with her mental health. Someone handed her an apron, and she slipped it over her shirt, covering the coffee stain. She had to focus. *You're Randi Woodruff, homebuilder extraordinaire, tool-belt-wearing how-to girl.*

"Tell props we need a new two-by-four," Tom barked at a passing crewman. "Look, I know you don't like our show closers, but don't go around breaking stuff. Thing is—"

She held up a palm. "I know. Viewers love the cutesy *how-to*s. Endears me to them."

Tom patted her cheek. "That and your good looks and charming personality. Now, I don't know what you, Brad, and our illustrious producer were chatting about—"

"Believe me, you don't want to."

"Or what's been bothering you all day. But we've got work to do and an impatient crew. Think you can pull yourself together for one more segment?"

She nodded, then breathed in deeply as Tom left the spotlighted patio, the scent of coffee mixing with pine and heat from the lights. Brad met her eyes from where he'd taken up residence by the picked-clean food table, hopefully catching the apology in her wave.

She could do this. Finish the taping, then escape to the mountain. Drag herself through one more episode ending, try to ignore the guilt these closing segments always caused. Like sandpaper scratching her heart each time she forced the words.

You made your bed . . . Yeah, sure, a bed of nails.

"Whenever you're ready," Tom boomed from off set.

Focus. She tucked a runaway curl behind one ear and stepped to the patio table in the corner of the set, connected with the camera.

Three, two . . . "I don't know about you, but sometimes no matter how careful I am, I end up with dents in my wood." Cue cute pout followed by we're-all-in-this-together expression. *See, easy.*

If she could only silence her conscience.

"But most dents are fixable. All you need are two things: water and a steam iron." She picked up the iron posed atop the table, then walked over to the newly placed board, practiced grin still in place. "Now, some people would be too impatient for this repair technique."

This was it. The line the whole sequence hinged on. *Don't think about what you're saying.* The glare of the set lights whited out her scenic surroundings, the faces of the crew. Just her and the camera. And the lie.

"My husband, for instance, bless his blasted heart, is so impatient he eats TV dinners half frozen." *My husband.* Sandpaper. Scratching. Scraping. *I'm sorry, God.*

"He may have taught me everything I know, but if it were up to him, we'd throw out this damaged slab. But I say, don't be so quick to pitch a good thing." Oh, if ever words held such layers. She hid a grimace, gestured to the lumber. "Now, with softwoods, like pine or cedar, just wet the dented area to swell and raise the sunken wood. But for hardwoods, you need an iron."

Her eyes landed on the groove in the oak board, a blight on an otherwise perfectly usable piece of wood. And suddenly all she could see was her own heart. Dented. Damaged. She closed her eyes against forming pools. She hadn't made it all day only to fall apart now with cameras rolling, everyone watching.

Quick, do the Maria von Trapp thing. Sleeping in, feather pillows, maple syrup . . .

But it didn't stop the screeching of her conscience, the emotions swirling inside her. The interview, Lincoln's news . . . the anniversary.

And then, movement. A flash of orange as a man strode along the side of the set. That profile! Crooked nose, high forehead, floppy hair. So like . . .

The pang in her heart pushed out a gasp as a whoosh of mountain wind painted goose bumps over her arms. The first raindrops spattered on the wooden slab. She dropped the iron.

"Robbie?"

Chapter 2

"You call this a story?"

Editor Greg Dooley's words bulleted through the phone line, a mixture of incredulity and anger. Matthew stifled a groan, pushing away from the table, wooden chair scraping over the laminate flooring of Jase and Izzy's kitchen.

He'd known, even as he stayed up typing into the middle of the night, waiting for the sound of Jase's car coming up the drive, his article couldn't hope to live up to Dooley's expectations.

And he had no one to blame but himself, letting Delia Jones get the best of him like he had. Besides, how was he supposed to write when all he'd been able to think about was Celine in the ER? *I should've been there.* They'd always had a special bond, he and his niece.

Instead, he'd spent the night playing baby-sitter for the neighbor kid his sister-in-law had been watching at the time of the accident. Jase dropped Matthew at the house before whisking off to the hospital to be with Izzy and Cee. While the neighbor kid slept, Matthew had slumped on the couch, worrying, plunking out an article he'd have been ashamed to show his high school journalism teacher.

"I don't know what to say, Dooley."

"We don't even have a single photo of the announcement."

Only a bird chirping outside the window interrupted the morning stillness of the house. The rest of the family still slept after their early-dawn return from the hospital, when Jase had carried in a bruised but otherwise okay Celine. Too beat to drive home, Matthew had crashed on the couch.

Now he moved aside his glass of orange juice and tortured himself with another look at the newspaper. *Actress Announces Late-race Write-in Campaign.* The blaring headline mocked him, and Jones's byline under the lead article—front page, top of the fold—blew the last of his dignity to bits.

He had to admit, Delia Jones had done okay for herself since he'd gotten her fired from the *Star Tribune*.

Matthew's stomach pinched. "I confess. I messed up. But I was so sure. I heard this rumor about Senator McKee, and I had to follow up on it. For the good of the magazine! I was only—"

"You were only playing Superman when all I ever asked for was Clark Kent."

Matthew stilled in his chair, the force in Dooley's voice blasting any attempt at argument. *I really messed up this time.*

He stood, carried his empty cereal bowl to the dishwasher. Sunlight so bright the kitchen's white cupboards glowed against pale yellow walls splashed into the room from the window over the sink. A thunderstorm would've been a better match for his mood, complete with hail and howling winds and brooding clouds.

"You used to have a nose for news like no one I know, Knox. But you spent an entire week hounding Margaret McKee. You should've sensed this story long before the actual announcement." Dooley's sigh spoke frustration. "At the very least, you should've turned in a story that made everyone else's look like bare bones. We should've read about who she had lunch with and how often she checks her e-mail and who painted her stinkin' nails!"

Matthew caught his reflection in the window—stubble-shadowed face, wrinkled tee borrowed from Jase, circles around his eyes. He turned, reached for the pitcher of juice to return to the refrigerator. "I'm sorry. I'm just . . . sorry." Why did the apology fall so flat when honest-to-goodness regret clamored inside him?

"And I'm sorry I keep letting an old college friendship cloud my common sense. I tossed you the story because my best reporter went on maternity leave before McKee agreed to our interview and I know the freelancing thing hasn't paid off for you lately—especially after . . . well, you know. But I guess you're still the same old Knox."

Matthew opened the fridge door with a heavy exhale, head dropping as Dooley's words found their mark, his sore spot still bruised from five years ago . . . or maybe fifteen.

Yes, that's right. It wasn't enough that life—no, Dad—played him for a fool once. The first time tore apart their family. The second, his career.

And the consequences clawed at him still.

"You let your father's past actions cloud your reporting."

"The article had 'conflict of interest' written all over it."

"You tried, convicted, and sentenced him in one headline. All because of what? His long-ago Houdini-dad act?"

As the cold of the refrigerator crept over his face, the voices from his past played one after another. Together they added up to one heaping reminder of just how far he'd fallen—from one-time Pulitzer finalist to local disgrace. Freelance writing for a national magazine that was barely a step up from a gossip rag.

"Still the same old Knox."

"You still there, Knox?" Dooley's voice, the humming light from the back of the fridge tugged him back to the present.

One hand still gripping the door handle, he raised his head and heaved the door closed. As he did, his fingers brushed a crinkled piece of notebook paper stuck to the refrigerator with a Snoopy magnet. Two stick figures—the tall one holding a kite, the short one smiling. Underneath, scribbled in his niece's nine-year-old scrawl, the words: *Uncle Matt and Cee fly a kite.*

Best thing his brother ever did, bringing Izzy, a single mother, and her daughter home from his teaching stint at Texas A&M. Celine was only five at the time, still recovering from her bout with meningitis.

Jase didn't have to play at the Superman thing. He just plain lived a heroic life.

"Knox?"

He blinked, turning from the fridge. "LucyLu's," he muttered.

"What?"

"Her nails, Margaret got them done at this froufrou place in downtown St. Paul called LucyLu's. She ate lunch at Periano's yesterday, and as far as checking her e-mail, she looks at her iPhone at least once every five minutes."

"Now you tell me." Something close to amusement tinged Dooley's words.

Matthew dropped back into his chair and flipped the newspaper over. Couldn't look at Delia's headline anymore. "Listen, don't pay me for the article I turned in. I blew it, and I don't blame you for being angry."

The pause on the other end of the line stretched, the sound of Dooley tapping his keyboard coming through the line. And then, "Fine, I can't believe I'm going to offer you this after you just blew the biggest scoop this side of Watergate—"

"Slight exaggeration, maybe?" Matthew cut in.

"You are in no position to mock my hyperbole. Listen, about six months ago, Lisa, my reporter who's out on maternity

31

leave now, came to me with an idea for a new story. Not a print article, mind you—at least not right away."

Matthew leaned back in his chair, feet propped on the tabletop. "Tell me more."

"We proposed a serial blog on the *Today* website, pitched it to the subject's manager over five months ago but never heard a thing. And then, a couple of days ago, he contacts me out of the blue, says they would like to make it happen. But it would require travel to North Carolina."

Matthew reached for the Cheerios box. "A serial blog?" Like, a daily journal or log of activities? Okay, so it wasn't Woodward and Bernstein material. And he'd promised himself when he accepted the Margaret McKee assignment it'd be his one and only foray into celebrity reporting. But if this interviewee was interesting . . . "Who's the subject?" He chomped on a handful of cereal.

"Randi Woodruff."

A Cheerio lodged in his throat, and he sputtered. "That woman from that home makeover show?" What was the show called? Izzy and Celine had a standing Sunday night date to watch it. Cee loved it so much she'd taken to saying she wanted to be an architect when she grew up. "You want me to interview a reality TV star?"

Dooley chuckled. "You say it like she's one of those girls from *The Bachelor*. Not the same thing, Knox. *From the Ground Up* is a legit home-repair show. And she builds homes for low-income people, does all kinds of charity work on the side. She's a do-gooder."

"Right, a regular Mother Teresa." Minus the habit, plus a tool belt. He'd caught the show a couple times and wondered if the perky star with the smoky eyes actually knew her stuff or if she was simply a pretty face playing *This Old House*.

"I can't pay much, either," Dooley went on. "But I can

promise you readership. Though her show's ratings haven't been impressive lately, there's been a burst of interest about Randi Woodruff herself. Lots of curiosity about the husband she always talks about—the one no one's ever seen."

Tabloid speculation at its best. And Dooley was asking him to join the silly fray. Not a chance. "Look, I appreciate the offer, especially considering last night and all. Generous of you, really. But I don't think it's my thing." Definitely not the heavyweight material he needed to make his career comeback.

Matthew dropped his feet from the tabletop as Celine padded into the room, her hair mussed and a line of stitches over one eyebrow. He offered his niece a smile as she settled in the chair across from his, sleep still tugging at her features. He lifted his right hand to tap his chin, then his open left palm, and finally his elbow.

American Sign Language for *Good morning.*

With both index fingers, she signed, *"Hang up."*

In a minute, he mouthed.

"This could be a big story," Dooley continued. "Yes, we've got the blog thing to do, but I'm still hunting for January's cover, if you catch my drift. So do what you do best: sniff. See if there are any skeletons in the closet. By the rumblings going around the entertainment media world, I think you might find some."

"As much as I appreciate the offer, I'm not an entertainment reporter. We all know that after the McKee fiasco. I think I'll hold out for something a little more meaty."

He felt the familiar attention of Celine's eyes on his face as he spoke. She read lips like a master, her way of "listening" since the meningitis stole her hearing.

"That's some pride you've got going, Knox. I know you've got Walter Cronkite aspirations, but even Walt had his fluff years."

"I'll consider it. All right?" About as seriously as he'd consider piercing his nose. But he owed Dooley at least a show of gratitude.

"Consider quickly. If I don't hear from you by tonight, I'm moving on."

They hung up and Matthew turned his full attention on Celine. "How do you feel today?" he said aloud, signing at the same time.

The look in her eyes was like a kick in the gut—hurt and a hint of lingering fear. His heart lurched for the hundredth time since last night. "Why didn't you come?" she said, voice low and with her familiar blending of words. Because she'd been speaking long before losing her hearing, she still used her voice.

"To the hospital? I wanted to, but Jase asked me to stay here with your friend from next door."

Celine slid out of her chair and rounded the table to stand in front of him. "You should've come."

He latched gazes with her and nodded. "I know. And I'll make it up to you."

Hands to her hips, she stuck her bottom lip out in a playful pout. "How?"

Love for the kid feathered through him. *Forget Dooley and a story in North Carolina.* This is where he belonged. Here with family, and with his niece, the one person who never failed to see past his screw-ups.

This is where Miranda belonged. Tucked in a hidden nook in the Smokies, away from the hurried pace of television taping. From the crazy ideas of her crazy producer. From the humiliation.

She'd actually believed it was *him*. Someone ought to tattoo the word *naïve* on her forehead.

Miranda's arm moved at rapid pace, prodding the sand-paper under her palm back and forth. The motion soothed, the scratching of the wood her lullaby. Long windows paneling her woodshop's west wall invited in the colors of the sunset, spilling oranges and reds against the opposite wall. A buzzing light bulb dangling overhead provided the shop's only other light.

At the tightening in her wrist, Miranda stilled. She moved from her kneeling position beside the antique chest of drawers to sit cross-legged, wood shavings and abandoned scraps of sandpaper blanketing the woodshop floor.

Up here, there was no probing into her privacy. No Robbie look-alikes, either. Last night's embarrassing episode still harassed her—the way she'd fastened her gaze on the man strolling along the edge of the set. How she'd called out his name. The circus of thoughts crowding in . . .

It can't be him . . . unless . . . he remembered the date! Unless Robbie, too, had woken up squeezed by the grip of unwelcome memories. *It would've been our anniversary. Three years. We would've celebrated with a vacation.* Or maybe they would've simply stayed home, enjoyed breakfast in bed, and then tackled a house project together. Working side by side the way they had when they first met.

Miranda blinked and pulled open the bottom chest drawer, resumed sanding its base. "Forget yesterday. Forget all of it."

"That easy, huh?"

A screech exploded from her at the surprise sound of a male voice in her workshop, and in one fluid movement, she reached for her hammer and lurched to her feet.

"Easy there, Mighty Mouse." Brad Walsh stumbled backward, knocking into her table saw, hands raised in surrender. "It's just me."

Miranda's heart pounded as she lowered the hammer.

"Sheesh, Walsh, what were you thinking, sneaking up on me like that?" She leaned over, hands on her knees. "I think I'm having a heart attack. My arm hurts. Aspirin."

"I read somewhere the pain-in-the-arm symptom doesn't happen for women. So if your arm *is* hurting, it's only 'cause of how furiously you were sanding. Like someone's life depended on how smooth you got that drawer."

She lifted her head. "*Someone's* life is going to depend on how quickly he explains his presence in my shop."

Brad folded his arms over his navy blue polo. "Two things: first, an apology." He lowered onto a workbench, voice turning serious. "It didn't hit me 'til I got home last night. The date, I mean. The anniversary. Things make a little more sense now."

She dropped beside him on the bench. "You mean the way I lit into you yesterday?"

"I mean the way your eyes were devoid of anything close to happiness. Sorry I didn't realize it sooner. I should've supported you instead of pushing your buttons."

She released her hammer, and it clinked to the floor. "Wasn't just the anniversary. There was the news about the show, Lincoln's crazy plan, and the interview earlier in the day. They asked such personal questions."

Brad patted her knee. "And the Robbie twin?"

She offered a shrug in place of an explanation. What must the crew think of her? When she'd seen the stranger on set during taping last night, she hadn't been able to stop herself from propelling forward. In the time it had taken to reach the patio's edge, the sky finally broke open in a blitz of pounding rain, moisture hammering Miranda's face, running in rivulets down her cheeks. She'd sidestepped a camera, ignoring her director's chiding and the sudden hustle of the crew. Had to know. Had to see the man's face.

She'd said his name once more, approaching from behind, damp clothing clinging to her skin and sending shivers throughout her body. She'd raised an arm, tapped his shoulder.

He'd turned. And the chill darted into her heart.

Not him. Of course. It never was.

"I could've sworn it was him." She shook her head as Brad stood and reached for her hands. "Guess I had Robbie on the brain."

He tugged her up from the bench. "Could've happened to anybody. C'mon. There's another reason I drove up tonight. I've got a surprise."

"Oh no, don't tell me you brought me a dog." She nudged the dresser drawer closed with her foot.

"Say what?"

She yanked on the light bulb string and the light blinked off. "Every year for the past three years, when my anniversary-that-almost-was rolls around, you suggest I get a dog. And while I'd love one, I'm not home enough to be a good owner."

Brad latched on to her arm, tugging her toward the shop door. "No dog, I promise."

Outside, the fiery hues of the sky washed her mountain clearing in a blaze of color. The leaves on the trees circling her property were just starting to turn, green fading into the promise of a colorful autumn. The home she'd begun building nearly three and a half years ago, when she still wore Robbie's ring and believed their love unbreakable, rose from the clearing—one half finished, livable; the other half nothing more than foundation and frame.

Fitting, really.

She stopped halfway to the house and blinked at the figure sitting on the front steps. "Liv? What are you doing here?" She turned to Brad, swatted at his arm. "And here I thought you brought me a sheepdog."

Miranda's best friend rose and gathered her into a hug. "Actually, he was leaning toward a mastiff. I talked him out of it."

Brad's nervous chuckle sounded from behind her. Liv released Miranda and tucked her hands into the pockets of her jean jacket, breath visible in the chill of the evening.

"So you're the surprise," Miranda said, stepping back.

"Half the surprise," Brad corrected. "I've got awesome news. We're going to celebrate."

"Sounds good, but please tell me y'all brought sustenance. Pretty sure the only food in my kitchen is a box of Pop-Tarts and some beef jerky that'll break your jaw."

Brad moved to his car, ducked in, and then returned with two paper bags. "The woman can build a house but has the nutritional habits of a toddler," he muttered, passing the women and climbing the porch.

"Can it, Walsh," Liv called after him. She tucked an arm through Miranda's. "We brought all the fixings for homemade pizza. And Brad didn't notice, but I also stuck in a package of Peanut Butter M&M's."

"My hero."

They entered the house, greeted by the sound of Brad already unloading groceries in the kitchen. Liv paused in the living room. "Hey, before we join Chef Walsh, you okay? You know, I'm still so mad at Robbie, I could rearrange his teeth." Twin strawberry-blond braids framed Liv's face, and feisty anger leaked from her voice.

Miranda burst into laughter. "Are you kidding me? You have trouble slapping mosquitoes. And you've never even met Robbie." Liv Hayes ran Miranda's favorite charity, a shelter in Asheville for orphaned children with special needs. She'd befriended Miranda during her "dark days" after Robbie left, encouraged her to volunteer at the shelter as a healthy distraction.

"But seriously, how are you? Brad filled me in on your mother of all bad days yesterday on the way up. You could've called me, you know."

Miranda's gaze roamed the room as she considered Liv's question. Overhead, thick redwood beams crisscrossed, and soft light gleamed from a hanging fixture. During the day, tall windows tugged in the colors of the outdoors, dramatizing the otherwise muted hues of Miranda's furniture. A fireplace and mantel edged one wall, and an open stairway lined the other. The opposite side of the room opened into the dining room. Beyond that, a kitchen and the unfinished portion of the house—what would've been a master suite.

Instead, Miranda slept in the small bedroom at the end of the otherwise incomplete lofted second floor.

This was supposed to be her and Robbie's dream house. After Robbie had woken up, she'd never quite had the heart to finish building.

"Yesterday was rough," she confirmed as they continued to the kitchen. "But you and Brad are here now. And you brought M&M's. Friendship and sugar—best therapy there is."

They walked in on Brad dumping a packet of yeast into a bowl, Miranda's ruffled apron tied around his waist. "Nice, Brad." Liv giggled. "So how long are you going to make us wait for your big news? You getting married or something?"

"Very funny." He wiped his hands on his apron and faced Miranda. "You, Miss Woodruff, have been nominated for the Giving Heart Award."

Miranda froze. "You're joking."

"I don't think so," Liv countered. "This is Brad, remember. He can't even tell knock-knock jokes."

Brad draped a towel over the bowl of dough and set it aside. "Completely serious. The foundation is making the announcement next Wednesday. And if ever a celebrity deserved an award for her charitable contributions, it's you, kid."

Liv squealed and threw her arms around Miranda. "Ah, see, there is always a light at the end of the tunnel. You're so going to win! Didn't Audrey Hepburn win the Giving Heart way back when?"

Brad chuckled. "You look shell-shocked, Rand."

"I'm flummoxed." A delayed grin finally spilled over her face. "Always wanted a reason to use that word."

"And what better reason!" Liv declared. "Let's get cracking on that celebratory pizza."

Miranda pulled a cutting board from the cupboard as Liv lined up toppings—onion, green pepper, jar of olives, fresh mushrooms. The Giving Heart Award. Who would've thought? The award had snowballed into a high level of prestige in the past few years. How in the world had the host of a little sleeper of a homebuilding show made the list of nominees? Especially one in danger of cancellation?

"You remember the prize is $100,000 to your favorite charity, right?" Brad asked as he kneaded the pizza dough.

"How awesome would it be to give that to Open Arms?"

Liv flipped the oven to preheat. "Very. We're in need of roof repairs."

"Oh, I could help you with that, silly. I'll get a few guys from the crew and—"

"Girls, at the moment, I'm the one who needs help." Brad lifted his hands, dough clinging to his fingers. "This is too sticky."

"You need more flour. Here, let me." Miranda relinquished her knife to Liv. "Brad, this is good news for the show, right? The network's not going to axe a show whose host is up for the Giving Heart. Maybe I can even talk Lincoln into dropping the husband thing." Hope slid in as she worked her fingers into the dough.

"That's not exactly the case," Brad said over the sound of

running water. He rubbed his hands together. "Lincoln's the one who was notified about the nomination. He called me. He thinks this is more reason than ever to come up with a husband to parade in front of the press."

"He's crazy!" Exasperation pushed Miranda's words out in a huff. "I can't conjure up a husband from thin air." She pounded a fist into the dough, knuckles connecting with the bottom of the mixing bowl. "I won't do it."

"Linc thinks viewers, and the foundation board, need to see your softer side—and that we need to quell the rumors that your mystery husband doesn't exist. After all, if you win, you'll be more popular than ever. Which means curiosity will rise to new levels. Either way, in his eyes, the husband scheme is how we'll save the show." He took a breath. "Which *is* what you want to do, right?"

Her fingers curled around the dough. He knew she did. Because somehow saving the show meant saving herself, her identity. Without *From the Ground Up*, who was Miranda Woodruff, anyway? Nothing but a jilted, practically family-less woodworker with half a house in the mountains. "Of course I do," she said in a whisper.

"Then the husband reveal could give you just the push you need."

Sure, right over a cliff.

Oh, how she wished, for the thousandth time, she'd never brought up Robbie's name back when she auditioned for the show. Wished she hadn't mentioned her post-college years in Brazil, hadn't told the panel of execs about constructing homes in Rocinha, one of Rio de Janeiro's urbanized slums. About the schools they'd built in rural communities. About the mission team leader, Roberto "Robbie" Pontero, who had pulled from her an architectural creativity—and a passion—she hadn't known she possessed.

"And who is this Robbie?"

She'd blinked when the executive asked the question during the audition. The words had slipped out of their own accord: *"My husband."*

Such a stupid lie, prompted solely by the guilt she'd felt at going against the convictions her grandparents had tried so hard to instill in her—living with a man she wasn't married to. And once the lie was out there, it stuck. Because the panel latched on immediately to the novelty of her foreign romance. She hadn't known the story would become such a part of the show, had told herself it was a harmless fib since she planned to marry within months anyway.

What was it Grandma Woodruff used to say? *"Best way to make God laugh? Tell him your plans."*

Only in Miranda's case, God probably wasn't laughing. Not when she'd made such a mess of things. Maybe it would've been better if she'd never auditioned in the first place, never beat out that other girl—Hollie Somebody—for the hosting spot.

"Let her be, Walsh," Liv piped up, edging into Miranda's wandering memories. "We came to have fun tonight, didn't we?"

Miranda lumped the dough into a rounded ball. "Liv's right. I'm starving. I'll think about the show and Lincoln and Robbie . . . tomorrow." Limp smirk. "At Tara."

"All right, Scarlett O'Hara. So you got any soda in the fridge?"

Brad nudged her arm as Liv crossed the kitchen. "Just consider it," he said gently. "Remember when one of the biggest show sponsors dropped out and you took charge and found an even bigger one? Remember how you fought the network execs so you could build in poorer areas of the country? Be *that* Randi Woodruff again. You've invested too much in this show to let it sink."

If only Robbie had thought the same about their relationship, she might not be in this situation.

But as Brad's words pricked her insides, a new ribbon of energy needled through Miranda. He was right. She'd spent far too long in the clutches of the past, determination lost to a pelting ache.

No more. The show needed a savior. And she needed the show. It was time to make a power play.

And unlike Robbie, she played for keeps.

Matthew swung his right arm back and then forward, fingers releasing the bowling ball into a thud and roll. The embarrassingly pink ball took its sweet time covering the distance of the lane. One measly pin down.

Par for the course these days. Wrong sport, but still. At least Izzy and Jase weren't there yet.

"You're really bad at this, Uncle Matt." His niece peered up at him from innocent blue eyes.

"It's the ball, Cee. If you would've let me use the red one like I wanted—"

"No," she cut in, pigtails swinging as she shook her head, hands signing along with her spoken words. "You're no good."

"Anybody ever tell you you've got incredible tact?" He ruffled Celine's bangs and reached for his ball when it spit out of the machine track.

"I don't know what tact is."

"My point exactly."

The smell of grease from the snack bar in the corner permeated the bowling alley. Neon lights rimmed the walls, and music thrummed through the speakers overhead. Too bad he hadn't been able to talk Cee into the aquarium instead. But she had insisted on bowling. And uncles were supposed to give in.

Just like journalists were supposed to write.

Sure, but did kitschy celebrity pieces even count? Throughout the day, he'd given Dooley's assignment offer its obligatory consideration, but he kept coming back to the same conclusion: too humiliating. Did blogging even count as journalism?

Matthew approached the lane, released his ball again, and for a moment things looked good. Straight down the middle until a last-minute curve sent it into the gutter.

"Like I said, you're really bad." This time giggles punctuated Celine's words.

Though Celine's eyes were on his face, he signed as he spoke. "Just you wait, Cee. When we get home we're playing Candy Land, and I'm gonna whomp you." Maybe no one would pay attention to the electronic scoreboard announcing his lack of skills.

"Matthew!" Izzy's call rose over the clutter of voices and falling pins in the bowling alley.

He handed Celine her purple ball, signed *"Your mom's here,"* and then turned. His sister-in-law bounced toward him, blond hair pulled into a high ponytail, bowling shoes slung over her shoulder by the laces.

"Where's Jase?" he asked as Izzy reached them.

"Doing some after-hours work at the gallery. Besides, things were decidedly cool between the two of you before you left this morning. Care to explain? Jase sure didn't."

Matthew turned to Celine, evading Izzy's question. "Need help, Cee?"

"I think not." Her latest phrase of choice. She sashayed up to the lane, bowling shoes tapping against the wood floor. She threw a near-perfect roll. Nine pins.

"Getting beat by my daughter," Izzy said from behind him. "Wow."

"Just having an off night."

Izzy plopped onto the bench behind the ball track while Celine lined up for her second throw. "So tell me, why are you hanging out with Cee instead of on a date? It's Saturday night."

He cast her a glare, then sat beside her. "Know what I love about you, Iz? Your kind respect for boundaries and privacy."

"What kind of sister-in-law would I be if I didn't pry?"

Celine hit her last pin and jumped up, clapping her hands. Matthew waited until she turned, eyes on him, to lift and twist his own hands in silent applause.

Izzy leaned in. "You're a good uncle, Matthew. She's lucky to have a friend like you."

"And I'm lucky Jase brought you two cowgirls back from Texas."

Izzy chuckled. "Yeah, I'm still a little mad about that during the fifth or sixth blizzard each Minnesota winter."

And then Celine stood in front of them, hands moving as she signed. "I'm hungry. You said we'd get pizza."

He nodded. "Right. Can you order for us, Iz? We've got one frame left each. We'll meet you over at the tables. Or did you want to play?"

Izzy shook her head. "Nah, I only paid for the shoes so they'd let me on the floor."

He glanced down at Celine as Izzy walked off. "Maybe I'll get a strike this time."

"I think not," she repeated.

She thought right. Another gutter ball. "Don't you dare laugh, Cee."

Minutes later their game ended. He didn't even bother looking at the score as they left the floor to join Izzy. "Man, the guy behind the counter just told me to go back to the ranch," Izzy drawled as they sat, drumming her nails on the tabletop.

Matthew eyed her Cowboys jersey. "I've been telling you for

45

years, you're in purple-and-gold territory. Flashing your Dallas duds ain't the best way to make friends up here." Matthew dropped a straw in Celine's glass and handed her a napkin, making sure her eyes were on his lips before speaking. "Pizza for the big winner, as requested."

"Maybe you should take bowling lessons, Uncle Matt. Then you wouldn't lose so bad." Izzy snorted at that, and Matthew tossed his straw wrapper at her.

He dished up a cheesy slice for Celine, then plopped a slice on his plate. "Pepperoni and mushroom, my favorite."

"Mine too," Celine added.

"Don't talk with your mouth full, kiddo," Izzy instructed before biting into her own slice. "So did you two have a good afternoon?"

Matthew studied Celine while she chattered about the day they'd spent at the park. Bangs hid the stitches over her eye, and with no visible bruises, no one would know she'd been in an accident the night before. Izzy told him earlier today the man who clipped Celine's bike had honked before making his turn. Of course, she hadn't heard.

Could've been so much worse.

"Iz," he blurted suddenly, swallowing a bite of pizza. "Have you scheduled the surgery yet?"

Jase and Izzy had been talking about cochlear implants for six months now. Because of the circumstances of Celine's hearing loss, she was a perfect candidate for the surgery, which could help her regain at least a degree of hearing. And after yesterday . . .

Izzy met his eyes over the rim of her soda glass. She lowered the glass to the table. "Cee, you want another piece of pizza? Or are you ready for a couple arcade games?"

Celine practically jumped out of the booth. "Games. But save me a piece."

Matthew dug into his pocket for a handful of change and passed it off to Celine. "Win me a teddy bear, all right?"

"You're too old for stuffed animals," Celine said before trouncing away.

Matthew turned to Izzy, forked in another bite. "What's up? Why'd you send Cee off?"

Izzy dropped a pizza crust onto her plate and pushed her plate away. "The surgery. It's not happening anymore. At least not anytime soon."

Matthew paused mid-chew. Not happening? But if it could help, if it meant Celine could hear honking cars . . . bowling pins knocking down . . . "Why? I thought you were only waiting for the insurance company."

Melancholy played over Izzy's face. "We got a letter from the company yesterday. They're declining coverage."

"That's ridiculous. The doctor said insurance usually covers cochlear implants."

"*Usually* was the operative word, I guess. And with things so bad at the gallery and my hours cut at the school, we don't have the money."

Matthew lowered his arm from the back of the booth, tense with disbelief. "Does Cee know?" Just the thought ripped at his heart.

Izzy shook her head. "Not yet. We're trying to believe for the best. Maybe if we save for a couple years, if things turn around . . . And the social worker at the hospital said we could file an appeal to the insurance company."

"But if you wait too long, isn't there a chance the surgery won't do as much good?"

Izzy pushed her empty glass to the middle of the table. "We're trusting God. It's all we can do at this point."

No, not good enough. And it wasn't all *he* could do. Resolve expanded inside him as cheers erupted from a nearby lane. "I have some savings, Iz. Not a lot, but it could help." And if nothing else, he'd downsize from his townhouse to a smaller apartment. Lower rent meant more money to push their way.

The dejection in Izzy's eyes softened into gratitude. "Not gonna happen, Matt. Jase would never—"

"Do you have any idea how many times Jase has been there for me over the years? It's about time I did something for him."

"What I really wish you'd do is take that story assignment in North Carolina. Go meet Randi Woodruff. Do you know how many people would kill for a chance like that? Have some fun." Her expression intensified. "Be an example to Celine of someone who doesn't give up just because they've hit a rough patch."

Izzy paused, then picked up her fork. "Besides, if Celine finds out you had the chance to interview her hero and didn't take it, she'd never forgive you. Have you seen the *From the Ground Up* poster she has in her bedroom? The tool set she insisted we buy her for her birthday?"

His eyes landed on Celine inserting quarters into an arcade game as the consideration trekked a slow path through him. Maybe he *should* take the assignment. But not for the reasons Izzy listed.

If Dooley was to be believed, there were skeletons to be unburied in Randi Woodruff's closet. The woman did have an interesting story, after all. Yes, he'd Googled her that afternoon. After three years in Brazil, she'd come home and within months landed the starring role on a new show. He'd read she'd beat out some other HGTV-type personality, had so impressed the network that they'd redesigned the whole show around her.

The husband mystery was intriguing, if nothing else. And though it was the last kind of journalism he'd ever aspired to, the gossip rags paid well for exposés. Plus, Dooley had hinted at a possible cover story.

If he had to temporarily ditch his journalistic integrity, so be it.

The decision made itself. He'd do it for Celine. For once, he'd play the hero.

Chapter 3

So this is what Big Bird felt like.

Miranda froze in front of the full-length mirror, five-foot-ten image blaring back at her like a horror movie in Technicolor. The sunflower yellow dress smoothed over her lithe form like a second skin and reached to her knees. Ruffled sleeves dolled up the look, and a cherry-red sash cinched her waist in place of her tool belt. "Whitney, I can't wear this dress. I'm a walking hot-dog condiment."

And then there were the heels. John Wayne would have had a better chance than she would of sashaying in front of a camera in the three-inchers.

"You're autumn chic," her assistant argued. "The point is to wow whatever morning-show host you'll be chatting it up with this morning." Whitney stepped back and gave an appraising once-over. "And trust me, this will do the trick."

Miranda braved one more look in the dressing-room mirror, her form spotlighted by the row of circle lights over the vanity behind her. She winced. "This isn't me. I should be wearing jeans and a tee and flan—"

Whitney halted her with a palm and shudder. "Don't even say that word."

"What? Flannel?" Miranda pushed a wayward curl behind

her ear and fiddled with the red bangles shackling her wrist. A ponytail tamed and held the rest of her black waves—that, at least, in keeping with the norm. It wasn't even the idea of a dress that bothered her so much. It was more the assumption that she couldn't be trusted to pick her own.

If she'd done the choosing . . . well, it would've been mid-night blue, like the color of the afghan Grandma Woodruff always used to fold over the back of her rocking chair. No sequins or frills, just enough flare to bow out at her knees and swish when she walked. In wedged sandals instead of the spikes she balanced on now.

"Someday, girl, I'm going to hike up to that mountain home of yours and steal every last scrap of flannel from the prop-erty," Whitney said. "And then I'll have a bonfire. Now show me your walk."

"Uh, I think I'd rather stay right here." Playing Mirror, mirror, on the wall, who's the fakest of them all.

Because it wasn't just her appearance putting on a false front today. Somehow she had to smile her way through an interview, all the while knowing Brad and Lincoln waited to pounce with her ready-made pretend husband. Apparently it was easier to find a willing stand-in than she'd figured.

If only they asked her before making the selection. Brad had called her with the news Monday evening.

"We found the guy from the other night, the one you thought was Robbie! His name is Blake Hunziker. Turns out he was with the catering crew."

Brad had called the catering company to get the man's name and contact information. He'd already contacted the guy, laid out their scheme, made the request. Just perfect. As if she hadn't embarrassed herself enough in front of the stranger the other night during her momentary bout of mistaken identity.

"Just meet with him, Rand. And don't think about it as

lying. He's just another character on the show." Brad's voice had skirted the edge of begging. *"You've described your husband enough on-screen that we needed to find a look-alike."*

Fight or flight? One way or another, today she'd either cave to Lincoln's plan or stand her ground. Neither sounded particularly fun. So should've downed a second Pop-Tart this morning.

"C'mon, Rand. Show me your stuff," Whitney ordered. "If you can build a house, you can walk in heels." Whit smacked her gum, arms crossed, waiting.

If Miranda had that much faith, she might still be in Brazil playing missionary. Or she'd at least remember the last time she warmed a church pew.

But at Whit's demanding stare, her own stubbornness reared. Miranda raised her head and took a tentative step. Fine, more like a hobble. Then another, gaze fixed on the window behind Whit, where dawn spread a pale sheen over the fog rising from the Smokies. She'd risen at three thirty this morning to make it to the set by five, while darkness still blanketed the mountains.

Three cups of coffee later, she was still droopy-eyed. Or maybe that was just the prospect of meeting a certain Mr. Blake Hunziker.

"You're not wearing work boots, girl," Whitney urged. "And you're not a horse. No plodding."

Miranda's eyes narrowed as she balanced herself with the folding chair facing the vanity.

"C'mon, you've got multiple publicity events coming up where you're going to have to play Southern belle. Walk with finesse, wiggle your hips. Think Marilyn Monroe."

Any more patronizing from her assistant and she might have to chuck a heel across the room.

"Randi Woodruff, can that really be you?" Brad breezed into the dressing room. "You'd look good in a nun's habit, but today?" He whistled. "Matt Lauer or whoever won't have words."

"You ever heard of knocking, Walsh?"

"You ever heard of accepting a compliment?" He picked up a Duke University cap from the vanity top. "Not planning to wear this, are ya? Doesn't match."

Miranda plucked the hat from him. At least for the moment, Brad's presence, annoying and endearing all at once, smoothed out her wrinkled emotions and the worry creasing her confidence. "Thank you for the hat advice. And the compliment."

Brad dropped into an overstuffed chair. "That's better. Now, we need to talk." He sent a pointed look Whitney's direction.

Whitney raised her hands in a surrender pose. "I can take a hint. But make her keep walking, Brad."

"No thanks. Five minutes in these shoes and already my toes are weeping." Miranda lifted one foot from her shoe, wiggling her toes, voice rising to a squeak. "Please, don't do this to us. Set us free!"

Brad snorted. "You're hilarious."

"No, she's stubborn," Whitney piped in. "Like a mule. Walks like one, too."

"Why, I oughta—"

Brad jumped from his chair, pulling her back by the shoulders while Whitney escaped the dressing room. "Easy, darling."

Miranda attempted to shake out of his grasp, but her shoes staked her in place. "Well, she's been heckling me all morning. I could find a new assistant, you know. And don't call me darling."

"You don't scare me when you're not wearing your tool belt."

"Pretty sure these heels could do some damage."

He glanced down. "Hmm. Point taken. Listen, can we sit for a minute?"

Miranda perched on the edge of the vanity, eyes moving

across the line of photos spanning the opposite wall. Photos of houses they'd worked on over the seasons, the families who inhabited them. Mixed in, images of the children from Open Arms, wide-eyed smiles and hands waving. "I know you and Linc want me to meet my so-called husband today. Because apparently to you *no* means *bring on the nuptials.*"

"Yes, it's true. Lincoln's champing at the bit to introduce you. We vetted the guy like a president would his potential VP. He's perfect."

"I'm more concerned about the timeline—such as, how long I'm going to be stuck in a fake marriage. You and Linc promised me an exit strategy."

"And we've got one. Besides, let me point out the fact that you've been stuck in a fake marriage for years now, Rand. We're just giving the guy a face. Anyway, we'll talk about that later." Brad crossed one leg over the other, fiddled with a shoelace. "There's something I forgot to tell you."

Miranda slid from the counter. "Like that there is, in fact, a purpose for high heels, and—"

"A reporter's coming," he cut in. "This morning."

"I have another interview today?"

Brad cocked his head, yanked the knot from his shoelace in a jerky move that spoke nervousness. "Today, yes. And for the next few days. Weeks, actually. Three or four weeks."

A trail of dread started in her brain and hiked its way to her throat. She straightened, ankles suddenly steady. "I don't understand."

"*Today* magazine wants to shadow you for an ongoing Web story. I think they called it a serial blog."

She had the sudden urge to pelt him with the nails from her tool belt pouch. Except thanks to Whitney she wasn't wearing it. "Shadow me? As in follow me around? And you're just now telling me?" She crossed her arms, bracelets digging into her flesh.

"It's going to be a daily blog. The timing couldn't be more perfect with the Giving Heart Award and all that. And now with the show in jeopardy, this is one more notch on the ladder to renewal. The editor pitched the story months ago, but I didn't really see any advantage in agreeing to his proposal. But when things started getting shaky with the show"—his words gushed, as if spilled quickly enough they might mop up her annoyance—"I thought it might ramp up viewer interest. So I contacted him and accepted his proposal."

"*You* accepted . . . ? Brad, I've got a show to save, an award to win, and a fake spouse to fit into the insane puzzle that is my life. And, oh yeah, I'm chatting it up with the national media in an hour. Now I'm supposed to deal with a reporter playing Lamont Cranston?"

Brad paused, eyebrows raised.

"From *The Shadow* radio program, novels, comics," she prodded. "Lamont Cranston is one of *The Shadow*'s aliases."

"You have the weirdest trivia floating around in your brain. I'm surprised there's room for all that woodworking knowledge."

She shakily stalked forward and stopped in front of Brad, staring him down. "Don't change the subject, Walsh."

"You're the one who went all *Jeopardy* on me."

"Isn't *Today* just another celebrity tabloid? Why would you agree to this when you know how hard I've worked to draw the line between my personal and public lives?"

"It may not be *TIME*, but *Today* isn't just another grocery-aisle magazine. They portray celebrities as real people. They cover world issues, news, even the occasional political piece."

"Yeah, when it involves scandal."

Brad met her eyes, a stern glint hardening his expression. "Listen, I'm sure the reporter won't be a problem. And the editor told me if you win the Giving Heart, you'll be the cover story for *Today*'s January issue. Think of what that will do for ratings."

Miranda exhaled, grasping for calm. But the choking feeling of panic wasn't so easily subdued. "I feel like things are spinning out of control," she forced out in ragged breaths.

"But they aren't." Brad stood and placed both hands on her shoulders. "Rand, ever since we found out about the possibility of the show getting cut, opportunity after opportunity has fallen into our laps. First the award, now the magazine feature. And that Blake guy—could it really be just a coincidence that he happened onto the set the other night looking so much like Robbie you almost threw yourself at him?"

"Are you saying there's some kind of divine destiny behind all this?" Somehow she doubted God would be all that supportive of a phony marriage played out on a national stage.

"I'm saying, where you see chaos, I see ducks lining up in a perfect row." He tipped her chin so her eyes met his. "And where you see a girl who can't walk in heels, I see the ridiculously talented woman who rose from obscurity to charm viewers across the country. The star who has years and years of success left in her if she'll just remember how to reach for it."

Miranda felt something close to a smile take over. "You know, I seriously don't deserve a friend like you." Brad might drive her crazy, but he always found a way to encourage her. Running into him after returning to the States, just when she'd found herself in need of a professional manager, it'd felt like a divine favor. Undeserved.

Brad stepped back. "Well, you might want to remember that when I tell you the part about the reporter staying in the cabin on your property."

Either Matthew truly deserved the title "unluckiest person in the world" or someone up there had it in for him. Probably both.

"No, no, no." He banged his head against his rental Jeep door as he drove. Then banged it again. A little harder than intended. Fine, throw in a bruise, too. Not like this day could get worse.

So much for a shortcut. He'd thought it smart, taking the back road over the Appalachian foothills rather than the winding highway around. The plan backfired when the altitude obscured his GPS. Now, thoroughly lost and plenty frustrated, he drove aimlessly.

Through the open window, fresh mountain air breezed over his face. Under other circumstances, he would be relishing the experience. No concrete, no horns honking, not a corporate suit in sight. Only pillowy clouds and blue ridges draped in a blanket of pine and cedar.

Matthew slapped a hand against the window frame. "Purple mountain majesties, forget it." Some good this scenic heaven did with its twisty roads leading him nowhere. If he missed this morning's meeting with the *From the Ground Up* execs, Dooley would have his head once and for all.

He still couldn't believe he'd even accepted the story assignment. But the look on Izzy's face Saturday night, the thought of Celine missing out on her surgery . . . Well, no way was he going to sit around and do nothing. He'd write that blog on Randi Woodruff and scout for secrets. All celebrities had them, right? He'd even humiliate himself and do the entertainment TV gossip circuit if need be, spill the star's story for the sake of cash flow.

Anything to help Celine. To do something, for once, that mattered.

Of course, he had to actually *find* Miss Homebuilding

Celebrity before he could get to work. Hope crept in at the sight of a vehicle up ahead. Maybe he'd find a local who could point him the right direction. But why was the truck stopped along the road?

He slowed his Jeep as he approached, and as he reached the vehicle ahead—an old Ford truck that looked like something off the set of *The Waltons*—the full situation registered. The river running parallel to the road had curved and spilled over up ahead, flooding the road. And the driver of the truck had driven right in.

He braked and shifted into Park. Was the driver still in the truck? He hopped out of his Jeep and walked up to the truck bed. The front end dipped into the water. As far as he could tell, no one sat in the driver's seat.

"Oh well. So much for luck."

A screech sounded from the truck bed as a head popped into view.

Matthew jerked, his own gasp jumping from his throat. "Whoa, you scared me!"

The woman in the truck bed sat up. "I scared you? I thought I was out here in the middle of nowhere, alone, and suddenly I hear this voice."

Alluring gray eyes, wide with shock, connected with his. So familiar . . . "You didn't hear me drive up?"

A shrug and half smile. "Guess I was in my own world. A nice feeling, actually . . ." Her voice trailed at the end.

"You look like you could use some help."

She slid from the truck bed, bare feet landing on grass, her yellow dress wrinkled. "You mean 'cause of the river slurping on my truck?" She chuckled. "Just needs a little push. I was going to do it myself, but I don't have to be back for another thirty minutes, so I was taking advantage of the opportunity. Plus, I don't mind making my manager squirm over my absence."

Her manager? She grinned as she spoke, sunlight casting a shine on her dark curls. Why did he feel like he'd met her before? Like he'd admired her smoky eyes . . .

His jaw dropped as it dawned on him. "You're Randi Woodruff."

Amusement played over her face as she rounded the truck. "At your service."

He hadn't expected the star-struck daze settling over him. Nor the sudden onset of nervousness. "You're, uh, taller in person than you look on TV."

Her laughter filled the mountain quiet. Her cheeks were rosy, probably from the autumn chill in the air. "You should see me in the heels they're trying to make me wear. A regular Sasquatch."

So not the word he'd have used to describe her.

She leaned against the truck. "Where you going taking the Ol' Pass Road? Other than us locals, people quit using it years ago."

"I'm lost. I'm trying to find Pine Cove . . . the set of your show, actually."

She gave him a curious glance, then stumbled as the front of the truck sank farther in the sludge underneath. His arms shot out to catch her before she tripped into the water. And when she looked up at him, every self-conscious nerve in him stood at attention. *Oh boy* . . .

Steady, Knox. He practically pushed her away. "Careful. You'll ruin your dress."

There was that celebrity smile again. "Don't I wish. Anyway, as long as you're here, if you want to help me out with the truck, I can get you to the Cove. You missed the turnoff. It's just a couple miles back."

"Sure thing. We can push this out easy."

"Since you've got some muscle on me, I'll steer." She plopped a bare foot into the mud surrounding the truck and climbed in.

"Just a sec, Miss, uh, Mrs. . . . Randi?" He knelt to untie his Converse shoes and roll up his pant legs.

"I'm Randi on set," she said out the truck window. "But I prefer Miranda."

He stood, met her eyes. "Miranda."

Laughter rang from the driver's seat as Miranda took in his rolled-up jeans. "Nice look, Huckleberry Finn."

"Funny. Mock all you want, but I'm not the one who drove my truck into a flooded roadway."

"I was daydreaming, all right?"

He stepped up to her open door. "About what?"

Her gaze shifted to the view outside her windshield. "Taking an entire month off work. Expanding my workshop. Buying a new cabinet saw with chrome-plated surfaces. Woodworking to my heart's content." She straightened in her seat, facing him once again. "Probably sounds silly."

He shook his head. "Not silly. Just not much like an ordinary vacation."

"Well, I've never been all that ordinary." Her comment hovered between nonchalant and something more. "All right, let's do this."

He pushed her door shut, then dipped a toe into the river. The cold sent shivers up his leg. She started the engine. He forced his other foot into the water and, standing knee-deep in the river, braced himself against the hood of her truck.

"Ready?" she called out the window.

"Stick it in Reverse and go for it."

He threw his weight into the vehicle, pushing until his back strained, mud squishing between his toes. The vehicle barely budged, and as soon as he let up, it settled back into its mud bed. He took a breath, pushed again, swallowing the taste of humiliation.

He felt the jerk of the truck as Miranda shifted into Park.

She jumped down from the truck. "New plan. Why don't I put it in Neutral? I'll help push and as soon as it's out, one of us can hop in and steer.

He shrugged. "All right."

She reached inside to shift into Neutral, then padded around to the front of the truck. She didn't even flinch as she waded into the water. They stretched their arms beside each other, palms atop the hood. He slid her a glance. "Why do you drive such a beast anyway?"

"It was my grandpa's. So sentiment or stubbornness, I don't know, but I love this rusting heap." She paused, eyes gazing past the truck to the winding stretch of tree-lined road, then shook her head. "Can't bring myself to get rid of it."

As cold numbed his feet, sympathy heated his heart. He'd done his cursory research about Randi—enough to know she'd lived with her grandparents for most of her childhood years while her parents did some kind of missionary work in South America.

"Well, let's save your truck before the murky river eats it."

She nodded.

But instead of pushing the truck, he slid his hand over hers. "Hey, what you said about not being ordinary—I think that's a good thing." *What are you doing, Knox?*

Her eyes climbed from her covered hand to his face. "Um. Thanks?"

Celine. He'd said it because of Celine. Because she, too, lived with that sense of being unordinary. Because it'd become second nature to voice his reassurance. He pulled his hand back. "On the count of three?"

She nodded again. "One . . . two . . . three—"

"By the way, I'm Matthew, the reporter from *Today*. I hear you have a cabin—"

At his words, she whipped her head in surprise, slipped

while he pushed. And as mud sprayed up into the air and the truck inched backward, he heard the "Oomph" as she landed in the water.

Oh man. Perhaps not the best timing for the introduction. "I'm sorry. I'm really—"

"My truck!" she sputtered through dripping hair.

The apology would have to wait. He hopped over Miranda— *So getting kicked off this story!*—jumped into the driver's seat, and yanked the truck into Reverse. Backing up beside his Jeep, he parked . . .

And watched through the windshield as Miranda rose from the water, dress clinging to her body, hair a dripping frame around her face.

"I'm sorry," he called again as he fumbled out of the car. "Sorry! Let me help—" He held out an arm.

She ignored it, lifting a hand instead to push the hair out of her face. "Oooh, Whitney's going to kill me."

He stood at the edge of the flooded portion of the road, creek water syruping over his toes. "Your dress—"

She waved off his worry with a fling of her hand. "I hated it the second I squeezed into it." She hugged her arms to herself as she plodded from the water and came to stand in front of him. She poked a dripping finger at his chest. "But you . . . I don't appreciate you waiting so long to tell me you're the reporter."

"I wasn't hiding it."

"You let me go on about Grandpa's truck. You could've at least identified yourself before starting the interview. And you think you're going to weasel your way into free lodging in my cabin?"

He'd laugh at her wrinkled nose if not for the fierce look in her eyes. "I'm not trying to weasel my way into anything. Your manager offered the cabin, and—"

She stomped her foot, water and mud spraying. "I know he did. Rat."

"Would it make you feel better if I fell in the water, too?" Stupid thing to offer. Like he had any desire to go swimming in icy water.

But she smiled at his offer. Very possibly a bad sign. "It just might, at that." She stepped forward, a gleam replacing the annoyance in her eyes.

"I was mostly kidding, you know."

She reached out. "Oh, really?"

He inched backward. "Miranda, please. I'm a journalist, a professional. I'm on the job right now." At least until she canned him.

"You did say you were here to shadow me. I was in the water, therefore—"

He ducked just as she lunged forward, but lost his footing in the process. Water splashed over his face as his backside settled into the flooded mud floor, Miranda's laughter following him down. "You're right. I do feel better!" She reached down and sent a wave of icy water toward him.

"Why, you . . ." He splashed her back and scrambled to his feet.

"Randi Woodruff, you get out of that water this instant!"

They froze in sync at the yell from the water's edge. Busted. And by a guy who, if he were a cartoon, would have had steam coming out of his ears about then. Matthew leaned toward Miranda. "Uh, I think we're in trouble."

"We? I have a television interview to do, and between my dress and the water, I look like a jaundiced river rat."

Angry Dude crossed his arms, eyes shooting darts at Matthew as he stalked forward to pull Miranda from the creek.

"Now, Brad, don't freak out," she consoled.

"In the truck."

Miranda offered Matthew a shrug, then climbed into her truck. The guy named Brad dropped into his own car, glared once more at Matthew, and motored off behind Miranda.

Matthew lifted an arm in a frantic wave, creek water dripping from his shirt. "Wait, I need to know how to get to—"

But they were already gone, with only the sound of Miranda's muffler trailing behind. Mud slicked around Matthew's ankles as he trudged from the creek. "Well," he sighed, shoulders dropping. "Welcome to North Carolina."

❦

"You've got to be kidding me."

"It's all I had in the truck, Walsh. Didn't have time to raid the dressing room." Head high, Miranda strode past a slack-jawed Brad, away from the studio porch where moments ago she'd sacrificed her last vestige of freedom from public scrutiny. A foundation spokesperson had made the award nomination announcement on the national morning news show. After a commercial, the show went to a live-feed interview with Miranda, staged in front of the set house.

"It's bad enough you decided to have a water fight before appearing on TV. Did you really have to make it worse with *that*?" Brad pointed to her long-sleeved T-shirt, the words *Harry's Fingerlickin' BBQ* splashed across the front.

"Hey, Harry's a friend of mine. He'll appreciate the publicity." At least she'd kept her left arm tight to her side during the interview, hiding the barbeque sauce stain from her last tangle with Harry's tangy ribs.

"Well, what's done is done, I suppose. Come on, Lincoln's waiting to introduce you to your new hubby."

She groaned through clenched teeth. "I feel like a teenage bride being led to meet the groom my parents arranged. What kind of dowry did you and Linc offer him?"

"Couple cows and a hundred bushels of grain."

Brad ushered her to the side door, but she stopped him with her hand on his arm. "This is crazy. How do we even know we can trust this guy? What would make him agree to do this?"

"Money? Fame? We'll take care of all his living expenses, plus pay him a great wage—as well as a tidy bonus if he sees this thing through. Apparently, he needs it. Appears to be a regular prodigal son—spent five years traveling around the world until he emptied his bank account."

"And that's who we're trusting?"

Brad pressed his lips together, pausing before answering. "Rand, we've interviewed him. We've done background research. We feel confident this is our guy. But at the end of the day, it's your call. Just meet him, okay?"

The sound of tires on gravel cut her off from answering. She recognized that Jeep and the guy behind the wheel. "Hey, that's the reporter."

"You mean the Marco to your Polo? Sure knows how to start things off on the right foot."

"The river incident wasn't entirely his fault." After all, Matthew Knox had only been trying to help. Kind of nice, actually. With her handy-girl skills, she hadn't had a man offer to help her out with so much as a light-bulb replacement since . . . she didn't even know when.

And then there'd been that moment, standing knee-deep in river sludge. *"What you said about not being ordinary—I think that's a good thing."*

A reporter's ploy, right? Hone in on the interviewee's insecurity, then coddle her into emotional goo. And yet, his voice, his expression, his hand on hers, all added up to some pretty convincing sincerity.

"Listen," Brad said. "I'll stall the reporter while you go meet Blake. Lincoln's waiting with him in the meeting room."

She nodded and entered the building, casting off thoughts of Matthew Knox. She stopped in front of the meeting room door. "For the good of the show," she muttered and swung the door open. "Hey, Linc."

"Ahh, Randi!" He stood, arms folded, in front of a white marker board covered in Lincoln's scribble. *Born in Charlotte, no siblings . . . college at Duke . . . three years in South America after college . . . met in Brazil . . . thirty years old.*

Ladies and gentlemen, her life condensed into dry-erase board notes.

"I caught your interview," Lincoln said. "Nice job. Though, interesting choice of attire. I especially liked the stain on your arm."

Oy, and she'd thought she'd been so careful.

"Randi Woodruff, meet Blake Hunziker."

Miranda barely heard Lincoln's voice as the figure rose from a chair at the head of the conference room table. The same face she'd seen last Friday, deep-set, dark eyes, mop of black hair, square shoulders—all uncanny in their resemblance to Robbie. But the likeness stopped at this man's carefree grin flanked by twin dimples.

He sidled around the table and held out his tanned arm. "Hi, um, honey. Darling. Sweetheart. Which do you prefer?" The man's dimples deepened with his teasing, a playful glint in his eyes.

"Randi will do," she said wryly, accepting his handshake.

"Really, this is all too perfect," Linc declared, clamping one hand on Miranda's shoulder, the other on Blake's. "You look good together."

Miranda stepped back. *For the good of the show.* If she just kept telling herself that . . .

"I go by Blaze, by the way. So how long have we been married?" Blake asked. He ran a hand through shaggy hair, the lazy smile never leaving his face, and then tucked his hands into the pockets of his board shorts. Wasn't it a little chilly to be dressing like a surfer?

"A few years, right, Rand?" Linc looked to her.

"Three as of last Friday," she said on autopilot. Couldn't take her eyes off Blake. It was like staring at a hologram of Robbie. Freud couldn't have deciphered the emotions twisting inside her at the moment.

It's only temporary. You can do it. She ripped her gaze from Blake. "For the record, Lincoln, I have serious reservations about this."

He nudged his glasses. "But you'll do it, right? I've already filled Blake in on everything."

"And I'm perfect for the job," Blake offered. "My parents are on a three-month safari in Africa—no joke. And I've spent the last five years country-hopping on one adventure after another, haven't kept in good touch with anyone. So friends, hometown folks, they won't have any reason to doubt this thing."

In other words, no ties, no one to question the logistics of their marriage.

"Siblings?" she asked.

For the tiniest moment, a shadow flickered over his face. "Not anymore."

She'd have stopped him right there if she could have, at that first glimpse of vulnerability from her husband-elect, but he'd already continued. "And another thing: I can cook like no one's business. You will be one well-fed wife during our little marriage, pumpkin." He fiddled with the zipper on the sweatshirt he wore over a bright orange T-shirt.

"Call me *pumpkin* again and our marriage won't make it past the honeymoon."

He donned a properly chagrined expression and dropped into his chair. "So, where do we go from here?"

Lincoln pulled out his cell phone. "I go to a meeting with the publicity team. You two lovebirds can take a few minutes to get to know each other."

Miranda's eyes pressed into slits. She ought to whack Linc.

No, she ought to about-face and leave the room, the surfer dude, and Lincoln's smug expression behind. But resolve anchored her in place. As much as she hated it, this *was* the best plan to save her show, her career . . . her identity.

As Lincoln exited, she lowered onto the chair at Blake's right. "So, uh, Blaze. That's an interesting nickname."

He leaned forward, elbows propped on his knees. "Yeah, little incident with a metal travel mug in a microwave. Then there was the time I singed off my eyebrows roasting marshmallows. Oh, and the fireworks seven, no eight, Fourth of Julys ago."

"Suddenly I'm worried about welcoming you into my house."

Blake grinned. "Don't. It's been three and a half years since my last fire. Hot air balloon. Operator error. In Switzerland. Ah, that was a doozy."

Apparently Jack London had nothing on this guy.

He rubbed his palms together. "So, look, this is a wild situation. One minute I've got a part-time stint with a catering company, the next I'm talked into my first acting gig in a role as your husband. But I like helping people—which, from the sound of it, is exactly what you need."

"I need some normalcy, that's what." Something told her this guy was anything but.

He leaned back in the couch, chuckled. "I can't promise that. But I can promise to stick to whatever story you want, play the perfect husband. You totally have my word."

For just a moment, a new thought teased her: *This could be fun.* Would it be so bad to show up at some glitzy restaurant on the arm of this, uh—fine, she'd admit it—hunk? To put up with his dimpled grins and crinkled, marble eyes?

Would it be so painful to act out the happy marriage she'd always dreamed of? "Why are you really doing this, Blaze?"

He must have recognized the imploring tone of her voice for what it was—a plea for assurance, for some kind of serious answer to convince her she wasn't about to make the mistake of her life. "When your manager approached me, at first I thought, 'Dude, I've spent a good deal of my life in someone else's shadow. This is my chance for the spotlight.' May not be noble, but it's a reason, right?" He shrugged, then softened. "But the truth is, I had a chance to help someone once, and I . . . failed. Ridiculous as it sounds, this felt like a second chance. A slightly insane one, but . . . Well, anyway, the paycheck's good, too."

Miranda studied him. He may brush off his own words, but she'd seen a spark just then, something honest and generous. He genuinely saw this as a noble cause, didn't he? "And y-you really think we can pull this off?"

"Babe, I once bungee-jumped off the Golden Gate Bridge. I think I can manage a few weeks of wedded bliss."

He propped his feet on the conference table, flip-flops in place of shoes, not even a hint of concern on his face. Maybe she could learn a thing or two from the man. "You don't think we're crazy trying to pull the wool over a whole country's eyes?"

"Oh, I think you're crazy, all right. I just happen to like crazy."

Oh, Lord, help me. But the prayer had no business flitting through her mind. She couldn't ask God to help her *lie.*

Not lie. Pretend. Remember what Brad said: " . . . *just another character on the show.*"

Somehow the thought didn't ease her conscience. *Someday when this is all over, God, I'll be the obedient, meek and mild woman I'm supposed to be. The person Mom and Dad always wanted me to be.* Maybe she'd go to church again, too. Rekindle the faith that had burned down to barely a flicker of late.

But for now, she had to do what she had to do.

"All right, Blaze. Consider yourself fake-married." She stood and reached behind her head to loosen her ponytail.

"Not so fast." Blake rose, mischievous smile in his eyes. "Shouldn't we say our vows?"

"Excuse me?"

He extended his arm. "Hand, please."

She complied, solely out of amused interest.

"I, Blaze Hunziker, take you, Randi Woodruff, to be my imaginary wife. For richer or for poorer—though I prefer richer; in sickness and in health—I never get sick; for as long as that guy named Lincoln shall order."

A duet of exhilaration and trepidation—possibly what it felt like just before jumping out of a plane—sang through Miranda. "You're a clown."

"Shh, this is a serious occasion. Now, do you, Randi Woodruff, take me, Blaze Hunziker, to be your imaginary husband, for richer or for poorer, in sickness and in health, for as long as you need me for your show?"

"I—"

"Randi! Good, you're still here." Brad burst into the room. "I've just been showing Matthew Knox around, and—" His voice clipped as his eyes swept over Miranda and Blaze, standing hand in hand in the center of the room. He tossed Miranda a mocking grin. "Well, isn't this a sweet moment."

It was then Miranda noticed Matthew standing behind Brad, jeans still wet around his ankles, messenger bag slung over his shoulder. And curiosity, plain as the white walls of the meeting room, spelled out in his raised eyebrows and tilted head.

Miranda dropped her hands, flush warming her cheeks.

"Rand, don't you want to introduce Blake and Matthew?" Brad prodded.

"I, uh . . . I do." Eyes to Blaze. His wink did nothing to quell the butterflies ramming into her stomach. *God, help me.* And this time she didn't take back the prayer. "Matthew, this is . . . my—" deep breath—"husband."

Let the farce begin.

Chapter 4

Sunlight streaked through the curtains of Miranda's bedroom window, spotlighting a trail across the redwood floor and over the quilt tangled around her legs. She rolled onto her back, stretching her arms and breathing in the morning air breezing into the room from the window she'd kept cracked open last night.

She sank back against her heap of pillows. Not too many more nights and temps would dip below freezing. But she'd cling to autumn as long as she could, drinking in its color and tasting its mountain chill. The air smelled of pine and leaves and . . .

Burning?

Miranda sniffed, nose crinkling and the last clutch of sleep releasing as she realized the distant scent of smoke came from her own house. "Blaze!"

She jerked to her feet, toes connecting with the cool wood floor before tripping over the blanket wound around her legs. She kicked herself free, then reached for the green fleece robe draped over her bedpost.

"Ooh, if that man is burning down my home, I'll . . ." She'd fake-divorce her fake husband—that's what.

She crossed the room in quick strides and barreled down the stairs. On a different day she'd have stopped to gulp in the sunrise still caressing the morning, its pinks and oranges cascading through the lanky windows fronting the house. But not with that man somewhere in the place, probably the kitchen. She passed a mess of sheets and blankets strewn across the living room floor.

Oh yes, she'd abandoned him to the couch last night, their first night, for all intents and purposes, as husband and wife. Maybe he'd tossed and turned all night. Maybe that's why he was playing arsonist in her kitchen now.

"Blake? Er, Blaze?" She thudded through the dining room, skidding to a halt in the opening to the kitchen. He stood shirtless over the stove, sinewy muscles threading down his arms and back. She felt the warmth spread over her cheeks even as she exhaled.

"Morning, sunshine. Thought I'd make you breakfast. I hope you like your flapjacks well done." The words rolled lazily from his tongue ahead of a yawn as he ran a hand through his floppy mop of black hair.

At least a frilly apron covered his torso. She cinched the belt of her robe, did not even want to think about what her own hair looked like. Or her face. Had she even washed off her makeup last night? They'd rolled in so late, and she'd had to find sheets for the bed in the cabin—

The cabin, the reporter! She slapped a hand to her forehead. She'd been so exhausted last night, she hadn't even checked out the condition of the cabin first. Just pointed it out and left Matthew Knox to explore it in all its neglected glory on his own.

"Hey, you okay, Woody?" Shirtless Blaze stepped toward her.

Miranda's gaze found its way past Blaze to the spatters of batter all over the wall behind the stove, the pile of blackened pancakes on the plate atop the counter. "Woody?" she asked warily.

"Short for Woodruff. Thought you might like the endearment, but judging by the way you're clenching and unclenching your fists, I guessed wrong." He tapped a spatula against his chin. "I tried *darling* and *sweetheart* yesterday. Scratch those. How about *honey*?"

"How about you hand over that spatula?"

"How about you come and get it?" He winked. "This is fun. Your turn. How about I . . ."

She reached out, loose fleece dangling around her arm. "Hand it over before we have to call the fire department. I really don't need you living up to your nickname while under my roof."

He jerked the spatula back. "Make me."

Her hand closed around the end of the spatula, cakey batter oozing through her fingers. "Let go, Blaze."

He kept a steady grip. "Our first married fight. This feels so official."

"Give it to me." Her elbow jabbed into his chest as she struggled for the utensil. And why was she smiling? This wasn't fun, it was a matter of safety. "C'mon, Blaze. You need to know, I wear the pants in this family."

He whirled, sending her spinning with him, and her hip hit the stove with an "Oomph."

"Sorry, buttercup, but all I see are bare legs under that robe."

"Why, you . . ." Still holding tight to her end of the spatula, she stomped on his foot. "Take that, Mr. Breakfast Burner."

"And here I thought you weren't a morning person, little missus."

Finally she gave up on the tug-of-war. But she wiggled a finger in front of his face. "You may be stronger than me now, but remember, I know where you sleep."

"Yes, the infamous couch to which all husbands under duress are banished."

Under duress? The laughter seeped out of her as his words took root. "Do you feel conned into this, Blaze? It's ridiculous, isn't it? We're not even twenty-four hours into this charade, and I'm convinced there's no way it can work. I don't even know you. Someone's bound to catch on. And, oh yeah, I've got a Geraldo Rivera type sleeping just a stone's throw away, and—"

Blaze placed a finger over her lips. "Calm, m'love. Save the worrying for later. You haven't even had breakfast yet."

She glanced around him at the stack of charred pancakes. "I'm not sure I want to."

Blaze rubbed a hand over the stubble shadowing his chin. "You know, I think I'm going to help you in more ways than one. I'll play your husband for the sake of your show *and* because I've been bored ever since returning to the States. But I think I'll also teach you to have fun."

Miranda folded her arms. "I'm perfectly capable of having fun—thank you very much."

Blaze shook his head before she finished. "People adept at fun don't use phrases like 'perfectly capable' and 'thank you very much.'"

"We need to talk seriously for a minute. I think we should set some ground rules. Starting with"—her eyes darted to his apron-covered chest—"clothes. Please wear them. At all times."

A grin lit his dark eyes. "What else?"

"I'm sorry you have to sleep on the couch, but as you probably noticed last night, I haven't finished building the rest of this house. So the couch is all I've got as far as guest space at the moment. But it's a must. Our relationship is strictly . . . professional." Because, yes, it was oh-so-professional to playact a marriage.

"Right. Clothes, couch. That's it?"

"Also, I think it'd be better for you to avoid any solo interviews with the media. Let me do as much of the talking as possible."

"My lips are sealed. Anything else? Too many more rules and I might need to start writing them down."

She released a half smile. "Just one more thing. No more cooking."

He gasped. "Punkin, I swear I'm a whiz in the kitchen. There's something up with your stove. I think the burner's got issues."

"The burner's fine. It's the cook." She swiped for the spatula again.

"Not a chance, doll."

"Another rule. Don't call me doll or punkin or—"

He hip-checked her away from the oven. "I've got pancakes to make."

She bumped him back. "You mean burn."

Blaze's arm circled around her, reaching for the bowl of batter and trapping her against the counter. He lifted the bowl over her head. "You were saying?"

"You wouldn't dare." She could kick herself for giggling. "I—"

A throat clearing from behind broke into their banter. Over Blaze's arm, Miranda gaped at the figure in the kitchen doorway. Matthew Knox stood in the opening, amusement mixed with embarrassment in his expression. And, oh dear, how long had he been standing there? And how much had he heard?

"Um, I knocked on the front door, but no one answered."

And the couch. He'd probably seen the blankets and sheets. Reporters were observant like that, weren't they? And he'd wonder . . .

"We were just . . ." *C'mon, think, girl.*

"Little morning routine we like to play," Blaze supplied. "She's at her most feisty in the morning."

Ooh, she'd whack him with the spatula—if she ever got ahold of it. Blaze turned to face Matthew, one arm slithering around her waist to her front, pulling her backward into a half hug.

Did she look as flushed as she felt? Apparently she'd forgotten to factor in the touchy-feely part of this whole thing. Of course, if the man had bothered to wear a shirt, this wouldn't be nearly as awkward. Gulping, she patted her hand over Blaze's.

"Married life. It's a roller-coaster ride." His voice brushed over the tip of her ear.

Matthew gave a hesitant nod. "Uh, mind if I grab a cup of coffee?" Poor man looked as uncomfortable as she felt.

Another rule: No hugging! Although, hubby sure smelled good—pancake batter and soap. And he wasn't unattractive. Quite the opposite, really. Not that she cared to admit it aloud. "Sure thing. Mugs are in the cupboard right over the coffeemaker."

As soon as Matthew turned to open the cupboard, she hissed at Blaze, "Hand off my stomach!" and pulled away. "So, Matthew, what's on your agenda today?"

He poured a cup of coffee. "Well, whatever you're doing. I'm your shadow from here on out." He took a sip and headed for the door. "See you later."

Lovely. A wacky husband infiltrating her house and a nosy reporter following her every move. If she survived this soap opera, she'd deserve a dozen Emmys.

That and freedom. At the sobering thought, she hugged her arms to herself. *Oh, please let Brad be right.* Let all the curiosity about her so-called husband die down at the end of this deception. Let the lingering effect of Robbie's past presence in her life finally—*finally*—fade.

Let spacey Blaze pull off his role. Let Matthew remain oblivious. Let her heart mend in the process.

"Oh, Rand, almost forgot." Blaze reached into the pocket of his apron and held up a crinkled envelope. "When I was digging around looking for a griddle, I checked the high cupboards over your refrigerator and found this on top of the fridge. I thought you might be looking for it."

No mistaking the handwriting on the envelope or the air mail stamp. It was on the tip of her tongue to tell Blaze it hadn't been misplaced. She'd meant to slip Mom's letter up there. Out of sight, out of mind. But saying so would only invite questions.

Questions she had no desire to answer.

So she pulled the letter from his outstretched hand, thanked him, and buried the envelope in the deep pocket of her robe.

"Installing crown molding can be a pain in the you-know-what. But if you have the right tools and take your time, I promise you can master it. Let's get started." Randi Woodruff's lithe form perched on the corner of a dining room table as she spoke. Three seafoam-green walls gave the staged room a beachfront feel, and set lights bathed the gathered crew in warmth.

Matthew observed the taping from behind the "fourth wall," fingers wrapped around the ice-cold Coke Brad Walsh handed him. Apparently Miranda's manager had forgiven him for his part in yesterday's creek incident. Either that or the man was waiting for the perfect time to hammer Matthew with a lecture.

"You should've heard Randi moan when Tom told her we needed to re-tape her crown-molding segment," Brad whispered. "It's the one project she hates with a passion."

But you'd never know it by the smile she flashed at the camera. Miranda glided across the set with a charming mix of grace and confidence. "Here are the tools you'll need for the job: power miter saw with 10-inch carbide-tipped blade, tape measure, pneumatic finishing nailer, framing square, coping saw . . ."

Matthew whistled. "Wow, I should've spent some time in a few hardware stores before coming down here."

"I hear ya there. Sometimes I have to remind her we didn't all grow up watching *Hometime* with our grandfathers."

Her grandfather, huh. Probably the one who'd left her the truck. "What do you know about her parents? I read they were missionaries. They still in—where was it?—Brazil?"

"Yes."

Was that tension in Brad's voice? Matthew slid him a look but met only folded arms and eyes still glued to the activity on set. "That a sore subject?"

"Not sore." Brad's shoulders stiffened, a tic in his jaw filling the pause before he spoke again. "But not all that popular, either. And it's not my story to tell."

Waves of curiosity whooshed in, salty and enticing. Matthew popped the tab on his can of Coke and took a long drink, carbonation fizzing down his throat.

On set, Randi climbed up a ladder. "The first thing we're going to do is use a chalk line to mark our installation lines along each wall." She held a piece of molding in place and marked its position with a pencil. "Modern crown molding actually traces back to the Renaissance when designers drew on elements of Greek and Roman architecture, using ornamental plaster and wood cornices to embellish the intersection of ceiling and wall."

Matthew followed her movements as she pulled an electronic thingy from her tool belt and said something about locating studs and joists. "She really knows her stuff, doesn't she?"

He felt Brad's glare as the manager's voice moved above a whisper. "Of course she does. What, did you think she was a fake?"

Man, the guy played uptight to a T. "No, I just . . ." Except, well, maybe.

Miranda's voice jutted into his fumbling reply. "Coped cuts are used where one piece of crown molding meets another at an inside corner. Coping is the process of cutting the end of a molding to mimic the profile milled into its face."

Matthew tossed Brad a sheepish grin, going for a mood-lightening tone. "Do you have any clue what she just said?"

But Brad didn't crack—pressed lips and stony stare ready at the defense. "Randi Woodruff has more talent in her pinky finger than most people accumulate in a lifetime."

Chill, buddy. I wasn't implying anything.

Miranda's instructions continued. "To create a snug-fitting joint, hold your coping saw at a five-degree angle away from the face of the molding and cut carefully along the marked edge."

Brad's rigid stance still leaking hostility beside him, Matthew downed the rest of his Coke. Time to mend fences. "Look, I didn't mean—"

"Hey, we're trying to tape here!" the show's director, Tom Somebody-or-other, yapped from where he leaned against a coffee cart. "Walsh, take the chitchat outside."

Brad tapped Matthew's shoulder. "Come with me."

"But I haven't finished learning about crown molding. It was just getting interesting. Cutting joints and sawing faces. It's like, Frankenstein meets *Extreme Makeover: Home Edition*."

Brad rolled his eyes, pointing at the exit. "Out."

Matthew turned, but not before meeting Miranda's amused gaze, her snicker rattling over the set as she stayed balanced atop her ladder. At least someone appreciated the humor—someone who managed to make Levi's and a plain white tee scream femininity. Even with that pencil between her teeth, her smile could have graced any magazine cover.

And would if he did his job right.

Brad gave him a light shove, and Matthew acquiesced, emerging into autumn's outdoor embrace. The colors of fall were beginning to deepen, as if an artist had smudged fresh paint over the landscape, blotting out the lingering green of summer.

Matthew matched Brad's stride. "This is a beautiful setting for the *From the Ground Up* set. Like going to work in a Thomas Kinkade piece."

Brad gestured to a patio set, surrounded by meticulous landscaping sloping down a scenic ravine. "Let's talk."

"Look, yesterday we sort of got off on the wrong foot. Today we still seem to be hobbling along on the same leg. How about we shift weight or something? Start over."

Brad dropped onto the rattan chair and motioned for Matthew to sit. "Fair enough." He opened the folder he'd been carrying since walking onto the set earlier. "Matthew Knox. Originally from Minneapolis, worked for the *Star Tribune* for five years. Pulitzer finalist in 2006. Impressive, by the way. Moved into the position of news editor in 2007 for a short six months before being bumped up to interim managing editor when your predecessor had heart surgery. And in 2008—"

Every muscle in Matthew pulled taut. "Pause, Principal Walsh. You've got a file on me?" And just how much did the guy know about . . . 2008?

Brad closed the folder with a snap. "Yes, I do. I'm picky about who spends time with Randi."

Matthew's hand tightened on the empty pop can he still held. "Hey, you okayed this blog project. I don't understand what's up with the interrogation act now."

"I okayed the project based on a proposal that listed the reporter as Lisa Spangle. She interviewed that one blond singer slash train wreck last year—made her look like Shirley Temple. Spangle's a softie."

"And she just had a baby, which is why I'm here. I'm simply a replacement. *Today* magazine isn't trying to pull anything on you."

"It's not the magazine I'm worried about."

Which meant Brad Walsh probably knew everything about the 2008 fiasco. In the distance, a woodpecker pounded out a rhythm. "I'm not out to play 'gotcha' journalism." Though, if the opportunity presented itself, wouldn't he take full advantage?

Absolutely. For Cee. And fine, okay, also for the career comeback. Not how he'd imagined it—and yes, it stabbed at his dignity—but when options were limited, what was a man supposed to do?

Brad's eyes focused on him, and Knox wondered what he saw. A wannabe writer in faded jeans, blue hooded sweatshirt, and Converse shoes? Someone too old to still be floundering in his career, questioning his life's purpose, his identity.

"You slammed your own father in a front-page exposé."

Brad's flat-toned statement dug into Matthew like claws, any response lost in the emotional puncture.

"We had a source." But the argument had as little weight now as it had five years ago.

"You pinned a target to his back with newsprint, only to find out weeks later he was innocent. That had to sting."

No, it had burned. And after it was all over, his career, his confidence, his reputation lay in ashes. He'd basically co-written the article, kept it under wraps until deadline. Didn't matter that it wasn't his name in the byline.

A distant scent of burning leaves wafted in with the breeze. Finally he found words. "The police were investigating my father. I wasn't blindly grasping at straws. You have no idea what you're talking about." No idea Matthew had more reason than anybody to suspect Gordon Knox of the scandalous embezzlement that rocked the Twin Cities financial district that summer. *Of course* he'd believed his businessman father capable of the scheme.

After all, the man had emptied the family bank account before leaving Mom years before. Not such a leap to believe he'd orchestrated the embezzlement scheme.

If his personal experience wasn't enough, there'd been his source—his father's former financial advisor. He'd come to Matthew claiming to have proof of Gordon Knox's illegal activities, said no one else would listen, no one else believed him.

Turned out, they were right not to listen. The State's case against his father crumbled quickly, and the real embezzler was convicted mere months after the crime.

But not before Matthew had green-lighted the scathing article that drew attention not only for its biting portrayal of Gordon Knox, but also for the shared last name of the subject and the paper's editor. Or as the *Star Tribune* publisher had described it seconds before inviting Matthew to resign, "glaringly obvious conflict of interest."

"My source was unreliable," Matthew said to Walsh.

"Your judgment was unreliable." Brad's tone was unflinching.

If the whole thing wasn't bad enough, the reporter whose name appeared under the article? Delia Jones. Matthew had fed her the article. And even worse, they'd gone out one night after a day of piecing together their research. He'd considered it a working dinner; she, a date. Either way, it didn't end well. He'd hurt the woman personally and professionally.

And while he had been given the chance to resign, she'd been sacked.

Was it any wonder she plagued him still?

Brad leaned forward, expression intense. "You play that kind of shoddy reporting with Randi, and I'll have you outta here so fast the Road Runner will be coming to you for advice."

"Point taken—on one condition."

Brad almost relaxed, apparently pleased at the outcome of his interrogation. "What's that?"

Matthew forced his voice into even tones. "Leave my father out of this from now on."

Because he'd learned the hard way, that was the best way to deal with Gordon Knox—who, as it turned out, had relocated to the South without so much as a good-bye after the case. *And history repeats itself.*

Brad shrugged. "All right, fine—consider the subject closed. And now, about what you said earlier, about Randi knowing her stuff, as if it was a surprise . . ."

That again? "I didn't mean anything by it."

Brad cocked an eyebrow.

"Okay, so maybe I wondered. But people always wonder about these TV types. Can Rachael Ray really cook? Can Martha Stewart really make her own candles?"

"If you insinuate Bob Ross couldn't actually paint, you'll throw me into a state of serious disillusionment." Finally the guy cracked a smile. "But seriously, have Randi show you her workshop sometime. Sure, she's a whiz at the home-improvement projects she does on television. But her real love is working with wood. It'll be good blog material for you."

They eased into conversation that belied the strain of only moments ago.

And yet, the folder in Brad's hands mocked Matthew. He clenched his pop can, squeezed it with a crunch. Would he never escape the stigma of his five-year-old fatal career move?

❦

Under a star-studded dusk, Miranda shuffled the path from the cabin to her house. Moonlight-tipped trees and shadowed ridges beckoned, the tension of the day begging to float off like the white of her breath in the evening chill.

But there wasn't time. Matthew might return any minute.

"What's the rush?" Blaze huffed from the opposite end of the antique trunk swinging between them. The weight of it pulled Miranda's arms taut. No way would she have been able to lug the thing without him. "You must really not want Knox to see whatever's in here."

A nighttime wind rustled through the trees circling her property. "Nothing important. Just personal. I'd rather not have a reporter digging through it."

The memory of the trunk in the cabin had hit her out of the blue after arriving home from work. She'd waited all evening for a chance to swipe it from Matthew's prying eyes, had practically choked on a sigh of relief when she heard his car rumble to life. The second his headlights disappeared down the road, she'd bolted from the house.

She hadn't expected the cabin to be locked, though. Who did Matthew think would break in? Smokey the Bear? And she'd given him her only set of cabin keys.

"I couldn't believe it when I saw you climbing in that window," Blaze said with a chuckle as they hefted the trunk up the porch stairs. "First you burst from the house like a greyhound, then you break into the reporter's cabin. This husband gig just keeps getting better and better."

Her forearms strained at the heaviness of the trunk. She shifted to free one hand and nudged open her front door. "It's not technically breaking in since it's *my* cabin."

Yes, perhaps removing one of the cabin's side windows and limboing in like an acrobat was extreme, but the contents of the trunk told more of her story than Matthew ever needed to see.

Inside the house, they dropped the trunk in the entryway. "I hope there's not a body inside. I'd hate to think I aided and abetted a murder," Blaze said.

Eventually they'd move it—maybe up to her bedroom or

her office next door. But for now, she needed to get back to the cabin, re-lock the front door, and replace the window. "Don't worry. This won't add to your criminal record."

"Not sure how I feel about the fact that you assume I already have one."

"I'll go clean up the crime scene. Watch for Matthew, and if you see him drive in before I'm back, stall him."

"Aye aye, oh, wife of mine." He saluted. "You can count on me." Tan legs poked from Blaze's shorts and his windswept hair brushed over his smiling eyes. The man did serious about as well as she did makeup.

She sprinted back to the cabin. The three-room structure had been the only building on the property when she'd purchased the land a little less than four years ago. For over six months she'd called it home, woken up every morning in the double bed edged up against one wall, covered in Grandma Woodruff's quilt . . . Robbie at her side.

Earlier, she'd been in such a hurry to retrieve the trunk, she hadn't allowed the tide of memories to rush over her. But this time, before she even walked through the door, the flashbacks returned so thick she could smell the sweet of the cedar walls, feel the poking springs of the old bed, hear the whispering voice of her guilt.

Miranda shook her head, dislodging the pull of the past.

The storm window sat on the ground where she'd left it, propped against a caulked wall. Quickly, she replaced it, then marched inside. She looked into the bedroom to make sure all was as she'd found it: Matthew's duffel bag in the corner on the rough-hewn floor, the doorless cutout closet empty, frayed braided rug at the foot of the bed.

Miranda's cheeks warmed at the sight of the bed sheets thrown back, the familiar chiding of her conscience like a gong. Because, while she and Robbie may have lived like it, they hadn't been married. Robbie—handsome, vibrant Robbie—had been irresistible. Her convictions, no match.

She took a breath now. Even without his clothes in the closet or his work boots lined up against the wall, the cabin still resonated with Robbie's presence.

Another labored breath. And then . . . she froze. The sound of footsteps on leaves, the crinkle of a grocery sack. The jiggling of the doorknob.

"Oh dear." How could Matthew be back so soon? She hadn't heard him drive up. So much for Blaze keeping watch. Oh, why hadn't she ever put a door on the bedroom closet? She could have hidden inside. Maybe under the bed. *And what, stay there all night?* Or maybe . . .

Too late. The door creaked open. Her heart thudded. *Think.*

Only one thing she could do. Miranda plastered on a smile and lifted her hand in a wave. "Hi!"

Matthew yelped and dropped the bundle in his arms. "What are you . . . I thought I locked . . . Way to freak me out, Woodruff."

"Sorry. Um, I thought I'd clean the place up a bit while you were out."

Suspicion crawled into his eyes above stubble-covered cheeks. He shook his head. "Not buying it. The place smelled like a forest when I got home earlier. Someone already went Pine-Sol ballistic."

That's right, Blaze had offered to clean the cabin while she and Matthew were out for the day. He'd also stocked her fridge with groceries and washed a load of towels. She should've brought home a fake husband years ago.

Matthew's eyebrows lifted a notch.

"Well, the truth is . . ." *Nothing, I got nothing.*

"I know what's going on here, so you might as well admit it."

See, this was why a person up to her neck in secrets didn't

play hostess to a sniffing reporter—even if said reporter could easily qualify as cute in his startled state.

Matthew bent to pick up his grocery sack. "You snuck out here so you could get a peek at my first blog for *Today*'s website."

She held back an instant grin. Saved by the man himself. "Yes." Serious face, apologetic eyes. This mock guilt was so much nicer than the real thing. "Yes, that is exactly what I was doing."

"Too late—already sent it. Sorry. But as long as you're here, want some ice cream? Sadly, the selection at the mini-mart was limited. We'll have to make due with Neapolitan."

He kicked the door shut behind him and walked to the kitchenette spanning one wall.

An old couch sat in one corner and a small round table occupied the center of the room, Matthew's laptop open atop it.

"I don't know if I should—"

"Or we could bring it over to the house in case Blaze wants some, too."

She thought of the trunk, likely still sitting in the entryway. "Uh no. He's a healthy eater." She had proof. Blaze had insisted on broccoli and apple slices with dinner tonight. "But, sure, I'll have a scoop. I never say no to ice cream."

"I can't go more than a few days without it myself. I think my internal organs would start shutting down."

"It's possible we share DNA."

Matthew pulled a bowl from the sink. "Found the dishes in one of the cupboards. Do you have guests out here often?"

No, she'd simply had no energy to clean the place out after Robbie left. Interesting, though, how seeing the ease of familiarity with which Matthew moved around the cabin blurred the ghost of Robbie.

"Thank you for letting me stay here, by the way," he said

as he dug a spoon into the box of ice cream. "Brad told me yesterday he'd neglected to okay the arrangement with you. I know he was expecting a female reporter. Hopefully this isn't too awkward."

Considering she also had a man sleeping on her couch, it was practically run-of-the-mill.

"I wanted to ask you about these dishes. They look like handmade pottery." Matthew tapped on the bowl, glaze swirls of red and blue and green ornamenting the upper rim. "I know you spent several years in Brazil. Is that where you got them?"

"Is this an interview?"

He handed her a bowl, pausing with a thoughtful study. "Nah. Off the clock."

"My parents brought that set home during one of their furloughs. They are missionaries in Sao Paulo, but they come home every four years."

He grabbed his own bowl and motioned for her to sit. "So you lived here in the States with your grandparents growing up, and then you joined your parents in South America after college?"

She choked on an icy bite of vanilla. "Joined them? No, I only saw them five or six times during my three years down there."

His quizzical expression fought with her reluctance to tell the story. Lord knew she'd have made any psychiatrist's day at the stacks of repressed memories piled inside.

But there was something about Matthew Knox's patient interest and relaxed gaze. The man may not have the magazine-cover looks of Robbie—or Blaze, for that matter—but that slow-spreading smile of his, under greenish-hazel eyes rimmed by eyelashes longer than any man had a right to have . . . Well, he drew her out.

Or maybe she'd breathed in too much Pine-Sol. "My mom

and dad brought me down to Brazil when I was seven. But I couldn't adjust. I was scared of every little noise at night, didn't like the food, couldn't communicate. Eventually they decided enough was enough."

He nodded. "So they took you home."

The words sped out before she could put on the brakes. "Sent me home. Put me on a nonstop flight to Charlotte."

His spoon landed on the table with a clink. "They abandoned you."

"They were trying to do the right thing. They promised when I was older, they'd send for me, but . . ." They never had. And for years, she'd battled the lies in her head: They didn't care about her. They loved their mission more than her.

That combined with her guilt at knowing they'd never approve of the lie she lived now was why, more often than not, she chose not to read their chatty letters and e-mail updates. It was too hard pretending all was fine. Thus, the letter still stuffed in her robe pocket up in her bedroom.

She locked eyes with Matthew. "I don't normally talk about this."

"To the press?"

"To anyone."

Something shifted in his jaw, and his voice turned husky. "I understand. My dad left us when I was fifteen. Not my favorite topic of discussion, either." His pause stretched, the quiet of the cabin marred only by the drip-dropping of the kitchenette's leaky faucet. And a connection, soft and appealing, filled the space between them. That look in his eyes, pure empathy.

Finally, Matthew cleared his throat. "So why'd you go back after college?"

She chewed on the question before answering. "The breaking point in Brazil for my parents was when they found me crying after getting beaned by a ball during a soccer game with the neighborhood kids. They'd encouraged me to play, wanted me to try fitting in. Didn't work so well." She allowed a smirk. "Ten years later I was named the captain of my high school soccer team. We took state two years in a row. A big part of the reason I returned was I wanted to prove to them—and myself, I guess—that I could overcome my fears."

The creases in the corners of his eyes and the dimple in his chin deepened, and he leaned toward her, the spice of his cologne enticing. "I like the way you work, Miranda Woodruff."

He held her gaze, perhaps understanding more than she'd intended to share. Like the hurt that even proving she could make it in Brazil hadn't wiped out.

Don't look so deep, Matthew.

She couldn't afford to have what he might find be revealed.

Chapter 5

Smudges of red and orange and brown blurred the landscape of the mountains. Matthew palmed the steering wheel, awe streaking a trail through his senses. It was as if he'd driven the rental Jeep into an Impressionist painting. Something Monet or Renoir would've brushed onto canvas.

To his right, Miranda's nose pressed to her window. A handkerchief tied at the back of her neck covered her hair, and she wore baggy overalls over a long-sleeved shirt. He felt his lips curve into a smile, and couldn't help himself. "Still not talking to me?"

She huffed, sending a few loose strands of hair floating.

"Come on, it was funny."

She turned to him, gray eyes narrowed. "I could've been injured."

"But you weren't."

"But I could've been." With a stubborn flounce of her handkerchief-covered ponytail, she crossed her arms.

Fine, okay, maybe he shouldn't have laughed at the woman when she'd tripped down the porch steps this morning. No, not tripped—flailed her way down. He'd been pressing Blaze for an interview, when Miranda had burst out of the house. Halfway down the stairs, her feet knotted and she skated on her backside to the ground.

He hadn't been able to contain his laughter.

"Miranda, I'm sorry I laughed when you fell down the steps." He spoke in measured tones now, forcing his mouth into a straight line. "And I'm glad you weren't hurt."

"Why? Because if I was, it might ruin your blog series?" Her bottom lip turned out in a pout.

"That's not the only reason. I also happen to be curious about where we're going this beautiful Friday morning—and why you were in such a hurry to stop me from talking to Blaze earlier."

"I wasn't—"

"Oh, yes you were. I know alarm when I see it."

She bit her lip, which he already recognized as her pondering look. "Um, what were the two of you talking about?"

"Nothing much. I was on my way to the house when he ran up behind me. Told me he's training for a marathon—barefoot."

"Brilliant idea, yeah?" Blaze had asked.

"S-sure. Brilliant." Or a symptom of a brain injury.

When Matthew asked Blaze if he could interview him for the blog, the man had turned all sorts of skittish—fidgeted with his stopwatch, swiped dots of sweat from his brow, mumbled something about a splinter in his foot.

And then Miranda had launched from the house.

Was there some reason Miranda and Blaze were nixing his attempt at an interview with Blaze?

"Did you happen to read my first blog post? It went live today."

Her shoulders relaxed as she uncrossed her arms. "No time, actually. I accidentally slept in. Took forever to fall asleep last night."

Her too? He'd lain awake long past midnight thinking about Miranda Woodruff's past, the hurt she thought she hid. But he'd also wondered whether or not, when it came time to write that January cover story, he'd have the necessary coldness to publicize her pain.

"My editor texted me it had thirty thousand hits in the first twenty minutes." A bona fide hit. Celine would have her surgery by year's end.

They motored around the ridge with the windows open, wind whipping the wooden cross hanging from the rental car's rearview mirror. A present from Celine. Never failed in its murmuring admonishment—for skipping church, losing his way . . . but most of all, for forgetting what it was like to open himself to God's presence.

"There it is, the lane for Jimmy and Audrey's." Miranda pointed.

"And they are . . . ?" He'd assumed they'd spend the day on set again, but she'd guided them the opposite direction of Pine Cove.

"Friends."

He steered onto the gravel, followed the bumpy road into a thick stand of trees, and slowed to a stop. The house in front of them, if it could be called that, was made up of ramshackle walls propping up a sagging roof and planks of wood jutting from the floor of the porch. The scent of cedar and pine, the trickling of what must be a nearby creek, drifted through his open window. None of that fit with the scene before him: dingy blanket abandoned on the porch steps, spindles missing from the railing, a shutter dangling from one window.

"It's not much to look at," Miranda conceded as she hopped to the ground. "But it's their home. Come on."

She took the stairs two at a time, sidestepping a loose board as she navigated the deathtrap of a porch. Matthew followed and waited behind her as she knocked on the rickety front door.

"Hello, Audrey? You home?"

The tapping of footsteps sounded from the house and the door swung open. "Randi?" Before he could catch a glimpse of the woman, she threw her arms around Miranda. "You came!"

"Of course I did. I said I would."

Audrey stepped back, and her eyes, pale blue and tired, turned on him. Straggles of mousy hair escaped a clip, and her brown dress hung from her small frame.

Miranda tugged on Matthew's arm, pulling him forward. "This is Matthew Knox. He's . . . a friend."

He held out his hand to Audrey. "Pleased to meet you."

Bare feet peeked from under the woman's dress. She placed a diminutive palm in his.

"I see Jimmy tarped the lumber I dropped off a couple weeks ago," Miranda pointed out. "Good move, especially with the slew of rain showers we've had."

"Jimmy is plenty smart like that." Audrey's thin lips stretched with her drawled words. She stepped aside to allow them into the house. "I couldn't believe it when I saw that truck coming down the road loaded with all that wood. Jimmy . . . he couldn't, either."

The pride in her voice didn't match her surroundings—uneven floors, hand-me-down furniture that had probably spanned generations, a broken pane of glass in the front room's one window. The house smelled of fried food and must. A framed photo of Audrey and a man who must be Jimmy sat on an end table.

"I was hoping I could see Lola before we get to work."

Audrey's wide grin pulled her gaunt cheeks tight. "Of course. It's about time for her to wake from her morning nap."

They trailed down an empty hallway, past a bedroom with a neatly made bed, its patchwork quilt the only color in the room. Though sparse and nearly dilapidated, the house was clean.

The next room held a crib. He paused in the doorway while Miranda and Audrey leaned over the baby bed.

"A little angel," Miranda whispered. She had softened the moment they stepped in the house, he realized, and now she fairly melted—cooing and talking in hushed tones with Audrey. He watched as Audrey lifted the sleeping baby and placed her in Miranda's arms. Miranda tilted forward to nuzzle the baby's head with her nose and place a kiss on the baby's cheek.

Beautiful . . .

"She is, isn't she?" Miranda spoke.

He blinked. *Oh.* He'd said it aloud. "How old is she?"

Audrey nodded. "Four months and one week. Her full name is Lola Danielle."

He moved to Miranda's side, rubbed the little peach-fuzz head. Caramel eyes stared back at him above cherub cheeks.

"So where is Jimmy today?" Miranda asked the question with her cheek pressed to Lola's.

Audrey's expression turned uncomfortable. "He went away with his pals. Sometimes he's gone three or four days, usually looking for work. Except this time . . . Well, it's only been a week. I'm sure he'll be home soon."

Anxious silence broke the tenderness of moments before.

"Well, I could stand here holding her forever, but that's not going to get your porch fixed." Miranda sighed. "I suppose I should get to work."

It took her another minute to surrender Lola to Audrey. When she did, she closed her arms around herself for a moment, a flicker of loneliness touching her eyes. But just as quickly, she unwound her arms and straightened her shoulders. "All right, Knox. Ready to help me?"

"Absolutely."

"I'll mix some lemonade," Audrey said, shifting the bundle

in her arms and leading them from the room. "And if there's anything I can do—"

"Oh no, you just enjoy your day with Lola. Leave the porch to us."

Matthew gulped the air outside, the expanse of the mountains such a contrast to the close quarters of the tiny house. Even the porch seemed to close in on him, and he quickened down the stairs.

"What I really want is to build her a new house," Miranda said from behind him.

He turned. "Why don't you?"

"Jimmy doesn't want it. I don't know if it's the idea of charity that bothers him or what."

"What he wants shouldn't matter nearly as much as what his baby needs." Especially if the man wasn't going to return. But Matthew shook his head, knocking the thought loose. Not everyone was like his father. "So, do you help out here often?"

"A couple times a month. More when I'm on break from taping."

"What do we do first?"

"Rip up the old boards. Some of them are okay, but anything wobbly or unstable goes."

She reached into the back seat of his Jeep and pulled out the toolbox he'd seen her throw in earlier. She paused. "I never really asked you if wanted to help. If you don't want to—"

"I do."

She handed him a hammer, a sparkle lighting her eyes. "Let's start tearing things up."

He grasped the hammer, plodded back up the porch, and knelt over the first loose board he saw. He dug the hammer claw underneath where the board wobbled and pulled. "How'd you meet Audrey?"

"At Open Arms, a children's shelter in Asheville where I

volunteer. Audrey's father kicked her out when she got pregnant. The way she tells it, Jimmy wanted her to move in with him, but she was worried her father might interfere. She hitch-hiked to Asheville and ended up at Open Arms, thinking maybe it was a home for displaced pregnant women. It isn't, but Livvy—the director and my friend—couldn't turn her away. Audrey stayed at Open Arms until recently, when Jimmy convinced her to get married and move back to the mountain."

His muscles strained to pull the board up. When he'd freed it, he chucked it into the yard. "How old is she?"

On the other side of the porch, Miranda stilled and met his eyes. "Eighteen."

His knees strained in his knelt position and he rocked back to sit. Eighteen. And living in a shack in the mountains. With a baby. And a husband who may or may not stick by her.

He leaned forward and hooked his hammer under another board, wood scraping against his fingers, promising blisters. "You know, you surprise me, Miranda."

"That a good thing or a bad thing?"

"Good. You're more than the tomboy you play on TV." He looked up to meet her eyes, unreadable but fascinating. When hit by the sun, they turned to a soft, almost-blue. Like a rainy sky.

She's married.

And he had no business putting words to the disturbing admiration clinking around in his brain.

"Um, thank you?" Cloudy uncertainty hazed over her face. "I mean, thank you."

"Welcome." *Married.*

And the key to his professional revival.

That's all.

He plowed the hammer claw under another protruding board. "So, tell me about tonight."

The uncertainty returned to her eyes. And the dinging of a distant warning bell continued somewhere in the back of his brain.

♨

"What's he like?" Liv's muffled voice called from the depths of Miranda's walk-in closet.

Miranda stood in the closet doorway, hands tucked into the pockets of her overalls. "Who, Blaze? He's a total flake. Belongs in a surfer flick with Annette Funicello at his side."

Liv emerged, arms draped with a rainbow of dresses and squeezed past Miranda. Miranda had forgotten she had such a storehouse of dresses. Other than the getup Whitney had forced her into the other day, she hadn't had occasion to hassle into a dress since . . . when?

Probably back in churchgoing days. Before the guilt anchored her home on Sunday mornings.

"And he looks like . . . ?" Liv paused.

"It's okay to say his name. Yes, he looks like Robbie. Though not as much now that I've been around him a couple days. And he's nothing like him. Robbie was all serious, even brooding sometimes. Blaze is lighthearted, carefree."

Liv dropped her armload onto the bed, plastic hangers clanking. "Think there's any possibility of . . . you know."

Miranda flopped onto the bed beside the pile of dresses. "Possibility of what?"

"Of you actually falling for your pretend guy."

Miranda burst into laughter. "There's more chance of Hades freezing over. Or pigs flying. Pick the cliché of your choice."

Liv shot her a defiant stare. "Hey, anytime you hear about a man and woman pretending to be married or getting engaged or married for convenience, they always end up falling in love for real." She held up a turquoise dress for inspection.

99

"Livvy, you're talking about movies." She waved off the dress. "This isn't a movie—it's my actual life."

"Which at the moment is looking very much like a Sandra Bullock flick. And you're right—nixing the turquoise number. Too *Little Mermaid*-ish." She laid the dress over a chair and flipped through the others.

"Besides, we already have an exit strategy for our . . . relationship. When the time is right, we'll leak a story about how the stress of public life was too much for us."

Livvy huffed. "So, fine, what about the other guy? The reporter. He's cute. Like a young Captain von Trapp."

"Well, I don't think he's married, so maybe if you sing a few bars of 'Do-Re-Mi . . .'"

Liv rolled her eyes and pulled a deep purple dress from the pile. "Gorgeous color."

Miranda shook her head. "Too flashy for tonight. We're eating on the terrace at the Timberlane." According to Brad it was a classy but laid-back restaurant where she and Blaze would get attention without looking as if they were, well, trying to get attention. Lincoln and Brad had planned the outing down to the last detail. She was surprised *they* hadn't picked out her dress.

"As for Matthew, he's . . ." Miranda searched for the word, conjuring the image of Matthew holding Lola during a lemonade break at Audrey's, twinkle lighting his eyes and boyish grin stretching his cheeks. "He's nice."

Liv smirked. "Vaguest word in Webster's dictionary."

Miranda traced the circled pattern of Grandma Woodruff's quilt atop her bed. "I thought he'd be a pain to have around, but he's so easygoing. Just fits in with whatever's going on around him. You should've seen the way he helped out at Audrey's house today. And last night, we had ice cream out in the cabin, and—"

"You mean your and Robbie's—"

"Yes. And somehow I ended up talking about South America and my parents, and he just . . . listened."

Liv laughed. "What's amazing to me isn't that he listened, but that you actually talked about it. Either you're turning over a new leaf or the man has some kind of superpower." Liv held up a black dress with white polka dots. "Now, this is cute."

"And probably four years old. I bought it right after we returned to the States. Thought it looked like something Audrey Hepburn would wear."

"You're right, it has *Roman Holiday* written all over it. Goes in the possibility pile." She paused, pursing her lips as if weighing her next words. "Rand, have you considered that this reporter might be trying to butter you up? He is out for a story, after all."

Miranda fingered the ruffled collar of the green dress atop the heap of dresses. "I don't think he's like that."

"She says without knowing a thing about the man."

"Not true. I know his dad left him when he was a teenager. And he has this niece, Celine, who he's crazy about."

In fact, he'd asked Audrey to take a photo of him posing with Miranda, which he'd texted to Celine. Apparently, she was a *From the Ground Up* fan.

Miranda also knew Matthew was a hard worker. He'd more than kept up today. He had a curiosity about him, too. Like on the way home from Audrey's when he'd joked about not paying enough attention in his high school shop class. *"What's a coping saw, anyway?"*

He'd given such attention to her answer. Like it—maybe she—really mattered.

"Your grin makes me nervous." Was that actually worry creasing Liv's forehead?

"What do you mean?" Miranda rose, an onset of discomfort

crawling through her. It was probably the thought of parading her imitation marriage tonight in Asheville.

"Just that Gregory Peck should be so lucky to get a smile like you just flashed from Audrey. And it has me wondering."

Miranda stood, reached for the polka-dot dress, held it up against herself. The straps of the sleeveless dress tied around the neck. The fabric pulled in at the waist, then flared to her knees. She'd need a wrap, considering the cool night.

Resolute, she nodded. "This one."

"You know you don't have to go through with this, don't you?" Liv's serious tone invited tension into the room.

"Dinner out? Lincoln insists. The sooner we give the public their first glimpse of my mysterious mister, the better."

"I mean the whole thing. It's a big part to play. Barbara Stanwyck might've made phony nuptials look cute in *Christmas in Connecticut*, but as you so assertively pointed out mere minutes ago, this is real life."

"Exactly. And for my real life to continue to include *From the Ground Up*, this is what I need to do." Miranda stepped into the dress as she spoke.

"After tonight, there's no going back. Once your and Blaze's picture is in a newspaper, on the front of a magazine, that's it. Exit strategy or not, he's your new Robbie, and the lie you've complained to me about all this time is cemented in place."

Liv's statement sent pinpricks needling through her. "How can you throw that in my face now?"

"I'm not accusing you of anything," Liv said softly, patiently, as if Miranda were one of her kids at Open Arms. She stepped up behind Miranda to tie the dress straps behind her neck. "But I'm worried you're losing yourself in a tangle of lies."

"Why didn't you say something on Saturday, when you and Brad came over?" She felt the heat of irritation taking over her face. And her alarm clock, blaring the hour in red numbers from her nightstand, nagged her. They needed to leave soon to make their restaurant reservation.

"Because at the time, I thought this thing might force you to stand up to your producer." Liv huffed a sigh and flopped against the pillows on her bed. "Or who knows, finally contact Robbie, get some closure."

Not possible. Because she didn't know where Robbie was. Wouldn't let herself care. And there was no such thing as closure anyway.

The rhythm of a branch hitting the windowpane pulled her back to the present. "What do you want me to say, Liv? That I'll give up everything I've worked for, not to mention letting down the whole crew, everyone who's invested in the show? Not happening."

"That's not—"

A knock at the door interrupted Liv's strained reply. "Miranda?"

Matthew. Disconcerting as the conversation had become, she welcomed the intrusion. She inched the door open. "Hey."

His eyes traveled the length of her in one admiring swoop. "And I thought you made overalls look good."

No missing Liv's whispered, "Oh, brother."

Miranda opened the door another inch, motioning behind her. "This is Liv, the friend I told you about who runs Open Arms."

He nodded. "Nice to meet you." His scrutiny flitted from Liv to the room behind her. What did he make of the place? Honey-colored walls, the greens and blues of Grandma's quilt on the bed, redwood furnishings. Did the room betray its single occupancy? What if the whole house did?

"So, did you need something?"

"I know tonight's sort of a PR thing for you. Have you considered it could get a little crazy afterward?"

"Not sure I follow."

"Follow . . . exactly. What if the paparazzi follow you home?"

"I'm not that big of a celebrity."

"My blog had over 450,000 hits today."

Shock slicked through her, pushing goose bumps to the surface of her bare arms. Behind her, Liv whistled.

"I was thinking, I might be able to help. Be your decoy. I'll take your truck. You and Blaze can slip away in my Jeep. Leaving in a different vehicle than you came in couldn't hurt."

"I appreciate the offer." Though it might be wishful thinking to assume she'd attract that much attention. Still, surprise warmth glided through her at Matthew's thoughtfulness.

"We'll just need to arrange a key swap. Outside the restaurant when you leave?"

"Sure. It's a date. A plan, I mean. Not a date. 'Cause I don't do dates 'cause I'm married. Not that I meant *date* that way anyway." Oh, someone just stuff a sock in her mouth already.

The corner of Matthew's mouth quirked and he turned.

Liv's smirk greeted her when she reentered her bedroom. "Don't do dates, huh. And what would you call tonight?"

"A publicity stunt."

Liv stood, crossed the room, and placed her arm around Miranda's shoulder, surveying her in the mirror. "You look fabulous. And remember I'm here for you no matter what."

"I wouldn't do it if I could think of another way to save the show. You know that, don't you?"

Liv turned, retrieving a sheer black wrap from a hook on the closet door. "Just be careful, all right? In the span of a couple days you've gone from secluded celebrity to having two men roaming your house."

"I can handle Blaze. As for Matthew, he's only after human-interest stuff. I'm not worried."

"Makes one of us."

"Liv—"

"I know, you'll be fine. Because you're Randi Woodruff. You can take a few pieces of wood and a hammer and construct a house, etcetera, etcetera."

"Your confidence is inspiring."

Livvy handed off the wrap, then reached around Miranda's head to pull out the tie holding her hair back. She fluffed Miranda's hair. "There, it looks perfect down and loose. You need a cute purse, though. I've got my red one downstairs. I'll go empty it."

Miranda ran a brush through her hair, slipped on her shoes, and paused for a final glance in the mirror. She ran both palms over her bare arms, stilled, and remembered.

One more thing to do.

She pulled on the glass knob of her vanity drawer, and with an unsteady hand, felt her way to the back until her fingers recognized the softness of velvet. She removed the box from the drawer and held it up in front of her face.

How long since she'd shoved the ring box out of sight, vowed never to pull it out again? A year and a half, two years? She'd gotten away without wearing a ring due to the practicalities of her job.

She'd given Matthew the usual explanation just today when she'd caught him looking at her hand.

"Jewelry is a no-no at work sites. I only wear mine when I know I'm not going to be around power tools and wood—on special occasions."

"So I suppose your date tonight counts as a special occasion."

It was the third time he'd asked about the date since they'd started working. His reporter's curiosity was obvious. Why—after years of not stepping out in public with her husband, when she was notorious for protecting her privacy—was she all of a sudden now okay with their being seen together? Not just okay but making an effort? That's what he wondered, right?

After brushing him off twice, she'd finally decided to shoot straight. While they'd worked on the porch, she told him about *From the Ground Up*'s iffy ratings and Lincoln's certainty that finally spotlighting her husband was the key to securing the show's future. As soon as she'd finished explaining, doubt started chipping away at her. She'd so easily slipped into trusting Matthew Knox. But what if he took what she'd just said and published it in tomorrow's blog? Made her out to be a publicity hound?

But he'd said little after her explanation.

"I suppose all that sounds fishy," she prodded.

He laid down his hammer. "Not really. Just kind of . . . unromantic."

Miranda blinked now, skimming her thumb over the ring box in her hands. She used to keep it on the nightstand, torture herself by creaking it open in weak moments.

Unromantic.

Matthew had no idea.

With her thumb, she popped open the case. The square-cut diamond inside glistened as keenly as the day Robbie had presented it to her. When he'd knelt, waited for her squeal, and pushed the ring into place.

Well, tonight she'd do the honors. Miranda plucked the ring from the case and slipped it over her finger.

"You look as uncomfortable as a snowman in the tropics."

Miranda gritted her teeth. The whiny saxophone of the jazz band inside floated to the outdoor terrace of the Timberlane restaurant. "That's hardly a complimentary thing to say to your wife."

Across the table, Blaze flashed his pearly whites. His hair covered his ears and brushed the collar of his button-down shirt, but he was freshly shaven. He even wore a tie—a lime green one, but still, it was the dressiest she'd seen him.

And the most mischievous. His eyes glimmered with playfulness as he reached across the table to pat her hand. Did he possess even a speck of understanding of the importance of this night?

"I'm just saying, you need to relax. Just because we're at an uptight restaurant doesn't mean you need to be."

"To you, this may only be a free meal at a ritzy joint, but tonight could make or break this marriage, which could, in turn, make or break my career." Her focus jumped from table to surrounding table. Were any of the journalists Brad mentioned here? Oh wow, was that Congressman Franklin a couple tables over? "What if nobody recognizes me, Blaze?"

Candlelight flickered in his dark eyes. "Then tomorrow we'll go somewhere else where the people are more observant." His dimples deepened with his goofy grin.

"Why do you keep smiling like that?"

"Because we're supposed to look like we're in love. Which is why you really should consider leaning forward a bit. Your posture might impress what's-her-name, you know that old manners lady . . ."

"Emily Post?"

"But it sure doesn't give the impression you're thrilled to be here with me."

A groan rumbled through her throat, but the man had a point. As their waiter approached, she forced her shoulders to relax and propped her elbows on the table, head tipped toward Blaze. "Better?" she whispered.

He only winked. The waiter placed their meals in front of them, gaze lingering on Miranda before he whisked away with their salad plates.

"See that? The dude definitely recognized you."

"Either that or I've got lettuce in my teeth." The sweet smell of apple-glazed pork made Miranda's mouth water. She spread a linen napkin on her lap, gripped her fork, and then paused when she noticed Blaze's stare. "What?"

"I've just figured out how we're going to convince everyone we're in love."

"How?"

He pointed his butter knife at her plate. "The way you just looked at that pork chop, babe? That's the look you need to give me when cameras point our way. Pure delight."

"I can't help it. I love me a good pork chop."

"If I'd known all it took to get you relaxed was a hunk of meat, I'd have started grilling from day one."

Miranda's mouth closed around a bite, a sigh of satisfaction escaping. Tender meat and an explosion of flavor almost made the pressure of this night worth it. "How's your steak?"

"Delectable."

They ate in silence for a few minutes, the clinking of silverware and glass along with hushed conversation from surrounding tables keeping them company. Heat piped in from vents overhead mixed with the outdoor chill, and moonlight slanted in, highlighting the shiny surfaces of the terrace.

"Can I ask you a question?" Blaze said, something close to serious in his lowered voice. "How in the world have you been able to keep up this mystery-husband thing for three years? Shouldn't someone have figured out the truth by now? How long were you planning to keep it up?"

Miranda swallowed, eyes darting to the surrounding tables. "Honestly, it hasn't been that hard. I'm not a Hollywood star. I don't have paparazzi following me around. I live in the mountains, Blaze. They probably couldn't find me if they tried." She rested her fork beside her plate. "It's only been recently that interest has really picked up."

"What if someone had asked to see a marriage certificate?"

She shook her head, voice soft as she leaned forward. "You're forgetting the story. We met and married in Brazil. That international explanation has always sufficed. As for how long I planned to keep it up, well, I didn't really. Have a plan, I mean. You have to understand, Blaze, it didn't start out as a lie. I really thought . . ."

Miranda sucked her next words in before emotion could intrude. She picked up her fork once more. "Can I ask *you* something?"

Blaze's head rose, the usual merriment that crinkled at the corners of his eyes replaced with consideration as he waited for her question.

"Why are you doing this? I have a vested interest, obviously, but what about you? I know you said something the other day about wanting a second chance to help someone, but this . . ." She gestured with both arms, voice lowering. "Isn't it a little extreme? You could've volunteered at the Red Cross or something. Instead you've put your life on hold to . . . play a part."

Blaze looked away. The thread of lights twinkling from the terrace roof cast a halo around his head. "Is it that hard to believe a guy like me might want to help someone?"

"It's not the money or the fame?"

He let out a derisive laugh. "I can think of better ways to get famous. And yeah, the boost to my bank account is nice, but I come from family money, so if I was that desperate . . ." His voice trailed.

Miranda cut into her pork chop. "Family money, huh. Like, you're from blue-blood stock? You don't look it."

His lips parted into a wry half smile. "Yes, well, my family would be in full agreement with you there."

Another bite. "This pork chop is like something from heaven." She waved her fork. "Vegetarians do not know what they're missing. What did you mean your family would agree?"

He eyed her plate. "Let's just say you're not the only one who's not on the best terms with the parents." He stretched his arm across the table, fork headed for her plate.

"What are you doing?"

"Taste testing." He swiped a bite.

Through Blaze's movement, she saw the flash of candlelight. "Blaze—"

"Married people do it all the time."

"Careful of the candle—"

The crackle of burning fabric and a swirl of gray rose up as Blaze settled back into his seat. He sniffed. "Hey, do you smell—?"

"Your arm!"

He yanked his arm into the air, an orange flare threatening to flame. "No," he moaned. "Not again."

Panic jerked Miranda into action. Her fingers closed in on the stem of her water glass, and she pitched its contents toward Blaze. Steam sizzled as the fire died. She lowered her glass to the table and stared at Blaze, water dripping from his face, darkening the fabric of his already-blackened sleeve.

"Good save, hon."

"Are you all right? And what did you mean, not again?"

He took one more glance at his singed shirt, then dropped his arm and shrugged. "Have you forgotten my nickname?"

Oh. Of course.

"Should I wave down a waiter and get you another glass of water?"

The man had just set his arm on fire and he was worried about her being thirsty? And speaking of waiters, shouldn't someone have come running at the sight of Blaze, uh, ablaze? Miranda scoped the place. No one ogled their table. No laughter. Not a single sign anyone had witnessed the near catastrophe.

"I can't believe it. It's like there's a dome of invisibility around our table. You started an actual fire and no one even noticed."

His eyebrows knit together. "Oh, right, that publicity thing. Sorry it's not working out."

Stung by her own insensitivity, she swung her gaze back to Blaze. "No, I'm sorry. Worrying about publicity when you could've been hurt. Did you burn your arm?"

"Nope. But do you think we should tell someone at the restaurant they need better smoke detectors? I'm big on smoke detectors. Which reminds me, when did you last change the batteries in the ones in your house?"

That comment probably should have frightened her. But the only worry rolling through her, inconsiderate though it may be, was the complete failure of their evening out. What would Lincoln say? What had she done wrong?

She bit her lip, eyes traveling the room once more, then landing on a figure moving toward their table. "What's he doing here?"

Blaze twisted in his seat to follow Miranda's gaze. "Knox? Dude must be hungry."

Matthew's walk bordered on a swagger as he approached their table. He smoothed a forest green tie that brought out the subtle jade hues of his eyes. Had he seen the fire? Come to assess the damage? His confident stride stopped at their table. "Say, aren't you Randi Woodruff, star of *From the Ground Up*? I love that show."

The forceful volume of his voice carried over the terrace. Miranda felt the confusion take over her face. "Um, Matthew? Ever heard of an indoor voice?"

"I'd play along if I were you," Matthew hissed through his teeth, cheesy smile still in place. "I can't believe I'm meeting you in person."

Blaze's "Ahh" reached over the table. Apparently he'd figured out Matthew's game. *Am I dense?*

"Yes, this is Randi Woodruff." Blaze's voice matched Matthew's in pitch, and what was with the full name? "What can we do for you?"

"Wait, you're her husband? I've always wondered about you!"

She felt the turning of eyes on their table, heard surrounding chatter quell to an interested buzz. Slowly, like the movement of feathery clouds filtering moonlight, Matthew's purpose dawned on her. He was acting, helping.

Making sure she didn't go unnoticed.

If he was helping her tonight, then he probably didn't plan to expose their publicity scheme in his blog tomorrow, right?

She almost launched herself at him in gratitude. For one tempting moment she imagined the arms that had both strained to pull up old porch wood and cradled little Lola now closed around her. *But he's the wrong man.* Miranda blinked, found words. "Why, yes, this is my husband, Blake."

"Could I get your autograph?"

She nodded, swallowed, waited as he pulled out a narrow notebook and pen. His reporter's notebook. She'd watched him fill the thing with notes ever since he arrived. Matthew placed it in front of her, opened to a blank page.

With Matthew's pen, she scribbled her name, paused. And then an additional note: *Thank you.* When she handed the notebook back, Matthew acknowledged the note with a wink.

And then she felt a tap on her back. She turned in her seat.

"Excuse me, did I just hear—" The man at the adjacent table broke into a grin. "I did hear right. Randi Woodruff. I'm Bob Yankee from the Asheville *Citizen-Times.*"

Miranda heard Matthew's footsteps as he walked away, his mission accomplished. Warmth blanketed her earlier worries at the realization he'd been watching out for her all along. Warmth and gratitude and . . .

And suddenly the concern in Liv's eyes made sense.

Chapter 6

If it was publicity Miranda and Blaze wanted, they were about to get it. Matthew slowed his Jeep to a crawl as he approached the photographers huddling outside the Pine Cove studio gate. The glaring morning sun glinted from the lenses of their cameras.

"You're officially fish food for the paparazzi now, Miranda," he said over his shoulder.

She jutted her head into the space between his seat and Blaze on the passenger side. "What?"

"Check it out, missus," Blaze drawled. "Our Saturday night splash sealed the deal. Get ready to do a parade wave."

Matthew heard scuffling in the back seat. "Not a chance." Miranda's voice was muffled. Was she hiding? Matthew stifled a laugh. "You're a celebrity. I thought this was the kind of stuff you famous types craved?"

"Movie stars, maybe."

The throng of photographers parted slowly as Matthew drove toward the gate. No cameras flashed, as sunlight provided all the light they needed, but the hollered questions made their way through his windows.

"Randi Woodruff, are you in there?"

"Is Mr. Woodruff available for interviews? Will he appear on the show?"

"How do you feel about the rumors?"

Matthew glanced over at Blaze. The man never flinched, his relaxed posture the complete opposite of the tension emanating from the back seat. How had Miranda ended up the star of *From the Ground Up* when her husband was the one with all the public panache?

When Matthew arrived at the gate, he opened his window and reached out to punch in the security code. But before his arm was even halfway out, a reporter stuffed his head through the window. "Ah, it *is* Randi Woodruff."

Matthew stuck his palm on the man's forehead and pushed him out. "Buddy, have some decency."

"Bodyguard, eh?"

Today, apparently, yes. He jabbed his finger at the security box, then rolled up the window. "What a circus."

"Nice move, though," Blaze commented. "Bet you gave him whiplash."

Matthew tapped the accelerator as the gate swung open. "Just hope he doesn't sue me."

Miranda's head came into view in his rearview mirror. "What'd Matthew do? I didn't see. By the way, do you know you've got quite the collection of soda cans on your floor back here?"

"Knox palmed the dude. And here I thought all our boy did was write. He's flexing his physical skills today."

While Blaze exaggerated, Matthew caught Miranda's eye in the mirror. She raised an eyebrow. He winked. She glanced away. "Well, that's three times you've come to the rescue now, Matthew. First you pushed my truck out of the river, then at the restaurant you brought the media to us, and today you got us away from them."

The restaurant thing. He certainly hadn't planned to butt in on Blaze and Miranda's evening. Ever since she'd explained *why* they were going on the date, he'd had a funny feeling in the pit of his stomach, his usual journalist's interest bordering on suspicion. She was using her own husband for publicity. And yet, Blaze was apparently okay with it—maybe even liked the idea.

But as he'd sat a few tables away Saturday night, watching Miranda's forlorn expression and slumped shoulders, he couldn't help himself. He'd pushed his chair back and wound his way through the tables dotting the terrace before he'd considered what he was doing.

Ever since, something had shifted between him and Miranda. An alliance of sorts. Yesterday, Sunday, they'd spent half the day on her porch—he dotting her with questions, Miranda answering with laid-back ease.

Why did she love building so much?

"I love wood. The way it feels under my fingertips. The way it doesn't die once a tree is cut down, but instead re-creates itself into something new and beautiful. And useful, too. Wood has an identity, and I get to help shape that identity when I build a house or a piece of furniture."

What was her favorite house she'd ever built?

Easy, the first home she ever completed in Brazil.

Not her own home?

"Well, I don't think it counts since I haven't finished it."

"Why don't you finish it?"

It was the only question she'd hesitated on. She'd mumbled something about it not being the right time, being busy. And then she'd gone inside.

As Matthew pulled into the parking lot, Blaze pounded him on the back. "Yup, Knox, you've been pretty handy to have around."

"I wouldn't speak too soon." Matthew angled to check his side mirror. "Our paparazzi friends made it through the gate before it closed."

Miranda groaned. "Swell."

He braked and parked in a visitor space in the lot and twisted to watch out the back window. Thankfully, someone else must have seen the scuttling mess of reporters, because they'd brought out the big dogs: three men in uniform. "You have security officers?"

"I guess so." Miranda's voice contained surprise.

Matthew jerked at the sharp rap on his window and turned to see Brad Walsh beckoning him to open the door. He obliged. "Hey, Walsh."

The man was beaming. "Good thinking having Knox drive today. While this may be the best thing that's ever happened to us PR-wise, the last thing we need is someone getting Randi's license-plate number."

Matthew slid out of the Jeep. "Actually, I only drove because Miranda's truck wouldn't start this morning."

But Brad had already moved to Miranda's door. "Come on out, kid. I want you to turn, give one wave to the media, and then Knox, you'll take her around to the back entrance."

Miranda peeked her head out of her open door. "But shouldn't Blaze—"

"Nope, Blaze here will be giving the media a statement."

"I will?"

"He will?"

Blaze and Miranda spoke at the same moment.

Brad gave a curt nod. "Hurry up and go."

Miranda was already moving toward the set, and Matthew hustled after her. The sharp bite of cold contradicted the bright colors of the day, sunshine streaking through the faintest trail of clouds, surrounding mountains ablaze in reds and oranges. As they reached the back of the house, Brad's voice drifted from across the lot. "Everyone, if you'll just shut up for a minute, Blake here will make a statement. Randi is on a tight schedule, so—"

Randi flung open the door. "Come on."

He ducked inside. "So apparently Brad was prepared for all this."

She folded her arms. "He could've called to let us know what was waiting here. Probably didn't because he knew I'd want to turn around. Crazy reporters." Her expression turned sheepish. "Sorry."

He shook his head. "No offense taken. Just know we're not all like that." Right. Because he'd only broken into a zoo building. Chased after a senator.

The sarcastic mental reminders drilled a hole in the wall he'd thought separated him from the paparazzi.

Was he just like those jokers outside, after all? So desperate for a story he'd intrude on a person's personal space and privacy? *You* are *living on her property. Hoping for a scoop to make January's print cover.*

But Miranda had willingly opened herself up to his presence. If anything, his blog was only helping her. And besides, every entry so far made the woman out in a positive light. No one could possibly accuse him of exploiting the opportunity.

"So what are you taping today?" he asked as he followed her down the narrow hallway at the back of the set house.

"No taping this morning, actually. I've got an interview about the award nomination. This afternoon we're doing a few retakes from some of last week's shoots."

"Sometime I'd like a tour of this place." It certainly wasn't like any studio he'd ever imagined. From the outside, it was just a huge house. From the inside, depending on what part of the house you were in, it looked either like a home under construction or an office building.

"It's a pretty cool studio," she said. "Here, let me show you one of my favorite rooms."

They ambled past the living and dining room sets, around a corner and down another hallway, a mix of scents trailing behind—coffee, cedar, and then the potent smell of paint.

Miranda stepped through an open doorway into a completely empty room. No furniture, no scaffolding or camera stands. Only four walls and three open windows, a few paint cans and rollers and what looked like a power painter. The mountain air cascading through the windows added a chill to the room but did nothing to dispel the pungent smell of paint.

"This room is solely for painting. Whenever we do a segment on proper painting techniques, mixing, choosing your colors, we do it here. But . . ." She used a mixing stick to pry open a can. "I also use it for stress relief." She dipped a brush in the bright orange liquid. She flopped the brush onto the wall, writing her name in large orange letters across the blue wall. Then she handed the brush to him. "Your turn."

He shrugged, slathering his own name across the opposite red wall. "So you do this whenever you want?"

"Yeah. Doesn't take long to cover it up when I'm done. It's almost as relaxing as working in the woodshop. And if I'm having a series of bad takes or things are going wrong on set, I just slip away, do a little painting, and *voilà*. It evens out my mental kinks."

She picked up the power paint sprayer and attached a paint container. She fiddled with the nozzle. "Hmm, it's stuck or something."

He dropped his brush. "Here, let me. I used one of these when I was helping Jase and Izzy paint their basement."

"No, I can do it."

"Let me, Miranda."

"Just because you displayed your oh-so-brute force with that peeping photographer outside—" She pulled the power sprayer and at the jerking movement, a flood of paint streamed from the nozzle, slapping onto Matthew's shirt, his face.

Miranda's jaw lowered, surprised silence filling the gap between them. And then an eruption of laughter pushed past her lips. "Oh my goodness. I'm sorry. Really. But . . ."

"Oh yes, it's so very funny." He wiped his palm across his face, leaving a streak of red across his hand.

Miranda still held the sprayer, bubbling giggles shaking her shoulders. "Sorry. I'm trying not to laugh."

"Yes, I can see that."

But the amusement in her sparkling eyes, the way her finger still posed over the trigger, told him she wasn't done. Why, she was actually thinking about doing it again!

Well, if it was a fight she wanted, he'd give it to her. "How *does* red look on me, Woodruff? Would you say it's my color?" He stepped backward as he spoke, knelt down to reach for the paint can and brush behind him.

"What are you doing, Knox?"

"Red might look good on me, but I'd say . . ." He glanced at the can in his hands now. "Ahh, blue, like your eyes."

Her nose crinkled as she backed away. "My eyes are gray."

"Not in the sun. In the sun they're as sky blue as this paint." He plopped his brush into the paint.

"You wouldn't."

"You underestimate me."

"I'm the one with the paint gun."

He whipped his brush in the air, flinging spatters of paint at her. They landed in tiny drops on her shoulders, her cheeks, her silky black hair. "Take that, Miranda!"

"Why, you—" And just as he knew she would, she sent a stream of red at him. He struck with his brush, painting a streak down her arm.

Intoxicating, almost giddy energy took over as they splashed and spewed paint at each other. The paint fumes and Miranda's nearness conspired to bully his common sense into nothing. Another river of red paint hit his chest, and he dropped his weapons, circling an arm around Miranda to pry the spray gun from her hands. She twisted, bumping an elbow against his stomach, her hair sticking to the paint on his face.

"Brad is so going to kill me!" Miranda said through a fit of hysterics. But she'd stopped trying to get away from him, instead standing in place inside his hold, giving in to her laughter, her arms turning to noodles as she lowered the paint gun.

"You got that right, Rand."

Matthew's head jerked up at the same time as Miranda's, and he got a mouthful of her hair. Uh-oh. Brad stood in the doorway, arms crossed, just like that day he'd found them in the flooded creek.

And behind Brad, a reporter, catching the whole thing on video.

"In the sun they're as sky blue as this paint."

Why couldn't Miranda get Matthew's voice out of her head and focus on the interview? They'd already gotten off to a terribly late start. She'd cleaned up as quickly as possible, leaving a rainbow of color streaking the tiled walls of the dressing-room shower.

Thankfully, she had a change of clothes, and Whitney was on hand to direct her makeup and hairstyle. Because, sure, that's exactly what the reporter from the local NBC affiliate cared about after witnessing her paint fight with Matthew.

Miranda forced herself to maintain eye contact with the fortyish reporter with a poof of blond hair sitting on the couch opposite her. Long dimples creased his cheeks like parentheses, and if she wasn't mistaken, he'd half flirted his way through this interview. Maybe after what he'd seen of her and Matthew he'd figured . . .

What? That she might be married but still enjoyed innocent dallying with whatever man happened to be around. False. Both halves of the sentence.

I was not flirting with Matthew.

The reporter, who'd introduced himself as Sam Toliver, leaned forward. "So, tell me about this husband who's made a sudden public appearance."

Miranda sucked in a breath. Why couldn't they have stuck to the easy questions? How did she feel about being nominated for the Giving Heart? What was her favorite charity?

"Well, his name is Blaze—Blake, actually. Blaze is an affectionate nickname." At least the reporter hadn't insisted on Blaze joining her for the interview. They hadn't had enough time to prepare for that yet. "Oh, and to set the record straight, I heard someone call him Mr. Woodruff earlier. His last name is Hunziker. I kept my maiden name for professional purposes. Anyway, he's a great guy and . . . a great blessing in my life."

The reporter winked. And unlike Matthew's wink earlier in the morning, Sam's felt slimy. "That's an awfully nebulous answer, Randi."

"I'm an unapologetically private person, Sam. Always have been."

"Yet you talk about your husband on your show. And you sure weren't in discreet mode the other night when you were spotted at the restaurant." The man's voice had altered from flirtatious to hard in a matter of a moment.

Miranda's oversized leather chair threatened to eat her up. What did Sam want her to say? Her gaze flitted to Lincoln, watching from behind the NBC camera. They should've coached her more for this. She was used to answering questions about wood density and brackets and blueprints. Not this.

"I talk about my husband because he helped shape who I am." The lie that had bothered her for years gutted her once again. Because it now had a face. "As for Saturday night, is it really such standout news for a husband and wife to go to dinner together?"

Sam's slow smirk spread as he straightened. "Well played, Randi."

Compliment or accusation? This reporter was nothing like Matthew, had none of Matthew's tact or kindness or . . . attractiveness. Her stomach tightened.

"Let's move on. There's been talk that *From the Ground Up* may not be renewed. Can you shed some light on the accuracy of the rumors?"

Oh, lovely. Can we go back to the questions about Blaze? "I prefer not to acknowledge rumors."

"So your public appearance with your husband had nothing to do with the rumors he didn't exist?"

Her fingers itched to squeeze into her palms, but she forced them to remain laced around her knee. Sam was jumping topics like a frog on lily pads, eager to snatch her up like a bug. Why didn't Lincoln step in, stop the subtle assault? She wished she could see if Brad was watching. And Matthew.

Most disconcerting of all was the realization of how close to the truth Sam crept.

"I'll level with you, Sam. People can think whatever they want about my marriage, my husband, and my reasons for dining out. All I have to say is, if I were the owner of the Timberlane, I'd be pretty happy about all the free publicity."

She caught Brad's eye, saw his proud nod of approval. Relief surged through her.

"And the rumors about the next season of *From the Ground Up*?" Sam prompted.

"We're currently taping season four. I'm confident of our future." Had she kept the doubt out of her voice?

"Then tell me this: What are we to make of the news that your network has heard a pitch from a new homebuilding show? I have the network president quoted as saying that he has, and I quote, 'a variety of well-crafted, entertaining options on the table for the spring schedule, including a potential home show.' What do you say to that?"

Miranda's pulse quickened as Sam read the quote. Her hands turned icy.

Nothing. She had nothing to say to that.

Only a blank stare. And a brand-new worry.

Matthew emerged from the bathroom attached to Miranda's dressing room, rubbing a towel against his hair. He jerked in surprise when he saw Brad sitting atop Miranda's vanity, his feet propped on the chair.

"Walsh, I didn't know you were going to wait for me."

"Yeah, I waited," Brad said.

Matthew draped his towel over a hook on the back of the bathroom door. "Did you think I was going to steal something?"

Brad had begrudgingly let Matthew into the room twenty minutes ago at Miranda's order. It had felt oddly intimate walking through her dressing room, making use of her private bathroom while she gave her interview.

Was it childish to feel the need to defend himself all over again to Walsh? *"I told you, she started it."*

He spotted her color-splotched dark jeans and light-green shirt with the ruffled sleeves abandoned on the floor. She'd actually dressed up for her interview today. And Matthew had ruined the look by turning her into an abstract painting.

Brad pressed his lips together in a stoic line. "I want to know what's going on with you and Miranda."

"What are you insinuating, Walsh?"

Brad's feet clunked to the floor, and he rose to stand eye level with Matthew. "Just that since the day you got here, you've been toying with her. It's the opposite of classy, flirting with someone who's unavailable. Unprofessional, too."

"We weren't—"

Matthew caught a glimpse of himself in the vanity mirror behind Brad. Tousled hair, stubble covering his cheeks. Izzy would've ordered him to shave by now. Stupid as it might sound, he sort of liked the rugged look. Give him a flannel shirt and he just might fit in here in the mountains.

But why did his eyes look so . . . energetic? Why the circles of red on his cheek?

He yanked his focus back to Brad. The man's expression hovered between smug and infuriated.

Matthew attempted a lame excuse. "We were just . . ." But he came up empty.

She's married.

And he'd known exactly what he was doing.

Brad's glare bored into Matthew's conscience. Miranda's manager stepped around him. "Let's go." But he stopped in the doorway. "She's off limits, Knox."

"I know that." He did.

But he also knew she was the first woman he'd felt drawn to in years.

He pulled the dressing room door closed behind him and followed Brad.

She's married.

And he was getting pretty sick of the reminder. Maybe

because it only spotlighted his own aloneness. Sheesh, Matthew hadn't made it past a third or fourth date since his mid-twenties. The couple times he'd been tempted to think he might've discovered "the" girl, he'd found himself breaking things off before he could mess them up.

"Hey, I just realized I left my phone in Miranda's bathroom," he called to Brad. "Be right back."

The man would probably follow him back. *Fine. Let him.*

He hurried toward the bathroom and located his phone on the counter, pushing aside his grating annoyance at Brad. The man was only watching out for Randi, right?

He pocketed his phone, then paused in the middle of the bathroom, the foamy scent of soap wafting. The temptation to linger in Miranda's dressing room tugged at him. What might he find here to aid his blog series? And how severely would Walsh punish him if he caught him snooping?

Before he could decide whether to act on the urge, the sound of the dressing room door opening filtered in. Walsh, most likely, coming to check up on him.

"Randi, you in here?"

That wasn't Brad's voice.

"Some guy was asking me about installing floorboards. Pretty sure I know more about the periodic table than that."

Matthew poked out of the bathroom. "Blaze?"

"Whoa, dude, you're not Randi."

Matthew's gait thudded to a stop in front of Blaze. "*You* don't know how to install floorboards?" Mr. Husband-who-taught-Randi-all-she-knew?

As if realizing a gaffe, Blaze sputtered out his defense. "I mean, sure, I know *how* to do it. Just don't have any desire to stick around for the fun. Know what I mean?" Blaze clapped a hand on Matthew's shoulder. "That's all Randi's thing now. I chased the woodworking bug out of my system a long time ago."

The woodworking *bug*? Hadn't the guy spent years building homes with Randi in Brazil? That didn't sound like a bug.

Blaze gave a nonchalant whistle, then shrugged. "Well, guess I'll go find Rand. Maybe she's still being interviewed."

Matthew followed Blaze from the room, no longer interested about what secrets Miranda's dressing room might hide . . . and instead all sorts of curious about Blaze.

Chapter 7

Miranda's house told a story Matthew couldn't follow.

He stood in the center of the unfinished portion of the house, its raised foundation and wood beams weathered yet sturdy. Studs and joists hinted at the outline of what would've been a master suite, according to Miranda. One she'd never gotten around to finishing.

Do you have a tale to tell, house? A heavy wind carried curled leaves in tiny waves across the grass.

Something felt off about this place. Melancholy hummed through the open space, hung from the rafters. Or maybe that was simply the clouds rumbling overhead in tones of disapproval.

Except that he'd done nothing wrong. Hadn't actually entered the house.

Though, with Miranda and Blaze off on another interview, if ever he wanted an opportunity to snoop, now was the time. And he couldn't deny the temptation.

Then there'd been Delia Jones's irritating e-mail.

Nice to see you've finally found your niche. When can I expect to see you hosting *Entertainment Tonight*?

Her sarcasm jumped off the screen, and his finger had slammed into the Delete button before he could fire off a nasty reply. Would the woman never forgive him?

You ruined her rep, Knox. Her byline on that article branded her. Although, she *had* bounced back with a fervor Matthew coveted, eventually landing a job at the St. Paul *Pioneer Press.*

With a heavy exhale, he made one more slow turn in the silent shell of a room. *Nothing to see here.* No breakthrough discovery to turn his gig into hard news or answer the questions that had gnawed at him since yesterday. Of course, he could just ask Randi.

Right, and ruin the trust that had developed between them.

Like the trust that had him considering poking through her house while she wasn't home? He dropped to the ground and circled to the front of the house, climbed the porch steps, each creak a scold.

Really shouldn't.

It's called investigative *reporting.*

It's called trespassing.

Matthew faced the front door, feet rooted in place. Delia's condescension gonged through his thoughts. He balled his fingers around the doorknob.

"Beat it! Just beat it!"

Matthew jumped as his cell phone ring tone squawked into the quiet. He plucked his phone from his pocket and, heart still hopscotching, snapped it open. "You just gave me a heart attack."

Jase's chuckle rang over the phone. "What're you doing that a phone call would freak you out?"

Matthew grasped the doorknob again, this time pulling the door open and stepping into the house before he could change his mind. "Hel-lo, I'm in the mountains. It's peaceful up here. So Michael Jackson's screeching is slightly off-putting. Please tell Izzy to stop messing with my ring tone, by the way."

"Right," Jase said flatly. "Because Izzy will listen so well. My wife delights in picking on you, little brother."

Inside Miranda's house, the smell of breakfast's bacon and eggs lingered. *"Always start off the day with a hearty breakfast,"* Blaze had admonished. Matthew had been joining Miranda and Blaze for meals in the past couple days.

See, Miranda *had* welcomed him into the house. Yet the hush of the empty interior draped him in guilt. Fine, so maybe she hadn't meant when she wasn't home.

"So, how's the blogging?" Jase asked.

Miranda's living room could have won some kind of architectural award with its high beams and angled ceiling, towering windows and redwood floorboards. Sparsely decorated, the room offered little in the way of hints about Miranda's personal life, though. Just one photo propped atop an end table—Miranda flanked by, he guessed, her grandparents.

"Today's post got the highest number of hits yet within the first hour." He ambled over to the bookcase lining one wall, fighting the feeling of being intrusive. The woman liked her classics: Jane Austen, the Brontë sisters, Mark Twain. Quite a few travel books, too. And a worn copy of *Gone with the Wind*. He'd expected at least a row of DIY home project volumes. "It's crazy how much people care about celebrities *and* their relationships."

"Not just any celebrity," Jase corrected. "This one's been intriguing the public about her husband for three seasons. It's about time she dished."

"But it's not like she owes anyone anything."

"All I'm saying is, she had to know what she was getting when she got into the TV thing. People were bound to wonder. Besides, you more than anyone should want all the details."

Matthew eyed the staircase, the taste of tantalizing curiosity overpowering his conscience. "I know details about her personal life are what make the blog, but I can't help wishing for something meatier."

He paused at the top of the stairs, Miranda's open bedroom door beckoning. His conscience screamed at him now. He flinched at the squeak of his shoes against the shiny wood floor. What if Miranda and Blaze returned early? What if she had a hidden security system?

"Meatier, like how?" Jase's voice intruded.

"Like . . . if I found out she built shoddy homes. Or if she couldn't build at all." Now, that would make a story.

But not a truthful one. Miranda's signature, the evidence of her talent was all over her home, from the carving of the woodwork along the base of the walls to the wood furnishings filling the place—he stopped outside her door—to the rocking chair in the corner of her bedroom. "An antique. I bet Miranda refurbished it," he mused.

"What? Where are you?"

His search moved from the rocking chair to the rest of her room. Pale gold walls wrapped around a space that sang feminine. And he couldn't have been more surprised. Lacy curtains matched the light blues and greens in the quilt on her bed, the hill of pillows.

"I'm standing outside Miranda Woodruff's bedroom. Trying to decide whether to cross the threshold."

"You're in her *house*? And she's not home?"

Matthew's silence answered the question.

"Don't do it, bro. A woman's bedroom is sacred territory. Once, I moved around the furniture in our bedroom while Izzy was still at work. She was so mad, I swear she purposely washed my wallet."

A painting of a seascape spanned one wall of Miranda's bedroom, and white sheer fabric wisped from the posts of her canopy bed. Girlish. Telling. The room even smelled like her, lavender and vanilla with a hint of wood.

Matthew about-faced. Jase was right. He had to draw a line somewhere. *Yeah, because sneaking around the woman's house isn't borderline illegal territory. Right.* "Why'd you rearrange the bedroom anyway?"

"Had a dentist appointment earlier in the day and read this article about fêng shui while I was in the waiting room."

"A bunch of baloney."

"Says the kid who always used to believe the toys in the cereal box would be as big as they looked on TV."

Yeah, well he'd lost his gullibility somewhere between Dad's last "Good night, son," and Mom's "He's not coming back."

Matthew moved to the next doorway. It opened into an office space, an antique rolltop desk edged up to one wall. Beside it, a trunk. Wait, he'd seen that before. Where?

"Listen, Matthew, I need to tell you something."

Matthew paused in the middle of the room. Had the trunk been downstairs before? Or . . .

In the cabin! Yes, in the bedroom, up against the wall. When had Miranda moved the trunk? And why? Suspicion poked holes in any lingering guilt over his unauthorized presence in Miranda's home. She wouldn't move the trunk unless . . .

She was hiding something.

"Matt, you even listening? I called for a reason. It's about Dad."

Matthew stiffened, a chill icing over his curiosity about the trunk. His thoughts skidded into each other. "What about him?" Something about his health? Was he back in the Twin Cities?

"He called. Wanted to talk to you. Said it was important."

"Important like he's finally decided to acknowledge Mom's

death?" Matthew sunk into the swivel chair at Miranda's desk. Three years since Mom's third bout with cancer stole her life. Gordon Knox hadn't responded to any of Jase's phone calls, not after the initial diagnosis, not in the days before the funeral. "Or maybe he'd like to rub my face in my ruined career?"

"Matt—"

Now that the floodgates opened, he couldn't stop the words. "No, I know. Turns out Mom had another bank account he forgot to empty, and he'd like to finish where he left off."

Acrid, the taste of resentment. But he could never quite swallow it.

Jase trekked on. "He gave me his phone number, e-mail, even a mailing address. He'd really like to hear from you."

"And I'd like to call him almost as much as I'd enjoy a frolic through a poison ivy patch."

Jase sighed. "You could e-mail."

"Or maybe walk barefoot through a field of thistles." It was time for this conversation to end. Jase had a gift for forgiving that Matthew could never understand. Look at how many times his brother had excused Matthew's screw-ups. But Matthew wasn't like that.

He couldn't forgive his dad.

Couldn't forgive himself.

Much as he might verbally accost his father for everything wrong in his life, deep down Matthew knew he had only himself to blame for his career failures.

But no more. He had purpose now. And he couldn't— wouldn't—let a random phone call from his father intrude on his opportunity to turn things around, help his family at the same time. Something Dad knew nothing about.

The sparse décor of Miranda's office sharpened into focus.

Cream walls, dark wood desk . . . and that trunk. Matthew shuffled his feet, rolling the desk chair over to the trunk.

"Geographically, he's just a hop away from you," Jase tried once more.

Matthew leaned forward to fiddle with the brass clasp on the trunk's lid. "I'm here on a job. No time for side trips, even if I wanted to." He lifted the lid, hinges creaking. Inside lay piles of photo albums, loose photographs scattered and tucked between books, some yellowed with age. And the shiny white of fabric . . . a wedding dress?

"So, what do I tell Dad if he calls again?"

"Tell him I'm busy." Matthew fingered through the trunk, closing in on a framed photo shoved down the side. He pulled it out.

"Come on, Matt, can't you even—"

Matthew slammed the trunk shut, a plume of dust rising and fading. "No, I can't, all right? I'm not you, Jase. I'm not . . . I'm just not interested. So let it go."

He could hear Jase's frustration before his brother even spoke again. And then, "I know you think you're on the brink of success. I know you think you're going to make some fast money and help us with the surgery."

"Izzy wasn't supposed to—"

"But you are never going to be the man you want to be until you face the man you're on the way to becoming."

"What's that supposed to mean?"

A harsh tenor took over Jase's voice. "Figure it out yourself. And I'm e-mailing you his contact info whether you want it or not."

The phone clicked into silence.

Matthew took an angry breath and shoved his phone into the pocket of his sweatshirt. Jase could play psychiatrist all he wanted up in Minnesota, but down in North Carolina Matthew had work to do. He looked down at the framed photo staring up at him from his lap. Work that had just turned interesting . . .

Because the man pictured with his arms around Miranda definitely wasn't Blaze.

☙

Hands wrapped around the Styrofoam cup she'd filled at the buffet table, Miranda forced her eyes to blink. The man strolling into the backstage waiting room could not be Blaze Hunziker. Not her Blaze.

The crew of the *Debbie Lane Show* hustled outside the doorway as he stopped in front of her. "How do I look?"

More like Robbie than he ever had before. She swallowed a burning gulp, bitter coffee prompting a wince. "Really . . . good." Nowhere to be seen were his usual flip-flops and ripped jeans. Instead, he wore black pants and a fitted black shirt. He'd slicked his dark hair back, even shaved, baby-smooth cheeks taking years off his face. She knew from the time they'd spent memorizing each other's back stories that he was twenty-nine, but today he looked barely twenty-one.

A man in headphones buzzed past the doorway.

"By the way, you don't look too shabby yourself."

She should say not, after an hour of Whitney's primping. Though the jeans Whitney had insisted she wear hugged her legs like a second skin, and her heeled boots, pulled on over her jeans, were about as practical for a homebuilder as a toddler's Playskool tool set. "I feel like Raggedy Ann trying to play Barbie."

"You've got Barbie beat by a long shot."

This "gig" was the first of a slew of talk-show appearances Brad had arranged for the next couple weeks. Though Miranda catered to the camera for her day job, publicity junkets were a different beast altogether. Uncertainty clawed at her nerves. Had she chewed a permanent mark into her bottom lip?

To make things worse, she hadn't been able to stop worrying since yesterday about the possibility of a new show replacing *From the Ground Up.* Were all these publicity efforts for naught?

Brad had assured her he'd look into the reporter's claims. But it was Lincoln's expression that concerned her the most—a blend of unease and anxiety, yes, but not a hint of surprise. Had he already heard about another home show in the works?

"Are you all right, Randi? Aren't you supposed to be used to this kind of thing? And when does this gig get off the ground?"

"I'm fine." She forced herself not to squeeze her Styrofoam cup. "I'm sure they'll come get us soon. Remember what we talked about?"

"Let you do the talking. Vague answers as much as possible. When in doubt, smile."

"Good husband."

"One thought."

Miranda threw back the last of her coffee. "What's that?"

"You're going to have to get a little more lovey-dovey."

Didn't he wish. "I'd rather take a power nailer to my own foot."

He pulled the coffee cup from her hands and chucked it at the garbage can. It bounced from the rim and landed on the floor. "Babe, I'm telling you, women pick up on stuff. You should know—you are one. They'll see right through us if you don't warm up a little."

Her fists found her waist. "So what exactly do you propose?"

His grin reeked of devilish joy. "We hold hands when we walk in. We give each other a few adoring looks during the interview." He paused, dramatic glint in his eyes. "And at least one kiss."

A man sticking his head through the door halted her gasp. "You're up in two minutes. Follow me."

"Don't even think about it," Miranda whispered as they exited the room. Although, if she were to consider kissing the man on national television, at least Blaze had the Antonio Banderas thing going on. If not for the guilt she couldn't seem to kick, it probably wouldn't be all that unpleasant.

"You know I'm right," he said into her ear, the minty scent of his shampoo lingering when he straightened. Did she actually just get goose bumps at his nearness? At a scolding look from the crewman, Miranda clamped down on her reply.

"I'm thrilled to the bone to welcome today's guests." Debbie Lane's voice carried to where they waited offstage as the host segued into an introduction. The woman flipped her bleached-blond mane and waved a hand. "Please join me in welcoming Randi Woodruff and her mystery man!"

Blaze's fingers closed around hers as the springy strains of the talk show theme song filled the set.

Here goes nothing. Together they stepped into the spotlight.

Twenty minutes later, Miranda's cheeks hurt from the grin she'd plastered in place. She crossed one jean-clad leg over the other and shifted in the purple leather chair. Blaze slouched in his own chair, a picture of relaxation with one hand resting over his stomach, the other covering her palm atop her own armrest.

It was like he breathed sedation. Did nothing faze him?

"Shameful, positively shameful, Randi Woodruff. I just can't believe it took you this long to share your hubby with the rest of the world." Debbi's singsong accusation was accompanied by the pattering of her fire-engine-red nails on a glass end table.

"Well, what can I say? My privacy is—always has been—very important to me. My marriage, too."

Blaze gave a consoling nod, squeezed her hand. There probably wasn't an ounce of fake in his grin. He was loving every cutesy moment. He'd beguiled the talk show host within two seconds of meeting her. And Miranda was pretty sure he'd caused every woman in the live audience to swoon before the first commercial break.

Ladies, if only you knew . . . Just this morning Blaze had told her one of his life's ambitions was to break the Guinness World Record for most bacon consumed in a twenty-four-hour period.

And yet, could she blame them all for buckling to his charm?

Debbie flipped her bleached-blond mane. "So tell us, why now? Why keep your handsome hottie under wraps for three years and then out of the blue let Jack out of the box, so to speak?"

Was that a ripple of suspicion in Debbie's lilting voice? Might be she was a bit more perceptive than Miranda had given her credit for. Perceptive but without an ounce of tact. *Handsome hottie?*

Miranda turned her smile on Blaze. She could almost hear his encouragement. *Work the camera, girl. That's right.* She faced Debbie again. "Well, we'd heard about some of those rumors out there. Someone told me there's even a www.wheresmirandasman.com." Brad had shared that little tidbit a few months ago, and she'd laughed it off the same way she would a question about whether Craftsman tools beat Bosch.

But that was before Lincoln had dropped the bomb about season four's uncertainty.

"I think all of us who live our lives in the public eye try to tell ourselves rumors and speculation about our personal lives don't matter. But I guess sometimes the desire to set the record straight outweighs even our desire for privacy."

Blaze's fingers intertwined with hers as he leaned forward. "And if I could interject—"

Oh dear. God, please stop him. There she went again, praying for divine intervention in a scheme that was anything but aboveboard. She squeezed Blaze's hand. Hard.

Debbie's eager nod set her hair bouncing, the flowery scent of her perfume wafting as she leaned forward. "Of course, Blake. We've heard far too little from you."

Another squeeze. "What my TV-star wife and I have is special." Blaze's voice strained as Miranda's fingernails poked his hand. But he kept going. "But working so hard to protect our privacy has meant we've spent a lot of time apart. That's been hard on our marriage. We decided if we wanted to have a healthy relationship, we needed some balance—even if it meant being seen together."

Before Miranda could stop it, a laugh pushed past her lips. No, a snort. A laugh-snort. A healthy relationship? In whose universe?

Debbie batted the impossibly long lashes that rimmed her wide blue eyes. Her forehead crinkled in question. "I'm not sure I understand your laughter, Randi. Your husband's comments, so well put, truly spoke to me."

Miranda released Blaze's hand. "Oh, they spoke to me, too." *Spoke a load of hooey.* "It's what he said about me being a TV star. I don't see myself that way."

"Well, I assure you, that's how we see you. You are a celebrity, honey, and a talented one, at that. But I have to tell you, it's even more fun seeing the romantic side of you than, well, the hammer-and-nails side."

Romantic, huh.

Blaze's grin turned sly. "Yes, the wife and I are nothing if not romantic."

"Oh, this is too cute." Debbie clapped her hands.

"Just because she may keep that side of her hidden on set doesn't mean it doesn't exist." Blaze turned to her, eyes twinkling and not so innocent just inches from her face. "Right, sweetheart?"

He's my "husband." He's ridiculously handsome. He's going to kiss me.

It'd been years since she'd been kissed. Might she actually be anticipating . . . ?

But the fact that Blaze was having the time of his life, playfully toying with her right in front of cameras, meant there was plenty of irritation mixed in with her heightened senses. Didn't matter. She had to do what she had to do.

"Right, Blake." She leaned forward, reluctance weighing her movement. Puckered.

The kiss was featherlight and soft. But it was enough for Debbie. She squealed as the audience cheered. Blaze winked.

"I'm just loving this," Debbie gushed. "It's time for another commercial break, but when we come back, it's the segment of the show I've been waiting for. A surprise for our lovebirds here."

Uh-oh, that didn't sound good.

"Randi and Blake may not be newlyweds, but to viewers seeing them together for the first time, they might as well be. Which is why we're going to play our own version of *The Newlywed Game* . . . right after this!"

Miranda's plastic smile stayed in place, but her confidence plummeted. Even Blaze's eyes held a hint of worry. Heaven help her, they'd need a lot more than a kiss to get them out of this.

The whir of Miranda's table saw in her workshop sang a soothing chorus after a day she'd love to forget. How anyone in America could believe her happily married after so many blunders on the *Debbie Lane Show*, she didn't know.

Yet she and Blaze had left Debbie still cooing.

Blaze . . . Ooh, if he ever tricked her into kissing him again, she'd go after him with a roll of duct tape. Tape those lips out of sight. His hands, too. Did he have to grip hers all the way through the show?

Actually, in all honesty, the kiss hadn't been horrible. Not a lot of chemistry, but she hadn't felt the need to scrub her lips clean or anything.

In a smooth motion, Miranda prodded a slab of wood under the saw blade. When she reached the end of the board, she straightened and flipped the switch.

Thing was, as worrisome as Debbie's little newlywed game was, it hadn't felt *all* bad. Clammy palms aside, for that one hour with Blaze at her side, she'd experienced a different kind of audience appreciation. For once, it wasn't her skill with wood and tools earning her recognition . . . but rather her womanhood.

She'd snagged the handsome husband. *She'd* scored the kind of wedded bliss others only dreamed of. *She* had the whole package: successful career, life mate, a happily-ever-after in the making.

If only it were real.

Miranda nudged her safety goggles up to her forehead as a knock sounded at the door. She glanced past the table saw to the workshop window—Matthew, smiling, waiting, as his breath produced puffs of white. She made her way through the maze of equipment and projects-in-progress and pulled open the door, greeted by a biting chill.

Matthew rubbed his hands together, nose red. "Hey. Can I come in?"

"Of course." She stepped aside, brushing off her shirt. She didn't need a mirror to know sawdust powdered her dark hair, and she probably had a trail of pink outlining her face where her goggles had been.

Fleece ski jacket still zipped to his chin, Matthew sniffed the air. "Do I smell cinnamon?"

"Apple cider. From my favorite orchard outside Pine Cove. They always save me a couple gallons from the first batch. I'll grab you a mug."

He followed her to the far end of the workshop, where she'd plugged a hot pot into the wall. She poured a mug of the amber liquid as Matthew dropped his bulky messenger bag and perched on a stool. The low hum of her space heater filled the air. "So, nice job on the show today," Matthew said. "I watched it on the old TV in the cabin."

She rolled her eyes as she handed him the steaming mug, fingers brushing his. "Are you kidding? If that had been the real *Newlywed Game*, Bob Eubanks would've laughed himself silly."

"Yeah, you did miss quite a few questions."

Eight out of fifteen, to be specific. "I guess we had an off day. We were both surprised by the game and . . ." She topped off her own mug and hefted herself onto a countertop, legs dangling over the edge. "I guess it only makes sense Blaze and I might seem a bit disconnected. So much of the time, I'm busy with the show."

And then there was the whole just-met-last-week thing. Hopefully Mr. Reporter bought her excuses.

"Well, either way, you still came off as a happy couple." Matthew sipped his drink, eyes roaming the room over the rim of his mug. Quiet settled over the workshop, only the soles of Miranda's shoes tapping against the under-counter cupboards filling in for conversation.

He's here for a reason.

It was obvious, the way he kept rubbing one palm against his jeans, taking a breath and stopping before releasing whatever question he had for her. Finally, he set his mug on her metal tool cart and reached for his bag.

"So, I wanted to ask you something."

"Okay. Go ahead."

"Am I interrupting your work?"

"This is relaxation, not work."

His eyes flitted to the saw where she'd been working. "What are you making?"

Surely that hadn't been the question he wanted to ask. "A new crib for Audrey's baby. Did you notice how old the one she has is? And it's the kind with the spokes a baby's head can get stuck in between. Of course, I'll have to convince Jimmy to accept it."

Matthew dropped his bag and stood, walked to the saw. "Looks like it's going to be quite the creation."

Miranda abandoned her mug and joined him at the saw. "I hope so."

"It probably sounds incredibly unmanly to admit this, but I've never used a table saw. Never built much of anything, unless you count working with my dad on his motorcycle."

"Are you calling *me* manly?" she teased.

And oh, the instant intensity in his eyes sent something swirling into her stomach so much warmer than her apple cider.

"Not in the least." The timbre in Matthew's voice was smooth as sanded wood. But in a blink and a moment, he broke the connection. "Show me how?"

"Sure. Umm . . ." She looked around for an extra pair of goggles, spotted a pair, and handed them to Matthew. "Safety first and all that."

For the next twenty minutes, she taught him the basics: Always look for knots, nails, or other foreign objects in the wood before beginning. Start the saw and let it reach maximum RPM before starting the cut. Feed the wood to the blade; don't push it. Keep the wood firmly against the guide fence.

He caught on quickly, asking about kickback and blade height and crosscuts. And even with the goggles subduing their visual connection, his nearness nipped at the barriers she'd tried so hard to keep in place.

When he pushed his goggles onto his forehead and flashed a smile that trekked to her heart before she could stop it, she knew she had to do something. She backed away, switched off the machine.

"Well, Teach, how'd I do?"

"Uh, good." She pulled off her goggles, moved to the counter, and gulped down the remainder of her now-cold cider. Didn't cool down the warmth she wore like a bodysuit.

"But not great."

"S-sure, great."

"Not amazing?"

At his tease, some of her nervous energy dissipated. "All right, if it'll make you happy, amazing."

He gave a curt nod. "That's better."

"Hey, what did you come here to ask me?"

His gaze strayed for an awkward moment before returning to her face. He picked up his messenger bag from the floor, then hesitated before pulling out a framed photo.

Wait, not *that* photo. . . . Where had he . . . ?

Well, she knew where he'd gotten it. There's only one place the photo would've been. In the trunk. In her office. In her house. "You searched my home?"

He winced. "Not extensively."

"What were you looking for? Incriminating files? Stolen goods? A chainsaw under my bed?"

He held up a palm. "I didn't step a foot into your bedroom."

"Wow, I feel so much better." Her heart thundered, the frame in her hand like a cement brick, weighty with significance.

"I need you to understand, Miranda, this isn't the kind of

reporting I usually do, this celebrity stuff. I'm a politics guy. Government. Hard news."

"So?"

"So it was halfway instinctive to go looking for a scoop. Maybe I was bored, or maybe it was my stupid need for recognition as a serious journalist, but I couldn't help—"

She hugged the photograph to her chest. "You could have. You absolutely could have. I don't care if you suspected I was the BTK killer. You—"

"He was arrested years ago."

"You had no right." But wasn't it her own fault for letting her guard down, for leaving him to roam her property at will? She should've insisted he come along with her and Blaze.

But after Saturday night, the way he'd stepped to her rescue in the restaurant, and then the other day, their paint fight at the studio, the way her heart so easily puddled into pleasure . . .

She'd needed those hours away.

"You're right. You're absolutely right. And I'm sorry. But . . . I do have to ask for an explanation. This guy isn't Blaze. And it looks an awful lot like an engagement picture."

"So . . . what? If I don't explain, you'll conjecture?"

He didn't answer, only probed her eyes with his. What choice did she have? She lowered the frame to see Robbie's smile, bold and vibrant and a little brooding. Just like she remembered, no matter how she tried to forget. She closed her eyes against the uprising of memories.

Didn't work. Because suddenly she was in Brazil, on her first day at Esperanca Construtores, warm with anticipation.

When she'd walked onto the site that day, there was no missing the man hoisting one end of a wall frame. Tanned skin shiny with perspiration, dark hair grazing his neck underneath a handkerchief tied around his head. And eyes like cocoa beans, flickering with energy. *Robbie* . . .

She'd listened that day as he instructed the rest of the crew in Portuguese, honeyed words oozing over her travel-wearied spirit, smoothing away her uncertainties. And then he'd turned his eyes on her, sent her a crooked smile, and switched to English. "Ah, you must be our new American."

Right then and there, with the Amazon sun beating through her work clothing, the clamor of a language she barely understood playing all around her, she'd tasted what had to be love. Or something awfully close.

"Miranda?"

It had taken everything in her to steady her voice, place her palm in his outstretched hand. *Yeah, I'm your American.*

How long had it taken Miranda to finally untangle her identity from that of Robbie's? To see herself as a full person, instead of one-half of a whole?

"Miranda?" Matthew's voice wrenched her from the memory. Her eyes snapped open to see a man nothing like Robbie. Not in looks. Certainly not in background. Yet with the same unyielding ability to pull her in.

Say something. You've got to fix this.

"Matthew, I . . ." She lowered slowly onto a workbench. Resigned. "I met Robbie in Brazil. He'd been there a couple years already. We connected, but, uh, Hope Builders team members weren't supposed to be involved romantically. So we worked at just being friends for a long time, but we gradually became . . . more than friends.

"And when things between Robbie and me became obvious, we were asked to leave." The humiliation of that day, standing before the mission board, still burned her. She'd tried to keep her feelings for Robbie at bay, but as her months in Brazil turned into years, she'd eventually given in. "After three years in Brazil, I kind of liked the idea of returning to the States. Robbie said he'd come with me, even proposed before we left Brazil."

Her world had tilted in that moment.

How quickly it'd all changed. She'd wanted to marry right away. Robbie had insisted they get settled in the States first. They'd set a date, and Miranda had counted the days . . . until there'd been nothing to count toward anymore.

"It was actually my stories about Robbie's and my work in Brazil that landed me the role on *From the Ground Up*. I only meant to audition for the crew. In fact, they'd almost settled on a different lead—Hollie Morris, I think her name was. Met her once—very awkward. But the execs liked my personality. Loved my stories about Robbie. Decided I should work them into the episodes. It was so well received."

Was she telling Matthew too much? And if so, why couldn't she stop the rushing flow of truth? It all came accompanied with such an odd sense of relief.

"I called Robbie my husband on the show because I figured by the time the episodes aired, I'd be married. Also . . ." She looked away. "It may seem old-fashioned to some, but I was feeling guilty about our living situation."

Her eyes landed on the photo again, and she remembered suddenly the love note he'd scrawled on the back of the photo. So unlike the final letter he'd written, left waiting for her when she'd arrived home that cool September night. She'd had news, the kind of news they should've celebrated with dancing and embraces.

Instead, she'd spied his rambling note sticking out between a JC Penney catalog and an electricity bill. With a hand to her stomach, she'd sunk onto their bed, a weeping mess as she read. *"You don't need me. There's no room for me in your life anymore."*

Without ever even trying, she'd memorized Robbie's cowardly letter word for word. Why was it that a person could forget a thousand moments over a lifetime but never purge the one memory she truly wanted to forget?

She blinked away the tears begging to fall now. Had to focus. Had to repair this the way she would a leaky showerhead or busted coffee table. "Anyway, he left before the wedding. But I met Blaze. And . . . and yes, he's a different man than the one I talked about in the first season. But he's *the* man in my life now." The same old scratching of her conscience played its sandpaper game. But shouldn't lying feel natural by now?

And why—*why*—despite the alarm that should have been sounding, did it feel so very good to let out at least a partial truth? Even knowing Matthew could use it to ruin her reputation if he wanted?

Maybe, for some uncanny reason, she trusted him with the pain of her past. And despite the painful memories, the emotional bruises, all that mattered was Matthew's next course of action. Her hope rallied. Because at least he'd come to her with his questions.

"You were in a tough spot." At his acknowledgement, her gaze shot to his. "I guess if I were in your shoes, I don't know what I would've done, either. Maybe it wasn't the most honest thing in the world to transition men and let the public think what they wanted . . ." He took a step toward her, his honesty at once sharp and sweet, like the smell of cinnamon still permeating the woodshop.

She braved the question. "What are you going to do?"

"I know what I *should* do," he murmured.

Run with the story, of course.

"Just not sure I *want* to."

Miranda's pulse slowed. "You mean . . . ?"

"I need to think." He took a step back, then cocked his head. "Where did you and Blaze marry? Didn't someone recognize you, your name, question it?"

"We thought of all that. So . . . we took a vacation. Got married in the Caribbean." One lie bred so many others.

"Marriage certificate?"

"I know we signed something. I'll look around and see if I can find it."

And the lie began again. . . .

He studied her a moment longer, then turned and left her alone.

Chapter 8

Miranda's body twisted at an odd angle in the close space of the studio bathroom. She stood to the side of the toilet, her hands at eye level, where she tightened the last screws of the over-the-toilet shelving unit.

Bathroom segments. The worst. Never mind that the set bathroom was triple the size that of most homes. With a craned camera lowered in her face, it still felt claustrophobic.

Add in the fact that she couldn't get last night's conversation with Matthew out of her mind, and this take was doomed from the start. She lowered the screwdriver and stepped around the toilet. "Sorry, Tom, I've got a crick in my neck like you wouldn't believe."

Tom called the cut. "Take five, Rand. We'll get it on the next take."

His patience had been unending today. She expected he, too, had heard Sam Toliver's hints about the new show. He knew the toll it was taking on her, on the whole cast and crew. Had they worked together for more than three years only to face an abrupt end?

In all her worry about her own career, she needed to remember many other livelihoods hinged on *From the Ground Up*'s continuance, as well.

In an attempt to avoid Matthew and Blaze, both of whom watched from the edge, Miranda escaped the confines of the bathroom and plucked a water bottle from the cooler by the catering table. She tipped her head back for a cool drink, wishing the water could wash away her worries as easily as it soothed her scratching throat.

When she lowered the bottle, Whitney stood in front of her with a blotting sponge.

"I messed up my makeup?"

"No, but you're perspiring like a glass of lemonade in humidity." Whitney dotted the sponge over Miranda's face.

"Lovely."

"Hey, I could've said you're sweating like a pig. What gives, anyway? Is it your husband watching making you nervous?"

Try the reporter standing next to him. "I'm fine."

"You've dropped your screwdriver twice, once into the toilet."

"I'm fine," she repeated. "And now my face is dry, so all's well in the world."

Whitney dropped the sponge in a wastebasket, skepticism flashing in her eyes. "Why'd your husband start coming to the set, anyway? Is it that journalist guy? Is Blake jealous? And you know what else is weird? I just realized the other day, I never knew your husband's name until he started showing up around here. Isn't that odd?"

Well, it's not as if Miranda and her assistant had ever been especially chummy. In fact, Miranda had always suspected the snippy woman didn't care for her all that much. Certainly didn't think much of her fashion choices.

"I suppose I talked about him so much on the show, I figured people didn't need to hear my gushing off set," Miranda said, the only answer she could think of to Whitney's queries. Whitney only shrugged.

Miranda took another drink of her water, then stretched,

arching her back, arms behind her. She'd be happy when this workday ended. Tonight she planned to stop by Open Arms and get in a couple hours of helping out with whatever projects Liv needed finished. The thought of more work should have exhausted her, but volunteering at the shelter always energized her.

Of course, she'd have Matthew along, documenting her every move. And while they'd certainly struck up a camaraderie, even bonded over the past few days, last night's confession added a whole new level of awkwardness to their relationship.

Not relationship. Acquaintance. Professional association.

She was still waiting for a phone call from Brad, letting her know Matthew had outed her switch of fiancés on his blog. Even if he didn't break the story now, surely he would later, when she couldn't come up with a marriage certificate. Would he buy it if she said Blaze had lost it? That wasn't so unbelievable, right?

At the sound of Tom's voice, she chugged one more drink of water, but the liquid jostled in her throat when she saw Matthew approaching. She coughed, sputtered.

"You all right?" he asked as he reached her.

"Fine." Her voice came out raspy, and she coughed again, then realized she was squeezing the water bottle so tightly, a trickle of water streamed down the side. "We're doing the next take, so I've got to go."

Uncertainty colored his hazel eyes. "Okay," he said slowly. "But I just . . . I wanted to say . . . are we okay?"

He asked the question with such sincerity. It touched her heart in a place she knew it shouldn't.

"Because I want to keep doing this blog. Let's be honest: Yes, I'd love a scoop. My career needs a boost. But I realized last night, if I spill your secret right now, the blog's over with.

Everyone else will snatch up the story. No one will care about my little serial anymore."

"So you're—what?—saving it for a bigger article down the road?" Would he admit it if he was?

"I don't know." He raked his fingers through his hair, lowering his voice. "I just . . . Well, so many things make sense now. The fact Blaze knows nothing about construction. How you two don't seem to have as much in common as the man you talk about in the first season. I'm glad you told me the truth. Knowing someone as private as you would tell me, that makes me *want* to be on your side. Even if it goes against my reporting instinct."

She deserved to be hit over the head with her own screwdriver. Pushed over the toilet and given a swirly. Because she had barely scratched the surface of the truth last night. And now Matthew looked at her as if she'd given him some kind of treasure.

Telling Matthew a piece of the truth last night might have come with a temporary sense of relief. But in the hours since, her guilt had ballooned.

"I've got to go," she said again. Because she had to focus. She had to do her job.

Even if it took another half a dozen takes.

Miranda's scream sliced through the cool evening air and jolted Matthew to attention. He dropped his rake and craned his neck to the tree house perched in the massive maple in the backyard of the Open Arms home.

"Miranda?"

In the corner of the yard, Blaze was oblivious, apparently lost in the drone of the leaf blower they'd found in the shed.

Another trill from overhead, the sound of scuffling. Matthew abandoned his pile of leaves and scaled the ladder into the tree house. "Hey, you all right?"

Oh, she definitely wasn't. A bird, flapping and panicky, flung from wall to wall, Miranda ducking, covering her head.

He climbed the rest of the way into the tree house as Miranda let out another squeal. "It's just a bird, Miranda. It won't hurt you."

The bird smacked into the wall. "It's trying to kill me."

It was as if he'd walked into a Hitchcock movie. Only, Miranda played a much cuter and slightly more hysterical Tippi. He grabbed a couple badminton rackets from the floor and prodded the bird toward an open window. Its wings fluttered, chirps escaping from its beak.

Miranda huddled in a corner. Where was a video camera when he needed it? He finally sheepdogged the bird out the window and then turned slowly toward his frazzled blog subject. And it boomed from him, hearty laughter.

"I can't believe . . . just a bird . . . you of all women . . . scared."

She smoothed a hand through her hair, shoulders straightening. "That thing zoomed in here like a dive bomber."

"Laughter . . . can't stop . . ."

She picked up one of the badminton rackets he'd dropped and whacked him lightly. "Go on. You've got raking to do."

"But I just saved you."

"Scram!"

He laughed all the way down the ladder, back to the pile of leaves he'd spent the past hour raking. He couldn't have asked for a more entertaining intrusion into his chore.

"Dude, your leaf pile is a kiddie pool to my ocean," Blaze said, coming up behind him. He carried the leaf blower like an AK-47, an orange extension cord wrapped around his shoulder.

Matthew lifted his rake to pry loose a clump of leaves.

"Maybe so, but there's something wistful and nostalgic about raking leaves. Reminds me of my childhood." The good part, anyway, before Dad's disappearance and Mom's cancer. "Leaf blowers sort of ruin the experience for me."

He caught a view of Miranda leaning out the window of the tree house. She swiped a paintbrush against the mini shutters framing the window, cerulean blue vibrant against the dark wood. The glow of the setting sun fell through branches and lingering leaves, landing on the back lawn of the Open Arms home in freckles of color.

It shouldn't surprise him, really, that Miranda had driven all the way across Asheville to volunteer at Open Arms after a full Monday of taping. Not after he'd witnessed her concern for that young family in the backwoods. Or the way she spent years of her life working in Brazil.

Maybe that's why he wanted to believe every word she'd said out in the workshop last night. Because compassion didn't mix with dishonesty.

But then, why the murmur of misgiving hovering under the surface? And why had she acted so nervous at the studio today?

Actually, the question he should have been asking was why he hadn't gone to Dooley with the truth about Miranda's marriage. Even if he chose not to blog about it immediately—in an effort to keep the blog going, buy time for further investigation, and maybe even find that Robbie guy—he should at least have let Dooley know he had material worthy of January's cover story.

But each time he contemplated it, Miranda would go and smile at him—or freak out at a bird—and he'd soften. Plus, there was another concern he hadn't considered until today. Cee adored the Randi Woodruff she saw on TV. She texted him practically every day, asking questions about Miranda, requesting photos. Did he really want to be the one to blow the image of her celebrity heroine? But that's what he'd have to do in January's article, right?

So instead of making a firm decision, he continued dallying around in indecision.

"Got to tell you, man, I never once raked leaves as a kid," Blaze said now. "We hired a service. Maybe I missed out."

Last fall, Matthew had spent three evenings over at Jase and Izzy's, raking leaves with Cee. They'd swept the yard clean, one heaping pile in the center of the lawn rising like the hill of grain at a co-op during harvest. And then they'd jumped, Cee unable to hear her own giggles, but Matthew gulping them in like a proud father as they landed in a mess of crunchy leaves and twigs.

"Blaze, do you and Miranda plan to have kids someday?"

Blaze's eyebrows shot up. "Getting personal there."

"I'm a reporter. We do that."

"I better let Randi answer that. I . . . we . . . tend to do things on her schedule."

Like getting married in a rush? Waiting to let the public in on it until it would benefit *From the Ground Up*?

Wait a second. Could Miranda have married Blaze *for* the show? Maybe that's why he'd felt unsettled about the whole thing.

He glanced up. She'd switched sides, now gliding fresh color over the cracked and faded paint of the opposite shutter. *Surely not*. Yet, now that his suspicion had a name, he had to confront it.

He nudged stray leaves toward the pile with his foot. "Well, if you won't answer that, tell me about your and Miranda's whirlwind courtship. For instance, how did your family react? Do you have family in the area? I know Miranda's parents are down in Brazil, but what about yours? Any siblings?"

For the first time since Matthew had met Blaze, a steely

sheen dropped over his expression like a shield. "Randi's your subject, Knox. Not me." Blaze flipped the switch on the leaf blower, and its gusty roar ended the conversation.

Questions gurgled to life as Blaze moved off, but Matthew swallowed them down. Because Blaze had a point. And because, after all, if he really wanted to know about Blaze's family, there was such a thing as the Internet.

As for his other questions . . .

He propped his rake against the tree. Miranda was bending over a paint can when he once again emerged into the structure. "You know, this tree house is like something out of *Swiss Family Robinson*."

Her head whirled at the sound of his voice. Wind fanned her hair, and the evening chill blushed her cheeks. "When I build a tree house, I build it right."

If only he could jet her up to Minnesota, he'd ask her to build one for Cee.

Now that a bird wasn't terrorizing the place, he scoped out the interior of the tree house, which was just as impressive as the outside—roomy, even homey, with curtains, knickknacks displayed on shelves, and two wooden chairs. "What's that for?" He pointed to a thick rope dangling from the ceiling. He followed its trail overhead. Some kind of pulley system?

Miranda's smile hinted at pride. "Watch this." She stepped close, the apple scent of her hair mingling with paint fumes, and gave the rope a steady pull. The metal hub jangled with the movement of the rope as a section of the tree house roof creaked open.

"You've got to be kidding me. A skylight in a tree house. It's like you saw inside my childhood imagination."

Miranda shook her head. "No, I saw inside my grandpa's imagination. When my parents sent me home from Brazil, my grandfather decided to cheer me up by building a tree house.

He bought one of those sets at the hardware store with the rainbow tarp, put the thing together in an afternoon."

A leaf drifted in from the open ceiling, landing between their feet. "It was a perfectly fine tree house, but the first time Grandpa climbed up with me, he took one look around and said, 'We can do better than this, Miranda.' And he did, customized that thing 'til it was the envy of the neighborhood. And that's when I first got bit by the carpentry bug."

"So you're giving the kids here at Open Arms the same fun your grandpa gave you." Tomorrow's blog post had just written itself. "This place—not just the tree house, but the whole facility—completely surprised me. I expected something a lot more institutional looking."

Instead, the shelter for orphans with special needs run by Miranda's friend Liv made its home in a Victorian house. The structure stood three stories high, painted canary yellow with crisp white shutters. A wraparound porch hugged its front and sides, and a balcony extended from French doors on the third level. Mums lined the path from the street to the entrance.

Thinking back to a couple hours ago, though, Matthew remembered it wasn't only the facility that surprised him, but also Blaze's reaction. Miranda's husband had gaped at the winding staircase that jutted into the mahogany-floored entryway, the curled carvings of the banister, the sight of the mammoth dining room table through an open doorway.

He'd stared as if he'd never seen the place before.

"Matthew, could you close the skylight?"

Miranda's voice pecked unheeded at his continued musing. Did Blaze never come along with Miranda to volunteer at Open Arms? Blaze joined Miranda for photo shoots and publicity junkets, but other than that, they seemed to live different lives. On Sunday, she'd spent half the day in her workshop and he'd taken off for town. While Miranda disappeared for several hours last night, Blaze went running.

"Earth to Knox." Miranda brushed past him to the floor opening where the ladder poked in. "Let's go help Blaze bag up the leaves and then hit the road. I'm dog tired."

Matthew turned, blurted the question pounding him like a gong. "Are you and Blaze for real?"

The paint can dangling from her hand squeaked as she turned slowly. "What?"

"I mean, is it a true relationship? Do you really . . . love each other?" A warning bell somewhere in the distant corners of his mind cautioned against anything more. Still, he pressed on. "Did you only marry Blaze for the show?"

Miranda's pause stretched, flexing the silence into something heavy and awkward. He knew he should wish the question back. But even more than he needed a story, Matthew wanted truth.

And her trust. Not so he could mine for blog fodder, but so he could discover . . . her. The fascinating woman with calloused hands and a bruised heart who built homes by day and played Good Samaritan at night.

"I can't believe you'd ask me that after what I told you last night."

If only the lighting weren't so dim inside the tree house, he might have read her eyes and discerned whether anger or hurt shadowed her words.

"But can you see why I wonder? How it might look?"

She turned her back to him, spoke slowly. "No. I didn't marry him for the show." She dropped to the floor, lowered herself to the ladder, and disappeared.

Leaving Matthew alone with the distrust he was coming to hate.

She hadn't lied. Not technically.

So why did Matthew's question bother her so? Half an hour later, it still pricked against the tender flesh of her emotions.

Miranda yanked the pull strings of a heavy-duty garbage bag ballooning with leaves. The last one in the box. Matthew had gone inside looking for more several minutes ago. She knotted the garbage bag handles, chucked it over with the others, and surveyed the yard. Only a few scattered piles left.

"No. I didn't marry him for the show."

That's right. Only pretended to.

The sun dipped low behind the Appalachian ridges, a streak of orange bold against a darkening sky. At her side, Blaze shook an errant tuft of hair from his face and pulled the hood of his sweatshirt over his head. "Brr. The weather's so shifty around here."

Halfway through the day, temps had reached the mid-fifties. Now they were headed for an overnight frost. "Thanks for all your help. This would've taken hours more on my own."

"Anything to help the wife. How would it look if I didn't come along?"

How, indeed. If his questions were any indication, Matthew had enough suspicions on his own. But what he'd said this morning, about wanting to keep the blog going—did that mean he truly didn't intend to write about what she'd told him last night? *At least not yet.* She couldn't let herself get comfortable. "Blaze, have you read any of Matthew's articles, his blogs?"

"Yeah, the dude's pretty good with his ABCs. Why, haven't you read them?"

She bit her lip, warming her hands inside the pockets of her fleece jacket. "I can't. It's weird, I know, but I'm . . . nervous. I don't usually know the people who interview me, so if the story rubs me wrong, it's no biggie. But Matthew, he's . . ."

Blaze cocked his head, raised eyebrows prodding her on.

She shrugged. "A friend, I guess. And sometimes you think you know how a friend sees you, but then you find out they actually see you differently than how you thought they saw you, and you wonder, is that how other people see me? See what I'm saying?"

He belted out a laugh. "I *see* why Matthew's the wordsmith and not you."

She elbowed him in the side. "Says the man whose vocabulary is monopolized by *dude*."

Blaze rubbed his palm over his stubbled chin, scratchy like the sound of sandpaper, before speaking again. "Want to know how else I see you?"

"I'm not sure." He'd already told her she didn't know how to have fun. Now what? She was too boring? Straightlaced? After all, she'd turned down his order to jump in a pile of leaves minutes ago.

"I see a woman who's pretending to be married to one guy while falling for someone else."

His words, like the cool of the night, chilled through her. She attempted a nonchalant giggle, but it came out a garbled cough. "What?"

His knees bent to bring him eye level with her. "You're falling for Knox. And it makes total sense, too. You're both creative types but in a different way—you with your wood, him with words. It draws you together."

No. No. *No.* "Thanks for the analysis, Dr. Love, but you're way off. I've known him all of one week. We're just friends."

"Universal code for 'I'm crazy about him but don't want you to know.' And you've spent more time with him in one week than many people do with family members in a month. Look me in the eye, sweetie-pie, and deny it."

"He's nosy a-and cocky and . . . nosy." And cute, even with

his blasted questions. And helpful and hardworking. "And he wouldn't know a Hitachi from a DeWalt."

"A what-y from a de-what?"

Another elbow in the side. Harder this time and accompanied by an exaggerated groan. "I'm going inside. Matthew should've been out here with more garbage bags five minutes ago."

Blaze's teasing laughter followed her inside. That, and the side effect of his words: worry. Because what if he saw something real?

I'm married. I'm married. I'm married.

She trailed through the mud room into the kitchen, the yeasty smell of homemade bread lingering in the air. Hadn't she told Matthew he'd find garbage bags here? Where had he wandered?

"Matthew?" she called, leaving the kitchen. "Liv?" Liv had been off to run errands with a few of the children when they first arrived, the rest of the kids on an outing with a volunteer group.

She moved down the first-floor corridor, then slowed outside the den when the sound of piano reached her ears. She recognized the song, a favorite: "Beautiful Dreamer."

She peeked into the room, surprise flitting through her at the sight of Matthew at the piano. His hands glided over the keys effortlessly. And standing beside the piano, the children who'd left earlier with Liv—Anya, Peter, Claire—their hands pressed against the back of the piano, smiling as they felt the vibration.

Listening.

Anya, Peter, and Claire were deaf.

With a gentle push against the door, Miranda padded into the room. She caught Matthew's eyes, saw the red creep into his cheeks. Liv watched from another corner of the room. Anya spotted Miranda and waved with one hand, then just as quickly returned her palm to the piano.

The song ended to the children's "clapping"—palms lifted, fluttering back and forth in ASL applause. Their faces lit up, eyes glowing, as their hands began to move in silent chatter. Oh, did they think Matthew was a volunteer sign interpreter?

And then her heart sighed as Matthew's own hands spun into motion. He spoke as he signed. "My name is Matthew." He spelled out his name one letter at a time. "What are your names?" It was possible she'd never seen anything sweeter.

"That reporter of yours is full of surprises," Liv spoke from behind her as the children signed their names.

"Indeed." But of course he'd mentioned his niece was deaf. So it wasn't surprising he knew ASL.

"How old are you?" Matthew asked.

"Ten, seven, and six," Miranda recited in a whisper as the children answered in sign. How often had she wished to communicate with these three, lamenting her lack of sign language skills, heart wincing as they stood by silently while she talked to the other children?

Oh, Liv knew basic sign language. And Claire, the oldest, could read lips. But more often than not, Miranda felt at a loss when trying to connect.

"All right, children. Into the kitchen for snacks. The others will be home soon," Liv signed and spoke.

As she herded the kids out, Matthew's fingers returned to the keyboard. He played a scale, upped an octave and played another. Miranda crossed the room and lowered onto the bench beside him. "Not only are you a writer, but you're also a concert pianist."

He chuckled. "Hardly. But I did take lessons 'til halfway through high school."

"I always wanted to learn. But by the time they took me in, Grandpa and Grandma were on a fixed income. Not enough money."

"Well, finally, something *I* can teach *you*."

Even though her eyes were on the black-and-white ivories, she could hear the smile in Matthew's smooth voice. Her heart quickened, and her conscience told her to stand up and leave. But Matthew pressed a key before she could move. "This is middle C."

"I know *that*. If that's all you're going to teach me—"

"Patience, grasshopper. What do you want to learn? 'Chopsticks'? Easiest song in the book."

Did he have any idea the effect he had on her? What was wrong with her, anyway? How could she shift so quickly from pining for Robbie to wishing . . .

She shook her head, felt the hair tickling her cheeks and Matthew's movement as he turned to face her.

"Not 'Chopsticks'? Okay. Well, I can teach you something else."

"No, that's not it." Miranda tried to stand, but her knees bumped into the underside of the piano and she wobbled—she'd turned into a klutz around this man—and sat back on the bench.

"It's about those questions I asked in the tree house. They weren't nice. I realize that. But I *am* a reporter."

"True. But this . . . *this* was nice." She looked from Matthew to the piano, back to his eyes. And that smile on his face, oh, she could seriously get used to it.

If she wanted to. But she didn't.

"It's just . . ." She lowered her head. "Not that many people know about Robbie. And now that I know you know, I feel . . . weird."

"Why? I don't think less of you because your first engagement didn't work out. I could tell you about some relationship blunders of my own."

"It's not that as much as . . . I've built up this identity for myself. And Robbie feels like a crack in that identity." Why was she being so honest with him? Hadn't she just decided to be more cautious?

"Is your reputation so important? I guess that's a dumb question, because you're a TV star, but it just seems . . ."

His voice trailed, and in the quiet she could hear the clomping of footsteps in the entryway. The other children must have returned from their outing. What Matthew didn't understand was this wasn't just about her reputation. It was about who she was, deep inside. And he'd seen a caged facet that was never meant to escape.

"Hey, if it'll make you feel better, I'll tell you about one of my less-than-proud moments," Matthew said. "Remember how I told you the other night about my dad ditching our family?"

Yes, out in the cabin. When she'd talked about her parents. It seemed they'd formed a pattern of sharing secrets.

"Well, about five years ago, I pretty much accused my father—in print—of embezzlement." His fingers grazed the top of the keys. "I ran a skewed article—one that I never should've pushed in the first place—and let a decade's worth of anger pretty much destroy my career. Had to resign. And worse, the reporter I'd assigned the article was fired."

She heard the regret dripping from his words, the shame.

"The ironic thing is, my dad apparently recovered from it all quite easily. He's running for office just a state away from here. Which kills me, considering . . ." He swept his hand over the bass keys, the noise harsh. "Why am I even talking about this? Oh, right. You, me, we're not all that different. We've both made mistakes."

The desire to lean her head on his shoulder, squeeze his hand, maybe let him teach her "Chopsticks," after all, overtook her. But before she could respond, the clearing of a throat in the doorway thrust her attention away. Blaze. "I found the bags and finished up, guys." He spoke in his usual lighthearted tone. But when she and Matthew rose, when Matthew bent over to tuck the bench underneath the piano, she saw the knowing look in Blaze's eyes.

And knew he wasn't all wrong.

Chapter 9

"Knox, all I'm saying is, take it up a notch."

Matthew closed his laptop with a frustrated exhale. His cell phone, set to speaker, lay on the conference room table in front of him, the *Today* editor's name displayed on the screen. "I thought you liked my blogs, said the website was getting record hits. Now you're saying the material's no good?"

He slipped his laptop into his messenger bag and stood. Earlier, the empty conference room of the *From the Ground Up* studio had seemed like the perfect place to write, pound out tomorrow's blog post while Miranda filmed a segment on window installation.

But Dooley's phone call ruined his focus.

"You're putting words in my mouth. Your posts are well-written and generally entertaining. Today, that story about Randi building a tree house with her grandfather, it was cute."

Somehow he doubted the word was a compliment. "It was meant to be insightful." And he'd labored on it last night after returning from Open Arms. Heard the wistful rhythm of Miranda's voice as he wrote.

"It was. But we're not the *New Yorker*, Knox. For the first week of posts, insightful worked. But if you want to hang on to your readers, you can't coast. Give us some flair. Put that reporter's nose to work and dig up some surprises."

What would Dooley say if Matthew told him he'd dug up a few already? *Blaze isn't the original mystery man. Miranda was kicked out of Hope Builders for being romantically involved with her team leader.*

He'd gone ahead and pretty much promised Miranda he wouldn't play whistle-blower on her . . . yet. She'd bewitched him, had somehow become much more attractive than the scandal he'd originally hoped for.

Matthew slung his bag over his shoulder. "I'm not going to make something up just for the sake of spice."

"Who's asking you to? If there's one thing I've learned in this biz, it's that there isn't a soul on earth not shielding some kind of secret or fault. You've shown us the talented, sentimental Randi Woodruff. All right. Now turn over the coin."

He should've never taken this assignment. He wasn't a blogger. And he certainly wasn't the kind of man who sold out a friend.

Which is where he'd made his biggest mistake—dropping his guard, letting Miranda sneak past his reporter's barrier.

Hearing voices outside the conference room door, Matthew picked up his phone and tapped the speaker off. "Okay, fine, I might have a minor lead."

"Yeah?"

"Miranda is convinced her show's in danger of cancelation."

"Okay," Dooley responded slowly, waiting.

He lowered his voice. "Well, if anybody wonders why she waited until now to put her husband on parade . . ." He trailed off, hating himself for what his words suggested. But wouldn't Miranda prefer a minor inference like this rather than exposure of the whole truth?

"Hmm. So she's using her husband in an attempt to save the show."

The voices grew louder outside the conference room. "I wouldn't put it in quite so crass of terms."

"You don't have to. Let the reader. Subtle implication is a beautiful thing, my friend."

"I don't remember you being so cold in college." Maybe he *should* back out. For Miranda. For his own integrity.

"The word is *smart*, Knox. And if you want the January cover story, that's exactly how you've got to play this: smart."

He was starting to care less and less about the January cover. But the paycheck? The follow-up interviews. His name in the spotlight and the subsequent lucrative possibilities?

You can play serious journalist later. It's about Cee's surgery now.

As the voices outside the room rose another level, Matthew crossed the space to the doorway. "Listen, I've got to go. But I'll give you more grit in tomorrow's post."

"Of course you will. And, Knox, be careful."

Matthew paused. "What's that mean?"

"It means usually you're the one bursting at the seams for an exposé."

"In politics, government, hard news, yes. But this—"

"People are intelligent. They read between the lines. Have you checked out the reader comments on your last couple blog posts?"

What in the world was Dooley getting at? "No, I haven't read the comments. But whatever you're suspecting—about me, I mean—you're wrong."

"Okay, then. But do yourself a favor. Read the comments section. Later, Knox."

Matthew pocketed his phone, bewilderment giving way to annoyance. Like he had time to scroll through five hundred comments. Not with Dooley breathing down his neck . . . and something going on outside the conference room.

He opened the door to find Miranda, her manager, and Lincoln Nash mid-argument, or at least what looked like an argument. Lincoln's arms were folded, Miranda's jaw set in defiance. "So, just like that, we're caving to rumors and—" She stopped when she saw Matthew. "Oh, hi."

"Knox, I forgot you were writing in there," Brad cut in. "Come with me. Let's talk about how you fit into Randi's schedule for the next few days." Brad nodded his head to the side, gesturing for Matthew to follow.

And ditch whatever interesting thing was happening here? But Miranda's pleading expression convinced him to acquiesce. He caught up with Brad.

"So, what's going on?"

They approached a humming vending machine, Miranda's and Lincoln's voices still trailing after them.

"If I tell you, I'd really rather it not hit cyberspace."

Matthew leveled Miranda's manager with an unapologetic grimace. "Can't promise that."

"At least you're honest." Brad shrugged, fishing into the pocket of his black pants and coming up with a handful of change. "Well, you'll find out one way or another. Lincoln's just told Miranda production on season four is halted until the network makes its final decision. She's not taking it well."

Down the hallway, Miranda was shaking her head as Lincoln spoke.

"I feel bad for her, but it isn't unexpected. Who would want to pay out on a show that hasn't been picked up for the next season?"

"True, but Randi's thinking with her emotions. She's thinking of the crew and their paychecks." Brad slipped his quarters into the vending machine. "She's also ticked off that the network is taking so long to make the decision. It's unusual not to know the spring lineup this late into the fall." He punched a button on the machine, and a candy bar dropped to the bottom with a thud.

"You're saying there might be more to the story, then?"

Brad shrugged again. "Rumor is the execs are all agog over a recent pitch for a new show, that they may not want to wait until next fall to give it a slot."

"Out with the old, in with the new. It seems crazy with Miranda's fan base." No wonder she walked around half the time tight with stress.

Brad pulled out the Snickers bar. "Well, if it's another building-type show, her audience would likely convert without too much grumbling. What's odd to me is that whoever pitched it did so to a network that already has a successful home show. Almost seems like . . . a personal dig. Who knows. I'd love to go mining for more information, but who's going to tell Randi Woodruff's manager about the competition?"

A personal dig? Against Miranda? An idea took root. "But they might tell a reporter. Especially one with *Today* magazine, one of the leading celeb mags."

A grin spread across Brad's cheeks as he started down the hallway. "For a reporter, you're an okay guy."

Matthew smirked. "Thanks . . . I think. Where you going?"

"To give Miranda her daily sugar supply. Might cheer her up." He turned back to Matthew.

"You know her well."

Brad stopped. "Well enough to know she doesn't need this on top of everything else."

Matthew would've thought this *was* the everything else.

"If there's one thing I've learned in this biz, it's that there isn't a soul on earth not shielding some kind of secret or fault."

Had he only scratched the surface of Miranda's secrets?

Gray skies looming, Miranda emerged from a grouping of trees. Rounding a bend and cresting the rise of terrain, she spotted the church, its white steeple piercing the sky. It stood in the center of a flat clearing, cut into the side of a craggy ridge.

How many times had she walked this path, approached the church building that, despite its simple architecture and faded white-washed walls, held an austere pose amid its mountain surroundings? At least a year's worth of Sundays.

But never during service times. Never risking a run-in with a regular attender.

And this was her first weeknight visit. What if she ran into a prayer group or something? She took a long, steady breath and reached for the handle of the heavy wooden door. It creaked open, promising silence, solitude. All she knew was she needed this—to get away, clear her head.

Maybe even pray about the anxieties pounding her like a heavy rain. No more production on their fourth season? It was as if Lincoln had pronounced an early death sentence on the show.

And then there's Matthew . . .

Anyway, for weeks she'd been meaning to leave an anonymous note at the church about Jimmy and Audrey. Their home wasn't more than two miles away, and if the church had any kind of outreach program, perhaps she could stop worrying about whether Audrey and her baby were eating enough.

Rays of colored light streamed in through the stained-glass windows. Wrapped in the quiet of the sanctuary, Miranda lowered onto a sun-warmed wooden pew. She breathed in the calm, felt the tautness of her emotions release as she leaned against the hard-backed seat.

She'd given up regular church attendance years ago, knowing full well her secret ruined any chance at finding community in a house of worship.

Make that *secrets.*

At the thought, the peace she'd grasped for upon entering the sanctuary doors seeped out in a slow escape. She might imagine she heard God's whispering during her weekly visits, even crave the once-comforting canopy of His love, but years had widened the gap between Miranda and the faith that used to feel as real as the rises and ridges of the mountains.

And yet, here she sat, with Jesus smiling at her in stained glass.

I love my career, God. I love my house in the mountains. I love making a difference. Don't you see I want to use my career to help people? Couldn't, just this once, the end justify the means?

No answer from the smiling Jesus.

She redirected her gaze, the pulpit—new since she'd last stopped in—catching her eye. She rose and walked down the aisle, past the altar. Her fingers connected with the rich wood, traced the grooved outlines of a lion, lamb, and dove carved into the front of the pulpit. Now, that was craftsmanship. "Beautiful." The word came out a whisper.

"Isn't it, though?"

She spun at the sound of the soft voice. Caught where she didn't belong. "I'm sorry. The doors were unlocked. I figured it was okay to come in."

The easy smile of the woman walking down the aisle released Miranda's chagrin. She wore a long-sleeved tee over running pants and Nikes.

"Of course it's okay. I'm Joni Watters, the pastor's wife. I see you appreciate fine woodworking?"

"Very much so." Calming, she held out a hand. "I'm Miranda."

"Nice to meet you. I didn't see a car outside, so you must've hiked. You live close?" Joni pulled earbuds from her ears and pocketed an iPod.

"Only a few miles away. Well, six or seven if you take the road. Can I ask who did the carving?"

"Hezekiah Sloane, Old Hez, we called him. A true artist. He carved most of it, but a professional woodworker finished it recently. You see, Hez died last winter."

Miranda slid her fingers along the markings on the pulpit. "How sad."

Joni chuckled. "Not really. He was ninety-three and had been predicting his own death for six years. Every Christmas Eve he'd come up to my husband just before the candlelight service and say, 'Brother John, I believe God told me this'll be my last Christmas. Make it a good one tonight.' And so John, Lord help him, would preach his best, but come the following Christmas, there Old Hez would be." Joni sighed and perched on the corner of the altar. "He had it right this year. He died in his sleep the day after New Year's."

Miranda circled back around the altar. "Guess he heard God wrong the previous years."

Joni studied her, gentle smile touching her eyes. "Ah, but he was listening. I think Hezekiah was simply eager to meet his Father. He lived a full, happy life, but something in that old man knew he wasn't made for this earth." She glanced at the stained-glass portrait of Jesus. "In other words, he'd found his true identity."

Joni spoke with a kind of calm assurance Miranda envied.

The woman's gaze returned to Miranda's. "And that, my friend, is my sermon for the day." Joni glanced away. "Morgan always used to joke that I should've been the preacher."

Morgan?

Joni must have read Miranda's question, because she answered before Miranda could ask it. "My daughter. She would've been twenty-two next month. She died in a skiing accident over spring break two years ago."

"I'm . . . so sorry." And just moments ago Miranda had coveted the woman's easygoing cheer. *So maybe we all wear masks.*

Except, apparently, the pulpit builder. Old Hez.

"Yes, well, I'd better finish my run before John comes searching for me. It was nice meeting you."

"Same here. And thanks for not minding me dropping by the church."

Joni replaced her earbuds. "Drop by anytime, Miranda Woodruff." She gave a small wave.

Only as the door scraped over the floor did it hit Miranda she should've mentioned Jimmy and Audrey. But the door had already rasped closed.

A light glowed from behind the tarp of Miranda's skeletal home addition, and she scrunched her nose in curiosity as she covered the remaining distance to the house. She'd stayed in the church until sunset made its first move. By the time she trekked home, the shadows of night had staked their claim.

An owl hooted in the distance as she approached the house, the sound of voices joining the owl's call. The familiar ruffle of laughter came from the other side of the tent-like addition covering. "Blaze?"

A hand slapped the tarp open. "Good, you're home."

The smell of Italian spices—oregano and basil—floated under her nose. Garlic, too, drawing a growl from her stomach. "Something smells heavenly."

Blaze reached his hand down to pull her up to the raised foundation. She grasped his palm and stepped up, catching sight of Matthew dishing up lasagna at a card table they must have found in a closet. Candlelight from a hodgepodge of candles lit the space. Had they collected every candle in the house?

"What's going on, guys? Did I forget a special occasion?"

Blaze's hand on her back guided her to the table. "Nope, m'lady. Not any more special than every night with you."

The saccharine tone of his voice pulled a chuckle from her, and she couldn't help glancing at Matthew. His eyes were on the plate in his hands, his face unreadable. But, oh, he looked handsome in a close-fitting black sweater that showed off the wide set of his shoulders.

She swallowed the thought. Blaze pulled out her chair, and she sat. "So there's no special reason at all for this?"

Matthew sat across from her, candlelight toying with the colors of his eyes—flickers of green and brown. She could almost taste the buttery garlic of the bread on her plate.

"Patience," Blaze ordered. "First, we say grace."

It was all Miranda could do to gulp back her surprise. Wouldn't do for Matthew to wonder why she was flummoxed at her husband's desire to pray. She accepted Blaze's outstretched hand at her left and Matthew's reaching across the table at her right.

"God, thanks for this day, for this good food, for beautiful weather. Lord, I pray for Randi. I know she got tough news today. Remind her that you've got a plan for her *and* for her show. And thanks for letting Knox join us, too. He's not near as annoying as he could've been, being a reporter and all."

Miranda's snort interrupted, and she peeked one eyelid open to see Matthew watching her, his own silent laugh sending puffs of air over the candles' flames.

"In your name we pray, amen." Blaze ended the prayer with a squeeze of Miranda's hand.

And for the first time, she detected a hint of maturity about the man she hadn't noticed before. Blaze was all right.

For a fake husband.

"One thing we haven't talked about since I've been here is your faith," Matthew said as he lifted his garlic bread. "But Blaze's prayer paved the way for the question. Are you two religious?"

Blaze looked to Miranda, and when she didn't answer, he started talking. "Well, I'm a Christian, but I'm still figuring out what exactly that means." Blaze slapped his napkin onto his lap. "I was on a backpacking trip in Europe. Ran into this group of Christians in a retreat at a chateau. Took less than twenty-four hours around them for me to realize they had something I didn't—something I wanted, needed."

"So you converted?" Matthew asked.

"I think so. I prayed, anyway. But ever since, I haven't really been sure—"

Blaze broke off abruptly, gaze turning distant, elbows on the table. He hadn't made a move to touch his food. For a moment, it seemed he might say more. Instead, he picked up his fork and nodded his head toward Miranda. "But anyway, she's the one you want to hear from."

Miranda's foot jerked to tap Blaze's ankle under the table. He shot her an innocent grin. She couldn't be all that annoyed with Blaze, anyway, not with the serious undertones in his voice just moments before. Besides, how could he know faith—and what wobbly pieces of her own remained—was the last thing she'd want to talk about?

Miranda closed her lips around a steaming bite of lasagna, buying time. But Matthew's patient study across the table lingered on the question. How to explain that she wanted to believe everything she'd grown up hearing—God's love, His son, Jesus, who died and rose again—but that believing required more than she could give?

She'd known it when she'd slept with Robbie.

She'd known it when she kept up the lie on her show.

She knew it now, with her false invention at her side, in the flesh.

"My parents were missionaries, as you know," she finally said. "So I grew up with faith. But like my . . . Blaze, I'm still trying to figure things out."

Maybe from the outside looking in, it appeared simple: just believe and tell the truth and let God take care of the rest. But how could she trust Him to do that when everyone else she'd ever trusted had abandoned her?

"What about you, Matthew? What do you believe?" Miranda turned the questions on him.

He pointed his fork at Blaze. "That this is the best lasagna I've ever tasted."

"Thanks, man, but answer the woman's question."

Nice one, Blaze.

"Okay, fine. I'm in the same club as the two of you. Still figuring things out. I definitely had my years of playing Doubting Thomas, but lately . . ." Matthew paused with his fork midair. "I think there's something about being out here in the mountains. Makes me think, if God can create something so amazing, then maybe He can work on a screw-up like me, yeah?"

A hush blanketed the table. Matthew's honesty added a new flavor to the evening, something savory and melty, like the perfect chocolate. Even better than Blaze's Italian feast. Miranda sipped from her glass of ice water.

When this is all over, God, I want to come back. I do.

Blaze cut into her prayer with a clearing of his throat. "Well, Knox, should we tell her why we're here tonight?"

"I thought you said there wasn't a special occasion?" What did her men have up their sleeves?

Her men? Um, no. Eventually they'd both leave. Miranda had to remember that.

"Not an occasion," Matthew said with a nod. "An announcement. Blaze and I . . . Well, all afternoon we brainstormed and—"

"We figured out how to save your show!" Blaze blurted.

Miranda crunched her teeth on her garlic bread. "Whaafh?" The word came out garbled.

"*Hopefully* save it," Matthew amended. "We're going to rally the troops in support of *From the Ground Up.* What's the fastest way to unite fans? The World Wide Web. We're going to start an Internet campaign."

Miranda gulped down her bread. "What's that entail?"

Blaze's fork clanked on his plate. "First off, I'm going to strangle your manager over the fact that you don't have a Facebook fan page yet."

Miranda chortled. "Please don't harm Brad. I told him a while back I didn't see the point of Facebook."

Blaze shook his head before she finished. "The point is, it's where the people are, honey. So it's where you have to be."

"Turns out Blaze here is a budding social media guru," Matthew pointed out.

A proud smile stretched Blaze's cheeks. "I've got ideas for improving your website and starting a YouTube channel. Matthew's going to make sure entertainment bloggers across the country are talking about you. He's got a great platform with his connections."

Matthew picked up where Blaze left off. "Tomorrow I'm going to blog about your show. I'm going to be honest and say it's in trouble."

Miranda dabbed at her mouth with her napkin. "Doubt Lincoln will like that."

"He'll have to deal. Because in addition to keeping my editor happy, the blog will get people talking. Your fans will come out of the woodwork. We'll get an online petition started, something to wow the network."

Miranda blinked back the gathering pools behind her eyelids. And it sure wasn't the spicy lasagna causing the tears. "You guys spent all afternoon talking about this?"

Matthew nodded. "Even worked up a PowerPoint to show Walsh."

Blaze reached out his hand to cover hers atop the table. "Sweetheart, we'll have you trending on Twitter by the end of the week."

She blinked again, swallowed. "I don't even know what that means, but . . . thank you. Both of you."

And suddenly, the thought of either one of them exiting from her life as quickly as they'd shown up felt like a sliver in an otherwise perfect night.

Chapter 10

"It's amazing up here."

The wonder in Matthew's voice drew a satisfied grin from Miranda. They stood on a rocky overhang, the view as breathtaking now as the first time she'd made the climb. Glorious sunbeams poured through the trees like waterfalls. A V of birds trekked southbound through the sky, their cadence of caws filling the landscape with melody.

Up here she could almost believe everything would be okay. *From the Ground Up* would be renewed. She'd win the Giving Heart Award. She'd wrangle out of her pretend marriage but somehow stay connected with lovable Blaze. She'd find her way back to God.

And Matthew?

She didn't know what to hope for there. That he'd never be any the wiser about the whole charade? What about the confusing feelings playing blender with her insides?

"I'm glad Brad suggested this," Miranda said. "He knows I would've gone crazy without work on a weekday."

"Are you kidding?" Matthew turned his hazel eyes on her. "You'd have found something to do. You'd build something out in your workshop or complete a half dozen projects at Open Arms. Or work on your house. Hey, that's what you should do with your surprise free time. Didn't you say you've been wanting to finish the addition for years?"

She shook her head. "Snow will fall before I could finish it. Besides, I haven't done enough to winterize it in the past. Some of the wood's gone soft. I'll have to tear it out before I can build."

Hands in the pockets of her flannel jacket, Miranda turned in time to see Liv joining them on the overhang. Her friend's pink puff vest and white sweater glowed against the browns and burgundies of autumn. The rosy sheen of her cheeks and strawberry blond pigtails added youthful appeal to her swaying walk.

It made Miranda feel like Ma Kettle next to Miss America.

"Not only is the view spectacular, but this would be a perfect spot for a photo of Miranda and Blaze," Brad said as he came up behind Liv.

"Right." Matthew pulled his cell phone from his backpack. "I'll take a candid, post it to the *Today* Facebook page, and it'll go viral in minutes."

"Matthew Knox, I like the way you think," Liv said.

A surprise jolt of jealousy zapped Miranda—at Liv's carefree tone, her ability to be herself. The glossy smile she wore like a model. And, fine, her rapport with Matthew. *Not fair, Rand. Not her fault she's single and attractive.*

Miranda felt Blaze's perusal. *"You're falling for him."* Ridiculous. Just because the mop-top surfer had lived in her house for over a week, he thought he could read her.

"After the photo, let's eat," Brad added. "I'm starving. And my feet hurt."

"I told you not to wear brand-new shoes," Miranda said while she slid Blaze's backpack from his shoulder and marched him into place on the overhang. He snaked an arm around her waist.

"Bothers you, doesn't it?" he whispered.

"What?" she hissed to Blaze as Matthew held out his phone to frame the shot.

"Your friend flirting it up with Knox. But don't feel bad, she's doing the same with Brad." He nudged his head toward where Liv now sat next to Brad.

"She's not flirting, she's just naturally . . . bubbly." And beautiful. A woman with purpose, who knew who she was. Loved God, loved life, her kids at Open Arms.

All right, so maybe a whisper of envy did echo through Miranda. But she couldn't allow it. Not when Liv was one of the few people who knew the whole truth about Miranda's life. Other than Brad, Liv had done more than anyone to help Miranda pick up the pieces after Robbie's rejection.

"Stand a little closer," Matthew requested, stepping back and pointing his camera.

Blaze tucked her nearer to his side. "You could tell him the truth."

"And risk him spilling it in one of his blog posts? I don't think so."

"All right, smile like you're on a second honeymoon." Matthew chuckled as he issued the command.

"Wonder what he'd say if he knew we never had a first," Blaze whispered through his grin.

Miranda gritted her teeth.

"Perfect." Matthew lowered the camera. "Now I think it'd be cool to do a side shot. You can both be looking out into the distance, real thoughtful-like. I'll get a close-up of your faces with the scenery around you."

Miranda moved into position. "I had no idea you were such a photographer, Knox." That's right, stick with his last name. Less personal, just in case what Blaze thought he saw in her— some kind of attraction to or connection with Matthew—had a spark of reality to it.

No, not a chance. If she was going to fake a marriage, she'd fake faithfulness, as well.

A breeze swept Blaze's disheveled waves of hair over his face, her own tresses whipping over her shoulder. Blaze stood at an angle beside her, one arm wrapping around her front. For once, she didn't fight his barging into her space.

Because playacting had suddenly become way more comfortable than sorting out her messy heart.

"Okay, now gaze out at the landscape like you're thinking about something you really love," Matthew suggested.

"Tacos," Blaze murmured.

"My workshop." And these piney mountains. Her friends. Grandma and Grandpa Woodruff.

Matthew snapped the photo and flashed a thumbs-up. And when Blaze released her, she heard her own sharp intake of breath.

Robbie. She hadn't thought his name when scrolling through her mental list.

Lord, am I . . . over him? But how could it happen just like that? Why, less than two weeks ago she'd faced their would-be wedding anniversary with the emotional stability of a soap opera character.

But now . . .

A few feet away, Liv laughed over something Brad said, and Matthew showed Blaze the photos on his phone. The sudden urge to shout out in joy over the uncoiling of her heart, her freedom, tumbling over her like the sunlight warming her skin.

"Rand, what's with the goofy smile?" Brad was standing now, moving toward her.

She wanted to hug him. And Livvy. Even Blaze.

And Matthew? Her gaze shifted to meet his questioning study.

"Just happy to be up here. To be with friends. To know

you're all in my corner." To know at least one room in her heart had tidied.

Brad slung an arm around her shoulder and guided her to Matthew and Blaze. "I want to see the pictures, too."

Matthew held out the camera, and Brad clicked through the photos. "Not bad, Knox."

"No kidding. I actually look . . ." She couldn't find the word. Even though the pictures showed her in flannel and denim, something in the angle or the lighting highlighted her eyes, her thick curls, the soft slant of her cheeks.

"You look like a magazine cover model," Brad finished.

She snickered. "Yeah, if you're talking about *ToolTime* or *Carpentry Expert.*"

Now Liv peered over their shoulders. "Nuh-uh, girlfriend. Try *Glamour* or *Vanity Fair.*"

"You got some photography skills, bro. That's for sure," Blaze said.

Matthew's demeanor spoke embarrassment. "My brother's the real photographer in our family." He sighed. "And if I'm honest, my father, too. He was a businessman by trade, but photography was a mega hobby of his."

The group fanned in a circle, Brad and Liv back on the hollowed log, and Miranda on the ground between Blaze and Matthew. Brad unzipped his backpack and tossed granola bars and string cheese to everyone.

"You say *was*," Liv prodded. "Is your father . . . gone?"

Even from a couple feet away, Miranda could feel Matthew's stiffening posture. "He and my mom divorced. So, I have no idea whether he's still doing the photography thing."

"That's sad," Liv said in a gentle tone, the same voice Miranda had heard her use with the kids at Open Arms. "Has it been a long time since you've seen him?"

Leave him be, Livvy. He doesn't like to talk about this.

But Matthew's answering voice surprised her. "Five years. He moved south."

"That's about how long it's been since you've seen your parents, isn't it, Rand?" Liv asked.

Livvy, I love you, but could you just stop already? "Yes."

Wise, discerning Brad piped in. "Well, my parents recently decided to take up a new hobby themselves. Beekeeping. I should be thankful because a few months ago it was belly dancing. I came back from our Fourth of July gathering scarred for life."

Blaze and Miranda laughed, but Liv still studied Matthew. "Where is your father now?" she asked Matthew.

Matthew cleared his throat before answering. "I just found out he's living in Knoxville. Running for office, actually."

Liv clapped her hands. "But that's so close. You should go see him. Oh, Matthew, what if you could reconcile?"

Couldn't Liv see the stony set to Matthew's jaw, the darkening of his eyes? Did she have any idea what it was like, the punching feeling of childhood hopes and hurts hardened into adult bruises?

"What if he's been waiting all these years to reconnect with you? And now you're only a few hours away from each other."

"Liv—" Miranda began, but Matthew's shuffling to his feet beside her stopped her.

"I think I'll go take a few more photos. I promised my niece . . ." His voice faded as he clomped away.

"What did I say?" Liv turned to Brad, but Brad only shook his head.

A scraping cool descended as clouds passed over the sun. She met Blaze's eyes, caught his subtle nod. *Go.*

Fine, so he *could* read her.

♥

Matthew heard the crunch of rock underfoot before he saw Miranda rounding the same clump of trees he'd passed through moments ago. He sat, back against a boulder the size of a small car, his Twins baseball cap shielding his eyes.

"Hand me your phone." Miranda's soft voice accompanied her shadow, now looming over him.

He tipped his head. Shrugged. "Okay." He pulled the device from the pocket of his fleece pullover, then watched as Miranda strode to where the landing ended in a dip. She clicked one shot, then another, moving the phone to capture the scenery in a series of views.

She returned. "Now Cee won't be disappointed."

He accepted the camera from Miranda, smile teasing his lips. Miranda lowered beside him. He'd been childish to walk away. After all, he'd been the one to bring up his father.

But lately he couldn't get Jase's phone call out of his head. *"He'd really like to hear from you."*

And Matthew would like to oblige about as much as he'd like to step off the side of the mountain, flail his way to a broken neck. But what if his father was sick? Had an emergency? Needed him?

Yeah, well, Gordon Knox's family had needed him, too. Mom's original cancer diagnosis had come just one month after Dad left. Matthew had been so sure the news would prompt Dad's return. But no.

Still, he probably looked like a moody kid, stalking off from the group like he had. He'd felt invaded by Liv's questions. From beside him, Miranda gave a contented sigh now. Maybe that's what she'd felt this past week, as his questions steered closer and closer to memories she'd obviously walled in.

He chose a photo to send Cee, typed in a message. "She's dying to meet you—Cee, I mean."

"You're a good uncle," Miranda said. "Not all uncles would text their nieces every day."

"Not all nieces are like Cee." He pocketed his phone. "I used to think fatherhood wasn't for me. After the way my own dad was, I figured I'd rather not gamble with someone else's life on the off chance I'd turn out like him. But Cee? She makes me think maybe I could be a good dad."

"I think you'd be more than a good dad, Matthew. I saw the way you were with Anya, Peter, and Claire." No hint of flattery, only sincerity in Miranda's voice.

"It's just I have this tendency to screw up. It's one thing when it's my own life, but a child's?" He tasted the vulnerability in his own words. Overhead, an eagle soared through drifting clouds.

He turned his head to the side, Miranda's profile coming into view—head leaning against the boulder, tipped to the sky, sun kissing her skin.

"Matthew, I'm sorry Liv pushed you. She comes from the perfect family. Her parents are like Ward and June Cleaver on happy pills and she has tight bonds with her siblings. She thinks familial perfection is possible for everyone."

Miranda lifted her hand to brush stray wisps of hair away from her face. "I've, um, been getting letters from my parents in the past few months. E-mails, too. Way more than normal. I made the mistake of telling Liv about it the other day, and she immediately launched into this hopeful outburst about how maybe they're reaching out and our relationship can be rekindled."

Her pinched forehead was proof of how she felt about that. "You disagree?"

"Honestly, I don't know. I keep waiting for something more than a chatty update about their lives. I know I should write back, but . . ." She shook her head before continuing. "We were supposed to be talking about you. And Liv. And how it must be the social worker in her that feels a need to fix hurting sons and daughters—whether they're five or thirty-five."

"I'm thirty."

A grin spread over her face and she nudged him with her elbow. "That's not the point."

"But it is. I'm thirty, and I'm still sometimes so angry at my dad. The kind of angry that makes you feel claustrophobic, trapped. Why am I not over this?"

He studied Miranda's profile, the emotions playing over her face. Empathy, compassion, understanding. Their pasts weren't anything alike, but the lingering effects were strikingly similar.

"Anyway, Jase wants me to go see Dad, thinks it'd be helpful if I get everything out in the open. All I can think is, it'd only be a repeat of the last time we saw each other."

Gordon Knox's face came into view, hair greased back and maverick sneer fuming in his eyes that day five years ago. *This is garbage, son. Straight-up garbage.* His father had held a copy of the *Star Tribune* in his hand, Delia's article screaming from the front page. And Matthew hadn't realized what he was doing until his fist connected with his father's jaw.

Miranda slid her hand over the dusty ground beneath them, fingers brushing over the top of his own before closing over it. What was she doing? *She's married.* The annoying voice of his conscience, or maybe just common sense, hadn't stopped repeating the reminder in days now.

But he didn't move his hand from under her hold. "You know what upsets me the most?" he murmured.

"Hmm?" Her eyes grazed over the blazing hues of the landscape.

"I'm turning out just like him."

"Your father? Why do you say that?"

He rotated his hand so his palm faced hers. "I mess everything up. I hurt people who care about me." He thought of Jase, angry at the zoo. His former co-workers at the *Tribune*. Even Miranda and the article Dooley wanted him to write. If he wrote it, he'd hurt her. If he didn't, he'd anger Dooley and mess up the plan to help with Cee's surgery. "I'm a screw-up."

She released his hands and shifted to a kneeling position as her eyes took hold of his. "That's a ridiculous thing to say, Matthew Knox. Let me tell you something. You keep forcing me to tell you my story. You ask me questions that annoy the socks off me, but once you get me talking, I can't stop. And it's pouring out of me, the past I've avoided for years."

She spoke with energy, enthusiasm, cheeks reddening. Her knees dug into the dirt. *So breathtakingly beautiful . . .*

"I've had these hurts clawing at me for so long, but now that I'm finally facing them, I'm finding a new freedom."

Hurts? She'd only told him about her parents. And that Robbie guy . . . But the intensity in her voice now confirmed what he'd reckoned all along: there was more. And he warred between asking or . . . pulling her into his lap.

She's married.

His conscience heightened to a scream.

She placed a palm on his shoulder, warmth he had no business feeling spreading through him. "*You* did that. You helped me. You and your irritating, nosy questions."

He'd also searched her house. Did she remember that? He'd goaded Blaze behind her back. He'd noted every averted glance, verbal slip, and fidgety movement. Tucked away every sign of surreptitious behavior for later study.

I'm not what you think, Miranda. He should tell her. Then maybe she'd pull her hand from his chest and lose that glimmer in her eyes. Save him from losing his last grip on his purpose here.

"And Celine, look at what you're doing for her. Anyone can see this isn't exactly the kind of reporting you relish. But you made the sacrifice, came down here to interview a B-list celebrity and make some quick money, all for her."

Her hand glided to his heart. And he couldn't stop his own from reaching up to cover hers. "Miranda—"

"You're not a screw-up. Not to me."

Her face was so close he could feel her breath. His chest pumped as her lips parted.

"Miranda," he gasped at the last second. "You're married."

She froze, face hovering in front of his for a millisecond before shock sparked her into movement. Her hand flew from his chest as if burning and she fell backward, backside thudding into the dirt, dust and pebbles spilling around her. Her arms jerked to the ground to steady her and she scrambled to her feet, horror mixed with humiliation creasing her forehead.

"I'm . . . I'm . . ." Her hands covered her cheeks, and instead of blushing, she'd paled to white.

He jumped up. "It's okay. We were just . . . having a moment. It was natural instinct, that's all, and—"

Back to him, she groaned. "I'm sorry. I'm so sorry."

He skirted around her, arms popping out to hold her in place before she could whirl away. "You don't have to apologize."

Her hands dropped from her face. "But I do. Matthew, I . . ." Her eyes pressed closed, and then opened, lashes fluttering until her gaze focused. "I'm not . . ." She bit her lip as vulnerability welled in her gray irises.

"You're not what? Sorry after all?" His lips hinted at a smile.

She took a long breath, squaring her shoulders. "I'm not—"

A scream gashed into the stillness of the forest, followed by a crash of branches and yelling. Miranda's mouth dropped open. "Livvy?"

"Come on." He grabbed her hand, pulling her into the grove.

But even as he quickened his pace, his heart raced. Not because of whatever lay ahead . . .

But what remained behind. An almost-kiss. Miranda's unspoken words. And in her eyes, the mixture of mystery and fear and . . . confession.

§

"Brad, can't you drive any faster?" Miranda heard the high-pitched whine of her voice but didn't care. Blaze's moan from the back seat of Brad's Camry conjured the picture of him on the ground, arm at an angle that could only mean serious pain.

"We're not going to get to the hospital any faster if we get in an accident, Rand—so just calm down."

"Calm down? The man fell out of a tree!"

She glanced out the passenger-side rearview mirror. Matthew still followed in his Jeep with Liv.

Her voice lowered to a hiss. "Poor Blaze. I feel awful."

Especially since he'd had to walk a good mile after the fall. None of their cell phones had enough signal up on the trail to call 9-1-1, so Brad had jogged back to the car, driven it as far up the trail as he could, and they'd met in the middle, Blaze assuring everyone he could make it.

"It's not like I haven't broken an arm before," he'd said through gritted teeth. "This is the third time. No, fourth. No, wait, third. That other time was a dislocated shoulder."

He'd talked all the way to the car. His way of dealing with the pain? Or a side effect of all the meds Liv had stuffed down his throat.

"I still can't believe Liv gave him all that Sudafed. He has a broken arm, not a head cold."

"She thought he'd be better off drowsy." Brad passed a station wagon.

He was drowsy, all right. Mumbling something about Michigan and his brother and pancakes.

She twisted in her seat. "It's going to be all right, Blaze. We'll get you to the ER and the doctor will fix your arm and—"

"Can't fix it now." Blaze lay on his back, broken arm cradled against his torso, the other flopped over his forehead. Dirt streaked across his face, sullied his zipped-up jacket. "Too late. He's gone."

"What?"

"The meds, Randi," Brad said. "Mixed with the pain, he probably doesn't know what he's saying."

"Drive faster." Oh, why'd he have to climb that tree? It was a miracle he hadn't been hurt worse. "I'm a horrible wife, Walsh."

"Pretend wife. And why would you think this is your fault? If it's anybody's fault, it's mine and Liv's. We should have stopped him when he asked us to time his climb."

She shook her head. "I know the kind of stunts he pulls. I could've talked him out of it. I should've been there."

Instead of chasing after Matthew and almost—

Oh, Lord, help me. She had almost told him everything. Worse, had almost kissed him. She could feel the flush taking over her face even now. Horror and humiliation cavorted in a frenzied mental dance. "I could just die."

"Say what?" Brad veered his vehicle onto Main Avenue of the small mountain town. The hospital there was small, but it was closer than Asheville's suburbs, and they'd get faster service.

"Nothing." She couldn't worry about Matthew now. Not with Blaze still mumbling in the back seat, face white.

"Nothing I can do now," Blaze murmured. "Too late."

"He's really out of it." She exhaled. "Are you sure it's just a broken arm? It looked so mangled. And what if he's got internal injuries?"

"I really think it was a clean break." Brad's voice softened. "It's nice of you to play the concerned wife, but truly, I think he'll be okay. And look, here's the hospital."

He pulled into the circle drive. Miranda shot out of the car the minute he shifted into Park. She ducked in the back seat. "Blaze, honey, it's time to go into the hospital. Come on."

"You called me honey," he slurred.

The doctor might have to pump his stomach in addition to setting his arm. How many pills had Liv given him? She wove her arm through Blaze's good arm, patting his shoulder with her other hand. "Let's get inside."

Footsteps padded on pavement behind her. Brad most likely—maybe Matthew and Liv, too. But she was focused on getting Blaze through the revolving door, into the emergency room. The receptionist was blessedly free, the waiting room, smelling of bleach and potpourri, empty of all but one other cluster of people.

Within minutes a nurse took Blaze back. The receptionist handed Miranda a clipboard and paperwork with a crooked smile that spoke recognition.

Yes, I'm Randi Woodruff. But please, not now. Miranda joined the others in the waiting area.

♡

"If pacing was an Olympic sport, you'd win gold, Miranda." Matthew rose from his vinyl chair. "He's going to be just fine."

She couldn't look at him. Didn't have words, either. Not after . . . She turned to the window.

"Listen," Matthew said, "I missed a few calls but can't get good reception in here. I'm going to step outside to catch up on my voice mails."

She waited until the whir of the revolving door promised

Matthew's absence and dropped into the seat next to Brad. "Where's Liv?"

"Same as Knox, on her phone. Checking in on Open Arms." He poked her arm. "So, you want to tell me?"

"Tell you what?" She pulled her flannel jacket tight around her, the waiting room's warmth no match for the blizzard of worries whirling in her. She fiddled with her hands.

"Why you and Knox are acting as awkward around each other as a couple of teens on their first date."

"Don't be ridiculous."

Across the room, a nurse called a name, and the other waiting room occupants rose to follow her down the corridor. The receptionist chattered away on the phone.

Brad shrugged, picked the clipboard up from the end table. "Fine. Let's get the paperwork filled out."

"Sorry I snapped at you."

"You're worried. I get it. Any clue what Blaze's middle name is?"

She pulled the clipboard from Brad's hands and slipped the pencil from the clip. "Lucas. Blake Lucas Hunziker."

She scanned the cover sheet. They'd swiped Blaze's wallet before he'd gone back, so they could rifle through it, fill in his birth date, maybe even find a health insurance card.

"What should I put for his address? Mine or the one on his license?"

"The one on his license. They'll want a copy of his license, so they should probably match."

"Yeah, but . . ." Oh well. Hopefully the hospital personnel wouldn't ask questions.

She looked farther down the sheet. Was he on any medications? Um, other than the cold meds Liv fed him, she hadn't seen him pop so much as a Tylenol. Allergies? She kept reading. Oh dear. Past surgeries? Medical history?

No stinkin' idea.

"I can't do this, Brad."

"You're right, you shouldn't guess. It's okay. We'll get Blaze to look at it after—"

She flopped the clipboard into the chair next to her, fighting a wave of nausea. "It's not just that. It's this whole thing. It's so wrong."

The receptionist's nasally giggle traveled across the room. Miranda propped her elbows on her knees, head hung, fingers massaging her temples. "What if Blaze's falling out of the tree is God trying to tell us something."

"Like what?"

"Like I'm an idiot for trying to pull this off."

Brad's chuckle grated on her nerves. "Rand, I think God could get the message across a lot more effectively than breaking Blaze's arm. This is just a hiccup. Don't give up on it now. And you're hardly an idiot."

"I absolutely am. Did you hear me with the receptionist? 'My husband's hurt.' My husband. Lied right to her face." She rubbed her hands over her knees, dirt staining the denim in patches of beige.

"You're not hurting anyone."

"We're . . . in . . . a . . . hospital."

"You didn't force Blaze to climb the tree. Didn't we already have this conversation?"

"And if you knew what I almost did . . ." She stood, head hammering now. Panic—that's what it was—creeping like something toxic up her throat. "I almost told Matthew the truth."

Brad's gaze shot to hers. "You didn't."

Something was humming now, like trapped wind. "Almost said it right to his face."

"Randi—"

She mimicked herself, exaggerated her own breathy voice. "'I'm not married. He's not really my husband.'" Sarcasm dripped from her words. "'It's all a big show.'"

A gasp. Only . . .

Only it came from behind her. Oh no. The humming, the revolving door . . .

Brad winced. She turned. Could almost hear the click in Matthew's brain as her eyes locked with his. Watched the dawning play out over his features as heated confusion turned to angry realization.

And maybe something even worse. Hurt.

"Matthew, I—"

But he whirled, disappeared the way he'd come.

Leaving heart-piercing shame in his wake.

Chapter 11

"He's not answering." Brad scraped his fingers through his hair, letting out a frustrated exhale. His knuckles were white around his phone.

Miranda hugged her arms to herself, shoulders hunched, the weight flattening her into inactivity. She leaned against a pillar outside the hospital, cement cold against her back. Her thoughts, her emotions, they were a tangle of wires connected to a ticking bomb. Pull the wrong one and she'd detonate.

"Knox isn't answering," Brad repeated, moving until he faced her square on.

"Of course he's not." Because she hadn't only accidentally confessed to her lie . . . she'd wounded Matthew. She'd seen it in the shadows passing over his face, the same look of betrayal she used to wear like a permanent accessory after Robbie.

Not possible. You and Robbie were a couple, together for a year and a half. You've barely known Matthew two weeks.

"Rand, this isn't the time to play the wilting lily. We've got to do something before he goes and ruins everything."

When had the sun slipped behind a mess of churlish clouds? "What can I do? You've tried calling him half a dozen times already."

Seconds after Matthew had disappeared from the waiting room, she and Brad had rushed after him. But he was already gunning out of the lot in his Jeep.

Now, more than half an hour later, Miranda couldn't seem to unfreeze. And Brad, poor panicked Brad, was about to lose it. "I'm so sorry, Brad," she said for the twentieth, maybe thirtieth, time. How could she have been so stupid? The hairs on her arms rose as an unforgiving breeze whipped under the hospital's canopied circle drive.

"Where's your phone?" Brad asked, ignoring her apology, barely veiled irritation heating his tone.

"In my bag." She pushed escaped strands of hair behind her ear. "Inside." Where she'd left her dignity.

Or had she lost that years ago, when she'd traded in truth for a pretty picture now broken?

Brad gripped her elbow. "Then we're going in. You're going to call him this time."

"Brad, if he didn't answer your calls, he certainly isn't going to answer mine."

"You two were friends." He lurched to a stop. "Maybe something else." And then he was in front of her again, the accusation in his eyes as piercing as the sound of the ambulance's siren bursting from the garage nearby. "Was something else going on, Randi?"

She yanked her arm away, escaped into the shelter of the revolving door. Oh, to just curl up on the floor, let the door spin and spin and spin until someone else had miraculously sorted out the clutter of her life.

Instead, when the door spit her out, her feet hit the flake-chipped flooring of the waiting room. She retrieved her bag, dug for her phone, heard Brad coming up behind her. "Think whatever you want, Walsh, but save the interrogation for another day. I'm calling him."

"Rand, you know I didn't mean—"

She cut him off with a raised hand as the rings of Matthew's phone sounded against her ear, one after another. And then his voice. "Hi, this is Matthew Knox. Sorry I'm not answering . . ." She took a breath, waited for the beep.

"It's me." A pregnant pause. "I don't even know what to say. Maybe by the time you call me back, I will. But . . ." Nothing. There was no excuse good enough. She tapped out of the call.

"You should've told him you could explain," Brad said.

"Like you already did a hundred times?"

He lowered his voice to a hush. "Do you even halfway understand what this could mean? Do you care?"

She punched a text message into her phone as Brad spoke.

Call me, Matthew. Please.

"Of course, I do. All it'd take is one call and he could have the media swarming. I'm so incredibly mad at myself." She dropped her phone into her bag. "But I've got to worry about Blaze now."

"Blaze is going to be fine. It's your career that may end up permanently fractured." They faced off—Miranda's feet planted shoulders length apart, Brad with crossed arms. "Randi, I'm speaking as your manager . . . and as your friend. You could be in serious trouble."

She softened her tone to match his. "I know, Brad. I . . . know." Miranda lowered her head to his shoulder, felt his arms unwind and one hand pat her back.

"We'll just have to regroup," he said. "We'll figure something out. Maybe Knox will decide he didn't hear what he thought he heard."

"Excuse me?" A nurse in maroon scrubs entered the lounge. "Blake will be ready to leave in a jiffy. Would one of you like to come back?"

Miranda met Brad's eyes. He nodded. "Yes, I'd like that," she answered, pulling her bag over her shoulder, grabbing the clipboard, and following the nurse down a shiny-floored corridor. A thick blue stripe ran the length of the wall, all the way to the patient room at the far end.

"Blake's in there," the nurse said. "The doctor is giving him some final instructions about taking care of his cast."

Miranda stepped through the door to see an exhausted Blaze, bobbing his head as the doctor spoke, a clean white cast encasing his arm.

"All right, we should be good to go, Blake. Take good care of that arm. We'll see you again in a few weeks."

Miranda approached the side of the exam table as the doctor left. Blaze's feet knocked against the metal edges, and he gave her one of his lopsided smiles. "Guess it pays to be ambidextrous, huh." The words rolled off his tongue way too easily, considering their location, the day's events, and the sling holding his casted arm.

"Are you really ambidextrous?"

"I think so, but my fourth-grade penmanship teacher might disagree." He hopped off the table. "Let's go. Hospitals make me queasy."

Miranda tilted her head to meet his eyes. "I'm really sorry this happened, Blaze. Truly."

"Not your fault, muffin. Come on."

"Wait a minute. You need to help me finish filling out this form." She held up the clipboard. "Let's see . . . They're asking for your previous surgeries."

Blaze looked over her shoulder at the form. "Oh, honey, we are going to need a lot more space than that. Maybe we should ask for another sheet of paper."

Fifteen minutes later, they handed the clipboard to the nurse. As she walked out of the room reading the form, her eyes widened and she mumbled something about showing it to the doctor. But no one told them to wait, so they quickly covered the length of the hallway. Miranda was surprised by the sound of voices growing as they neared the waiting area. "Wow, the ER must have filled up in the past few minutes," she mused. They rounded the corner . . .

And a flash of light blinded her. The click of cameras. Voices hurling questions. And Brad's call raising above them all. "People, back off. Back. Off."

When the stars cleared from her eyes, she caught sight of the sheepish receptionist perched behind her desk.

"Randi, what happened? Was it an accident on set?"

"I thought *From the Ground Up* suspended taping?"

"Is a broken arm your husband's only injury?"

They were still calling him her husband.

She slung her arm through Blaze's good elbow, and they shoved through the crowd. *Wait!* "Brad, where's Liv?" she called as they barreled outside, the press flocking behind. In all the chaos of the past hour, she'd completely forgotten her friend.

"She found Wi-Fi access at a coffee shop across the street. We'll pick her up."

They fell into Brad's car.

And finally, twenty minutes later, after they'd picked up Liv and headed out of town, Miranda pulled her phone from her bag. No missed calls. No messages. No texts. She checked to make sure the ringer was on. Then opened a new text message, found Matthew's number, and typed two words:

I'm sorry.

With one hand Matthew navigated the snaking highway, following the directions of his GPS. With the other, he hit speed dial on his cell and lifted it to his ear. This was probably stupid. All of it: the drive, the phone call.

But so was faking a marriage for the sake of television ratings.

The phone rang. Once, twice, three times. *Answer, man. This isn't a call you want to miss.* Four, five, six rings. *Do I really want to do this?*

He'd spent the first forty minutes of the drive with a tic in his jaw, the kind of fury beating through him he hadn't felt since his father shoved his erroneous article at his face five years ago.

The next forty minutes, he'd debated with himself. Then he fished out his phone.

"This is Greg Dooley. Leave a message."

Matthew waited for the beep. "It's Knox. I've got your story. Call me." He chucked his phone into the passenger seat and eyed the GPS. Less than half an hour to his destination.

He reached for the flimsy plastic cup in his cup holder. Fountain pop from a gas station, now flat. He flipped off the lid, pushed the straw aside, and drank.

It wasn't right, what Miranda was doing. He wasn't just angry about the lie itself. He'd kept quiet about that whole Robbie thing, had even gallantly thought he was helping the woman. His blind trust had kept him from seeing that her secrets went so much deeper.

And now he had no clue how to direct his reaction. After he'd stalked out of the hospital a couple hours ago, he'd slammed the door of the Jeep, then simply started driving. Aimless, twisted up inside like a tangled yo-yo.

Because as infuriated as he was toward Miranda, he couldn't deny the thin ribbon of relief also winding its way through him. *She's not married.* His conscience recited the new mantra like the "Hallelujah Chorus." And he hated himself for it.

Whatever forbidden feeling you thought you felt before—thought she might feel—it wasn't real. Because she's not real.

Why he'd suddenly gotten the urge to hit the Interstate, to finally do what Jase had begged him to, he had no idea. Maybe because Jase, unlike the woman who'd so skillfully caught him in her web, could actually be trusted.

The western sun stung his eyes, and with an angry swipe, he lowered the visor.

Yes. When Dooley called him back, he'd spill the whole thing. No more Mr. Nice Reporter. He'd tell all, and then they'd decide how to break the story—on the blog or another way.

His phone chirped from the passenger seat. Good. Dooley got his voice mail. He pulled it to his ear. "Knox here."

"Uncle Matt!" Cee's voice bubbled with glee.

He inhaled, every muscle knotted and tense. *Switch gears, man.* He couldn't disappoint Cee. Not when he knew how much she loved using the speech-to-text relay phone service Jase and Izzy had purchased.

"Hey, sweetheart. It's so good to talk to you," he answered, knowing she'd read his words as the relay service transcribed them, relieved that she wouldn't hear the strain in his voice.

"I miss you. When are you coming back?"

He wanted to say soon. Playing the gullible fool grew old the minute he heard Miranda's sarcastic proclamation. *"It's all a big show."*

His GPS directed him onto an exit ramp leading into suburban Knoxville.

"I'm not sure, Cee. Did you get the postcard I sent?"

After a pause, she spoke. "Yes. I hung it on the refrigerator. I wish you were here. I'm watching a movie tonight."

Not for the first time, he tried to imagine watching a movie without sound. Only closed-captioning to explain what was happening on-screen. But if Cee had the cochlear implant surgery, it could transform her movie experience. He could actually take her to a theater.

And now he had a story, ripe with juicy deceit—just the

cash cow they needed to help fund the surgery. Except it might break Cee's heart in the process. Not to mention Miranda's.

"What movie?"

"Your favorite cartoon. *The Incredibles.*"

About a family of forgotten superheroes, the father frustrated, disappointed by the cards life dealt him. Matthew let out a slow sigh and turned onto Maple Street. Just a few blocks . . . "Hey, I heard you got your stitches out."

"Yeah, and it didn't even hurt."

Some things didn't.

Some things did.

He squinted, reading the numbers as he passed each house. 1945. 1947. 1949. There, 1951. "Uncle Matt, I want to meet Randi Woodruff. Is she with you now? Can I talk to her?"

"Sorry, kiddo, she's not."

"But can I meet her sometime?"

If Matthew did what he knew he should—tell her story, all of it—there was no way Miranda would want anything to do with him or his family. "I don't know, hon. Hey, is your dad around?"

"Yup. Dad!"

Despite his stormy mood, he smiled at her yell.

"Here he is. Come home soon, Uncle Matt." He heard the rustle of the transferring of the phone, the beep of the text service turning off, and then his brother's voice. "Hey, Matt."

"I'm sitting in front of his house, Jase."

Jase's pause lasted only a second. "Seriously?"

Matthew stared at the suburban home across the street. The beige structure and immaculate landscaping couldn't have stood in starker contrast to the cabin he'd been sleeping in for the past week. Or that shack in the mountains he and Miranda had visited. Fancy brickwork created a trail to the front door, potted ferns and hanging flower baskets adding splashes of color along the porch. A two-story deck jutted out behind the house, and a privacy fence likely encased an in-ground pool.

Only the best for Gordon Knox.

"What made you finally do it?"

"Impulse."

"You mean you didn't call him first? E-mail? You're just showing up out of the blue?"

"Fitting, don't you think? Same way he left." Matthew's seat belt cut into his chest. He reached for the release and freed himself from the buckle's stranglehold, then opened his window to let in fresh air. "Look, I asked Cee to put you on for moral support. But if you haven't got any to give—"

"All right, all right. If nothing else, I'm glad you're . . . making an effort, even if it comes as a shock."

Shock? He could empathize. "I don't know why I'm here. I have no desire to see the man."

"But he wants to see you. Who knows, maybe it's a good thing. Just try to approach it with a clear head. Lay the past aside as much as you can. Hear the man out."

Right. He could do that. Couldn't he? "Thanks, bro."

They hung up, and Matthew eyed the house again. Jase was right. He should've called. He should've formulated a reason for being there. Was it to spew years of pent-up frustration or to seek reconciliation? Both? His forehead dropped forward to bump the steering wheel. Clear head? Hardly.

But he'd come all this way . . .

He reached for his door handle, but before he pushed the door open, a couple emerged from the home. *Dad.*

Gordon Knox wore a dinner jacket over stylish jeans, the woman on his arm in a long dress and black coat. Walking behind the couple was a teenage girl, colorful bag slung over her shoulders and knee-high boots clacking against the porch steps. Laughter trailed their walk to the black SUV in the driveway.

Matthew felt the air seep from his lungs.

Suddenly, Gordon Knox looked over, eyes scanning the street and locking on Matthew. Matthew was tempted to duck his head back into the car and roll up the window. But curiosity—or maybe stubbornness—kept his focus in place.

Five seconds stretched into ten.

His father took a step forward. "Matthew?"

He couldn't find words. Why had he thought this was a good idea? But he'd driven all this way . . .

His father said something to the woman Matthew assumed to be his new wife, then crossed the street, slowing as he reached Matthew's Jeep. "It is you."

"Jase gave me your address."

"I'm glad. Although a call would've been good. Did Jase give you my number? We're already late for dinner."

Matthew nodded. *Dinner. Right.*

"But listen, I'll be in Asheville for a conference next week. Jase told me you're in the area. Could we meet?"

He felt like a fool. An angry, tired idiot who'd just trekked half a state for a thirty-second conversation with a man who now acted as if the past didn't exist. "Okay."

"Okay. Give me a call."

His father tapped the car's rim, gave a small wave, and crossed the street.

Okay . . .

Matthew shifted into Drive and sped down the road without a look in his rearview mirror.

Miranda fluffed a pillow and gently slid it under Blaze's casted arm. He leaned back against the pile of pillows she'd already assembled on her bed behind him.

"I would've been fine on the couch," he said, eyes closed

and his usual crooked grin in place. "I've already caused you enough trouble. I didn't need to take your bed, too."

She sat on Grandma's rocking chair. "You caused me trouble? Blaze, you quit your catering job, packed a suitcase, and moved to my place in the middle of nowhere. You've put up with interviews and photo shoots, and now you're covered in bruises and suffering a broken arm. All because of me."

One eye cracked open. "Not because of you. Because somewhere between the most radical hike ever through the Andes Mountains a few years ago and now, I lost my tree-climbing finesse."

His golden skin seemed darker in the dim light of her bedroom, and a day's stubble covered his cheeks.

"The Andes Mountains, huh."

"Yeah, that was the last time I scaled a tree. Made it all the way up that time."

She brushed a lock of black hair from his forehead. "What haven't you done, Blaze Hunziker?"

For once, he didn't have a reply. Not a funny anecdote or unbelievable story about his crazy adventures. Not even a joke or teasing endearment. She inched her rocking chair closer to the bed. "I realized today how little I really know about you. I have all these basic facts we memorized, but there's a lot more, isn't there?"

No response, only a breezy sigh. He sank farther into the pillows.

"When you were all fuzzy on meds, you mentioned a brother. And when we first met, you said you didn't have siblings . . . anymore. What's your story?"

When he still didn't respond, she figured he'd fallen asleep and rose, careful not to knock into the bedside stand. She stood in the center of the bedroom, torn between turning in early down on the couch and waiting up for Matthew's return.

That is, if he did return. But surely he'd at least come back for his things in the cabin.

"Hey," Blaze's voice floated from the bed.

"I thought you were asleep."

He pinched the bridge of his nose and his eyes fluttered open. "I'll tell you my story someday. But first, I think you need to figure out your own." Gone was the usual spark of playfulness in his voice.

"What if I don't know how?" She surprised herself with the question.

He shifted under Grandma's quilt. "How'd you learn to build houses?"

"What?"

"And how'd you learn how to do all that sweet stuff with wood?"

What did that have to do with anything? "Well, my grandpa taught me a lot, and of course college, internships, working in Brazil. But a lot of it, honestly, came naturally."

He shifted his broken arm. "So, instinct. Go with your gut. You'll figure it out." He closed his eyes with a smile. "'Night, dumpling."

She stared at him, watching the rise and fall of his chest as his breathing heavied with sleep. *"Go with your gut. You'll figure it out."* How many times had she done just that and found herself in a major mess?

No, she couldn't count on her own logic or emotions to figure out where to go from here. She needed help, guidance.

Miranda tiptoed to the door, leaving it open a crack before descending to the first floor. Hunger tugged at her stomach. In the pantry she found a loaf of bread and a jar of peanut butter. She pulled them both from the shelf, then thought twice and replaced the bread. She grabbed a spoon from the silverware drawer and twisted the lid from the jar.

This had always been her comfort food. Grandma Woodruff used to hand her a spoon, hold out an open jar, and say, "Dig in, darling. Peanut butter is good for the soul."

No, you were good for the soul, Grandma.

If only she were here now. Miranda burrowed her spoon into the Skippy jar, trying to conjure up more memories of Grandma, but years had blurred so many of the mental images.

The Bible! Right after Grandma died, whenever Miranda had wanted to feel close to her, she'd pull Grandma's Bible from the bookshelf. Read the notes in the margins, skim the highlighted verses.

She plopped the spoon in her mouth, abandoned the peanut butter jar, and retraced her steps into the living room. There it was, Grandma's Bible nestled between *A Tale of Two Cities* and her boxed *Chronicles of Narnia* set. She slid it from the shelf, grabbed a blanket from the back of the living room couch, and then padded to the front door and slipped out.

Moonlight cast a halo around her mountain clearing and spread a sheen over the grass underfoot, still damp from an early-evening rain. With the Bible under her arm, Miranda pulled the spoon from her mouth, sticky peanut butter coating her tongue. She rounded the house, coming up on the unfinished part of the house, tarp flapping in the breeze.

Wood beams and a cement foundation created an empty frame. *Someday . . .* She placed the spoon between her lips like a sucker and hoisted herself onto the cement floor of the incomplete structure. An animal—maybe a squirrel or a chipmunk—rustled through a nearby tree.

She settled, her back against a thick beam, blanket over her knees, Bible in her lap. Now what?

"Psalms, honey. When you're feeling lost or confused, flip open to the Psalms and let David's prayers be yours." Grand-

ma's voice again, so clear tonight. Would she ever hear God's voice as clearly as the voices of her past?

She opened the Bible at the middle. Started reading. Read aimlessly for five minutes, maybe ten. Why couldn't she find the comfort in this book her grandmother always used to? Wispy clouds trekked across the sky, muting the light of the moon, blanketing the stars. When she looked back down, her eyes landed on Psalm 138:8.

"The Lord will fulfill his purpose for me; your love, O Lord, endures forever—do not abandon the works of your hands."

Abandon the works of His hand. The way she'd abandoned this skeleton of a home addition? A mountain wind skidded through the framed room, scuffing her cheeks and tangling her hair. The crinkle and slap of plastic tarp whipping against the frame filled the silence.

"The Lord will fulfill his purpose for me." But would He really? Especially when she'd built the foundation of her identity on a lie?

I want to believe your love endures forever, God. But the woman I've become can't possibly be the person you intended.

She'd trapped herself. And how could freedom from her false identity possibly be worth the cost? Her show, her career, her reputation, her crew . . . all would suffer if she fought against who she'd become. She closed the Bible.

The sound of tires on gravel cut into her solitude, joined by the harsh yellow of headlights. Matthew.

Maybe I won't have a choice. Maybe Matthew will force me out of the lie.

Quiet hovered after he cut the engine. Did he see her sitting there? A lonely figure in a hollow room.

She heard the clank of his door shutting, then footsteps swishing through wet grass and leaves. She sucked in a breath as he moved toward her, the urge to flee what would surely end up as an interrogation battling with her desperation to know. . . .

Would he tell?

But of course he would. How could he not?

He pulled himself onto the raised foundation, blocking the light of the moon. "Why?"

Just that one word made her wish she'd gone with her first impulse and escaped into the house. "Could you not stand over me like that? It makes me feel . . . small."

He lowered to the cement, legs dangling over the side. Now, in the pale moonlight, she could see the pinch in his eyes and the set of his jaw.

"I wasn't sure you'd come back."

"Yeah, well, I follow through on my assignments. You're my assignment. So."

The way he said the word *assignment* sent the message loud and clear. It's what she should've expected. Didn't mean it didn't sting.

"You and Blaze aren't married."

She shook her head.

"You're faking it."

Nod.

"For the show."

Another nod.

He turned to face her. "So now it makes sense why you couldn't produce a marriage certificate. Seems like a long-shot gamble to me. You really didn't think someone would eventually figure it out? How long were you going to keep it up? How'd Blaze get drawn into it? And why didn't you just drop the 'I'm married' act years ago? Men probably would've flooded North Carolina for a chance at you."

His rapid-fire questions shot holes in her ability to put up a defense. "There's more to the story, Knox."

"Then tell me." The command felt more like a plea. "Why?"

She thrust the Bible off her lap. "Because I wanted to, all right? I like my show. I like my success. I like the person I am when I'm wowing viewers."

It was time she admitted it. It was easier to lie about who she was than face what she wasn't: Wanted. Enough. A worthy daughter . . . wife . . .

A *mother*. Oh, how long it'd been since she allowed that word space in her heart.

Now she stood. Let the self-righteous journalist feel small for once. "That's the answer to your question, Matthew. I wanted to. Because I like people thinking that, at the end of the day, I'm going home to a handsome husband who adores me, rather than an empty house that only reminds me of the man who discarded me and our . . ." No, she couldn't go there.

But did he see it wasn't all coldhearted and calculated? Oh, it probably didn't make a difference in the end, not to his story. But something in her needed Matthew to *know*.

"I wanted the country to believe about me what I couldn't believe myself—that I'm worth holding on to."

"Miranda . . ." But he didn't finish. Just lowered his head in a move that spoke judgment.

Okay. She jumped to the ground, turned her back, started to walk away—leaving her Bible, her blanket, the last of her hope. Except . . .

Except, no. She had to at least ask. Fight. Be strong.

She whipped around. "Please don't tell, Matthew. I have no right to ask, I know, but please. Or at least, if you're set on it, give me a few days to prepare. Consider this me begging. I'll do anything."

He raised his head, a tiny chink in his stony glare. "Anything?"

One nod. One sliver of hope.

Chapter 12

"This one! This is the biggest pumpkin in the whole world!"

Despite the cement-like wall that'd gone up between her and Matthew in the past two days, Miranda couldn't help the grin spreading across her cheeks at the sight of Matthew's niece. The child had Matthew by the hand, guiding him to her pumpkin of choice at the patch outside Minneapolis.

Cee's cerulean blue eyes glimmered under the autumn sun, pigtails framing a pixie face and a clan of Disney princesses parading across her hooded sweatshirt.

"That's a beauty of a pumpkin, Cee," Matthew signed as he spoke aloud, then bent to a crouch and pulled a pocketknife from the pocket of his black army-style jacket.

"That girl idolizes him," Matthew's sister-in-law, Izzy, said as she came up beside Miranda. "He's like a big brother, best friend, and first crush all rolled into one. Although, I do think she's gotten over the idea of marrying him."

Matthew hauled the pumpkin into his arms, pretending to wobble at the weight, scrunching his face into exaggerated strain. Cee's giggles floated through the patch like golden harvest dust. "He's a good uncle," Miranda agreed.

Even if he had treated Miranda like a leper during the past two days.

Miranda hadn't been able to believe it when Matthew had issued his bargain: Go with him to Minnesota to meet his niece, and he'd hold the truth about her sham of a marriage close to his chest . . . for now.

"That's all? You want me to meet your family?" She'd asked, then regretted the words the second they escaped her lips. It wasn't as if he'd asked her to meet his family as . . . someone special. Oh no, she had no misconceptions about where they stood. He'd made that plenty clear.

"I follow through on my assignments. You're my assignment."

Matthew despised her. And honestly, she couldn't blame him. But did he have to ooze such outright hostility? He'd barely spoken a word during the plane ride that morning. While they'd waited for Izzy and Cee, he'd stood so rigid that if she'd knocked him over, he'd have fallen like a slab of wood.

And don't think she hadn't considered it.

Izzy had acknowledged Miranda's presence on the way to the pumpkin patch, regaling Miranda with stories of life as a Texan transplanted up north. Jase, too, had given her a hearty welcome and chatted with her as they drove past tawny fields and farmers at work.

"You just had to pick the hugest pumpkin in all of Minnesota," Jase was saying now as he ambled over to his daughter and brother. "I suppose you're going to make me carry it to the car."

Jase matched Matthew's height almost exactly, but a hint of red tinged his hair and his Roman nose sloped to a point. At the airport, he'd greeted Matthew with a tight bear hug. And Miranda hadn't missed the way he studied his younger brother as Matthew introduced her. It was easy to see the older sibling in Jase.

Matthew, his brother and sister-in-law, Cee—they were a small family, but a tight-knit one. If only Matthew would stop freezing her out, she might truly enjoy this day away. That morning at the Asheville airport, even with its stale smell and suffocating crowd, there'd been something refreshing about leaving her home world.

For this one short day, there was no television show. No fake husband. No paparazzi. At least not yet. She tugged her baseball cap lower over her eyes.

"Worried someone might recognize you?" Izzy asked. Matthew's sister-in-law was built like the cowgirl Matthew said she was—long legs and broad shoulders, her blond hair pulled into a ponytail. *A woman after my own heart.*

"Just a little. I wouldn't want to ruin Cee's day by drawing attention to myself."

"I can't believe you came all this way just to grant Cee's wish," Izzy marveled. "To think you're going to hop on a plane tonight and head back."

"I don't know if Matthew told you, but taping has been suspended on my show. So at this point, I'm a woman of leisure. Besides, he's talked a ton about Cee and all of you. He's seen so much of my life, it's fun to get a glimpse of his."

"Well, you've made Cee's day, probably her year. You know, she's been telling all her friends to tell their parents and their friends to leave a comment on the blog Matthew wrote earlier this week about saving your show. You've got *two* persistent Knoxes on your side."

Except that Matthew probably wasn't on her side anymore, even if the Internet campaign he'd started was going strong. Miranda hadn't read that blog post that kicked off the petition, but Blaze had told her before their hike that Matthew had shucked off any pretense of unbiased journalism and basically pled with his audience to show their support for *From the Ground Up.*

He probably regretted writing it now.

"Okay, we've got our pumpkin," Matthew announced as he lugged the pumpkin. "Now what?"

"The hay bale maze!" Cee spoke, her hands moving rapidly. "I want to go with Randi."

Something warm and maternal sparked in Miranda, warding off the chill of the Midwest wind . . . and Matthew's ire. Like she'd seen Matthew do, she waited until Cee's eyes were trained on her face to speak. "It'd be my pleasure. You'll make sure we don't get lost, right?"

Cee gave a serious nod. "I know the way."

"She should. She's already been through the thing three times this fall," Jase said.

"How about Jase and I go pay for the pumpkin and load it up?" Izzy suggested. "You two can take Cee through the maze, and we'll meet you back at the car."

Miranda caught Matthew's eye. He grunted his agreement. Was the man going to play caveman all day? They followed Cee to the structure. The hay bale walls stood at least six feet high, casting shadows over the ground.

"This is some maze. I'm impressed," Miranda said as they started out. "Wouldn't it be scary in the dark?"

Cee skipped along.

"She can't read your lips if she can't see your face, Rand." Matthew walked on the other side of Cee, about as far away from Miranda as he could manage. Both hands were jabbed into his jacket pocket.

"Maybe I was talking to you. Although, why I would, I have no idea. You give the silent treatment better than any thirteen-year-old girl." And no, she hadn't missed the way he'd reverted to the shortened, less-personal version of her name. "You're the one who wanted me to come today. I'm sorry if I'm totally ruining it for you, but I came because you asked me to."

"You came because you don't want me to tell anyone you're a liar."

Miranda stopped, dark hurt trekking a path straight to her heart. No, his judgment didn't surprise her. But its sharpness did. "Maybe you should just do it. Publish the truth about Blaze and me. Whatever might happen couldn't be worse than your high-and-mighty treatment. I'm sorry I'm not the picture of moral perfection you obviously expected."

The musty smell of the hay pricked her eyes and fogged her thoughts. What was Matthew looking for from her?

Up ahead from a fork in the path, Cee whirled around. "Come on, keep up!" She turned to the right.

"Are you sure that's the right way?" Matthew called after her. But Cee had already galloped ahead. He turned back to Miranda.

She stood rooted in place, arms folded, a shield against his disapproval. He dropped his hands from his pockets, his tight stance loosening. "I'm the last person to expect perfection." He rubbed his hand over his chin. "But honesty . . . I value it. So yeah, I'm having trouble getting over the fact that everything I thought I knew about you is a lie."

Miranda rolled her eyes. "Really, I hadn't picked up on that."

"But you're right. I asked you to make this trip with me, and I've been freezing you out all day. Which is very"—his jaw released into a half grin—"thirteen-year-old girlish of me." He took a step toward her. "Maybe we can just forget about everything back in North Carolina. For today, at least."

Relief slid in. Miranda pulled a stringy piece of hay from a bale, twiddled it in her fingers. "I'd like that."

Cee burst around the corner. "I was wrong. It's that way." She took off once more.

Matthew nudged his head. "Come on. We'd better keep up before I lose my niece."

The space between them had whittled to only a couple feet. "Hey, I don't know if I can forget about *everything* back in North Carolina. I promised Blaze I'd call and check up on him sometime." She'd told Blaze on the way home from the hospital that Matthew knew the whole truth about their non-relationship. "Can't believe we left the poor guy home two days after he broke his arm."

"Yeah, but he insisted." Matthew waved at Cee up ahead, assurance that they wouldn't fall behind again. "And he seems to be fairly used to getting around with injuries."

"The man is crazy."

"How'd you come up with him, anyway? Of all the people you could've chosen to be your husband, why Blaze?"

Miranda released her piece of hay into the wind. There wasn't anything she could tell him now more damaging than he already knew. Might as well. "It all started with a case of mistaken identity. See, just a few days before you showed up, we were on set and . . ."

Was it just Miranda, or did Matthew keep loosening as they spoke? He drifted closer to her side, his shoulder brushing hers as they turned a corner.

"So what's up with the two of you?"

Jase asked the question the second Miranda disappeared into Cee's bedroom. The pair had talked about soccer all the way home from the pumpkin patch, and now Cee wanted to show Miranda her team pictures from the summer league.

"What do you mean what's up with us?" Matthew followed Jase down the hallway.

"I mean when you first got here, you treated her with all the warmth of a prison warden. By the time you escaped the hay maze, you were chatting it up."

They descended the staircase to the first floor, and Jase led the way to the living room. "We called a truce."

"Why do you need a truce?" Jase flopped onto the plum-colored couch.

"You ask too many questions."

"I'm a concerned older brother."

Matthew settled into a recliner. He'd enjoyed the mountains, but there was something comforting about being back at home. Well, not technically *his* home. But he spent about as much time at Jase and Izzy's as his own townhouse. He could have blamed it on Cee, but truthfully, sometimes his bachelor pad felt plain-old lonely.

"She's got secrets, Jase. And I don't know what to do with them."

"Like, big secrets?"

Matthew locked his fingers behind his head, elbows pointed out. "Like, the stuff of national headlines." Already, Dooley was foaming at the mouth. The editor had called at the crack of dawn yesterday, as soon as he'd heard Matthew's message from the night before.

Matthew had fumbled for an excuse, told Dooley he'd jumped the gun with his cryptic message. He never should've called the editor so quickly in the heat of his anger after first learning the truth about Miranda and Blaze. He'd finally—barely—appeased Dooley by promising an entry on the rival show being considered by the network. He'd hinted at it in his earlier blog, and Brad seemed to think there was something fishy there. Maybe he could dig it up, to stall for time.

Jase nodded slowly, eyes on the football game on the wide-screen TV. "She sure seems nice."

"Oh, don't get me wrong, she is." More than nice, actually. Kind. Compassionate. With a voice like honey and the kind of laugh a person couldn't get tired of. "Now that I know the truth about her, it's like everything's changed. And yet . . . it hasn't."

Because underneath the lies, she was still her.

And he was still him.

And there was still that uncanny connection stringing them together.

"You like her." Jase said it matter-of-factly.

Matthew didn't bother with an answer.

"She's married."

"Oh, but she's not." It slipped out quickly, accidentally.

Or maybe he'd meant to say it. Maybe he'd needed to tell someone. Someone who could help him push through the obnoxious choir in his head that, on the one hand, chided him for being duped, and on the other hand, swayed in a happy dance at the reality of it all: She was available. Kind of.

Jase leaned forward, whistled. "Seriously? Did she get divorced or something? Then who's that guy on the tab covers?"

"Long story, man."

"And you promised not to tell." Jase read him like a book.

Matthew nodded, and his gaze drifted to the window. Outside, the last of autumn's color clung to the maple tree in Jase and Izzy's front yard. This had been a beautiful day to make the trip. Cee's smile when she'd spotted him in the airport, the way she'd flung herself into his arms—totally worth the hassle of rising early to catch a red-eye flight.

"I could make money off this story," Matthew admitted. "I could get paid for interviews. Could really put a dent in the cost for Cee's surgery."

"Matt—"

"I know what you're going to say, that you won't accept my money. But that's stupid. Think about how many times you've had my back. Obviously I want to help with this."

"That's not it."

"Why do you even think I took this story in the first place? I know Izzy's hours have been cut back and things at the gallery aren't good."

"I'm selling the gallery."

The recliner springs moaned as Matthew jerked. "What? Y-you can't."

"I have to. I'm not moving pieces like when it first opened. Blame the economy, blame whatever you want, but the place is leaking money."

"Yeah, but it was your dream. You saved for over a decade to open it."

"And it's been a fun few years. But my family is my dream now. They come first. There's a teaching spot open at the U of M next semester. I've already accepted."

Jase spoke with straight practicality, but he had to be hurting. He'd invested so much in that place. Matthew had been there on opening day, had watched straightlaced, reserved Jase practically bounce through the place as he greeted customers, artists, photographers.

"Isn't there anything I can do?"

"It's already done. I had an offer on the space within two weeks of putting it up for sale."

Two weeks? That meant Jase had been moving on this before Matthew even left town. Why hadn't he said something?

"It's a miracle, actually, a reasonable offer coming in that quickly, in this economy. To Izzy and me, it confirmed this is God's will."

"It's God's will you give up on your dream?" Sarcasm laced his words. Maybe he hadn't been Mr. Super Christian lately, but that didn't sound like the God he'd learned about growing up. Did God give people dreams only to yank them back?

He leaned his head against the recliner's headrest. Is that what Miranda wrestled? Did she feel as if God had taken away her original dream—marriage to that guy from Brazil—and is that why she went to such crazy lengths to hold on to what she had left?

Whereas Jase went ahead and surrendered. Laid his dream on the altar when it became too much. What now?

"Will the money you get from the sale make Cee's surgery a possibility?"

Jase sighed. "It'll help. And the university has a great health insurance policy, though it won't kick in until February. After that, we'll see. We're still praying about it. Celine is happy, well adjusted. We want what's best for her, but we have to trust that God knows what He's doing."

Trust. It always came down to that. And rarely did it work out.

Jase turned off the TV with a click of the remote, then leaned forward, elbows on his knees. "Hey, little brother, don't look so down. It's not all bad news. Izzy and I were going to tell you at dinner, but you seem to need the news now." Jase paused, light flooding his eyes. "Izzy's pregnant."

Matthew burst from the recliner. "Jase, are you serious?"

Jase looked up. "I'll joke about a lot of things, but my wife carrying our child? Uh-uh. We're due in May."

"Well, then, stand up so I can hug you, bro!"

They embraced with hearty pats on the back.

"An uncle all over again. I like this." He squinted against the sun pouring into the room. "But the gallery. I am sorry, Jase."

"Don't be. It was fun while it lasted. But with Iz pregnant, now more than ever, we need an income we can count on. Sure, it'll be hard to see the place empty out. But I like teaching. It'll be great."

Although Jase's confidence rang genuine, Matthew detected the barest hint of forced optimism. So strange, the combination of pure joy and disappointment over the end of his brother's dream. But like Jase said, he had a new dream now: his family.

A new dream.

What if Miranda could escape the trap of her lie and find a new dream?

What if I could?

"Maybe we should take Miranda by the gallery on the way back to the airport tonight. She's got a few blank walls in her house."

Jase clapped his hand on Matthew's shoulder. "Yeah, back to her. And you. And the fact that she's not married."

"We're not going there, dude."

Jase crossed his arms. "Fine. Izzy'll get it out of you eventually anyway. I'm going to go check on Cee, make sure she's not forcing your celebrity into building her a new bedroom or anything."

"And I'm going to find Izzy and congratulate her. You do know if you have a boy I expect you to name him after me."

Jase's chuckle bounded through the house. While his brother climbed the stairs, Matthew headed toward the kitchen. But he stopped short at the sound of Miranda's voice. She must have come down already.

He peered around the corner. Izzy and Miranda stood on opposite sides of the island counter in the middle of the kitchen, cutting boards and a variety of vegetables ready to be chopped.

"I thought I was going to die of boredom chaperoning that dance. But then this new guy walks in. Someone tells me he's a visiting professor in the art department. A photographer." Izzy chopped an onion as she spoke. "I'm telling you, by the end of our first dance, I'd decided I'd marry him."

Miranda giggled. "That quickly, huh?"

"I think it was the dancing. Dance with the right guy and—wham—you just know."

"That so?"

"Sure. Haven't you ever gone to a dance with your husband? Didn't it do all kinds of funny stuff to your stomach?"

Are you going to lie to her? The silent question pricked Matthew.

"I've never been to a dance, actually." Miranda's tone spoke nonchalance, but even from where he stood, Matthew could see the tightening of her wrist as she sliced through the cucumber.

"Why not? Not even your high-school prom?"

Miranda shook her head, her knife rapping into the wooden board with each cut. "No. I remember wanting to go. Or at least considering it. And I really thought someone would ask me, too. I had all these guy friends from shop class. But each time one of them came up to me, right when I thought they were going to ask, they'd ask me for advice on which cheerleader they should take or how they should invite another girl."

Miranda had stopped slicing as she spoke. Across the island, Izzy bit her bottom lip, waited.

Finally, Miranda shrugged, waved her knife with a chuckle. "It's a silly thing to remember. Not like it mattered in the bigger picture of my life. Although, to this day, I don't know how to dance. And that freaks me out considering this Giving Heart gala thing includes dancing." She pointed the knife at herself. "But look at me. Do I look like a girl who belongs in a dress on a dance floor?"

Yes . . .

"Yes, what, Uncle Matt?"

He glanced down. Cee stood in front of him, wearing her soccer uniform and socks pulled to her knees. *"Yes, you look awesome in your uniform,"* he signed without speaking.

"But I didn't even ask you that," she signed back.

"I read your mind."

Like he'd read between the lines of Miranda's question to the insecurities obviously still nagging her. And it made the thought of adding one more scar to the mix by publicizing Miranda's fake marriage feel all sorts of dirty.

That's right—as much as he wanted a story, as much as he wanted to be there for Cee, he realized now he didn't want to do it at the expense of Miranda's heart. Maybe he could find some other angle.

But he couldn't be the latest in the string of men who'd hurt Randi Woodruff.

Even if it cost him his career comeback. Maybe, like Jase, it was time he sacrificed one dream and found another. He took hold of Cee's hand and strolled into the kitchen.

❦

Matthew had never seen Miranda laugh so freely. In the span of a few hours, she'd latched on to his family like a little girl with a new doll. She'd listened with intent focus while Cee shared her dream of becoming an architect and built her up with words of encouragement.

Then he'd taken on Miranda and Cee in a game of soccer in the backyard. He'd let Cee barrel past him every time she dribbled toward the homemade goal—the hammock hanging between a tree and a pole.

But when Miranda raced toward the goal, he darted in front of her, egging her on with playful taunts.

Later, the party of five had laughed through a dinner of steak and veggies and then a half dozen rounds of Uno Attack.

Finally, they'd loaded up into Jase's car, Cee squeezed in between Matthew and Miranda in the back seat. On the way to the airport, they stopped at the gallery, where Miranda purchased an eight-hundred-dollar print. Whether she actually liked the artwork as much as her gushing suggested or she'd picked up on the For Sale sign in the window, Matthew couldn't tell.

All he knew was, watching Miranda hug Cee, then Izzy, then Jase, she'd needed this day. He might have coerced her into it for Cee's sake, but she had benefited, too.

And me, too. Once he'd stopped pouting, it had been the best day he could remember in a long time.

He leaned down to kiss Izzy's cheek. "Congrats again, sis."

"I hope you're prepared for your baby-sitting duties to double."

"I think I'm up for the job."

He hugged Jase next, then bent down in front of Cee. "You're going to make the best big sister in the world."

She plunked her hands on his shoulders. "I know, silly."

He pulled her into a hug.

Fifteen minutes later, he and Miranda made it through Security and located their terminal. They found two empty seats and settled to wait for their flight. Matthew raked his fingers through his hair. "Man, that was a fun but long day."

"Hey, Matthew, do you know anything about smartphones?"

"What do you need to know?"

She pulled out her phone. "Well, supposedly I can e-mail from this thing. But I've never used it."

He chuckled while he tapped on her phone. "The girl who makes using a table saw look easier than brushing her teeth doesn't know how to send an e-mail from her phone. Love it."

She jabbed him with her elbow but smiled.

"Here you go. Your e-mail system was already set up. I opened a new message for you." He handed her phone back. "Who are you e-mailing?"

"Silly reporter. Always asking questions."

He watched her tap out the message. Slowly. He grinned. "Fine. Don't tell me."

She kept tapping. "If you must know . . . my parents."

"Really?"

She looked up, met his eyes. "Really. Just to, um, say hi, I guess."

He held her gaze. "Well, Liv will be proud of you." And she wasn't the only one.

Miranda bit her lip over a half smile, then went back to typing her message. Minutes passed until the sound of the television pulled his attention. "Hey, Miranda, check out the TV." A rerun of *From the Ground Up.*

She pocketed her phone, looked up, and groaned. "I remember that episode." On screen, she lay on her back, head poking under a kitchen sink. "Drain work drives me crazy. I'm a carpenter, not a plumber."

They watched in silence, airport activity barely a hum so late at night. Exhaustion from their eighteen-hour-day tugged at Matthew's mind, his eyelids drifting closed.

"My real life is as fake as that kitchen set," Miranda's voice glided into his sleepiness.

"Huh?" He lifted one eyelid.

"That kitchen. The cupboards are hollow, no china or utensils stored inside. The counters are all movable, depending on the scene. The refrigerator and stove aren't hooked up. It's all . . . fake. Shallow." Weariness formed her words as she slouched in her chair.

"Remember, today we're not thinking about any of that. And it's"—he checked his watch—"eleven forty-four. We've still got sixteen minutes of today left."

The whir of an airplane taking off outside the window diminished the sound of the television, the airport's hum. Matthew lifted his hand from his lap and covered Miranda's palm on the armrest.

Chapter 13

The morning had started out in a blur of phone calls and hurried activity.

"How fast can you get to the set, Rand?" Brad blurted the question without so much as a good-morning when she'd answered the phone, her voice raspy from a night of way too little sleep. She and Matthew hadn't rolled in to her property until after 3:00.

"Sasha Perot's guest for her show today cancelled, and she wants you to fill in."

Miranda had flung her feet to the floor. Sunlight poured in through her bedroom windows. What time was it, anyway?

"The set? But Sasha tapes in Chicago."

Sasha Perot, owner of SteelWorks Kitchen Appliance and Accessories, and host of *We Can Women*, a live how-to show, had guested on *From the Ground Up* at least a half dozen times throughout the years.

"They'll satellite you in. This is good publicity, kid. The topic is kitchen design. I already called Linc, got his permission to use the studio kitchen. He told me to call Tom, which I did, so he and some of the crew are getting it ready as we speak."

All pitching in to help their front woman, paycheck or no. "What time do we go live?"

And so here she was, leaning against an island counter in a relaxed pose entirely contrary to the weekend's swirl of emotions still twisting inside her.

"Thirty seconds, Rand," a crewman said, whisking past.

From the monitor a few feet away, Sasha introduced the segment. The woman's glossy black hair and eclectic jewelry screamed urban suave. ". . . which is why I'm so glad Randi Woodruff, host of *From the Ground Up*, is joining us today to talk all things kitcheny. Randi, thanks for joining us via satellite."

Can't mess this up. You're live. Thank goodness for Whitney and her cosmetics case. For once Miranda appreciated the makeup plastered over her face. Even she had cringed at the circles under her eyes this morning.

"You're welcome, Sasha, and thanks for having me on the show. Kitchens, possibly more than any room remodel, take extra care and planning." She moved across the set without missing a beat. "Not only do you have to consider practical and aesthetic appliance arrangement, but you also have to take into account plumbing lines, electrical wiring, and of course, your personal use of the kitchen."

She caught Tom's thumbs-up from where he stood off set. Nearby, Brad shot her a smile of approval.

They'd all rushed to make this happen. But did it even matter? If Matthew broke the story about her lies, surely the network would can the show. Oh sure, he'd made a bargain to keep her secret for the time being, and she'd gone with him to Minneapolis. But could she really expect him to hold out forever? He had his own career to consider.

All the people she cared about would be hurt when the story broke. And what about poor Blaze? They'd never planned to stay fake-married indefinitely, but if her secret came out and the whole country knew about her ruse, what would *his* future hold?

The truth pummeled her, even as she performed on auto-pilot, moving to the center of the kitchen space, bobbing her head at Sasha's commentary.

"To create a truly distinctive space, first consider what might serve as the focal point of your kitchen," Sasha was saying. "Randi, what would you say is this particular kitchen's focal point?"

They'd talked about this before taping, but in the minutes since, their plan had tangled with her knotted emotions. *Focal point . . . Oh!* "Without a doubt, I'd say the bank of windows on this long wall. You could really take advantage of that with an eye-catching counter. And what cook doesn't appreciate a runway of a counter?"

"Randi, talk to us about cabinetry. I know your first love is woodworking, so you probably have fabulous ideas for kitchen cupboards."

Miranda brushed a hand over the oak cabinets at eye level. "While budgets will differ from household to household, I often tell people the one area not to skimp on in a room remodel is carpentry. Cabinets can make or break the aesthetics of a kitchen. So if you can afford it, I do suggest customizing."

"Do you have some tips for cabinet makeovers on a budget?"

"Absolutely. One of the easiest things you can do if your cabinets have become old hat is to refinish or even repaint the doors and frames yourself. Be sure to prep the surfaces first by cleaning thoroughly and then sanding them down with fine-grit sandpaper. This process assures the paint will stick." The instructions flowed effortlessly. "Another simple tip to give your cabinets a face-lift is to replace or clean the knobs and hinges. And consider buffing them with a clear wax."

If only life and all its bumps and grooves was as easily reno-vated. A little sanding here and smoothing there, a layer of refinisher to remove the stain.

Five minutes later, the segment ended when *We Can Women* went to its final commercial break. Miranda settled onto a barstool at the island counter, shoulders relaxing for the first time since waking up this morning. At least she could do something right, even if it was only babbling about countertops and cabinets.

"Good job," Tom said, leaving his perch. "You're as natural on camera as you are at a table saw."

"You mean I've learned how to put on the perk." She gave him a tired smile. "Remember how awkward I was those first few months on set? I was sure the execs had picked the wrong person for the job."

"Not going to lie, Woodruff, I had my doubts, too. You had a doozy of a time remembering not to turn your back to the camera." He settled onto the barstool next to her. "But you turned out all right."

She laid her palms flat against the smooth granite counter top, its swirls of gray and green pulling her vision out of focus. "You know what else I remember?"

"You're not going to get sentimental on me now, are you?" He groaned.

"Hush. I'll never forget Valentine's Day a couple years ago. Seemed like everybody in the studio was getting flowers and candy and stuffed animals. Everybody had a date. Everybody had . . . someone." She'd made one excuse after the other as to why her own "husband" hadn't been as thoughtful. But Tom, being the only one on set who'd known the truth about her marital status, had seen right through her. She turned to meet Tom's eyes now. "You found me alone in my dressing room."

"Sulking," he interjected.

"Reflecting," she countered. "Fine, sulking. And you came in, sat down, and pinned me with your classic no-nonsense stare. And you said, 'Rand, someday, some man is going to fall so hard for you he'll need CPR just to revive him.'"

"I said that?" Tom raked a finger through his whiskers. "Doesn't sound like me."

"Don't pretend you don't remember. And then I said something about the slim chances of a man looking past my tool belt and work boots. And you said . . ." Her voice faded as the memory came into focus.

The way the liquid in her eyes pooled. The chill of the winter day outside her dressing room window reaching to her heart. The leather of Tom's work gloves on her shoulders.

"'The right man won't be looking past your tool belt and work boots. He'll look right at 'em. He'll love you for 'em.'" She repeated the words now, the same sense of comfort blanketing her today as it had then, warm and hopeful.

Tom coughed. "Still don't remember." He stood and lowered his voice. "But, mind you, it was the truth then and it's the truth now. Now I'm going to go enjoy the rest of my day off. The missus and I are going antiquing. I'll see you when we're back to filming."

If we come back.

He tipped his head and ambled away.

They had to come back. Because despite her gut-wrenchingly honest confession to Matthew on Friday, *From the Ground Up* wasn't only about Randi Woodruff. There was Tom and Whitney and Rog, the head cameraman. The props crew, the marketing team, the interns all hopeful at the start of their careers.

She'd figure something out.

"Rand, phone," Brad said, joining her on the set platform. He held out his phone. "It's Sasha."

She cocked her head in question. Brad only shrugged and handed her the phone.

"Hi, Sasha."

"Randi, thanks again for helping us out so last minute. No one would've known that segment was thrown together in less time than my stylist takes on my hair."

Miranda chuckled. "Of course, no problem. I was happy to help."

"Listen, I consider you a colleague. Our work, our shows, they're different enough that I don't see you as competition. And I respect you as a professional."

"That's nice to hear."

"Which is why I called to tell you this. I debated it, but your willingness to help out today convinced me it's the right thing to do."

Miranda's curiosity ballooned. Brad mouthed that he'd be right back and trotted off.

"You've heard about the new home show being pitched to the network."

Ohhh. That. "Yes, we'd heard rumblings."

"Well, someone connected to the show set up a meeting with me a couple weeks ago. They asked for sponsorship. I'd guest on the show throughout the season, and they'd use SteelWorks appliances exclusively."

Miranda's palm thudded to the countertop. "Why are you telling me this?"

"Because the whole thing rubbed me wrong. I asked a few questions, and—Randi, I'm going to tell you straight up—they're gunning for you. I don't know why, but they want to make a splash big enough to drown *From the Ground Up.*"

But why? And who? She searched for possibilities but came up dry. Who would have it in for her? "I knew things weren't looking good for us, but . . . I'm stumped."

"I'd like to give you names, but I fear that would be going too far." Sasha's raspy laugh carried over the phone. "Instead, I've got an offer for you. I like *From the Ground Up.* I like you. I've had my financial gurus come up with a sponsorship package for you. It's already in the mail. Check it out, see if you're interested."

"Oh, wow, Sasha. I don't know what to say."

"Don't get too grateful yet, hon. We've got conditions, of course. For instance, I saw that Whirlpool fridge of yours. It's gotta go." Sasha laughed again. "But it's an attractive package. At least a little something to make the network think twice about axing you too fast. We need to look out for each other in this biz."

Miranda slipped off the barstool, hope sliding in like rolls of mist over the mountains. "I truly appreciate this, Sasha. Thank you."

They ended the call, and Miranda found Brad outside, wiping a dusty streak from his car. "I might have good news, Walsh." She relayed Sasha's news, optimism growing at Brad's enthusiastic response.

Of course, there was still the new show on the block—and Matthew, too—to reckon with, but she still felt a glimmer of hope.

And then she thought of the e-mail she'd sent Mom and Dad last night. She'd second-guessed sending it all through the flight home, while Matthew nodded off beside her. Was opening that door of her heart worth it? If they knew the truth about her life these days, would they still try to reconnect?

When it came down to it, though, she couldn't control any of it. Could only hope. Pray.

Now, there was a thought.

"What are you up to for the rest of the day?" Brad said as he lowered into his car.

"Going home to check on Blaze." And then a walk . . . to the church.

"What are you not telling me?"

Matthew held his phone to his ear as he emerged from Miranda's cabin and crossed her property to the house. Greg Dooley's suspicious question goaded him.

"You leave me a cryptic message last week that gets my heart rate going, then put me off all weekend. You know what that does to a man?"

"No, what?"

"It turns him into a snapping turtle. The wife won't talk to me now, and my secretary's in hiding, too."

Underfoot, the grass still glistened from the thaw of last night's frost. The air was crisp, the sky white. Coming snow, he could taste it, crisp and cold. The Midwesterner in him well recognized the approach of winter.

"I told you, I pulled the trigger too fast with that message. I thought I'd landed on a scoop. Now . . . I'm not so sure."

He glanced at the driveway, where Miranda usually parked her heap of a truck. Gone. He thought he'd heard it rumble away earlier.

"You sounded anything but uncertain when you left that message."

"I was hot under the collar. Remember, this is Matthew Knox you're talking to. I have a history of getting ahead of myself." Normally he didn't like admitting it, but today it made for a nice defense. "Besides, the blog is still getting a ridiculous amount of hits, right? That post last week about the dire straits of *From the Ground Up*, that's still getting good play."

"I just want to know why I can't get over the feeling you're not telling me something. Am I going to regret giving you this assignment, Knox?"

"No. Listen, I need to go. I *promise*, I'm working on something." *Something* being the key word. Something worthy of a cover story.

He hung up.

Miranda needed to win the Giving Heart Award—that's all there was to it. That would be worthy of the cover. And he could write a nice, happy story. It wouldn't earn him big bucks. He'd have to find another way to help Jase and Izzy afford the surgery. But after seeing Cee with Miranda, he knew he couldn't write an exposé.

Of course, there was always the possibility of there being a story behind that rival show. He'd made a few calls, poked around enough to get a few details on the new pitch. All he had was a name, but maybe there was enough of a story there to satisfy Dooley.

But for now, Matthew had something else to focus on.

The porch steps creaked as he climbed to the front door. Blaze's relaxed grin greeted him on the other side of the screen door. "Dude, what's up? How was your trip? Miranda headed out for the day, and I'm bored to death."

Matthew pocketed his phone, forced himself to forget Dooley's insistence.

"Well, say good-bye to boredom. Because I need a little help."

Sunset danced in a whirl of pale color as Miranda turned Grandpa's truck toward home. Cotton-candy pinks and blues hovered over the mountain horizon, fading into purple overhead. She hadn't planned to spend so much time at the church. But she'd run into Joni Watters again and ended up helping her paint the basement Sunday school rooms as the woman spoke of the daughter she'd lost.

How different it'd felt listening to someone else's hurts—and joys, too—rather than dwelling on her own. She rolled around the pastor's wife's stories in her mind, tasted Joni's vulnerability for the gift it was. People usually came to Miranda for advice on stripping paint and weatherizing their deck, not to bare their hearts.

Except for Matthew. When he'd spoken of his damaged relationship with his father, he'd let her see inside. Yesterday, he'd further opened the door to his personal life with their brief trip to Minneapolis.

And look what she'd done with his trust. Trampled all over it with lies.

It had been nice to spend time with Joni. Miranda's only fumble had come when her new friend invited her to church on Sunday.

"I—I don't think so. But thank you."

Joni didn't dig for the reason. But why did Miranda get the feeling the pastor's wife guessed more than mere reluctance kept her away? She probably even knew Miranda had been coming by the church on Sunday afternoons for months now.

She pulled into her driveway, gaze immediately moving to Matthew's cabin. Yes, she'd begun to think of it as his. With a heavy breath, she trudged to the house, up the porch steps.

Strains of an orchestra waltz drifted from the house. She pulled open the front door. And gaped.

Blaze and Matthew stood in the middle of her emptied living room—the couch pushed up against the east wall, the fuzzy rug that usually decorated the floor in front of the fireplace rolled up and standing in the corner. Streamers dangled from the corners of the room.

Blaze stabbed a thumb in Matthew's direction. "His idea."

End tables, leather recliner, and floor lamp, all huddled by the staircase.

"What's the deal?"

Matthew stuck his hands in his back pockets. "Well, see, I had this idea."

"To make over my living space?"

"To teach you to dance. And, um, give you the prom you never had."

Oh. "Matthew, you don't have to—"

"I might have overheard you telling Izzy you're worried about the dancing at the gala. Izzy begged Jase to take dancing lessons before their wedding, and Jase coerced me into going along." He swung both hands up and down in front of him. "So what you see before you is an expert dancer."

No, she saw the reporter who could topple the very thing she was desperate to save if he spilled her secrets to his drooling editor. And he wanted to dance?

"Just so you know, muffin, I could totally pop-n-lock like a blinged-out rapper if my arm didn't weigh ten pounds in this cast," Blaze said, dropping onto the out-of-place recliner. Now that Matthew knew the truth about them, they were able to drop the "couple" act at home.

"I appreciate this. I do. But . . ." She looked from Blaze to Matthew. "Don't we need to talk?" Even with all the time they'd spent together yesterday, her revelation still hung between them.

"Believe it or not, it's possible to dance and talk at the same time. Now shrug out of your jacket." He walked to the iPod dock on her fireplace mantel. "What's your preference? Old Blue Eyes or Bing Crosby?"

A tinge of enthusiasm tickled through her. "Who's the easiest to dance to?"

"Either's great, but for starters, we'll go with Bing. The first step I'm going to teach you is the box step, because you'll use it in all kinds of ballroom dances: waltz, rumba, foxtrot, quickstep. We'll start with the waltz."

"Lame," Blaze said as he pulled the lever for the recliner. He leaned back, amusement dripping from his voice.

"Should I make him leave?" Matthew asked Miranda, taking a step closer to her.

"No. He's forgetting I know where he sleeps. Behave, Blaze. Matthew's trying to help me."

He crossed his arms behind his head. "Relaxing. Zipping my lips. Minding my own business."

"That's better. So, what do we do, Matthew? Aren't you going to start the music?"

"Uh-uh, I was just getting it ready for later. You learn the box step, then we add music. So . . ." Discomfort flickered through his eyes but disappeared before it had a chance to spread. "I'll place my right hand on your waist." He did. "You put your left hand here." He pointed to his right shoulder. "And with your right hand . . ." His fingers closed around hers.

He smelled like soap and fabric softener. Stubble shadowed his cheeks and jaw. And did his eyes ever stop shifting colors?

Close quarters.

Why? Why was he doing this for her?

"Now, on the first beat, I'll step forward with my left foot. You step back with your right."

He stepped forward. She didn't step back. And her chin bumped against his shoulder as a nervous giggle pushed past her lips. "Sorry." Warmth flashed up her neck.

"It's okay. Let's try again."

This time she remembered to shift her foot back. Then followed as Matthew taught her the rest of the moves. She caught on quickly after the first couple attempts.

"See, nothing to it, Miranda."

"Maybe there's hope for me. Though, that was only one step."

Matthew clicked on the iPod. "Never you worry. I'll turn you into Grace Kelly yet."

"You mean you're going to dye my hair blond and send me off to marry the prince of Monaco?"

He took his place in front of her, hand settling on her waist, and rolled his eyes. "I mean, you'll feel graceful."

Bing Crosby's crooning floated through the room.

"Now, just follow me."

Did he notice the callouses toughening the skin of her palms? Or the freckles Whitney always attempted to hide under a layer or five of makeup?

"You're doing well."

"I bet you say that to all the girls you teach to dance."

"Only the ones wearing work boots," Blaze called.

"Can it, Casty," she shot back.

"Now, that wasn't very graceful." The recliner creaked as he leaned back.

"Ignore him," Matthew said. "Just focus on me."

But, see, that's what got her into trouble. For days, she'd focused on Matthew—started to like the way he tagged along, drew her out, made her feel important by taking notes when she talked. She'd forgotten *why* he took the notes. His assignment.

"I follow through on my assignments. You're my assignment."

At the memory of his bitter words, she stumbled, dropped her hand from his shoulder.

"Something wrong?"

She met his eyes. "We're pretending."

His glance darted to the side, to Blaze now fiddling one-handed with the iPod dock remote. "I . . . I know. You already told me."

"I mean us, you and me. I dropped a bombshell on you, and there's this crater of emotion underfoot and we're still tiptoeing around it. I appreciate this lesson. But please tell me what you're going to do."

At some point during her pleas, he'd released her waist.

Blaze, oblivious to the conversation, rose. "Stupid arm is itching again. I need something to do. Who's hungry? I'm cooking. One armed, that is. This'll be fun."

He left the room without waiting for an answer. Matthew kept his eyes on her face.

"Whatever you think of me, I understand. I do," she said. "I don't think a whole lot of myself these days."

Matthew stepped an inch closer. Why didn't he say something?

"I'm not going to beg you to keep my secret anymore. You're a reporter, and you've got a job to do. But if you could just let me know—"

Suddenly he lifted his hands to her cheeks, and before she knew what was happening, he lowered his head, cut her off just like that, and kissed her—kissed her as if she hadn't made a royal fool of herself, as if he hadn't seen her ugliest side. And just as she warmed to the idea—closed her eyes, leaned into him—he broke away.

"What," she gasped, breathy, flustered, "was that?"

He'd dropped his hands but still stood only a breath away. "I . . . I . . . don't . . ."

Oh, for crying out loud. She threw herself at him, arms around his neck, and kissed him just as she'd ached for the day of their hike. Before everything went so wrong. She felt his hands on her back, tucking her into an embrace full of promise and warmth and . . .

The doorbell rang, and they sprang apart. She lifted her eyes to meet his. *What now?*

"Fireworks," he said.

She pulled together a half grin as the doorbell sounded again. "What? That kiss or the way we popped apart?"

"Both, I think." His cheeks were so red they could have planted him on a street corner with the word *STOP* painted in white.

What was that? He'd kissed her. And then she'd kissed him. And . . .

"Who's at the door?" Blaze called, coming in from the kitchen.

Legs good and wobbly, Miranda made it to the front door, flung it open.

And her world tilted once more.

"Randi."

Just like always, in just one word, he completely undid her.

"Robbie?"

Chapter 14

Robbie was standing in her kitchen.

Robbie was standing in her kitchen pouring muddy black coffee into her favorite mug.

Uncertainty and confusion hardened through her like plaster, leaving Miranda an unmoving statue in the doorway. Robbie lowered the mug before drinking, eyes traveling the length of her, pausing on her fuzzy slippers. He smiled.

"That's my cup." She should've made him leave an hour ago. Should've closed the door in his face.

Robbie blinked. "Oh, sorry." Pause. "Here, I've not taken a drink yet." He offered the mug like a peace offering as he spoke with that familiar hint of accent in his voice. Robbie had dual citizenship. He'd spent most of his school years living with his father in South America, summers in the U.S. with his mother. With all the back and forth, he'd acquired the vocal flavor of a world traveler.

He shouldn't be here. Not now, not after all this time.

She'd hoped to emerge from her bathroom to find the evening's events only a dream. Well, not *all* of them. The moment in the living room with Matthew, his kiss, *her* kiss. The feeling of his arms around her. Didn't want to forget that.

Should. But didn't.

Then Robbie had shown up. Knocked the wind out of her and replaced it with tension, thick and heady.

"I am sorry to show up so suddenly," he'd said, moonlight framing his form in her doorway. "I've always been spontaneous. You remember, yes?"

"I remember a lot."

The music from Matthew's iPod had faded as the song ended, only silence draped in awkward strain filling in. Finally Robbie spoke again, "I was in the area. I thought it might be nice to visit you. I . . . missed you."

Words, reason, common sense, they'd all fled together. And she had followed suit, whirling on her heels, climbing the staircase as if it led to a safe haven where her past couldn't intrude. She'd heard a knock minutes later, Matthew's soft voice at her door.

"You all right, Miranda? Do you want Blaze and me to send him away?"

She'd creaked open the door. "No, I guess not. But I'm tired and I smell like paint. I'm going to shower. Tell him I'll be down in a while."

Matthew had nodded slowly, as if he wanted to argue, but hesitated.

"And . . . you and Blaze . . . maybe you could grab supper in Pine Cove while Robbie and I . . . talk."

The unmistakable hurt in his eyes at that last part had been palpable. "Are you sure . . . ?" he began but left the question dangling, finally nodding and turning.

Now here she stood, against her better judgment, wearing comfortable purple fleece pants and a white cotton shirt. Too comfortable. If only she'd pulled on her work pants and boots, she might feel a little more in control. *Tool belt, too. A hammer might come in handy.*

Oh, why had she suggested Matthew and Blaze leave?

Robbie studied her through cocoa-bean eyes from his spot beside the kitchen sink. Hands hidden in his pockets, one leg crossed over the other. He didn't move, as if wary that she might spring into attack.

She lifted the mug he'd handed her, gulped the coffee like water. The liquid scalded her throat on the way down, and she sputtered. *Hot. Too much. Choking.* Tears sprang to her eyes.

"Randi, you all right?" Robbie unfroze, moving to her side, patting her back.

One more cough and she could breathe again. Only instead of coffee, now Robbie's palm burned her back. She jumped, the remainder of her coffee splashing over the edge of her mug. And those tears, why couldn't they leave her alone?

Desperation formed words. "Wh-what are you doing here?" The question came out a feathery whisper. *No.* No, she wouldn't play the stuttering weakling.

"You're strong, unbreakable." Robbie's own words, once jarring and grim in the letter he'd left her, filled her now with a resolute energy. He'd wounded her enough. "Talk."

He raked a hand through his wavy hair and opened his mouth. Closed it. Opened. "I rehearsed this. Lot of good that did."

Miranda's hands found their way to her waist. She wasn't about to make this easy for him. "Maybe I can help you start. Where have you been the past three years?"

He leaned against the sink. "I went back to Brazil, at first. Spent time with my family. Then I went to work with a contractor friend of my father's. Now I live in California."

She used to imagine this conversation, grilling him about his life since leaving her. She would picture the emptiness in his eyes, the loneliness, the regret. And she'd always wavered in imagining her reaction. Would she comfort herself with his misery or let herself be swept away by a tide of sympathy?

Turned out it was neither.

All she felt was an incredible emptiness. And cold, inside and out. She balled her fists up into the sleeves of her shirt.

"Do you have to look at me like that?" he finally said.

"Like what?" She cocked her head.

"Like I just sawed off your right arm." Something close to challenge brimmed in his eyes.

"You left without a word." She paused between each syllable, tone heavy with accusation.

"I left a note."

"Are you kidding me?" Her voice rose decibels. "Well then, that makes everything a-okay. Thanks so much for that heartfelt notice that our time together had come to an end."

He looked away, lips pressed, then found her eyes again. "So, we are going to do this now?"

"Well, what else did you come here for, Robbie?"

The corners of his mouth lifted, but his eyes remained hard. "It's been a long time since anyone called me Robbie."

"*Roberto*, I moved on. I'm not above admitting you broke my heart, but I moved on. I don't know why you had to come here. I'm in a better place. If you take this from me, too, I don't know what I'll do."

"Too? I did not take anything you didn't willingly give. Do not put that on me, Miranda."

He has no idea. Had he ever watched her show? Did he know how she'd gushed about him in those early episodes? And did he have any clue what she'd suspected in those last days before he left? Had he even noticed her giddiness?

The words gummed up in her throat, sticky and scorching. In slow motion, she lowered to a chair at the kitchen table. "I just don't understand why you had to come here. I mean, you stayed away for three years and—" She stopped when she saw him shaking his head. "What?"

"I did not stay away for three years."

Surprise silenced her. What did he mean by that? He'd been back?

"I returned six months after I left," he said, head lowered. "I felt horrible. I wanted to apologize. To see if . . ." He looked up. "To see if we might still have a chance."

No, that couldn't be true. If he'd returned, why didn't he see her? Why hadn't he sought her out? Oh, Lord, what if he had? Would she have . . . would they have . . . ? And all of this with Blaze, the show, none of it would be a problem now.

And Matthew? "I don't understand."

"I found your journal. You were not home. I still had a key to the cabin. Inside, I found a box, and the journal was there. I read it, and I knew there was no place for me here anymore. At least I thought so."

Realization descended. *Oh, God, help me.* He *did* know. He knew about . . .

Now his words came out in a flood, rushing over her, drowning her in the kind of hurt she couldn't outswim. "You must understand, you asked me to sleep at the house instead of with you in the cabin. You became secretive. You were always at work. I thought . . . you were pulling away from me. I had no idea you thought you were . . ."

He paused before the next part, and the pain of knowing what was coming sliced through her. "Pregnant."

At the word, she sprang from her chair, tears damming again behind her eyes. She shook her head. "No, no, I don't want to talk about this."

"We have to."

"We don't. There's nothing to talk about anyway. If you read my journal, then you know. I wasn't pregnant. It was a mistake. End of story. And you can't just show up on my doorstep demanding answers when you disappeared the way you did. Just . . . go. Please."

"My father died," he blurted.

Her emotions stilled, her heart quieted. Despite the mix of anger and despair swishing inside her, she allowed herself to look at him, really see him. The circles under his eyes. The pounds missing from his frame since she'd seen him last. The regret pulling at his every feature.

He'd been amazingly close to his father, in a way Miranda had admired. Even coveted, at times.

"I'm sorry, Robbie," she whispered.

"I only wanted to be around someone who would understand. I was not able to get back to Brazil before he died. After the funeral . . . I could not stay."

Another man she might have embraced, might have spoken words of comfort or faith. But how was she supposed to respond to the man who'd broken her heart?

"One day, Miranda. That is all I ask. Let me spend one day with you remembering the good times."

No. No, don't let him in. Someone else can comfort him.

"Okay. You can sleep on the couch."

Why? Why are you doing this?

Perhaps because she understood loneliness was a lethal addition to hurt. She remembered far too well the morning she'd awoken to realize there was no pregnancy. And there was no man at her side to share her disappointment.

Sunshine filled his eyes despite the darkness blackening the kitchen window. "I'll get my things from my car."

When he turned, she closed her eyes. But his voice returned. "Oh, I should tell you—I know you're not married to that man."

Her eyes shot open. "What . . . h-how?"

His eyes went straight to her hand. The ring. *His* ring.

And as Robbie walked away from her a second time, it wasn't hurt or pain or even anxiety cutting through her.

It was fear.

❦

Sunlight fell into the cabin bedroom like a waterfall, hitting Matthew's eyes and cajoling him awake. He yawned and stretched, flopping his arms out, only to have his right arm flung back at him. His palm landed on his chest, and a grunt sounded beside him. He jumped, the bedsprings whining. "What the—"

"Lord have mercy, dude, you toss way too much in your sleep."

As Matthew's heartbeat calmed, Blaze's sleepy voice from the other side of the bed carried in the memory of last night. Miranda's ex-fiancé showing up. The hours he and Blaze waited at the roadside café in Pine Cove, trying to stay out of the way. Finally, their return to see that Prius still sitting in the driveway.

They'd padded up the porch, knocked lightly. Miranda had creaked open the door. "Hey, guys." Telltale puffiness rimmed her eyes, but she offered a smile.

"He's still here?" Matthew asked.

She'd motioned behind her to the man's sleeping form on the couch. "He asked for a day. Can you sleep in the cabin, Blaze?"

A day? What did that mean? A day to do what?

"And, um, I told him the whole story about Blaze."

"You what?"

She was shaking her head, already beginning to close the door. "He'd already figured it out. He . . . knows me. A day—that's all he wants."

A cold wind had played haunting music through the trees as Matthew and Blaze walked the path to the cabin after leaving the house. The translucent white of a harvest moon illustrated the otherwise blank canvas of dusk's sky. The Midwest would probably always be home in his heart, but it wouldn't be hard for these mountains to take up residence right alongside Minnesota. They pulled a person in, wrapped him up in a quilt of beauty and wonder.

Why, then, had that walk from the house to the cabin felt like a funeral procession?

Because he'd allowed himself to think he might have a place here, that's why. By shielding Miranda's secret, teaching her to dance, he'd thought he was winning a place in her life.

Only to be usurped by the man she hadn't been able to let go of in three years.

"Miranda's couch is definitely better than sharing a bed with you," Blaze now said drowsily. "If that Robbie guy is sticking around, one of us has to find somewhere else to stay."

"If he stays, I'll be happy to." What was Miranda thinking, opening her home to him?

Matthew stepped onto the chilled wood floor, still wearing his jeans from the night before. He glanced out the window, spotted the Prius still mocking him from the driveway. But Miranda's truck was gone. "I'm going to run over to the house for coffee. I'm out."

Blaze mumbled an okay and rolled onto his side.

Frost still whited the lawn, glistening against unfiltered sunlight. At the house, Matthew found a note taped to the door.

Robbie and I are going to Audrey's house. Be back later. —M

Impossible to read between the lines. Or maybe there wasn't anything to read. She was spending the day with the man. Okay. Not okay. It gutted him. Had last night's kiss meant anything?

Apparently not.

Matthew forgot about the coffee, skulked back to the cabin, and grabbed his messenger bag. "Blaze, I'm going to Asheville."

Blaze's mumbled reply followed Matthew out of the cabin. He slammed the door of his Jeep.

"Someone actually lives here?"

Robbie's voice was incredulous from the passenger seat, and Miranda couldn't blame him. Audrey's home looked more dilapidated than ever. Clothing, apparently hung out to dry, draped over the porch railing she and Matthew had repaired the last time they were there. A white frost glistened over the clothing, the lawn. And that pile of lumber Miranda had dropped by weeks ago, meant for roof repair, was still on the lawn, covered with tarp.

Robbie trailed behind her as she made her way up the porch, knocked on the door. Robbie. She still had trouble believing he'd slept on her couch last night, not Blaze—he'd shared a cup of coffee with her this morning, then accompanied her to the shack, not Matthew.

She still couldn't process his nonchalant reaction to her explanation about Blaze. "You did what you thought you had to in order to save the show. If I hadn't left you, you never would've had to."

At least he acknowledged that. But she'd started wondering more and more these past few weeks if both she and Robbie were wrong—she hadn't *had* to keep up the ruse. Oh, she'd told herself it was her only option. But truth had always been an option. She just didn't want to face it.

"Nobody should live in a dump like this," Robbie muttered as Miranda knocked again. "Remember all the houses we built in Brazil?"

As if she could erase those years from her memory.

Don't let him too far in.

She'd repeated the reminder over and over already this morning. *Just one day. Because he's hurting.*

"I remember." Her voice blended with the cries of Audrey's baby from inside the house. Why didn't Audrey answer the door?

She knocked a third time. When there was still no answer, she reached for the doorknob. Audrey's baby was crying like something was seriously wrong. And if the woman wasn't answering the door . . .

The knob gave, and she pushed, creaking open the door. Immediately, a sour smell wafted from the house. Miranda wrinkled her nose but stepped forward. "Hello?"

More clothing hung in the living room—over a lampshade, on the back of the dilapidated sofa. The baby's cries continued.

"Perhaps the baby's mother isn't home," Robbie offered.

Anger sliced through Miranda at the thought, and she marched down the hallway toward the sound of Lola's cries. "Look for Audrey," she said over her shoulder.

"Where do I look?" Robbie called after her. "This place is not big enough to hide."

Miranda hurried into the nursery, Lola's screams piercing her ears. "It's okay, it's okay," she said gently. She reached for the infant, lifted her from the crib, gasped. Heat radiated from her skin. "Oh, honey, you're sick."

The baby's cries became coughs. Miranda closed her eyes as she held her against her chest, palm cradling Lola's head, her hair sticky and wet.

Robbie walked in. "There is no one else here." He stopped. "That cough sounds bad."

"It is bad. I can feel the croup in her chest through her back. I don't know what to do." And she was so very hot. Miranda swayed, whispering, worrying as Lola continued to cough and cry. What should she do?

And why was Robbie staring at her like that? Feet rooted in place. Eyes glazed and lips pressed tight. "We could've had this," he whispered.

Yes.

No!

She blinked, swallowed a lump in her throat, and then swallowed again. "I'm going to help you, Lola. I don't know how, but . . ."

The smack of the front door sounded through the house. Next thing Miranda knew Audrey was in the nursery, stringy hair framing her pale cheeks, purple circles sagging under her eyes. She stared wordlessly.

"Where have you been?" Miranda blurted the words, then clamped her mouth shut. No need to scare the girl. "Lola's very sick. Why did you leave her alone?"

"She kept crying," Audrey murmured listlessly. "Crying and coughing and crying. I couldn't . . . I needed to . . . I just went on a walk." She blinked, seemed to snap to life at the sight of Robbie watching from the corner of the room. "Who is that?"

Miranda ignored the question. "Audrey, have you taken Lola's temperature? She's burning up."

"No."

"Do you have a family doctor? I think we need to call someone."

Audrey only shrugged. Miranda's worry unfolded into an all-out dread. "Take Lola. I'm going to make a call."

"Can't you hold her a little longer? I'm awfully tired."

She could've yelled. Maybe did. Who would know with Lola's pitiful cries filling the room? With one hand balancing the baby, Miranda whipped her phone from her pocket with the other. She jabbed the number she'd entered into her contacts the other day and propped the phone between her ear and shoulder.

"Why are you here?" Audrey asked again. "Is it about Jimmy?"

She shook her head as the phone rang in her ear. *Come on, pick up!* "No. When was the last time you saw him?"

Audrey shrugged limply. "A few weeks ago."

"You mean he hasn't been here since—"

"Hey, Miranda!" A perky voice interrupted her.

Thank God. "Izzy, I need help."

❦

"Matthew, what are you doing here?"

Liv's pumps clacked against the wood floor of Open Arms' entryway. Matthew fiddled with the canvas strap of the messenger bag slung over his arm. Maybe he should've called Miranda's friend before showing up at her place of employment.

Liv halted in front of him, her pink wrap dress so unlike anything Miranda would wear. How had the two become friends, anyway?

"Sorry to show up without calling or anything," Matthew said. He held out his hand.

"You seriously want me to shake your hand? Isn't that a little formal?" But Liv grasped his palm anyway and gave a hearty shake.

"Sorry. Habit of the trade, I guess."

"The trade. So you came for, what, an interview?"

Matthew shook his head, irritation at his own lack of poise prickling him. These past few days had thrown him so far off his groove, it was like he walked through a house of mirrors.

Why am I even here?

"No, not an interview exactly," he answered Liv. The piney scent of evergreen and fir filled the open entryway. "Hey, why does it smell like a Christmas tree farm in here?"

"All the kids have daily chores. Today's was polishing all the woodwork in the house. They may have used enough Old English to fuel a car. So, what can I do for you?"

She could start by explaining her best friend. What made a woman welcome a man who'd broken her heart back into her life?

He flipped open his bag and pulled out a set of DVDs.

"The other day when we were here, you mentioned what a hard time a couple of the newer counselors have had picking up ASL. Some of the kids, too. When my brother married my sister-in-law and brought Celine home, he needed to learn. I wanted to, as well. So we found this DVD set online. Total miracle worker. I was in Minneapolis over the weekend, so I picked it up." He held out the plastic case.

"Oh, Matthew, this is great. I knew there had to be something out there to help us. Truly, thanks so much." She paused, one toe tapping against the floor. Then, "But did you really drive all the way out here just to deliver this? Not that I'm not grateful. Seriously, it was so thoughtful of you. But I fancy myself a good people-reader and—"

The chimes of a child's laughter sounded overhead, followed by the patter of footsteps running down the hall.

"I should let you get back to work." Matthew closed his bag. It was silly to come here. Liv wouldn't spill on her bestie.

"Nice try, Knox, but I'm not going to let you go all Artful Dodger on me. Come on back to my office." She was already heading toward the French doors leading into what Miranda had told him used to be a parlor. It had been remodeled into a grouping of offices years ago.

He shrugged and followed Liv into a closet of an office, lavender-colored walls brightening the small space. Behind Liv's desk, a kaleidoscope of kids' drawings crowded a hanging bulletin board. A lit candle on her desk replaced the smell of furniture polish with vanilla.

Liv reached into a miniature fridge and pulled out a Diet Coke. "Want some?"

"Sure, thanks." His stomach reminded him he'd skipped breakfast. A Coke would do for now.

Liv dropped into her swivel chair. "You obviously came to talk about Rand. So talk."

He lowered onto the chair across from her. Only he over-estimated its height, his backside bumping onto the seat when his knees buckled. An "Oomph" escaped from his lips as he landed.

Liv lifted a fist to her mouth to cover her giggle. "Sorry, I've usually got kids in here. There's a lever under the chair to raise it."

"As if I didn't feel like enough of an idiot."

"I don't allow the kids to use the word *idiot*. Now, like I said, talk."

"You're bossy."

"And you're upset. So spill."

Why did he feel like a patient in a psychiatrist's office? Miranda *had* said Liv liked to fix people's problems. "You know I know she's not married to Blaze, right?"

"Yeah, I was in the car when she told Blaze on the way back from the hospital."

"Right." He popped the tab on his soda. "Her fiancé came back."

Liv's hand knocked into her pop can and it fizzed over onto her desk. She grabbed a couple Kleenexes and wiped up the spill. "Sorry. That surprised me."

"Surprised all of us. He just showed up out of the blue last night."

"Robbie. You should've brought him here. I'd love to kick the guy in the teeth."

Somehow he had trouble picturing the blonde in the pink

dress so much as sticking her tongue out. "Yeah, well, that wasn't Miranda's response. He spent the night and now they're off working together for the day."

Concern etched into Liv's face, pulling her lips into a frown. "I don't like that."

"Me neither. I don't get why she'd allow him back. What kind of hold does he have over her?"

Liv lifted her pop can to take a drink, then slowly lowered it onto the desk. "I didn't know Rand before he left. But we've talked about it since then. It's usually me coercing her into it. Getting her to talk is like pulling teeth, yeah?"

Actually, that hadn't really been Matthew's experience. How many evenings had they spent out on the porch or in her workshop, chatting to the tune of sandpaper against wood?

"Miranda fell for that man oh-so-hard in Brazil. If you ask me, she was still hurting from the loss of her grandparents *and* the fact that her parents were so distant. Robbie became a lifeline. And when he left . . ."

Liv didn't need to finish. Matthew had seen all the evidence already of Miranda's pain. "So why let him back into her life now?"

Liv shook her head. "I don't know. Maybe she needs closure. Maybe there are things she needs to say to him. Like . . ." She paused, uncertainty hovering in her unspoken words.

"Go on," he urged. "I want to understand. Not as a reporter. As her friend." As the man who'd kissed her last night. Who ached to make things better for her.

"She thought she was pregnant when Robbie left. Found out a few weeks later it was just a false alarm."

Surprise whooshed through Matthew. That and . . . hurt. Hurt at the reminder of the way Miranda had given herself to the man. And hurt for her—how she'd faced not only rejection but certainly confusion, as well.

"Look, Matthew, Miranda needs someone like you on her side. Someone who sees and values her strengths, but who can also handle her weaknesses. She needs someone who will allow her to stand on her own two feet at the same time as he cares for her, provides for her, gives her someone to lean on. Don't give up on her."

He leaned forward, his untasted can of pop encased in both hands. "What are you saying?"

"I'm saying, don't abandon her now." Liv smiled. "She likes you more than she's liked any man for a loooong time. Believe me. Robbie coming back? It's just a blip. I'm sure of it."

A seed of determination bloomed into the full thing. He stood, knowing what he needed to do, to say.

Chapter 15

"This reminds me of old times, Rand."

Miranda found her footing on the roof of Audrey and Jimmy's shack, the sound of Robbie's voice carrying on a wind that threatened autumn's coldest day yet. It whipped her ponytail, sending her hair into her face. Maybe this hadn't been the best day to replace Audrey's roof.

But she and Lola couldn't live in the house through the winter without it. And considering how long he had been gone, it was unlikely Jimmy would be returning.

At least little Lola's fever had broken. Thanks to Izzy's calm instructions over the phone, Miranda had been able to coax down the fever with crushed-up Tylenol and a cold cloth to the baby's forehead. She'd also called the pastor's wife, Joni, remembering the woman said she used to be a nurse. Joni had stopped by a few hours ago, examined Lola and listened to her lungs. "I think she'll be just fine. I brought some cough medicine and Vicks VapoRub."

Audrey, finally, had taken over caring for her baby.

"Rand?"

She looked up. Robbie had moved to her side. The knees of his jeans were black from climbing around on the roof, prying off weather-beaten shingles.

"Old times, yes?" he asked again. "Although, in Brazil we usually used clay roof tiles."

His voice still had that honey texture she'd fallen for years ago. And he'd obviously taken care of himself since she'd seen him last. She hadn't missed the bulge of muscles in his arms and back as he yanked out nails and row after row of shingles.

Is that all it had been back then? Physical attraction?

"Yes, I guess it does remind me of old times."

"Remember the time we were working on top of a house and a thunderstorm pelted us?" Under his arm, he held a stack of shingles, ready to be laid. They'd already installed a waterproof edging and asphalt-felt underlayment. With such a small house, the project was going quickly.

"I remember," she said. "I was so worried about getting hit by lightning."

His laughter boomed, like a Santa, which, considering their location, brought a smile to her face. And it must have encouraged Robbie, because he took a step closer. "I like working with you again. We make a good team."

"Robbie."

"I wish . . ."

What? That he hadn't run out on her? Would they still be working together today?

It must have been more than physical. We were a good team. In fact, they'd earned a reputation as the dynamic duo at Hope Builders. Well, until a new reputation forced them out.

Maybe it was the thrill of rebelling.

But she *had* loved him. It may have been an immature, reckless love. Still, it was love.

And the way he was looking at her now, it was like he wished he could bring that love back into existence. Just a few weeks ago, so had she.

A lot had changed in a few weeks.

Which probably meant she shouldn't be so trusting of her feelings, not if they could reshape so quickly. She reached down for a bundle of shingles. "We should finish. Poor Blaze is probably growing bored back at the house."

Robbie lowered to his knees, lined up the first shingle along the vertical chalk line they'd snapped along the center of the roof. She laid a shingle on the opposite side of the chalk line.

Silence drifted on the breeze until Robbie spoke again. "Could you tell me about the days before I left? When you thought . . ." He let the question linger.

Miranda sighed, wanting only to finish this job and escape home. But he'd helped all day. Kept his distance. Maybe . . . maybe there would be healing in the telling. "There was about a week where I threw up every morning. At first I thought I was just sick, but then I started counting the weeks since, well, you know. I just assumed." And guilt had clawed its way through her. *Pregnant out of wedlock.*

The terminology might be from a different generation, but morals didn't have an expiration date. She and Robbie, they'd done things backward.

She spilled her suspicions to Brad first. Instead of criticizing her, he'd reminded her about grace and forgiveness and all the things she'd figured were out of reach since she started wandering from the proverbial narrow path.

She'd clung to his words. Decided they'd make things right. They'd move up the wedding date. Find a church. Start living the moral lifestyle their baby—their *child*—would need.

"Remember the day I came home from work and asked if you'd want to move into the house early?"

He nodded, folding his arms. "I couldn't understand why you suddenly wanted to live separately."

"Robbie, a hundred feet away from each other is hardly separate. But I thought we had a baby on the way, and I was trying to do the right thing. Sleeping in different bedrooms seemed like a good start."

"Why didn't you just tell me you thought you were pregnant?"

Her knees strained at her crouched position, and she lowered to sit, fingers still closed around her hammer. "I was working up to it. But you got so angry when I asked about changing our sleeping arrangements. And I knew you were frustrated about your job search."

She stilled in front of him. "But then Lincoln pitched this idea of you appearing on the season finale. I'd talked you up, you know, and you'd become this legend of sorts. So that night I had a plan. I was going to tell you about the show and the baby all at once, make it really special. But when I came home . . ."

He closed his eyes. "I was not there."

She nodded her head, expecting the same old blend of sorrow and anger to crackle through her like the empty branches *rap-a-tap*ping in the wind.

Instead, all she felt was . . . sympathy? In all the times she'd imagined this conversation, kindness had never been a part of her response.

"Randi, I—"

The sound of a vehicle crunching over gravel cut off Robbie's next words. Miranda peered over the edge of the roof. Matthew's Jeep came into sight. Was Blaze in the passenger seat?

"That's the reporter, Matthew," she said. "Mind if I go down and talk to him?" Why was she asking permission?

And why the pattering of her heart at the sight of Matthew behind the wheel? Fine, she knew why. Underneath the emotions simmering from the strange string of events in the past twenty-four hours lay the reminder of their kiss.

She descended the ladder on wobbly legs.

When Matthew cut the engine, the sound of Robbie pounding

nails filled the gap. Matthew stepped out. She squinted to study the face of the passenger through the windshield. Jimmy?

Surprise and joy blended together to raise the pitch of her voice. "No way!" And before she could stop herself, she launched into his arms for a hug. "Audrey will be so excited! How . . . where . . . ?"

Matthew grinned. "Sitting in a truck stop halfway between here and Asheville. Drowning himself in a root beer, of all things. I recognized him from the photo in Audrey's living room. I think it scared him half to death when I came up to him."

Over Matthew's shoulder, she could see Jimmy's slumped posture, his straw hair poking over his ears. He looked like a kid sitting there. Barely old enough to catch a girl's eye, let alone be a father.

"I'm tempted to give him a lecture he won't soon forget," she said, but Matthew's hand on her arm stopped her. The sound of pounding nails paused.

"Miranda, we talked. And I think . . . he's going to be okay."

Matthew had brought the wandering prodigal home. Matthew, who'd been so skeptical about the whole situation. Did the look on her face express the admiration dancing inside her? "You talked to him. Mr. He'll-never-come-back, she's-better-off-without-him?"

"He was off looking for work, felt too ashamed to come back when he couldn't find anything." Matthew's hazel eyes brimmed with something she couldn't quite identify. But they pulled her in, magnetic, mesmerizing. "I told him about my own dad, actually. I told him the real shame would be if Lola ended up without her dad around."

Jimmy stepped out of the Jeep, and Miranda heard Audrey's squeals from the porch.

The crack of Robbie's hammer hitting metal pierced the sky once more.

"He's still here," Matthew said.

Miranda only nodded.

She and Robbie finished the roofing job within an hour after Matthew's arrival, while Matthew made phone calls and packed up their tools as darkness fell.

Matthew insisted on leaving his rental Jeep with Jimmy and Audrey. "Just in case Lola gets sick again in the night. They need a way to get into town." Since Jimmy's Chevy had broken down a week ago, and Miranda's truck wasn't always reliable, he insisted it was the best option.

Miranda guided her truck around the ridge she knew by heart. Robbie's heavy breathing sounded from the back seat. The man was plain exhausted. Considering he'd traveled to Brazil and back in the past week for his father's funeral, and then to North Carolina, she supposed she didn't blame him.

But he was supposed to leave tonight and didn't seem to be working toward that.

"So how long is he sticking around?" Matthew asked softly.

Her truck sputtered along the road as she considered Matthew's question. She glanced in the rearview mirror. Sometime during the day, Robbie had rolled up a handkerchief and tied it around his forehead the way he used to do in Brazil. Only now a mop of black hair escaped and flopped over one eye. His cheek pressed against the window.

"I really don't know."

But before she could elaborate, her truck made a choking sound. The engine rumbled as the frame shook. Robbie stirred in the back seat.

"That doesn't sound good," Matthew said.

"Brilliant deduction, Watson." She eased up on the accelerator, but the groaning of the truck continued. Finally, when steam rose from the hood, she pulled to the side of the road, braked and parked. "Great. Just . . . great."

"What's wrong?" Robbie murmured, eyes still closed.

"I don't know, but I'm going to check it out."

She plodded to the front of the truck and flipped up the hood. Steam, hot and hazy, hit her face. She surveyed the engine, but who was she kidding? She could build a house, but the innards of a truck were foreign territory.

Matthew's footsteps sounded along the gravel shoulder. His head ducked under the hood next to her. "Hmm, looks like your carburetor wires are crossed with the engine gauges and the fuel pump is—"

"You have no clue what you're talking about." She met his eyes, mirrored his grin.

"Guilty as charged. I don't know what a carburetor looks like. Couldn't even spell it."

She clucked her tongue. "And you call yourself a writer."

He slammed the hood while she pulled out her phone and called Blaze. A couple minutes later, she rounded the truck to the sound of Robbie's continued snores and found Matthew pulling a blanket from her back seat. "Blaze promised he can drive one-armed. He'll probably be here in fifteen, twenty minutes."

Matthew held up the blanket. "And I've got a plan for the meantime. Come on."

She followed him to the back of the truck. He lowered the tailgate and hoisted himself up. "M'lady?" he said, offering his hand.

"What are we doing?"

He pulled her up, then spread the blanket on the truck bed. "Stargazing. Look up. It's like a circus of stars up there."

He was right. They dotted the sky in clusters, no clouds to dim their sparkle. She sat on the blanket, the chill of the metal truck bed reaching through, and pulled her thin fleece jacket tight.

"Too cold?" Matthew asked. "Here." He began to pull off his black coat.

"No, no. Then you'll be cold. Keep it on."

He placed his coat around her shoulders. "Yes, but I'll feel like a gentleman."

"A cold gentleman."

"I'm warm-blooded."

"You're . . . kind. Thanks."

He lay on his back, arm pointing to the sky. "Look, there's the Big Dipper."

Sitting cross-legged beside him, she followed his gaze. "And the Little."

"And I think that might be Orion. He's the bear, right? Or, wait, no, the hunter with the bow? If you put the Big Dipper and something else together, doesn't that make something else?"

She giggled. "I have a feeling you know your constellations about as well as the inside of a truck engine."

"Yes, but what I don't know, I make up for in charm, don't you think?"

Well, he was the only man who ever had her sitting on a truck bed under the stars. On either side of the road, the mountains rose up like sentries, guarding their privacy. Their tree-lined crags made for dancing soldiers as a mountain wind created the night's music.

Charming, yes. Maybe even romantic.

Except for the man sleeping in the back seat of the truck.

Neck tightening, she moved to lie on her back, knees pointed to the sky.

"Um, if Robbie wakes up . . ." Matthew prompted.

"Believe me, he won't. Once he starts snoring, he's out."

She could feel the prickle of tension her telling words produced. But eventually, the quiet smoothed over the awkwardness.

"Hey, Miranda?"

"Yeah?" She practically purred, relaxation kneading her muscles for the first time in days.

"Why did you let him stay?"

She groaned. "This feels so perfect. Do we have to ruin it by talking about that?" Silence expanded until she gave in. "He's always been able to convince me to do just about anything. I don't know why. I fancy myself this strong girl, you know. The tomboy who can take care of herself. But Robbie . . ." She turned her eyes back to the star-speckled sky. "He wrecks my common sense, always has. Look at me, I've still got his ring all these years later. Even if I am pretending it came from my stand-in spouse."

Matthew's fingers closed around her wrist, his touch tingling through her. He lifted her hand up. "I didn't realize that was really Robbie's ring."

"He did. That's how he knew I wasn't really married to Blaze." The diamond twinkled against the backdrop of the sky. "I should've gotten rid of it years ago."

"Why didn't you?" He lowered her hand, but kept his fingers intertwined with hers.

"At first, because I kept hoping he'd come back. And then, I suppose, because I was never quite ready to move on."

The quiet wrapped around them, comforting, the only sound a distant purr of a vehicle. Could she just stay here—guarded from pressure or worry, quilt beneath her, blanket of stars above?

And Matthew.

"You know Friday when I left you at the hospital?"

"When you stalked away ready to blow your cork, you mean?" She tipped her head with a half smile.

"When I needed some time to digest your news, I mean. I drove to Knoxville."

Her smile turned full. "Knox went to Knoxville."

"Ha, funny. I drove to my dad's house."

"Did you see him?"

"No. I mean yes, I saw him. But I barely even talked to him." His fingertips traced her knuckles. "Didn't even get out of my Jeep, couldn't. Half cowardice, half anger, half some semblance of wisdom that crept in from nowhere."

"That's some interesting arithmetic you've got going on there."

His head inched closer. "I guess I bring it up because I'm a little tired, too, of carrying around my regrets. I messed up so badly with how I handled that article about my father years ago. I've messed up my career and disappointed my brother and cost a colleague her job."

A piece of her heart cracked at his admission, at the vulnerability unhidden by his wry words.

"So you're saying we've both got issues."

"I'm saying we both probably need a little grace. And not the fancy-footworking kind."

Grace. A divine reality she still embraced deep down. Despite her failings as a missionary and lack of church attendance and mistakes with Robbie, she believed.

But didn't grace first require repentance? And didn't repentance require a decision to turn from one's wrongful actions? And for Miranda, didn't that require giving up the marriage act?

In which case, it also meant giving up her show. How could God ask her to give up the one thing that made her who she was?

"Get this," Matthew said. "I actually called my dad tonight while you two were finishing up. I don't know if it was finding

Jimmy or what that made me do it. Maybe it was seeing you e-mail your parents the other night. He's going to be in Asheville for a conference this week. That's part of why he called my brother. He'd seen my blog, knew I was in Asheville, too. I agreed to meet him."

"I think that's great, Matthew."

"Well, I guess this is the week for reunions. You and Robbie. Jimmy and Audrey. My father and me. It should be interesting, if nothing else."

The sound of an approaching vehicle grew closer. A honk. Rubber on gravel.

Matthew unlaced his fingers, propped up on his elbow to face her. "How about, even though we're both on rocky ground faith-wise, we pray for each other. I'll pray that you know how to handle Robbie . . . and Blaze . . . and the show. And you can pray for me. About tomorrow."

Her voice lowered to a whisper. "I'd like that."

The slam of a car door. Blaze's voice. "Your knight in white is here."

Chapter 16

Matthew glanced around the hotel lobby. To his right, the hotel elevator dinged and emptied, spilling people and luggage all around him. His father had asked to meet at the hotel he was staying in for his conference.

Miranda had driven Matthew back out to Audrey's place late that morning in her repaired truck. They checked in on Lola. No fever, and her cough had all but disappeared, so Matthew picked up his Jeep.

Another trill of the elevator, the sliding of the doors. He dropped onto a cushioned bench and tapped his phone.

I'm in the lobby.

The scent of chlorine from a splashing indoor waterfall wafted over him as he waited for his father's response. A bellboy strode past pushing a cart full of luggage. Sunbeams from the overhead skylights bounced off the plastic leaves of the greenery decorating the busy lobby.

Everyone has a place to go. But where did he belong anymore? His story was completely up in the air. Dooley was probably ready to have his head.

His phone beeped.

Morning session is almost over. I'll be out soon. Looking forward to seeing you, son.

Matthew wasn't sure he could say the same. He decided to grab a coffee while he was waiting and started toward the Starbucks he'd noticed on his way in.

But skidded to a halt when he saw a woman crossing the lobby. He gasped.

Delia Jones?

Probably just a look-alike. Didn't they say everyone had one?

He ducked behind the waterfall display, out of her peripheral vision. She stopped at the concierge desk. *Come on, turn. Let me see your profile.* Just a coincidence, surely.

And then she angled enough that he could see her reflection in the mirror behind the desk. Even from a distance, it was enough to know. No denying it. He knew that toothy grin, her flaming red hair.

"Think, Knox," he whispered. "What's she doing here?" And how long could he keep hiding behind the waterfall? Tiny pricks of water hit his face as he debated what to do next.

He glanced around the lobby, scanning for an escape route. If he could get back to the elevator undetected, he could—

And then he saw another woman.

Oh no. No, no, no. Not Miranda, too. She'd said she was heading back to the house when they'd left Audrey's. Robbie was still there, after all. And Blaze.

But here she was, the revolving door spitting her right into the lion's den. If Delia saw her, she'd pounce.

Because that's why Delia was here, wasn't it? She probably resented how well his blog was doing and wanted a piece of the story for herself, or simply wanted to ruin things for him, like usual.

But he wouldn't let her. Taking his chance, he swooped toward the atrium, where Miranda was heading straight toward the concierge desk. If he hurried, he could cut her off before she got to—

Wait. What if she was here to meet Delia? What if Delia had already contacted her, arranged an interview? Of course she had! Delia was just the kind of sneak to do something like that. And Miranda couldn't have any idea what she was getting into. Delia would sniff out the truth and skewer Miranda's career.

He moved again, praying Delia didn't turn around or notice his reflection in the mirror. "Miranda," he whispered as he reached her, one arm automatically making its way around her waist. "Come with me."

"Whoa. What's the hurry, Knox?"

He dragged her with him, her feet shuffling. "Just obey." She resisted, tugging free of his hold. But only for a second. He gripped her elbow, still pulling. It couldn't be much longer before Delia finished her business at the desk.

"What is wrong with you?" she hissed. "I'm not your dog. Don't tell me to obey you."

"True, you're much too pretty to be a dog. But . . . trust me. You don't want to talk to her."

"Don't try to sweet-talk me when you're dragging me across a hotel lobby." She struggled against his hold. "I don't know what you're talking about. Let go of me."

He only held tighter. Almost to the waterfall display, out of sight, safe. "Miranda, please, you don't know what she's like. You don't want to let her interview you."

"What are you talking about? Who—" She yanked, pulled . . . lost her balance.

And the sound of her screech ended in a splash. Water slopped over the edge of the waterfall base.

In slow motion, she rose from the water—so like that first day he'd met her, out on that flooded road. Water streaked down her face, her sputters lost in the sound of the fountain. She stepped onto the carpet, shoes squishing. "Why . . . do you always . . . do this to me?"

Water dripped from her sweater, her jeans, soaking his Converse shoes. "I'm sooo sorry, Miranda. I thought . . . you were . . . and Delia . . ." He whipped his head around, hopping from one ogling face to another. Muffled chuckles dotted the room. But no Delia.

Thank you, God.

Miranda shook her head, moisture flicking onto his face. Her eyebrows peaked and she stomped her foot. "Well, speak up."

Relief slid through him to see Delia had left the lobby, tempting laughter on its heels. *Don't you dare, Knox.* "I really am sorry."

She stabbed a finger at his chest. "I don't know who you think I'm here to see, but I came for you. For moral support when you meet your dad."

Oh. He couldn't help smiling so big his cheeks hurt. "That's, um, sweet, Miranda. Really, it is. But I have no idea how it's going to go, and you're . . ." *Beautiful, even soaking wet.*

Her eyes narrowed, and she pushed past him, shoes squeaking as she stalked through the lobby.

He turned to meet the stares. "Nothing to see here, folks. Nothing to see."

And for the life of him, he couldn't stop grinning.

⟡

"Can I help?"

Miranda wrapped one arm around her metal ladder and looked to the ground where Robbie stood, head tipped. He wore a stylish, fitted black coat that, together with his dark eyes, gray scarf, and dark hair, could've landed him a modeling gig. Handsome as the day she'd met him.

After leaving the hotel, she'd returned home with every intention of asking Robbie to leave. It was too confusing having him and Blaze and Matthew around. But nerves had kept her from the task, and she'd escaped outside.

She motioned to the remaining storm windows propped against the exterior of her house. "I only have a few left. Ground floor. If you want."

He picked up a window, sent her a grin. "I want."

I wonder how Matthew's time with his dad is going.

Matthew had followed her from the hotel lobby out to the Ford sedan she hardly ever drove, apologizing over and over for bumping her into the fountain. And then thanking her for coming.

"Seriously, it means a lot to me, Miranda." Sunlight kissed his skin and turned his brown hair golden. "Come on back inside."

"But I'm soaking wet. Besides, I think the concierge recognized me when we walked out. I'd better go before a media frenzy begins."

Matthew had pulled her into a hug before letting her go.

Now she jiggled the window she'd just placed, making sure it was stable before climbing down the ladder.

"I would have come outside to help earlier if I'd known you were working on the house," Robbie said as she reached for the last window. He'd already installed two. "Why isn't Blaze helping?"

"Broken arm, remember?"

"Oh, right. Where's the reporter?"

"In Asheville."

"He does not like me," Robbie said, wiping dust from his hands and moving to her side.

Her arms strained as she lifted the heavy window. "Who?"

Robbie's arms pitched forward to pull the window from her grasp. "Let me, Rand. And I mean the reporter."

She wanted to argue, yank the window back. She could do this herself. Had all three winters since Robbie left. But he was stronger and just as stubborn as her. And he barely grunted when he hefted the window.

"Why do you say that?" Hadn't Matthew been perfectly polite last night?

A gust of wind, carrying a scent of pine and cold, played with Robbie's hair, and he shrugged. "I know because of the way he looked at me. Like I am a tiger ready . . . ready to eat up an unsuspecting human."

"A bear would be a better description, Robbie. We don't have many tigers around here."

Robbie finished with the window, then turned to peer at her. "Do you ever think about going back to Brazil?"

"Not really. Sometimes I think about going down to visit my parents. But they've never actually invited me."

He brushed his hands together. "I saw them at my father's funeral."

Her eyes widened. "Really? I didn't realize you stayed in touch with them." She'd let them know things hadn't worked out with Robbie. But she had no idea if they'd ever watched her shows, kept up with her life enough to know about her marriage act. "How, uh, how did they seem?"

He leaned against the side of the house. "Well, they told me how you send a donation to their mission each year."

She shrugged. "Seems like the least I can do."

"They said they've been trying to contact you. They miss you."

And other than sending a spur-of-the-moment e-mail the other day, she'd ignored the letters and phone calls. She turned, reached for the ladder.

"I will get it," Robbie said, reaching around her. They walked quietly around the house, the silence of the mountains shrouding her alcove in peace.

"Miranda, why did you never finish the house?"

She shrugged. "It never felt right."

The musky scent of his cologne invaded her senses as they

stopped to study the skeleton of the addition. "You had big plans for it. Jacuzzi in the master bedroom. Skylights."

"Remember how you wanted a walk-in closet?"

"And you made fun of me for having more clothes than you," he added.

They faced each other, the sweet-and-sour mixture of emotions so thick in the air between them, Miranda could taste it. "How long are you going to keep pretending?" Robbie's voice was suddenly deep, intense, and his gaze ripped into her calm.

"What?"

"I have watched every episode, Randi. Every episode. When you talk about your husband, you are talking about me. At some point, someone is going to figure out you're not talking about that man with the broken arm." He dropped the ladder, and it jangled to the ground. He inched closer. "You are mixing my history with his face." His breath came in puffs of white that brushed over her cheeks.

She tried to back away, but Robbie lifted his hands to her shoulders. She refused to meet his eyes.

"I need to know. Do you still love me?"

Her head whipped up, jaw dropping. "Why would you ask that?"

"Because I still love you."

Her inhale was so sharp, mountain air scraped at her throat. She could feel its prick hit her heart.

She used to imagine Robbie returning to say those words, looking at her exactly as he did now—chocolate eyes promising a sweet return to the romance they used to share. This was the part when she was supposed to throw herself into his arms, tell him she forgave him. Tell him she'd saved his ring in hopes of this day.

His ring. Its diamond dug into her flesh now, her hand clenched into a fist.

"Say something," he urged softly.

All she wanted to do was run away. "No." She whispered the word. And then, finally, asked him to leave.

॰

"Miranda's not home?"

After returning from Asheville, Matthew found Blaze doing one-armed jumping jacks in Miranda's living room. Nausea plagued his stomach. Somehow he'd allowed himself to believe meeting his father might go well.

He'd been royally wrong.

"No, she went on a walk. Probably to that church she told us about." Blaze shook the hair out of his eyes.

"And Robbie?"

Blaze beamed. "She kicked him out."

At that, at least, he could smile. "It's about time. I think I might go find her."

"Have at it, dude."

Matthew stopped before exiting the house. "You've had a pretty boring go of it lately, haven't you? Everybody's been running around, and you've just been hanging out."

Blaze pointed to his head. "Thinking time. It's good for me."

Not for the first time, questions about Blaze's real life—the one he lived when he wasn't faking it as Miranda's husband—poked at him. Miranda had said there was an exit strategy for their pretend marriage, but just how long had Blaze committed to this thing? Was he beginning to feel trapped, maybe regretting his decision?

But Blaze waved him out the door before he could ask his questions. "Go on. Randi's probably in need of company."

"I don't know where the church is."

"Miranda went down that path. Maybe if you follow it, you'll end up there."

Matthew shrugged. Might as well. Outside, the wind tousled his hair, and he buttoned his black jacket the rest of the way. He needed to clear his head of this rotten day but couldn't stop the flashback playing like a movie reel . . .

He'd seen his father before Gordon Knox saw him. The man stepped into the hotel lobby, scanning the expansive room. Matthew took a breath, waved and waited.

"You look different, son," his father said when he reached him. Gordon Knox's teeth, either caps or the work of some hard-core bleach, glowed white against a tanned face. His still-thick hair was more salt than pepper now, and extra lines creased his face.

"I guess five years will do that." The words broke free before he could second-guess them. Did they come out as accusatory as they'd sounded in his head?

His father's face gave no hint. "Yes, I suppose that is how long it's been."

The speech Matthew had rehearsed on the way fell by the wayside as his father grasped his hand. "So what's your conference for?"

"Oh, some silly thing on community utilities management. Comes at a bad time with the campaign and all. Election is only two weeks away. But if I'm elected, it'll be good experience. Jase did tell you about my city council run, right?"

"He mentioned it."

"How is Jase, anyway?"

"Fine. He's had some business setbacks, though."

"Hmm. Anything I can help with?"

About fifteen years too late for that, wasn't he? "I don't think so."

"I saw a Starbucks. Let's grab a cup of Joe."

Matthew followed his father's long strides, the smell of coffee whetting his appetite.

Gordon scouted the coffee shop, seemed to find what he was looking for, and guided the way to a booth. Which is when Matthew's eyes landed on the figure already sitting there.

Delia.

And she wore conniving like a piece of clothing, from her taunting, toothy smile to the way her fire-engine-red nails tapped the Formica table. He jerked to face his father.

Gordon motioned to the booth. "Sit, son. I believe you two know each other."

Blindsided, Matthew did as his father ordered. He slid in across from Delia.

"I'm going to grab a latte. Son, Ms. Jones, can I get you anything?"

"Grande skinny mocha, no whipped cream," Delia said.

Matthew only shook his head. "What are you doing here?" he asked as his father walked to the counter.

"Mr. Knox called me. I came."

He didn't know whether to believe her or shoot questions at her like bullets.

"Enjoying playing lightweight celebrity blogger?" Delia asked.

"What turned you into such a crank, Delia?"

"Maybe having my editor take me out on a date, and then— rather than calling, maybe asking for a second date like a normal guy might do—he force-feeds me an article that gets me fired. That might do it, don't you think?"

He started to open his mouth, but she stopped him. "And don't give me the 'we had a source' argument. I tired of that long ago."

He hadn't planned to mention the faulty source. Whether she would believe it or not, he'd been about to apologize for the dinner-date misunderstanding. But she wouldn't have accepted the apology anyway. Delia's scowl seeped disdain, and if it weren't for the curiosity clawing him, Matthew would have walked out right then.

Instead, they'd waited in silence for his father.

And when Gordon Knox returned, he got right to business.

"Son, the reason I wanted to talk to you is twofold. First, remember my Ducati? I had it detailed a few months ago."

His father had contacted him because of a *motorcycle*? Confusion fought with a reel of memories, all the same: the sound of the bike's muffler as his dad rode away. So many evenings he'd watched from the window as Gordon Knox took off on his nightly ride, then lain awake in bed listening for his return.

Until one night . . . he didn't.

"Yeah, I guess I remember."

"And remember how I always said one day it'd be yours."

"I don't remember that."

Except . . . except maybe he did.

"Dad, I want a Ducati, too."

"Someday, son, you'll have one. And not just any bike, but this one."

So clear now, the memory. He must've repressed it years ago. Or had simply given up on the promise ever coming true. And in the process of disappointment, forgotten.

"It's time for you to have it. You can come pick it up in Knoxville or I'll ship it to you. Whole lot of value in that thing."

And then it rushed him, the anger. It pushed at the restraints he'd thought in place. No more. "I don't want your bike. If you think it makes up for years of neglect, you're wrong. And just so you know, it's not neglect of me I'm angry about. It's Mom. She was sick and you—"

"Matthew, my goal here is not to rehash the past."

"Well, maybe it needs to be rehashed." He hated that Delia was sitting there watching this beside his father. Gordon Knox hadn't only insulted him with this ridiculous sham of a re-union, he'd invited his rival to watch.

"It needs to be healed, is what," his father inserted. "And that's why Ms. Jones is here. I want us to call a truce. A public truce. End this painful estrangement. Become a family again."

Delia's nose wrinkled. "Why would I want to be a part of that?"

"I'd like you to write about it. I know you suffered in that mix-up with the article. I thought, who better to record my reconciliation with my son?"

Oh. Slowly, like an ugly puzzle coming together, the pieces connected in Matthew's mind. This was all a part of his father's campaign. He hadn't called Jase because he wanted to reconnect with his sons. He wanted a publicity stunt.

Matthew could feel the tension in his jaw snap. "I can't believe you would—"

"Son—"

"Would you stop calling me that?" The words exploded from him, probably too loudly, probably enough to disturb the coffee shop's other customers. But his father had wanted a public reunion, didn't he?

It could be public without being positive.

Slowly, his father leaned forward, his palms flat on the table. "It's what you are." His tone spoke challenge.

"Maybe. But when you gave up your role, I gave up mine. You left. You took all the money. You didn't go to Mom's funeral. And now you want me to agree to some hokey article to shore up your city council campaign?" He stood, pushed out of the booth. "Thanks, but no thanks. I wouldn't wish you on any city."

His father's eyes narrowed. "Think about what you're doing. This could be as good for you as for me. It's not like your career's headed anywhere."

The hurt, same as always, hammered him. *Screw-up. Failure.* Fists balled at his sides, Matthew closed his eyes. Only for a moment. Just long enough to make the decision.

Been trapped in this place too long. His father's grip. His failure's grasp.

He met Gordon's eyes. "I don't want the motorcycle."

He turned, his legs carrying him from the Starbucks and through the hotel, the sun washing his face when he stepped onto the parking lot. Each step echoed his decision. *Done. Done. Done.*

But Delia's voice stopped him before he entered his Jeep. "Knox, wait."

He reached for his door handle.

"Hold on—just wait."

Against his better judgment, he paused, waiting for her to reach him. When she did, he pressed his body against the side of the Jeep to keep as much space between them as possible. "What?"

"I didn't know that's what this meeting was about. Sure, I was curious, especially when he bought me a plane ticket, but I'm not so low that I would've accepted that kind of story."

The sun-warmed metal of his Jeep burned his back. "Fine."

"But as long as I'm here . . ."

"What do you want?"

"I want in," she snapped. "I'm like any red-blooded journalist, Knox. I'm just like you."

If that was true, he should do society a favor and find a cave to hide out in for the rest of his life. The altitude had gotten to her.

"I'm sick of Minneapolis. Even though I talked my way into a job at the *Pioneer Press*, everyone there still remembers. I want to move up. Let me in on the Woodruff story. It'll be Knox and Jones, partners in storytelling crime again. What do you say?"

She was kidding, right? He rubbed clammy palms over his jeans and cocked an eyebrow. "Last time we worked together was a disaster—"

"Not my fault."

"And you've done all you could to hassle me ever since."

"Nothing personal."

"Yeah, right. So if you think I'll let you anywhere near Miranda Woodruff, you're crazy. I'm not an idiot."

"Debatable."

Fine, he'd stepped right into that.

"I know you're gunning for more than a blog, Knox. Dooley's probably baiting you with a chance for the February cover, right?"

"January," he conceded.

"I want in," she repeated. "And you're going to let me in because you owe me."

And that's when he'd finally yanked on his Jeep's door handle. Called it quits. Headed home.

Home . . .

Somehow the mountains really had started to feel like home. They'd pulled him in, wrapped him up in a quilt of beauty and wonder.

And maybe hope. If God could sculpt these ridges into such perfection, surely He could sculpt a person, too. Root out the parts so prone to screwing up. Remake a man into something . . . worthy.

Matthew's feet crunched over leaves and twigs, moonlight painting a path in front of him. He'd become so lost in his reverie, he hadn't even realized he'd reached the church. At least, he assumed it was the church.

Worthy of whom, Matthew?

He stopped, watched the white of his breath float until it disappeared. *Is that you, God?*

Worthy of whom?

His colleagues. His family. His father. No, not his father. Miranda.

Or maybe you, God.

He started forward again, toward the church, the cold now sneaking past his jacket. *My identity has always been about trying to be better. Trying not to be the screw-up. Trying to succeed.*

And that's probably why he'd stayed away from church, let his faith fade for such a long time. Because his attempts never panned out.

But maybe it's not about trying anymore. Maybe it was never supposed to be. Maybe I'm simply supposed to let you build me like you built these mountains. Like Miranda and one of her houses.

He stopped in front of the church, its white walls glowing against moonlight. Miranda sat on the front steps. "Hey, you," he said.

"Hey, yourself. How was seeing your dad?"

"Horrible. How about your day?"

"Horrible."

He gestured to the step. "May I?" She nodded, and he lowered, the step narrow enough that his thigh brushed hers as he sat. "You know, we're kind of a wreck, the two of us."

"Don't I know it."

She reached for his hand then, leaned in. And sighed.

Chapter 17

The featherlight dress fell in satiny wisps over Miranda's shoulders, her waist, breezing to her ankles until only her toes peeked from under the midnight-blue ripples.

"Yikes, Miranda." Liv squeaked out the words, pushing Miranda toward the full-length mirror attached to her closet door. "Look at yourself."

She couldn't. She probably resembled a clown. Worse, Raggedy Ann trying to fit into a china doll collection. Jeans, boots, her tool belt and favorite flannel—that's what she belonged in. Not this Vera Whoever creation. She couldn't make herself look.

From behind her, Liv's hands closed around Miranda's arms and shook. "Open your eyes, silly." Her bare feet shuffled over the hardwood floor as Liv nudged her closer to the mirror. "Or I'll spread the word about your date with the reporter tonight."

Her eyes shot open as she whirled, slippery fabric swishing around her legs. "You wouldn't! And it's not a date. It's not even—"

"Then get ahold of yourself and check out how you look in the dress."

Miranda mirrored Liv's crossed arms with her own. "Promise you won't breathe a word to anyone. I'm supposed to still be married." At least in the eyes of everyone except Liv, Matthew,

Blaze, Robbie, Brad, Lincoln, Tom . . . The network of those in the know was getting bigger and bigger.

Liv picked up a DVD case from the nightstand, mock sincerity lighting her eyes. "I swear on the awesomeness of this movie, your favorite and mine, I won't say a thing."

"I'd prefer you not spread the word about my love for Captain von Trapp, either," Miranda muttered, turning obediently. "I'd lose all credibility with the crew if—"

She quieted as the figure staring back at her stilled, the only movement her slowly unfolding arms. The dress hugged her upper body, sheer straps crisscrossing over her shoulders, leaving her arms bare. From there, it dropped over her waist in a graceful line to the floor. "I look . . . like a girl." With actual *curves*.

"I'd say *woman*." Liv stepped up beside her. "You're breathtaking. And will be even more so when we fix your hair and dab on some makeup."

And heels. She'd wear heels tonight because suddenly something had loosened in her heart. Or maybe her brain. Yeah, probably that, considering her history with heels. But the dress wouldn't look right with anything else. It had to look right, because . . .

She fingered the tendril of hair tickling her cheek.

Because of Matthew Knox.

And if she stopped to dwell on that realization, she'd go and analyze her way to an ulcer. Better not to study it just yet. "We need to hurry. I'm supposed to meet Matthew in an hour, and it's a forty-five-minute drive, at least." She reached behind her head to loosen her ponytail.

Liv stepped up to help. "Here, let me. And stay calm. I'll have you photo ready in minutes."

She shook her head. "Uh-uh, no photos tonight. Matthew promised me where we're going is off the beaten path."

He'd offered the assurance over the phone this morning, then told her to look on the porch—where she'd found the garment bag draped over the railing. She'd unzipped it while still on the phone, ran a hand over the shimmery fabric. "How . . . why . . . I thought you were saving your money for Cee's surgery?"

"I figure this is an investment. I teach you to dance, you survive the Giving Heart gala."

She'd checked the tag inside the dress. Her size. How had he known? But she'd known the answer without having to ask— Liv. "I'm not seeing how that's an investment." A rustling breeze played with the chimes dangling from the porch overhang.

"Oh yes, well, you promise to dance with me at the gala, I write my best blog yet, and I reckon Barbara Walters will be calling me to ask what it was like dancing with *the* Randi Woodruff. I will, of course, require compensation for such an interview. Good idea, huh?"

Oh yeah. "It's beautiful." The color of night when the sun dipped behind the Smokies.

"Well, I thought with your gray eyes and dark hair . . ." His words had petered out as he cleared his throat, silence stretching like the emotions expanding in her chest. Fluttery and unfamiliar after so many years tucked away.

Now, up in her bedroom, wearing the dress Matthew picked out, those *feelings*—whatever they were—glided through her again, tasting new and sweet, like the honey Grandma used to buy straight from the local beekeeper.

"So he asked you on a date two nights ago when you were out walking, then disappeared for a few hours yesterday, and then called you this morning, from the cabin on your own property, to get you out onto the porch so you'd find the dress?"

Miranda couldn't stop the grin stretching her cheeks. "That's about how it went."

Liv shook her head and whistled. "If you ever get yourself

out of this fake-marriage business, that Knox is a keeper. Now, sit, Rand, and I'll do your hair." Liv prodded her toward the Victorian stool in front of the antique vanity. "Up or down?"

"You're asking me? If fashion savvy had been a subject in school, I'd have flunked out." And yet, the dress alone had her feeling runway worthy.

"Well, which way do you think Matthew would prefer?"

She met Liv's eyes in the mirror above the vanity. "I don't know."

"You're a horrible liar, Woodruff." Liv picked up a brush and pulled it through Miranda's hair.

Last-name treatment. Livvy definitely saw through her. Which meant she might as well confess. "The other day we were working on Audrey's house, and by the end of the day, all my hair had come out of the ponytail. He made the comment I should wear it down more."

Liv stopped with the brush midair. "You're so completely smitten."

"Not true."

"Deny it all you want, honey, but I have eyes. Even Brad noticed—"

"Brad? What does he know? And when were you talking to him?"

She watched Livvy blink at the mirror. And what was with the blush? "Oh, my goodness. Don't tell me . . . Seriously?"

Livvy tugged the brush through Miranda's hair. And none too gently.

"Are you two . . ."

"He just calls sometimes. That's all." Yank.

"And?"

"And we talk." Pull.

"And?" Snarl. "Oww, careful there. It'll completely ruin the effect of the dress if I show up tonight bald."

"Sorry," Liv mumbled. "But I have nothing to say, all right? We've talked a few times. That's it. And he wants to volunteer at Open Arms. And I'm his 'plus one' at the gala tomorrow night. That's it. And he's coming to church with me on Sunday."

"Let me guess . . . That's it?" Laughter tumbled from her lips.

Liv jerked a makeup bag from her purse on the quilt-topped bed "Laugh all you want, Woodruff, but I'm not the one denying a crush on a guy who bought her an evening gown. While, I might add, harboring a fake husband. *And* who just got rid of her former fiancé."

Miranda clamped down on her giggles and twisted on the stool to face Liv. "I'm pathetic."

Livvy dusted her cheeks with blush. "You're conflicted— that's what."

"Robbie wanted to get back together."

"I can't believe it. I also can't believe you didn't invite me over while he was here. I'd have loved to give him a piece of my mind. And my fist." Liv reached into her bag, pulled out a tube of eyeliner. "Eyes closed."

"Well, it's possible you may still have a chance. He made it clear when he left he'd be sticking around town for a while."

Liv harrumphed.

"Why'd he do it?" Miranda asked softly, opening her eyes as Liv stepped back.

"Who, Robbie? Come back? Didn't you say his father died and—"

"No, Matthew." She motioned to the dress. "This. Tonight."

Liv lowered onto the edge of the bed, leaning over, hands on Miranda's knees. "You know why."

"He's helping me get ready for the award ceremony. I told him about not feeling graceful. So he's . . . helping. I know that."

Even before she finished, Liv's head swayed back and forth. "Be honest, Rand."

Choking panic wafted up, like the time she'd gotten lost in the market in San Paulo, suffocated by the mixture of foreign words and smells. "I shouldn't go. Even if there was no Blaze, there'd still be the show and the fact that supposedly I'm married and . . ."

Liv clucked her tongue and produced a tube of lipstick. "Don't be silly. You're thinking too hard. You're dying to go. Even Blaze wants you to go." She held out the lipstick. "Put it on."

Dying to go, yes. Because Matthew brought her to life in a way no one had since Robbie. He listened. He talked. He *saw*. Exactly what, she still wasn't sure. But it was enough to know he was looking. Not at a homebuilder. Not at a television star. At *her*.

She closed her fingers around the lipstick, puckered, felt the color deepen in a sticky, smooth stain.

"How do I look?"

"Like a finally-happy woman ready for a first date."

"A first date with a man who's been chronicling my life for three weeks. Should be interesting."

"Should be amazing. Now go forget everything else and have a wonderful time."

Matthew paced in front of the abandoned building he'd taken over for tonight's date. Miranda should have been there by now. What if she was driving around lost? What if the dress didn't fit? What if she hated it?

Nah, she'd called it beautiful earlier.

Shoes! What if she didn't have any shoes to go with the dress? He was such a *guy*. Didn't even think about that. Knowing Miranda, she probably had a closet full of boots and that's all.

The obnoxious caw of a bird streamed through the trees. He'd heard about this place the night he'd picked up Jimmy at that truck stop. It was a lone building set back from the main road, about twenty miles north of Pine Cove.

Even if Miranda did make it out there, to the middle of nowhere, complete with shoes, what if she thought this whole setup was hokey?

His pacing came to a halt at the sound of tires rolling over gravel. She'd made it. Matthew glanced down to his shiny shoes, up his black pants and tuxedo jacket, then to the plastic-encased wrist corsage he held in one hand. A deep-burgundy rose, which the florist said symbolized *unconscious beauty*. Couldn't have been more perfect.

Now if only the rest of the night could sail the same tide of perfection.

He was at Miranda's door before she'd even cut the engine. He opened the door and she stepped out.

"Hey, Matthew."

The sight of her made him drop the flower box. It landed at his feet, and as he knelt to pick it up, he caught a glimpse of the strappy, heeled sandals poking from beneath the dress he'd picked out. He lifted his head.

"Good . . . shoes." Words . . . stuck.

But who could blame him? With *her* standing in front of him all . . . gorgeous and stuff. He rose, his gaze capturing each inch of Miranda until it stopped at the smirk in her eyes. "Were you worried I'd show up barefoot?" she drawled, lifting one corner of her mouth.

Oh boy. She'd worn lipstick, of her own free will. Unless Whitney or Liv or someone had forced her. But no, she could take on any of them. Yep, the color accenting her grin was her own doing. And knowing that was . . . enticing.

"Say something, Knox. It's not every day I ditch my Levi's

for a gown." Her voice softened. "A really, really pretty one. Thank you."

"You're . . ." It's like something disconnected between his brain and his mouth.

"I think the word you're looking for is *welcome*," she offered, now eyeing the corsage. "Is that for me?"

"No." Maybe he should blink or something so his admiration didn't come off as ogling.

"Uh, so *you're* going to wear it?"

"No, I mean, *welcome* isn't the word I was looking for." Finally an entire sentence. "Beautiful. That's what I meant to . . ." He thrust the corsage box toward her. "So . . . here."

Her dimpled grin widened as she accepted the box and slipped the corsage over her wrist. *Idiot*. He should've done that. *Get ahold of yourself, man*.

"So, where are we, anyway? You'd think I'd know about this place." She was gazing at the one-story structure, probably dissecting its construction. She looked at buildings completely differently from the way others did.

"Let's go inside and I'll show you." He held out his elbow, and she tucked her arm through his. At last, a smooth move. And even though there wasn't anyone else around to see, he still felt a puff of pride at having her at his side. They ducked under a low-hanging porch roof.

"I heard about this building from some locals. Used to be called Everly Hall. Apparently it was the happening-est place in the area during Prohibition, complete with a distillery in the back room."

They paused in the doorway. "You mean it's a speakeasy?"

Matthew grinned. "Was. Tonight it's a ballroom."

Inside, the twinkle of Christmas lights lit up the room, thanks to the battery-powered generator he'd purchased yesterday. He'd bought at least a dozen coils of lights and spent hours today stringing them around the room. Thanks to his iPod, the smooth tones of a big-band dance number echoed through the room.

Over in the corner, he'd set up a card table and covered it with a white tablecloth. A pair of candles flickered in the center. He'd picked up their dinner spread from a restaurant Miranda had once mentioned as a favorite.

"This is . . ." She stopped in the middle of the room, turning in a full circle before finishing her sentence. "Amazing. How in the world did you . . ."

Her voice trailed as he reached her side. "So I did all right? You don't think it's hokey?"

"Try incredible." Specks of light danced in her eyes.

He led her to the table and pulled out her chair, then paused as a waltz picked up where the previous song left off. "Actually, the food will stay warm a little longer. Should we have a dance first?"

"I don't know if our one dance lesson prepared me for this." She bit her lip, the same uncertainty feathering over her face now as that first day, standing knee-deep in creek water, when she'd talked about her grandpa's truck, unknowingly spilling her heart . . . and in the process, capturing his.

"That's why we're here." Part of it, anyway. Possibly a very minor part. The bigger reason being his exploding desire to spend every minute he could with this woman before he had to go home. "I'm going to finish teaching you."

"At least there's nobody here. I can't embarrass you. Myself, yes. You, no."

"Not a chance. Besides, even if this room were packed, by this point in my life, I'm pretty unembarrassable." He reached for her hand. "Remind me to tell you about the time Jase and I got caught breaking into a zoo building while trying to be all Hardy Boys sleuth-like."

He pulled her toward the center of the room.

"That's hilarious. How long ago was that?" She tipped her head back, smoky eyes beaming.

"Uh, what?" Maybe if he didn't look at her he'd make it through an entire conversation. But then, well, he wouldn't get to look at her. Not so sure the trade-off was worth it.

"When you and your brother broke into the zoo. What were you, like, teens?" She stepped closer, placed her right hand on his shoulder, poised to move into the dance just as he'd taught her.

"I'd rather not say."

"No way, you were older? Adults? Oh, don't tell me you were on an assignment."

Left hand to her waist, right arm raised, fingers closed around hers. With a step, he nudged them into the nonexistent pool of dancers on the floor. She stiffened only for a moment, then eased into the floating movement. The tap of their footsteps accompanied the music.

"How long ago was it? Were you just starting out as a reporter? An eager-beaver journalist hot on the trail of his first story?"

"I shouldn't have brought it up."

"And why was Jase with you?"

"I lost my camera."

"Tell me, when was it?"

She missed a step as she joked, and instinctively he tightened his hold on her before she could stumble. "Careful there, Miss Curiosity." He pulled her in, moving to the sway of the strings, breathing in the lilac scent of Miranda's perfume. Her favorite . . . quickly becoming his.

"So are you going to tell me?" she said over his shoulder.

"Tell you what?"

A shadow flickered in the doorway, and for a moment his heartbeat picked up. Was someone there?

"The zoo story, Matthew. Do I get to hear it?" Miranda tilted her head, her teasing grin coming to a slow fade as they locked eyes. "You okay?"

No, of course no one was there. They were alone. "I'm perfect, Miss Woodruff." Absolutely perfect.

Except for one tiny thing. *I can't do that article.* He'd known it for days but hesitated over making the final decision.

She leaned in again, letting him carry them along to the music.

He had to do it—back out of the article, maybe even the blog. He'd call Dooley tomorrow and endure the tongue-lashing. But it'd be worth it. Because he was gone. So far gone, "conflict of interest" took on a whole new meaning.

"Anyone ever tell you that you exaggerate, Miranda Woodruff?"

Matthew spoke the words into her ear, his cheek brushing hers and the scent of his aftershave lingering as he guided her into an easy whirl. They'd finished their meal, Miranda gushing the whole time over her favorite restaurant's food. And then he'd coaxed her into another dance, which turned into two, and then three. "I exaggerate?"

"Yes. You're a much better dancer than you led me to believe."

"Not really. You're just easy to follow. That, and I slipped out of my shoes back at the table."

His head jerked down. "Really? What if I step on your toes?"

"You haven't so far."

She met Matthew's gaze as the music stopped, something telling in his hazel eyes with specks of green. And if it had been tangible, she'd have grabbed at it, held it tight. Instead, another number began, this one slow and lazy, and she closed the inches between them and laid her head on his shoulder. She imagined the room as it might have been back in the 1920s: flashes of deep red from the drapery ornamenting the room, the gold shine of ceiling lights bouncing off the instruments of the band, a rainbow of dresses dotted by the black of tuxedos . . .

But no, this was better. She closed her eyes and molded her movement to his.

"Absolutely perfect," he'd said. Absolutely right.

I could stay here. Forget ratings and awards and lies.

"You know, if there's a rumba on my iPod, we might be done for." Matthew led her from the perimeter of the floor into the center. "We never got to that during dance lessons for Izzy and Jase's wedding." He chuckled, his breath feathering over her cheek.

Absolutely perfect . . .

"Miranda?"

"Hmm?"

"I'm supposed to go home in a couple days."

Suddenly the smooth floor under her feet turned ragged. One foot tangled over the other. Not the first time since they'd started dancing. And just like every other time, Matthew's arms tightened, and his movement slowed until she found her stride . . . and the warmth crept over her face. "Sorry."

"My leaving bothers you that much, does it?"

Didn't have to see his face to hear the smile. "Who said it bothered me?"

"Your feet."

My, but he was smug. A good dancer, but smug. "My feet are simply ill-suited to dancing."

"Your feet are cute."

"Are not. They're calloused and ugly. And I haven't painted my toenails since I was five."

"They're cute."

297

"Stop looking at them."

He lifted his eyes to hers, and as his gaze inched down her face and landed on her lips, every thought save one disintegrated: *He's going to kiss me. Right here in the middle of the dance floor in an abandoned speakeasy.*

Her eyelids eased closed. Her head tilted as Matthew closed the space between them and . . .

His foot came down on hers.

"Oww!"

Matthew jerked back, dropping both his arms. "Sorry. I'm sorry!"

"It's okay, I'm fine. A few broken toes, that's all."

"Seriously? Ice, we need ice."

"Matthew, it's all—"

"Just like me to ruin the night."

"You didn't ruin anything." Except maybe her ability to walk. She took a gingerly step forward. *Hmm, not bad.* Another step. "See, I'm totally fine."

"You should get your shoes."

"Trust me, the heels are more of a danger to me than you are. I've still got all my toes. And look." She lifted her foot, wiggled her toes. "They still work." She replaced her hand on his shoulder.

"You really want to keep dancing?"

Such a simple question shouldn't burrow so deep into her heart. But the intensity in his voice spoke more than his words. She squeaked out a "yes" and took a step closer.

Lord, what's happening?

Matthew's hand encircled hers.

As if I'm not already in enough of a web. Now this . . . what? Infatuation? No, definitely more than that. Deeper.

"Hey, I should teach you to dip." The forced lightness in his tone was obvious. But she'd accept the reprieve, because suddenly the giddiness, the emotion, the connection she felt with Matthew carried a new layer: fear.

It filtered through her, foggy, blurring any chance of easy hope for this blooming, uh, friendship. *He's going to leave. Just like Robbie.* Sure, in this moment, he might fancy himself taken with her. Might even be caught up in a momentary star-studded whirlwind. But eventually he'd leave, return to his home and family in Minnesota. And once again, she'd be alone, rejection her only companion.

"The best time to dip is when the music swells. I'll lean forward, you lean back. Let my arms support you. Pretend we're in a crowd of onlookers and flash that TV-screen smile."

"Okay. You'll tell me when?"

"I'll tell you when."

They circled the floor, her movements smoothing out, crushed toes forgotten. The almost-kiss, so totally not.

The music crescendoed.

"Ready, Miranda?"

His arm around her waist tightened. She leaned back into his firm hold, then felt herself pulled back up.

"Very nice," Matthew whispered, his face only a breath away from hers, his smile reaching past her resolve. "And on your first try."

"I don't want you to go." The words tumbled out, unstoppable.

He scrunched his brow. "You don't . . ."

She shook her head. Around them, lights twinkled as the hollow room listened.

"Why not?" His voice was husky.

"I just don't." *Please don't ask me to explain.* Because she couldn't. Or maybe she could. But saying it aloud was just too much of a risk. Even now, if he turned away, she'd shatter like glass.

His eyes found her lips again. A second chance. She tucked her feet under her dress. No breaking the spell this time.

The kiss was soft, sweet. Unintrusive. Her arms slid around his neck as he kissed her again, this one deeper, longer, perfect. And when she broke it off, the dazed look in his eyes matched the contented sighing of her heart. "Well, I'll take that any day over broken toes."

His laugh shook her as he pulled her close again. "In that case, there's more where that came from."

"Is that so?" Full-on flirt. Who knew she had it in her?

"Yes, ma'am." His arms tightened, head lowered, lips met hers.

A flash of light and movement. Her eyes blazed open as she pulled away from Matthew. His own gaze shot over her shoulder as another unmistakable camera flash lit up his face. "Jones!" he gasped.

She whirled . . . and caught a glimpse of a woman's retreating form.

Had she followed them?

A reporter, maybe paparazzi. But whoever it was didn't stick around. She disappeared from the doorway before Miranda could move. And did Matthew recognize her? Wait, was it the same reporter Matthew had tried to hide her from the other day?

She turned back to Matthew. "Who was that?"

And then it sunk in, like an anchor tugging her to reality. Whoever she was, this Jones, she'd caught them kissing. On camera. And Miranda, supposedly married . . .

Matthew raked a hand through his hair, shook his head. "I'm sorry. I'm so sorry."

"Sorry for what?" Her stomach lurched. "Did you know she was going to show up?"

He froze. "You can't possibly think that I—"

"Staged this? How else does a reporter find us in the middle of nowhere? A reporter you know?"

His eyes searched hers, his hurt clear. He spoke slowly. "Miranda, if I wanted to break a story about you, I wouldn't have to go to all this work. I've got enough ammo as is."

Miranda slid one hand up and down her bare arm, goose bumps raised at the sting in Matthew's words. She'd allowed herself to forget all he knew, the damage he could do with one blog post. One article.

But that may not even matter anymore. Not if the pictures that reporter just took found an audience.

"Matthew . . ." she started, but he wouldn't look at her.

He only blew out the candles on their makeshift table and turned as he jogged toward the door. "I'm going after her."

Chapter 18

"Miranda? You in here?"

Miranda awoke slowly, the nagging pain in her side prodding her to consciousness—that and the voice jutting into her dreams.

"I sure hope you're out here. Otherwise, I'm going to be seriously worried."

Blaze? She shifted to free herself from the wooden arm jabbing into her waist. Her back, her neck, her whole body protested at her movement. She groaned as the hard back of her chair and the smell of sawdust reminded her where she was.

Note to self: I'm too old to be sleeping out in the workshop.

And then the memory of last night moved in like the gray light of the outdoors. For one hopeful moment, she wondered if it had all been a bad dream. No reckless kiss, no sinister camera flash. But one glance down at the midnight blue dress peeking out from under her blanket assured her the nightmare was pure reality.

How late had she worked last night, attempting to smooth out her emotions as she sanded away the nicks all along the surface of the dresser she refinished?

"Ahh!" Blaze's annoyed growl sounded along with the crash of something metal. Probably a can of varnish.

"I'm back here, Blaze."

The sound of his bumping against equipment and furniture tracked his movement. "There you are. Babe, do you have any idea how worried I was when I woke up this morning and couldn't find you?"

She leaned back, propping her feet on the edge of the tool cart in front of her chair. "Sorry. But don't call me babe. Makes me feel like a pig."

He plopped onto the stool beside her table saw. "Yeah, but that pig could talk. And he starred in, what, two, three movies?"

She pulled her blanket up to her chin. "He's a pig."

"He's cute. As are you."

She raised an eyebrow.

"What? You're wearing high heels and a ball gown with a pair of safety goggles on your forehead. It makes for a great picture."

Picture! Oh dear, had the pictures that reporter took last night hit the Internet already? She reached for her phone from her purse on the floor, checked the display. Four voice mails and eight unread text messages . . . all from Matthew.

Huh, if all the messages were from Matthew—none from Brad or Lincoln or Liv—then maybe whoever had taken those photos hadn't gone public with them. Had Matthew stopped it from happening?

She sat up straight. How could she have accused Matthew of being a part of scheming with another reporter last night? Well, she'd been in shock. She could've believed just about anything. The Easter Bunny, tooth fairy, Santa . . . *Yes, Virginia, men do let you down.*

But Matthew?

"Hey, Randi, seriously, you all right?" Blaze's eyes were filled with genuine concern.

"Last night was . . . bad. Something happened. I blamed Matthew."

"So that's why the guy never showed up. I wondered."

"He didn't come back?"

Blaze shook his head. "Didn't see his car, and he didn't answer at the cabin." He leaned forward to gently tug off her goggles with his un-casted hand. He chuckled. "You better hope those lines on your forehead fade before the gala tonight."

She lifted her hand to her face, traced the pattern the goggles left from one side of her hairline to the other. The Giving Heart gala—so not what she felt like doing tonight.

She quirked a grin. "Think I could get away with keeping on this dress and going as is?"

"The dress, maybe, but the sawdust in your hair might raise a few eyebrows." He pulled the goggles over his head and sat, posed with his arms folded. "What do you think? Do I look like a serious carpenter?"

"First carpenter I ever met who wears shorts at the end of October. Aren't you freezing?"

"You're the one in a sleeveless dress."

She snuggled farther into the cocoon of her blanket. "I *am* cold. My toes feel like icicles."

He pulled on the lever underneath his stool, and it whistled as he lowered. He grabbed one of her feet before she could protest.

"What are you doing?"

He clamped her foot between his one palm and the fingers of his casted arm and started rubbing. "Warming your feet."

"This is weird."

He shook his head. "It'd be weird if I was your former fiancé, who obviously still likes you. And it'd be weird if I was Knox, who's got the biggest crush on you this side of anywhere. But I'm just your pretend husband, so it's all good, hon."

Her muscles tightened at the mention of Robbie. No, Matthew. No, both. "Blaze—"

"Maybe I shouldn't have said it out loud, but come on, it's obvious. You're in one mess of a love triangle. Make that square, if you count me. You're going to have to make some hard decisions." He switched feet.

"What decisions? The way I see it, I'm left with little choice in this whole thing."

He dropped her foot. "Your toes are practically blue." He shook off his shoe and reached down to peel off his sock, brought it up to her foot.

"Where you going with that, buddy?"

"They're clean, I promise."

"I'm not wearing your socks."

"I'll turn it inside out."

"Really, Blaze, I'm fine. I'll go to the house and put on some real clothes."

He grabbed her ankle. She shook it. "Now, come on, Mrs. Woodruff. Make that Mrs. Hunziker. Listen to your hubby. He knows what's best for you."

"I don't need your socks."

He only held on tighter, his fingers sneaking to the arch of her foot. "Wear the socks, or hubby tickles you 'til you cry."

"This is abuse!"

He tickled her.

She screeched. "Blaze!"

"I mean it, missy. Blaze just wants to take care of you."

"Blaze should stop talking in third person!" She whacked at him as he forced a sock over her foot.

"So this is Blaze."

Miranda froze at the sound of the female voice. She hadn't heard the door open, nor the approach of the figures highlighted from behind by pale rays streaming in from the window.

She squinted, ankle still encased in Blaze's hand and hair falling around her face from the playful struggle.

"Miranda."

Robbie? Of course. He just couldn't stay away.

But strangely, he wasn't the one she couldn't look away from. She gulped and found her voice. "Mom?"

At the first hint of sunrise, Matthew emerged from his Jeep and marched toward the Asheville Marriott. Weighty clouds dimmed the sky in a swirl of silver, a mountain haze fogging the landscape.

He'd have had a better night's sleep if he'd actually checked in to the hotel when he arrived shortly after midnight. But assuming Delia was still here, he hadn't wanted to miss her if she made an early departure.

A valet dipped his head in greeting as Matthew passed. *Yes, I know I'm a wreck.* He still wore his tux, though he'd loosened his bow tie and ditched the jacket.

He pushed through the revolving door and dropped onto the first maroon bench he saw in the lobby. He'd stand guard all day if he had to. Because it wasn't happening this time. He wouldn't mess everything up, hurt someone he cared about. It's why he'd spent half the night on the phone, bugging Dooley, bugging the lawyer Dooley recommended. He had enough ammo now to keep Delia from leaking those photos—if she hadn't already.

If only he could find her. He'd left half a dozen messages on her cell phone. Somehow he'd stop her—protect Miranda.

Never mind the sting of Miranda's actions last night. Oh, she hadn't completely accused him with words, only implied. But the look in her eyes said it clearly enough.

It's not fair, Miranda. Not after how I've kept your secret all this time.

His shoes tapped against the carpet as he waited. Fatigue tempted one eye closed, then the other. He blinked. No, couldn't sleep. He might miss—

"Matthew Knox. Fancy meeting you here."

His head whipped up and his mouth dropped open as the familiar voice snaked into his concentration. "Delia." Her name came out flat, listless.

"All rested up after your evening of dancing?" she asked with a self-satisfied smirk. "I had no idea you were such a Fred Astaire type. I'd call you Twinkletoes, but something tells me you might not appreciate the endearment."

"Speaking of things I don't appreciate . . ." He stood. "You're not going to use those photos."

Her sardonic laugh had its intended effect, rankling his determination. "Don't be naïve. I hit the jackpot, and you know it. Although, I have to admit, I'm curious. That kiss—was it the real thing or was it part of some scheme to get Woodruff to open up? Either way, it's a great story."

If she wasn't a woman, the fists balling at his sides might not have stayed there. "I've already got a lawyer writing up a defamation suit. So unless you've got a hankering to hang out in a courthouse, you'll forget the whole thing."

"Hankering? You've been down south too long." She stepped closer, her spiked heels giving her enough height to face him eye to eye. "Your blog might be cute, Knox. Your name might be a hot thing at the moment. But your comeback's coming to an end."

How to convince her to drop this? Wasn't there something he could do? Apparently the idea of a lawsuit didn't faze the woman. The splashing of the atrium fountain, an impatient patron dinging the concierge bell, the need for sleep, it all muddled his brain. *Think, Knox.* "Jones, please."

"Please what? Have compassion on the man who let his

personal ambition and desire for revenge against his father ruin *my* career?"

That's it!

He grabbed Delia's wrist, pulled her to the bench. "Just listen. I'll do it. I'll do the story with my dad, and you can write it." Dread ran a marathon through his head at even the idea, but it would be worth it. For Miranda, it would be worth it.

"Write it for the AP, whomever. Former Pulitzer finalist on his way to a fine journalism career throws it all away to get back at his father. He causes his own downfall. Now, years later, his magnanimous father reaches out in forgiveness." Yeah right, more like in the name of Gordon Knox's own personal interests. But Delia's stillness, the way her pursed lips released, signaled her interest. "Father and son reconcile. Gordon Knox goes on to a blooming political career."

Delia chewed on the inside of her cheek, then shifted to face him, her elbow propped on the back of the bench. "I could write that story anyway, Knox. Only with a different angle. Father reaches out to son—son refuses."

"It'd be one-sided."

She shrugged. "As was the attempt at reconciliation. Besides, at best, the story has regional appeal. Randi Woodruff, that's national news."

"It's national *tabloid* news. I know you, Jones. We worked together for years. You're like me—there's teeth to your reporting. You're a hard-news journalist, not a bottom-feeder."

"You say that, and yet, you're writing for *Today*."

"Not anymore. I'm writing one last blog entry after the Giving Heart ceremony, but I'm done after that."

"What about the cover story?"

He shook his head. "Not doing it. Not the way Dooley wants." He scooted an inch closer to Delia. "Miranda Woodruff is a good person, Delia. Please, don't attempt to ruin her life the way I tried to ruin my father's. I only ended up hurting myself . . . and you."

Delia peered at him. "It *was* for real, wasn't it? That kiss."

Yes. "She's a good person," he repeated. Even if she had jumped straight to thinking the worst of him last night.

Delia folded her arms and nodded. Nodded again. She stood. "Let me think about it. I wasn't going to make any kind of move today anyway. I want to see how the awards turn out tonight. Besides, I'm following up on a different lead, too. Something about a new show to possibly replace *From the Ground Up*."

"I've been looking into that, too. Haven't gotten too far yet."

All he had was a name—Hollie Morris, the woman who had once been a shoo-in for the *From the Ground Up* gig before Miranda arrived on the scene.

The way he figured it, she may have created the new show just to get back at Miranda. But that was as far as he'd taken his research—because he'd become sidetracked, caught up in feelings for a woman who apparently still might not trust him.

Man, what if I'm doing all this and at the end of the day have only a good-bye to show for it?

"Anyway," Delia said, "I guess I'm willing to wait it out. Maybe a better story will present itself—better than America's tomboy darling cheating on her hubby."

His first urge was to argue that last part, but he swallowed his retort. "Thank you," he said instead. "Really."

"I only said I'd consider it."

But it was hope enough for today. He thanked Delia again, even shook her hand, then hurried to his car.

It's going to be okay, Miranda. Everything's going to be fine. As long as that better story really panned out. He'd ask Miranda about Hollie Morris. See if the woman had held a grudge. But assuming Delia had gotten as far in her research as he had, would she really consider the maneuvering of Hollie

Morris more intriguing than, as she said, a story about America's tomboy darling cheating?

Except she wasn't cheating. Why, if Delia knew the truth . . .

Wait . . .

What if she *could* know? What if Matthew could convince Miranda to stop role-playing in a pretend marriage? To just come out with the truth? She'd be free of her lies . . .

Free to be in a real relationship.

He turned onto the road leading out of Asheville, his hope rising like mist from the valley.

Mom was holding a framed photo of Grandma and Grandpa Woodruff when Miranda came down the stairs. Miranda had traded last night's dress for a pair of worn jeans and a pullover fleece. Might as well get comfy for these couple free hours before she'd need to leave for Asheville to catch her jet to Nashville for the gala.

Then again, standing in the same room as Mom felt anything but comfortable.

"Your father misses them so much," Mom said as she replaced the frame on the end table beside Miranda's couch. "I know he regrets hurrying back to Brazil so quickly after your grandma's funeral. If he'd known his dad was going to follow so closely . . ."

Low-slung clouds outside hurled gray and shadow instead of sunlight through the living room's tall windows. Miranda hugged her arms to herself, wishing words would come, waiting for the emotional reaction she knew she should be having right now.

Mom is here. In North Carolina. At my house.

And she didn't know what she was supposed to be feeling.

"I'm sorry to show up so suddenly." Mom's words were a repeat of earlier in the workshop. Miranda had almost knocked

Blaze over as she stood up, one of his socks pushed halfway up her ankle.

Mom had hugged her, her touch light and uncertain. And then Miranda had fumbled through an introduction of Blaze. "He's a . . . friend." It was one thing to lie to the press. Another to her mother. She couldn't make herself.

"You don't have to apologize," she said now.

Mom turned a slow circle around the room. "I cannot believe my daughter built this place. It's beautiful, Miranda. It truly is."

Miranda. Her nickname had never stuck with Mom and Dad. "Well, it would be nicer if I'd actually finish it someday." She shifted her weight from one foot to the other. "Um, how's Dad?"

"He's probably sitting in our flat pouting right now about not being here. But we just started a church plant, and his back pain's been flaring up. He saw a doctor last week who pretty much ordered him to take it easy. We didn't think an eight-hour plane ride would be good for him. But I promise you, it killed him to stay behind."

Mom settled onto the beige couch, pulling her feet up under her knees. Her dark hair, same shade as Miranda's, hung free and wavy, and she wore a long, belted sweater over loose linen pants. She had to have flown overnight, but there was barely a hint of travel weariness about her. Instead, a faint swirl of hope danced in her blue eyes.

"Please, Miranda. Sit with me? Talk?"

But Miranda couldn't sit yet, couldn't relax. Her skittish emotions might be tiptoeing around each other, but there was no denying the hard glint of resentment vying for center. Words she'd never said—accusations, pain—jammed in her throat. Could she really give her hurt voice now, when Mom had come all this way?

"Why are you here?" She blurted the question, arms still folded and legs refusing to bend.

Mom seemed momentarily surprised at the question but covered it with a soft smile. "I've wanted to see where you live, Miranda. I've missed being a part of your life."

"Were you ever a part of my life?"

A clear pinch of pain played across Mom's face, and Miranda almost wished the question back. Because truly, it wasn't a fair question, was it? Mom had given her life. She'd clothed and fed and cared for her those early years. And even when in her deepest pain—as a kid waiting for her parents to finally send for her, as a teen more in need of a mother than ever, as a heartbroken adult—she'd always known deep down that her parents loved her, maybe even missed her.

But it didn't stop the ache of their absence.

"Your father and I wish we'd done things differently, found a way to make it work for you to stay with us or come to visit you more often. I should've called you every week . . . every day. I should've made sure you knew my mother's heart never stopped beating for you."

The sound of Robbie clinking around in the kitchen jutted in. Miranda's stomach growled. She finally sat, the recliner's leather cool through the fabric of her jeans. "I don't want to be angry at you."

"It's okay to be angry. Let's be honest with each other. If you want to know the truth, I've had my moments of being upset with you in this past year. Every time a letter or e-mail went unanswered, a phone call unreturned. I started to think you wanted nothing to do with us."

A sliver of guilt wove through Miranda's mess of thoughts. And yet at the same time, she felt something unfolding in her heart—a willingness to have this conversation. To maybe, finally, say what needed to be said, to release the hurt she'd held on to for too long.

Just like she'd finally let go of Robbie.

"When I got your e-mail, Miranda, I dropped everything. I printed it out, found Cliff. We read it together, and . . ." Mom's gaze held Miranda's. "We just held each other and wept."

"Why?" The question was barely a whisper. She couldn't even picture it. Her parents, the bold missionaries, the tireless workers . . . crying? And she certainly hadn't said anything riveting in the e-mail.

Liquid glistened in Mom's eyes, and her voice shook with emotion. "We missed you. We missed our daughter."

Tears pricked the backs of Miranda's eyelids. She unfolded her arms and allowed herself to sink deeper into the recliner's embrace.

Mom dabbed at the corners of her eyes with her sleeve's edge. "Then when Robbie called, said he thought you might be in trouble, and told us about this gala thing, I bought a plane ticket."

Robbie had called her parents? Miranda thought back to the day she'd finally asked him to leave, the day he'd told her he still loved her. He'd argued with her, pushed her, attempted to sway her as he once had. He'd finally left, anger clearly displayed in his march to his car.

But underneath his ire, he must have been concerned enough about her to call her parents. Or perhaps he hoped Mom and Dad would help his cause. Either way . . .

Mom shifted, leather creaking underneath her.

"I . . . I feel bad that you spent money on a plane ticket. I know finances are always tight."

Mom was shaking her head before Miranda finished, eyes still glassy. "I know it might not be easy, Miranda. We might have to start back at the very beginning, get to know each other all over again. But I want to try." She leaned forward, reaching one hand to Miranda's knee. "Please, can we try?"

Miranda blinked, one tear and then another finally finding

their way down her cheeks. "There's so much you don't know. Robbie and me . . . and my show . . . and Blaze . . ." A sob caught in her throat.

Mom grasped Miranda's hands, gently tugging her to the couch, to her side, and wrapped her arms around her daughter. "Now would be a great time to tell me."

❧

Matthew drove over the speed limit all the way to Miranda's, rehearsing words he'd somehow find a way to say when he arrived.

Think about it, Miranda. All you ever seem to worry about is what you'll lose if you tell the truth. But what about what you might gain?

He parked in front of her house, dodged raindrops that had finally begun to fall. He took the steps two at a time up the porch and heard the voices drifting from the kitchen when he entered the house.

Halfway through the living room, he stopped. That wasn't Blaze's voice. He recognized that accent. And come to think of it, the blue Prius was in the driveway again, wasn't it?

Had Matthew gotten rid of one problem only to find another? He started forward again, marching through the dining room . . . and then froze. Disbelieving.

Because there stood Miranda, leaning forward to wrap her arms around Robbie's neck, her murmured "Thank you" like a sucker punch to Matthew's stomach. He blinked, forced his eyes back open . . . only to see her kiss the guy's cheek.

He turned, the weight of a hundred *why*s on his shoulder, and retreated from the house the way he'd come, down the porch steps to his waiting Jeep. He pounded his fist on the rain-slicked metal of the door, drops pattering on the vehicle's roof, down his cheeks.

314

How many times was he supposed to forgive her? The lies? The unspoken accusation last night? Now this? And he'd been ready to ask her to consider giving it all up for . . . what? Him?

Taking a deep breath, his chest tight, nerves taut, he let himself into the Jeep and wrenched his digital recorder from his bag. While he drove, he started composing out loud.

Chapter 19

Tonight everything would change.

The full-length mirror in the Nashville Convention Center ladies' room displayed a woman Miranda barely recognized. Every hair in place. A makeup job Whitney would've been proud of—shimmery blue over her eyes and rosy cheeks. The deep-purple-almost-black of her dress held close to her skin from her shoulders to her waist, where it gathered and belled the rest of the way to the floor.

Not quite as perfect as the dress Matthew had given her. But close.

"You look gorgeous." Miranda's mother's seafoam eyes met hers in the mirror. She still couldn't believe it. Mom had come all this way. And at Robbie's urging, nonetheless.

"I'm a bundle of nerves." And she would have felt so much better if Matthew had returned even one of her calls or texts. She never should have accused him last night. Surely he'd show up at the gala. Even if he hadn't returned to the cabin. Or met them at the Asheville airport for their private flight. Or, as of yet, checked in at the press desk inside the convention center.

Miranda knew. She'd checked.

Had he been busy all day tracking down the reporter who'd taken those photos last night? Even in the emotion of Mom's return, her niggling dread at what would happen when those photos were released hadn't gone away.

"I can think of only one thing you're missing," her mother said now, pulling her arm from behind her to reveal a jewelry box.

"Mom, you didn't have to."

"I didn't. Your father did. He wanted to be here."

That morning, after slowly breaking past the barriers time and geography and emotion had erected, Miranda had told her mom everything. And what amazed her more than anything was the fact that Mom hadn't criticized, hadn't scolded, had barely batted an eye.

"Everything's such a wreck," Miranda had said as they listened to the cadence of the rain hitting the living room windows. "I'm in so deep."

"There's nothing so deep God can't pull you out," Mom had replied after a pause. "Sometimes, though, it means doing the hard things. Because how can you grasp His hand if you're holding so tight to the prison bars? What do you want, daughter? What do you truly want?"

Miranda replayed her answer in her mind now as she popped the jewelry case open with her thumb.

To just be me. The real thing. No more lies. Freedom.

And Matthew. It was the first time she'd admitted it without hesitation.

Inside the velvet box, she found a dainty silver charm bracelet. Dangling from the diamond-studded links, a series of tiny charms—a hammer, a house, a boot, a saw. Tears pricked Miranda's eyes. "It's perfect." She lifted the bracelet from its case and held out her wrist for her mom to clasp the bracelet in place.

One morning conversation and one bracelet didn't erase years of feeling betrayed and abandoned. But they were on their way to healing—something Miranda couldn't have imagined just a day ago.

A gaggle of women entered the women's room then. Miranda heard the whisper as they passed. "That's Randi Woodruff!"

She shared a grin with her mother. "Let's go. We're missing the dancing."

"I knew you were a celebrity, dear, but experiencing your fame firsthand is quite the experience."

Miranda chuckled as they headed toward the ballroom. Her mom had looked just as bewildered when she'd realized their flight from Asheville was a private jet. And when a pool of photographers met them at the Nashville airport. And when Brad and Lincoln whisked them into a limo.

A jazz band played a brassy tune behind the chatter of guests as they entered the ballroom. A dance floor filled the front of the room, and clusters of white-topped tables covered the rest. Flowery perfume swirled with the sweet smell of champagne.

"Oh my," Lena whispered.

"This way, Mom." Miranda led the way to one of the front tables, where she'd spotted Brad and Liv, Lincoln and his date, Blaze . . . and Robbie.

Yes, Miranda had obtained a last-minute ticket for Robbie. Not so much because she desired his attendance, but because it had been amazingly considerate of him to encourage her parents to visit her. Also, despite all that had happened in the in-between years, he had been a part of her life when *From the Ground Up* began. It was possible she wouldn't be here today without him.

They'd even shared a tender moment this morning in her kitchen. They'd always have the past between them. But it didn't mean she couldn't appreciate his show of concern.

Liv squealed as they reached the table. "Randi Woodruff, you are the picture of elegance. Ooh, and show me your bracelet!"

Miranda hugged her friend. "Look at you two. My best friends here. Together. As a couple."

"Don't start, kid," Brad said as he hugged her.

"You can't expect me not to be happy about this."

"Tonight is about you," Brad argued.

"Fine. But we're *so* talking about this tomorrow."

He leaned in then and lowered his voice. "Actually, can we talk business for one second? Thanks to Knox, I've got info on that new show."

She gripped his arm. "You've heard from Knox today?"

Brad's brow wrinkled in confusion. "You haven't?"

She shook her head, itching to pester him with questions. But he spoke first.

"It's Hollie Morris. The other show, she's at the helm."

"The woman I beat out in the audition?"

Brad nodded. "Makes all kinds of sense now, doesn't it? Fits in with what Sasha from SteelWorks said. I couldn't figure out why such a show would target a network that already has a successful home show. But if she still holds a grudge and knows your ratings aren't the best, well—" He broke off suddenly. "Shoot, why did I even bring this up? It's your big night. I'm an idiot."

"You're not." Besides, she was more concerned about Matthew's whereabouts than what Hollie Morris was planning. And why had he called Brad about what he'd found out and not her?

But Matthew would show up soon. He would.

Miranda forced her attention to Blaze. He'd shaved and spruced himself up for tonight. His broad shoulders filled his white dress shirt, and his black leather shoes shined. His tuxedo jacket hung free over his left arm, still in a sling. "You're looking mighty handsome, Blaze Hunziker," she drawled. "All the women will be jealous of me."

His blush spanned all the way from his cheeks down to his collar. "Just wanted to make my woman proud."

She reached up to straighten his bow tie. "Mission accomplished."

He studied her, a depth she'd only recently come to recognize in his brown eyes. "It's been fun, Miranda."

"After all this time, he finally uses my full name."

She greeted Lincoln next, introduced her mom to those she hadn't met yet, and thanked Robbie once more for contacting her parents.

"You know why I did it, yes?" he said, voice low enough for her ears only.

She tilted her head.

"You don't have to say anything now. But later . . ." His eyes suggested an impossible possibility.

Oh, Robbie. Somehow she'd have to kindly let him know it really, truly was over. Despite his grand gesture.

She escaped the table then, moving around the room, hugging other industry friends, meeting new people, taking time to find and greet the other nominees.

All the while, she strained for a glimpse of Matthew. He'd probably spent the day tracking down whoever had taken those photos last night and had decided to travel separately to give her space.

He'll be here. He wouldn't abandon her tonight of all nights.

But if he was at the gala, he was avoiding her.

Miranda finally made her way back to her table when the ballroom lights dimmed and the music softened. Her mom grasped her hand when she sat. "This is it, honey."

Brad gave her a thumbs-up, Blaze a wink.

"It'll be you, for sure," Liv mouthed.

Matthew? Where's Matthew?

The president of the foundation walked onto the stage, her heels clacking against wood as she took her place behind the glass podium. "Good evening, ladies and gentlemen. My name is Gemma Cornish, and on behalf of the Giving Heart Foundation, thank you all for coming tonight."

Gemma gave a brief history of the Giving Heart Award, the importance of those in the national spotlight paving the way for citizen volunteerism and compassion, an overview of the selection process.

And then the lights blackened for video introductions of all three nominees. Screens flanking the stage lit up. Miranda barely heard documentary-style footage about Rachel Stilles, a Hollywood actress who'd been in a half-dozen blockbusters in the past two years, and her work for the Red Cross. Nor was she able to pay attention to the piece on Harry Creighton, the star of an Emmy-winning sitcom, and his support for a cancer center's research program.

Even as her own segment played, showing clips of her show, her work on the homes she'd built for families in need, her volunteer efforts at Open Arms, her mind was elsewhere.

God, if I win, please, help me to go through with it. With the plan . . .

And Matthew. *Please let him be here.*

The screens went black. Gemma took her place behind the podium once more. "All three of our nominees have hearts of gold and have chosen to use their national platforms to truly make a difference. Our decision was very difficult."

Gemma paused, took a breath. "But we did, of course, make a decision. And it's my pleasure to announce the winner of the 2013 Giving Heart Award . . ."

Mom's hand squeezed hers.

Breathe, Miranda.

". . . Randi Woodruff, host of *From the Ground Up!*"

The applause thundered as Miranda rose, surprise mingling with delight, mingling with . . .

Nerves. So tight they squeezed her lungs and wobbled her knees. She met her mom's glistening eyes. *Steady.* By a miracle she made it up the stairs to the platform and across the stage to Gemma. The foundation president hugged her, presented a plaque and an envelope containing the check for $100,000.

But then Gemma stepped aside and nudged Miranda to the podium. She stepped up to the microphone. Did it pick up the thumping of her heart? The breaths coming in tiny puffs?

"The truth will set you free."

Mom's words sang through her mind. It was time to do what she'd come to do.

"Wow, this is such an incredible honor." Her voice sounded strange in the mic, tinny and shaky. "Harry, Rachel, you are both just as deserving, and it's a privilege to count myself in your company."

Spotlights blinded her view, whiting out the faces of the audience.

"I have so many people to thank. My best friend, Liv Hayes, director of the Open Arms shelter for children with special needs, where this check in my hands is going. You inspire me, Liv. My executive producer, Lincoln Nash, the show's director, Tom Bass, and the rest of the executives and crew who make *From the Ground Up* possible, thank you. Brad Walsh, you're the best manager a girl could ask for and an amazing friend, too.

"My mom, Lena Woodruff, who's here tonight, and my dad, Clifford, who is back in Brazil, where they serve as missionaries. I love you both. And . . . I thank God. For not giving up on me."

One breath. Two.

"And finally . . ."

Could she do it? Three breaths. Four.

What do you want, Miranda? What do you really want?

She gripped the glass edges of the podium. Lincoln would be furious. Everyone else, confused.

The truth will set you free.

One more inhale, and with it, resolve. "Finally, I'd like to thank the man who, through his friendship, through his constant reaching out in kindness to those he cares about, through his many, many strengths and, yes, a few quirks, too, has truly captured my heart."

Whispers feathered through the room. Sighs and laughter met with the snapping of another spotlight.

"This man walked into my life just when I needed someone. And even though I can't say thank you enough for all he's done for me, I'm going to try. Thank you . . ."

The spotlight swayed, found Miranda's table.

". . . ever so much to the man I—"

Two figures rose.

". . . love."

Blaze. Robbie. Both stood haloed by the spotlight, twin confusion playing over their faces as the crowd gasped.

No. Not them.

Humiliation twisted its way to Miranda's core, joined by a searing disappointment. She dropped her hands from the podium, losing her voice before his name could escape from his lips.

And at the back of the room, a flicker of movement caught her eye as the ballroom door thudded to a close under the buzzing red of the Exit sign.

The airport was quiet, only a murmur of distant voices and the sound of luggage wheels purring over the carpet.

A woman padded past Matthew, her glance traveling up and down his body.

Yes, I'm in a tuxedo. Yes, I know I look ridiculous.

In front of him, expansive windows displayed the Asheville skyline, a twinkle of lights set against the backdrop of the mountains.

"Flight 1041 to Chicago now boarding passengers in Section A. Section A passengers now boarding to Chicago." The voice came over loudspeakers and Matthew stood. Chicago, then Minneapolis, then home.

He glanced once more at the North Carolina view, then turned away and boarded his plane.

Chapter 20

Tires crackled over gravel as Robbie's Prius disappeared down the lane. A heavy wind hurled itself against Miranda's face, tangling in her hair. Pale sunlight was no match for the late-October chill that had painted the ground a frosty white. A glistening blanket still rested in place this afternoon.

"Good-bye, Robbie." She whispered the words, letting autumn's breath carry away her farewell.

Robbie hadn't understood. But he'd gone.

"I'm really sorry, Rand." Blaze's voice came from behind. He stood on her porch steps, hands hidden in the pockets of his hooded sweatshirt, the luggage from their one-night stay in Nashville at his feet. Apology and regret swam together in his eyes. "If I'd known, I never would've—"

She should have warned them of what she was planning to say—but she hadn't been certain she would go through with her plan. "You couldn't have known. It's not your fault." Not his fault he *and* Robbie had stood during her declaration of love. They'd had this conversation twice already. Once last night when they'd finally escaped the onslaught of press after her humiliating acceptance speech. Again in the plane on the way home.

"I thought . . ." The low-toned cadence of wind chimes filled in where his voice left off.

He'd thought he was playing his part as expected. And Robbie, obviously, had assumed he'd earned himself a spot back into Miranda's heart.

What Blaze didn't realize was, it wasn't so much the embarrassment of having two men stand during the program that ripped into Miranda's heart. It was more the fact that a third had walked out.

She hadn't been able to see the person who'd disappeared from the ballroom just as Matthew Knox's name climbed up her throat. But somehow, she knew.

So here she was, standing in the cold on her expansive property, which once again only reminded her how alone she really was. Just like the first time Robbie left.

And not at all like then. Because this time around, she had brought the rejection on herself with deceit. One deliberate lie after another. She couldn't blame Matthew for turning his back on her. Not one tiny bit.

And she couldn't blame the press for going camera-happy as Blaze and Robbie had stood there last night staring at each other in confusion. She hadn't even finished her speech. Only mumbled an abrupt thank-you and fled the stage. She could only guess what the media was saying.

The beeping of a cell phone cut into the quiet now. It wasn't Miranda's. She'd turned it off last night, having the thumping desire to never turn it on again.

Blaze slid his phone from his pocket and read the text message. "Brad wants to talk to you. He's worried."

"Could you tell him I'm fine? Just not very talkative. I think I'll take a walk."

Her steps crunched over the hard sheen of frost underfoot.

"Miranda," Blaze called. He padded down the porch steps, hustled to her side. "Don't you want to know? Don't you wonder what the press is saying?"

"I could make a pretty good guess. 'Randi Woodruff Makes a Fool of Herself.' 'Marriage Troubles in Randi-Land?' Does that sound about right?"

"So you said you wanted to thank the man you love. So more than one guy stood. Nobody died. We can explain it."

"But that's just it. I'm tired of coming up with false explanations."

Blaze stood his ground, his demeanor for once stern. "Last night you were prepared to stand up in front of a celebrity audience and confess the truth—that you're not really married, that you've fallen for a guy you just met. What's different today than last night?"

The answer sprang to her lips. "What's different is Matthew's gone."

Blaze flung his good arm in frustration. "Because he thought you were talking about me! Or Robbie. Doesn't matter. Call him up and tell him the truth."

How could Blaze understand? What did he want her to do? She might be Randi Woodruff, the homebuilder, the award winner. She might be able to handle blueprints and crews and power tools.

But she couldn't handle rejection. Not again.

Blaze gripped her shoulder. "Last night you planned a grand gesture, the kind of thing most of us wish we were brave enough to do—wished we even had reason to do. You were ready to sacrifice your show, your career, your reputation if it meant a future with Knox. Don't give up on that."

Miranda pulled away. "You don't get it. Matthew walked away. It's done. And what I have left is *From the Ground Up.* It's the constant in my life. So no, I'm not going to lay it down on the altar of futile wishes."

Blaze's eyes searched hers. "You are not your show, Rand."

"And you're not my husband." The words flew from her lips—hurtful, she knew, by the wince Blaze tried to hide.

But he nodded, lips pressed and jaw set. Behind him, the mountain landscape had lost its color. "Your mom said she was putting on a pot of tea. Think I'll join her." He turned slowly.

"Blaze—"

"It's okay. You're right," he said over his shoulder. Then he stopped and faced her once more. "But I am, too. And one of these days, you're going to stop defining yourself by your career. Or your past. Or whatever man happens to disappoint you at the time."

Miranda sucked in a sharp breath as his verbal darts hit on target. Only when Blaze disappeared into the house did her first tear fall.

⚭

"Knox, you're a genius."

Dooley's enthusiasm was enough to grind up the last of Matthew's energy. Weariness after his night of flights glazed over him. "Genius?" Try idiot. Phone to his ear, Matthew plodded from his bedroom and into his townhouse living room. Beige walls matched his spirits.

"You went dark, man, just when everyone started talking about you."

Matthew dropped onto his aging couch, Miranda's voice suddenly spinning through his mind. *"A high-quality sofa is always heavier because of its sturdy frame, which is constructed of kiln-dried hardwood free from knots."*

Free from knots.

"Look, I'm sorry I didn't get today's blog post done. I just couldn't decide what to—"

Dooley cut him off. "Don't you get it? I'm not calling because I'm annoyed. Yes, I had a moment of worry when I realized you hadn't posted anything today. But now, with all the rumors . . ."

Worry trickled in. Had Delia released those photos after all? Matthew fought the sluggish fog confusing his thoughts, forced his eyes open. His gaze landed on the overgrown spider plant by his patio doors. Limp leaves hung from a yellow vine. He couldn't even keep a plant alive. "What rumors?"

"About you and Randi Woodruff."

"Delia—"

"No, not her. First, it was the comments section on your blog. Did you seriously never read those? Commenters have been speculating that our blogger had a little crush on his subject for weeks now. But the biggie is the fact that at the gala last night Randi Woodruff all but admitted she's in love with someone who *isn't* her husband."

Matthew swallowed the reply that jumped up his throat. Miranda hadn't confessed any such thing. Unless . . . had she said more after he'd walked out?

"Come on, you were there. Two guys stood, but she didn't acknowledge either one. Soo . . ."

Matthew finally caught on. "She wasn't talking about me, if that's what you're thinking."

"That's exactly what I'm thinking. I'm not stupid. I've read all your blogs. I've listened to you justify her obvious husband-parading at every turn. You went campaign-crazy trying to help save her show." Dooley paused. "And then there are the photos you begged our lawyer to stop. You got her to fall for you, my friend. I knew you were a risk-taker sort of journalist, but I had no idea you'd go this far."

He was going to throw up. "I did not do this on purpose. There's nothing genius about it."

Dooley filled his pause with a slow whistle. "You mean you actually fell for her? A married woman?"

"Let it go, Dooley." He stood and paced the room, fighting the image in his head of Miranda in Robbie's arms. "I can guarantee you she wasn't talking about me up on that stage last night."

Dooley gave an irritated grunt. "Then why didn't you post your final blog this morning? I thought you were playing coy with the press."

"I wasn't playing anything." Tired frustration finally boiled over in his voice. "I'm done. That's all."

"You owe me a blog post, Knox. And a cover story."

"Do we have to talk about this now? I've had three hours of sleep." Matthew moved toward his bedroom once more, plodding past the tuxedo he'd discarded in the wee hours of the morning. His foot caught on the jacket, and when he jerked it loose, something plastic slipped from the pocket.

"You're not doing this to me again. First Margaret McKee, now Randi Woodruff. You're imploding, Knox."

Matthew knelt and picked up the flash drive. He'd had the thing in his pocket at the gala. It contained the story he'd written yesterday afternoon about Miranda, a regular tell-all. After he'd seen Miranda and Robbie together in her kitchen, he'd let his annoyance write the article, and for a few heated hours, he'd had every intention of sending it to Dooley.

Now?

Now exhaustion muddied his determination. And the memory of Miranda up on that stage, the relief and pleasure and hope dancing over her face, tore into his anger.

"If it's conflict of interest you're worried about—" Dooley began.

"It's not." He held the flash drive in front of his face. Send it and sear Miranda's reputation to ashes? Toss it and forget his instant career comeback? Matthew lowered into his bed, let his head fall against a pillow, and lifted his legs onto the mattress. "Can we talk about this later?"

"Oh, we'll talk. And you'll deliver. I invested in you. I gave you an instant career boost. You're not going to screw this up."

Screw-up. He'd never escape it, the label, the identity. Matthew buried his head under his pillow. All he wanted was sleep.

And to forget the past month.

Not true, and you know it.

Matthew ended the call, Dooley's voice still barking, and tossed his phone across the bed. He'd deal with it all later.

But just as his eyes drifted closed, a rap on his front door yanked him from the start of what would've surely been a restless sleep. *If* he'd even been able to turn off his sparring thoughts. He forced his feet to the floor, knowing as he covered the distance from his bed to the door who he'd find on the other side.

"It's about time," Cee spoke and signed at the same time as he pulled the door open. Her wide blue eyes glowed in the light of his living room, a stream of the sun's rays pouring in behind her.

He gave her a hug, her head tipped back so she could see his moving lips. "Don't tell me you learned to drive while I was gone. How'd you get here?"

"Surprise!" Izzy tracked through his front door, a steaming dish in her hands. And Jase behind her, his arms filled with more dishes. He should've known when he texted Jase to let him know he was home that they'd show up.

"What is going on?" Did he appear as bedraggled as he felt? He looked down at his bare feet, wrinkled jeans.

"We came straight from church to bring you Sunday dinner." Izzy set the dish on his counter and turned.

Jase emptied his load and gave Matthew a one-armed hug. "Good to have you back for more than a day this time. Cee's been listless without her uncle-hero."

Hero, huh. "And I missed all of you. Especially you." He

ruffled Cee's hair, then raked his hand through his own. "I reek of airplane. Do I have time to grab a shower before dinner?"

"Yep." Izzy held up a Pillsbury tube. "I still have to bake the rolls."

"Hey, Cee," he spoke and signed simultaneously, "there's a gift for you in my computer bag."

Something Miranda had carved—a figurine of a dog. Cee had been begging for a real dog for years. He heard her "Ooh" as he rounded the corner to the bathroom.

"Hey, Matt," Jase said, following him down the hall.

"I know, the dog was a bad choice. Only gives her more ammo for begging."

A chuckle rolled from Jase's lips. "It's not that. Besides, she's stopped begging ever since we told her she's going to have a baby sister or brother." Jase gripped the doorframe to the bathroom as Matthew rummaged for a towel. "You, uh . . . you okay?"

Matthew caught a glimpse of his reflection in the mirror over the sink as he turned—shadowed cheeks, tired eyes. *No wonder she didn't pick you.* "Fine. Why? You've seen me look worse than this."

"Nothing to do with your looks. Your walk—it's like a man defeated."

Matthew leaned over the sink. "I messed everything up. Like alw—"

"Don't say it." Jase stepped into the bathroom, his reflection joining Matthew's. "Little brother, you have got to get over thinking you're a failure."

"Jase, I need a shower, not a pep talk."

Jase shook his head, gaze stern. "What you need is to try to see yourself the way the rest of us do. You are Superman to Cee—supportive, entertaining, always there for her. And Izzy—you've become the sibling she never had. I'll never forget that weekend I was traveling when our basement flooded and you came to Izzy's rescue. Man, there is no one I'd trust my family with more."

Matthew met Jase's eyes in the mirror. "But—"

"No buts. And me. When I brought Izzy and Celine home, you were the one who listened when I had trouble adjusting to such a huge life change. You're the one who learned ASL with me, who accepted my new family as your own. And don't think I don't know you encouraged Randi Woodruff to buy that print last week."

At Randi's name, Matthew hung his head.

"And speaking of her," Jase continued his speech. "You were her friend when she needed one. She told Izzy as much. You kept her secrets."

Except not entirely. Jase didn't know about that flash drive sitting on his bedside table with the article Dooley expected.

"Underneath your dogged reporter exterior, brother, you've got a noble heart and a sensitive spirit. If you won't take my word for it, take Izzy's." Jase's expression turned sheepish. "I told her what you told me last week, all about Randi Wood-ruff's fake marriage. She ah-ha'd like it wasn't even much of a surprise. She's the one who told me I had to talk some sense into you today."

Matthew's first smile since leaving North Carolina found his lips. "She is a good judge of character. She married you." And as if on wheels, the weight of emotions so heavy they physically hurt began a slow roll. "I wish I knew what to do next."

Jase gave him a hearty pat on the back. "I've got an idea. Let God back in. And trust that whatever He's got in store for you next, you're up to it."

Minutes turned into miles until Miranda found herself standing in front of the church. Blaze's words had followed her all the way to the church, the humming of the wind their soundtrack.

Accusations, they'd seemed. But now?

As she heaved open the heavy wood door, felt the rush of quiet pull her in, the truth hushed over her. *Blaze is right.* She'd lost the core of her identity under layer after layer of self-donned façades.

Randi the tomboy.

Randi the happily married.

Randi the celebrity.

Randi the . . . *rejected.*

She lowered into her pew, halfway down the aisle. *What happened to Miranda?* And should she even be here, in a house of worship, when the house of her heart was in such disarray? *God, how do I clean up the mess?*

So many times she'd perched in this same pew, in this little church tucked into its mountainous nook, always hungry for the touch of the God her parents served but mindful of the wall her sins built.

Suddenly the sound of movement, shuffling feet, jutted into her solitude. Someone slid into the pew beside Miranda, the bench creaking from the weight.

A whisper. "We had a feeling we'd find you here."

Mom? "How'd you know?"

"He may not be your husband, but he knows you. Look." She pointed to where Blaze moved down the side aisle toward their row.

Miranda's brow furrowed.

And then, more footsteps. Joni Watters settled into the pew in front of Miranda. Others, folks Miranda had never met, dotted the sanctuary. And was that Jimmy and Audrey walking down the aisle now?

Miranda leaned close to her mother. "I'm confused. What's going on?"

"Looks like church to me."

"Their services are in the morning. That's why I come in the afternoon."

"Hush," her mom said, just as Blaze took his seat on Miranda's right.

"We should leave. I don't fit here. If they all knew—"

"We know more than you think, Miranda," Joni said over her shoulder as a man, probably her husband, took his place behind the pulpit. "We've got TVs. We read newspapers. Believe it or not, some of us are even so technologically inclined as to read blogs. Now pipe down and listen. Whatever it is that's kept you from joining the services all these years, we can handle. Talking in church . . . not so much."

Joni straightened, and Miranda leaned back against her seat. Was this a joke or something?

"Who am I?" Pastor Watters said from the pulpit. "It's the question many of us start asking as adolescents. And where we find the answer makes all the difference. Today I'm going to tell you where to find that answer. It starts right there."

He pointed to the stained-glass face of Jesus, its reflection casting a rainbow of color over the front of the church. Miranda's mom clasped her hand.

Miranda glanced at Blaze and met his wink.

This wasn't a joke at all, was it? They were doing church. For her.

"Some of you knew Old Hez, a long-time member of this congregation. And you may know he crafted this pulpit." The pastor tapped the side of the wood structure. "What you may not know is that I spent hours helping Hezekiah strip the ugly pulpit we used to have to make this one. His arthritis was bad, but he was determined.

"Originally this thing was so overly stained it almost glowed in the dark." The pastor stepped from behind the pulpit as his audience laughed. He leaned against its side. "You could hardly tell what kind of wood it was under the stain."

Miranda leaned forward, gaze tracing every detail of the pulpit now. They would've used a coat of stripper first to soften the old stain. Then probably a stiff bristle brush or scraper. Finally, a lacquer thinner . . .

"When we wiped off the last of the stain, I wasn't sure what to think," Pastor Watters said. "Suddenly I could see nooks and grooves I hadn't noticed before, some from our own scraping, I'm sure. But Old Hez, he saw something else entirely."

The pastor paused, and Miranda felt her breath catch.

"He said, 'Pastor, you were ready to get rid of this old pulpit because all you saw was that ugly stain. But all along, underneath was a sturdy, strong wood. The kind of wood that's made to last. Just took a little stripping away for you to see it.'"

The pastor stepped down from the stage. "Here's the thing, friends: Hez saw the beauty all along, even when the curve of the wood's grain was hidden behind a stain."

All right, God. I'm listening.

"And it makes me think, what does God see in us that we don't? That matters. Because when all the stuff we're hiding behind is stripped away, it's what He sees that's left. So what does He see?"

His creation. Forgiven. Whole. Enough.

Miranda couldn't hold in the tears gathering in her eyes. Didn't even try.

Chapter 21

He was actually doing this. Willingly. Waiting for Delia Jones.

Matthew sat on a cold cement bench outside the Minnesota Zoo, the collar of his jacket flipped up to his chin. Was it really just over a month ago he'd attended the fund-raising gig here? That fiasco seemed forever ago.

Seemed like yesterday.

The snap of heels against cement drew his attention. She stood in front of him wearing a trench coat cinched at her waist and hair slicked into a severe ponytail, sharpening her already high cheekbones. "Hi, Delia."

"You came. I'm impressed."

He smiled despite her sarcasm and scooted to make room on the bench. After a guarded moment, she lowered beside him.

"If this is about the article with my dad, I did call him the other day. It's too late to do his campaign any good, but he's still interested." Gordon Knox had lost the election this past Tuesday, but Matthew had a feeling the man already had his eye on the future.

It hadn't been all that pleasant of a phone call—certainly not easy, but necessary.

"That's not why I asked to meet. I'm going to give it to you straight, Knox." She folded one leg over the other. "I couldn't just let the Randi Woodruff story go."

Matthew swallowed a gulp. How long until the day when every mention of Miranda's name ceased to pinch a nerve? "Please don't tell me you're releasing those photos."

She shook her head. "Not exactly. You know what happened at the gala with the two guys standing, right? I recognized the husband. The other, I didn't. So I did a little checking. Name's Roberto Pontero. He's—"

"Miranda's former fiancé. I know."

Delia clucked her tongue. "You see the potential for a story, yeah? Who is this guy? Why was he at the gala? He must be hiding out, because no one has the story. So, I figured I'll trade my photos for the full scoop. Only problem is, I can't get past Woodruff's manager. He insists she's not doing any interviews and won't even hear me out."

The bench rasped as Matthew shifted. "And you think I can get to her."

She shrugged. "You looked awfully cozy that night at that dance hall."

Matthew allowed room for silence to descend. For days, he'd ignored Dooley's calls, but here it was again—the opportunity laid out in plain terms. Expose Miranda. Hoist his own career.

Or don't.

It would've made sense to publish the story. If nothing else, it might stop the endless speculation about Miranda's love life ever since the gala.

But he'd already made the decision. Made it the day he slipped his flash drive into an envelope and dropped it in the mailbox.

"Delia." His jaw twitched as he spoke her name. "I didn't come here so we could talk work. I came to say I'm sorry."

She folded her hands in her lap. "You won't do the article with me."

"No, I mean, I'm sorry for everything. I'm sorry for taking you on that one date and then pretending like it never happened. I'm sorry for dragging you into the story about my father. I'm sorry for not working harder to make sure you came out of that mess unscathed."

With each sentence, she fidgeted more, twisting her hands in her lap, disbelief mixing with confusion in her green eyes. "What's your angle?"

"No angle. Just an apology. I know it's late, and maybe it doesn't mean anything to you. But I needed to say it." Because maybe he couldn't change the wrong in his past, but he could do the right thing now. "I truly am sorry. I know it doesn't make up for anything, but uh, when you called, I had a random idea. That is, I got you something."

He held out the small gift bag.

She couldn't have looked more surprised if he'd bent down on one knee to propose. She accepted the gift, suspicion still lacing her movement. But her fingers crinkled through the tissue paper and pulled up the tickets. She gave him a questioning look.

"I remember you saying you'd never been to a Vikings game. You probably have by now but—"

"I haven't," she cut in. "I . . . don't know what to say."

"Well, just say you'll enjoy the game."

She clenched the tickets, forehead still wrinkled but eyes a little softer. "This doesn't mean we're friends or anything."

"Of course not. I'd have had to get you season passes for that."

She offered him an honest-to-goodness smile then and slipped the tickets into her pocket.

"And about the article—"

"I know it's not happening. I figured as much even before I asked. But you can't blame a reporter for trying."

No, maybe you couldn't. "And the photos?"

She rolled her eyes. "If you can apologize and buy me Vikings tickets, I guess the least I can do is delete them." She said it reluctantly, but with enough sincerity to assure him she meant it. "Truth is, I don't think I like the *National Enquirer* life any more than you do."

Their parting handshake was stiff, but unless Matthew was imagining things, Delia squeezed his hand before letting go. And as she walked away, he tipped his head to the brilliant blue of the sky. *Well, God, I now know the impossible can indeed be possible.*

The honk of a car horn pulled Matthew from his joy. In the parking lot, Jase, Izzy, and Cee spilled from their car. Matthew jogged to meet them.

"You know, there was a day not so long ago when you said you'd never be able to bring your daughter to the zoo."

Jase rolled his eyes. "We're not breaking into any buildings today, little brother."

Cee grabbed his hand and tugged him toward the entrance.

Miranda swept her hand through a tangle of leaves and twigs clogging the rain gutters of Open Arms. Her work gloves scraped along the bottom of the metal gutter running across the east side of the house. The day was unusually warm, sunlight bouncing off the white of the house and an autumn breeze sifting through her hair.

It felt odd to be winterizing the shelter on an afternoon as pleasant as this. But amid the emotional roller-coaster ride of the week since she'd won the Giving Heart Award, November had crept in. Besides, Miranda needed to be busy.

She pulled out a handful of matted leaves and deposited them in the bag hooked around the ladder. When she reached in again, her fingers felt soft cloth instead of snarled sticks and leaves. A smile played over her face as she pulled out a tennis ball.

One hand still gripping the ladder, she tossed the ball over her shoulder.

"Hey!"

She twisted on the ladder with a start. "Brad?" He held his arm in the air, ball in hand. "Did you catch that? Nice."

"It was either that or get beaned in the face."

She climbed down the ladder, turning to Brad with a teasing grin. "Here to see Liv-vy?" She drew out Liv's name in a singsong voice.

Red crept over his cheeks. "That subject is off limits. And no, I'm here for you."

"Unfair. My two best friends are dating, and you tell me I'm not allowed to talk to you about it? What fun is that?"

"I'm more interested in my dignity than your fun, Rand. But speaking of Liv, she tells me you've been working all day."

"Yep," she nodded, blowing a wisp of hair from her eyes. "So far I've put in the storm windows, wrapped the basement pipes, and caulked a few leaks. Open Arms is ready for winter."

Brad perched one leg on a tree stump the Open Arms kids always designated as base during games of tag. "Tom said you spent all day yesterday doing odds and ends at the studio. And I have it on good authority you're also helping re-roof a local church."

She pulled off her work gloves and slapped them against her palm. "You're giving me that disapproving-dad look. Like that time in our college speech class when I gave the speech on felling trees."

"You brought a chain saw as your prop," he said, voice deadpan. "Today you'd probably be arrested for that." He cocked one eyebrow. "I'm just wondering if you're avoiding something. Home, maybe? Yourself?"

"How about prying friends?"

He chuckled. "Don't talk to me about prying, Miss 'I want to know everything about you and Liv.'"

She pocketed her gloves and tucked her hair behind her ears. "Brad, I'm fine, really. Life is slowly getting back to normal. Mom left for Brazil yesterday, though not before making me promise to fly down for Christmas. Blaze is heading out this week. And I haven't heard from Robbie since the day after the gala. I think I can consider him gone for good."

"And Matthew?"

Her eyes lowered to the browning grass littered with leaves that had fallen since Matthew and Blaze helped her rake. Maybe the kids would want to help this time around. They could make a game of it. "I can probably say the same about Matthew," she finally answered.

"That he's gone for good? That would really surprise me."

"Well." She leaned against the side of the house. "Could we go back to talking about how I'm avoiding something?"

Brad let her off the hook with a sigh. "Actually, there's something else I need to talk to you about."

A thrumming heavy with apprehension began in her head and worked its way to her heart. He'd heard, hadn't he? The fate of *From the Ground Up* had been decided. Her fate . . .

No. I'm done thinking that way. No more equating her life with a television show that may or may not see new life come January. "Should I sit down for this?"

He dropped his foot from the tree stump to the ground. "Yeah, pull up a stump."

She sat, folded her hands around her knees, and waited. Brad combed his fingers through his hair, his shadow shielding Miranda from the glare of the sun.

"So, I got a call from Lincoln, who got a call from one of the network bigwigs."

"Okay."

He took a breath. "There's not going to be a fourth season in January." The air whooshed from her lungs, but he spoke again before she could react. "But they're giving us a two-hour Sunday-night special in March. Apparently they were ready to drop us entirely, but Knox's blog combined with, well, all the publicity—good and bad—from the gala must have convinced them there might still be something to be gained. So *if* ratings are good, they'll consider a retooled, likely shortened, fourth season in the summer."

A Sunday-night special. A potential summer run. Either a death knell on the way to cancellation or a lifeline. "So . . ."

"So it was basically a non-decision. Nothing promised, but nothing entirely nixed." He paused, crouching to eye level with her, he studied her. "You all right?"

The thrumming faded as heat from the sun rushed over her. "Yeah. I really am."

"Even though things are pretty much still up in the air?"

"Even though."

Brad bit his lip for a moment, and then, "There's more, actually. Hollie Morris's show was picked up by a different network—which may have contributed to why we've still got a shot. But Lincoln said we have to view Hollie's show as serious competition—pull out all the stops. He wants you to do all the media rounds, talk shows." He took another breath. "And he wants you to give an explanation about what happened at the gala, an official statement about your marriage and—"

"There is no more marriage. I'm done with that." No more façade.

"They might throw your contract in your face."

"Think it could be a deal breaker?"

Brad nodded as he rose. "Possibly. After all, interest in your personal life has hit a whole new high."

Of course it had. Between her Giving Heart win and her

spectacle of an acceptance speech, she'd opened herself up to public scrutiny. And then there were the rumblings about Matthew's sudden disappearance from cyberspace. Not that she'd stopped by his blog. But she had ears.

"I love *From the Ground Up*, but it's not worth lying anymore."

Silence stretched between them until Miranda reached her arms up, a signal for Brad to pull her to her feet. "Can I have a few days to think before we agree to anything? My contract is up for renewal this spring. Maybe I should do the special and then just . . . let it go."

Brad opened his mouth, closed it. Then, "It's your choice, Rand. We've all got your back, whatever you decide."

She nodded and released a sigh, looked to the house, then back to Brad. "So, Liv made chocolate chip cookies this morning. She hates to bake almost more than I do."

"I love chocolate chip cookies."

"Exactly."

He tipped his head. "Are you sure—"

"I'm fine. I promise. But you're a good manager and friend to make sure. Besides, I'm about done with the gutters. I'm going to finish and head out." She stepped into his hug. "And one more thing. If you want to win Livvy's complete devotion, watch *The Sound of Music* with her sometime."

He groaned. "That movie's like eight hours long. I don't think so."

"Three hours. And you know you will."

He moved toward the porch, paused, then spun. "Actually, there's one more thing."

"I'm not getting a dog."

He grinned and reached into his pocket. He held a flash drive in front of her. "I've been debating whether to give this to you. I wasn't sure . . ."

"What is it?"

"I think Matthew sent it to me so we could rest assured."

"Matthew?"

"Just open the document named after you."

America has spent three seasons getting to know Randi Wood-ruff, host of *From the Ground Up*, through the glare of television screens.

I've spent three weeks getting to know her in person. No screen of separation.

So I thought.

Miranda closed her eyes against the pain Matthew's words conjured. She sat cross-legged on her bed, hunched over her laptop, the flash drive plugged into her USB port. A lit candle on her bedside stand scented her room with vanilla.

Why had Brad given this to her? Hadn't he known Matthew's article would slice into her determination to put the past month behind her?

Forget the past month. How about the past three years?

Yes, that's what she meant to do. Start over, with honesty as her focus. Oh, how good it felt to face the future in the arms of truth.

Which is why Miranda was tempted to clamp the laptop closed. Why relive the angst?

And yet, lingering questions jabbed at her. Why hadn't Matthew published the article? Certainly she would have heard about it if he had. Was he saving it for future use? And perhaps the biggest question: Why send it to Brad?

Curiosity sent her eyes back to the screen. And despite her better logic, she continued reading. She read as Matthew revealed the truth about her marriage, as he delved into the truth

345

about why she left Brazil—both times—and how she fell into her role on *From the Ground Up*.

How odd to read a story about herself containing more fact than she'd ever revealed in three years of public life. And by a man who'd known her only weeks.

She unfolded her legs, let one dangle over the side of the bed as she read. The candle crackled, its sweet aroma mirroring the feelings wiggling their way through her. Nonsensical feelings. Because she should have been infuriated at the way Matthew spilled her secrets in Times New Roman font. She should have felt betrayed.

But for once, rejection didn't walk its usual path through her emotions. Instead, sour though the truth may be, Matthew's honest portrayal honeyed into her heart. He wrote beautifully, insightfully. He'd *seen* her. All of her. Enough to capture her in vivid words.

Her gaze landed on his closing paragraphs.

If Randi Woodruff is so afraid of showing the viewing public the real woman beneath her fame, I have to ask myself, what else is she afraid of?

Is it fear that holds her back from finishing her own home?

Is it fear that sends her to church only when she's certain she'll find the sanctuary empty?

And is it fear that traps her in the comfort of a fake relationship rather than braving the possibility of true love?

Yes. First she breathed the word, then spoke it out loud. "Yes."

"Yes, what?"

Miranda's gaze swung to the doorway of her bedroom. Blaze. He wore his standard faded jeans and zippered hoodie. The cast covering his left arm was covered in signatures, a duffel bag slung over his shoulder.

"It's that time already?"

"'Fraid so, kiddo. Our wedded bliss is about to meet its demise." He exaggerated a sad face. "I know you'll miss me. If you like, I can snip a lock of hair for you to remember me by."

She tossed a throw pillow at him. "Save your hair. But . . . I will miss you." Yes, she could admit it.

He dropped his bag in the doorway and flopped onto her bed. "Me or my cooking?"

"Both."

"Well, so you know, I packed your freezer with food. You're set for two weeks, at least."

Sunlight poured in from the window, highlighting the tan of his skin, the tiny crinkles at the corners of his eyes. "Why'd you do it, Blaze?"

He cocked his head. "Do what?"

"All this. Spend a month living here, playing house, keeping secrets you had no obligation to keep?"

"You already asked me that, remember? That night at the restaurant."

"Yeah, but instead of answering, you went and set your arm on fire."

His chuckles bounced the mattress until finally he sighed and leveled her with sincerity. "I guess it was because I know what it's like to feel trapped by a secret."

"And yet you helped me keep mine."

He shrugged, his back against her bedroom wall. "When a person goes to such crazy lengths to keep a secret, they can't be far away from having the whole thing blow up. Maybe I just wanted to be around for the explosion." His grin drew her laughter, but gradually quiet settled over the space. "Thing is, now that you've gone and faced your stuff, I'm pretty sure I can't get out of facing mine any longer."

"You're going home? Michigan, right?" Why hadn't she thought to ask him more about his past? His family?

He nodded with a long sigh. "Yup. I can already hear the hometown gossip chain: Prodigal son returns after disgracing himself in a fake marriage."

Miranda hung her head. "Sorry."

"Hey, you don't need to apologize. I jumped at the chance. Remember? Besides, anything they're saying about me now can't compare to . . ." His voice trailed off.

She felt the urge to pry, but he pointed to her laptop before she could. "What are you working on?"

"Way to change the subject. You get to know my secrets, but I don't get to know yours?"

"Not yet. But I'll stay in touch. Deal?"

"Deal. And I wasn't working. Actually, I was reading Matthew's article."

Blaze's eyebrows popped up. "No way. Dude, I thought he hadn't published anything since the gala."

"He hasn't. I, uh, don't think he's going to."

"May I?" He reached for the laptop. Minutes later, he whistled. "Wow."

"I know. He's a good writer."

Blaze's eyes danced over his crooked grin. "Not what I was wowing, Rand."

She rose from the bed. "C'mon. Let's get you to the airport."

"Now who's changing the subject?" Blaze closed the laptop. "He pegged you, honey."

She stilled. "I know."

"And that is one doozy of an article."

She knew that, too.

"Now that you've read it, what're you going to do?"

That, she didn't know. Except . . .

An idea took root. "Blaze, what would it mean for you

if this article was published? I know what it'd mean for me, but—"

He stood. "Hey, don't worry about me. If the worst people ever say about me is I spent a month pretending to be Randi Woodruff's husband, I think I'll be all right."

She bit her lip. There was the crew to consider. The offer from the network. Even the people at the Giving Heart Foundation. How would they look if she did what she was considering?

But maybe the better question to ask was, what might the future look like if she did?

Chapter 22

"Can't believe it, Matthew. You actually accepted it." Jase whistled. "She's a beauty."

A cold wind hit Matthew's face as he lifted the helmet from his head and propped it under his arm. The motorcycle still shined—clean leather, gleaming chrome. It smelled of polish and memories.

"Not gonna lie, it felt like a kick in the gut to call Dad and tell him I'd changed my mind."

Jase bent to run a hand along the side fairing. When he straightened, he turned a quizzical eye on Matthew. "What made you do it? And more importantly, can I take it for a spin?"

"'Course you can." Matthew thrust the helmet toward Jase. "But you have to be careful. I'm not keeping it. Only reason I accepted it is so I could sell it."

Jase scrunched his brow. "Really? Is that fair to Dad?"

"He knows my plan, didn't argue. I think maybe he sees it as his way of helping, too."

"Helping . . . ?" Jase shook his head as Matthew's meaning dawned on him. "Uh-uh. No way."

"Yes way. This bike is worth over ten thousand dollars. The insurance company is going to make you pay, what, thirty thousand before they'll cover the rest of Cee's surgery? This gets us a third of the way there."

"You're amazing for offering, bro, but I don't think I can accept it."

"Fine, then I'll give it to Cee. She's not too proud to take it."

Overhead clouds paled the sky. Bare trees leaned in the wind. Matthew tapped the seat of the bike. "So, you want to take a ride before I head over to the Ducati dealer?"

"First things first." Jase threw an arm around Matthew, slapping his back in a brotherly hug. "You know I had to at least try to argue."

"Of course."

The rap of a screen door smacking shut in the wind sounded from the house. Matthew turned. "You are not letting my husband ride that bike!" Izzy called from the doorway.

But when Matthew glanced at Jase, his brother had already pulled the helmet on. "Sorry, honey, can't hear you," his muffled voice called back. He slung one leg over the bike, then leaned in. "Hey, try to talk Izzy down before I get back, all right? She's giving me a death glare from the porch."

Matthew chuckled as Jase motored off, then headed for the house. "Don't worry, Iz, he's going like forty-five miles an hour."

She clucked her tongue. "Yeah, but you're putting ideas in his head." She sighed. "Come on in. I made brownies. You can tell me how the job search is going, what your plans are."

"I don't have much of a plan yet." He stepped into the house, but before the door closed behind him, the sound of another engine drew a backward glance.

"Who's that?" Izzy said, looking past Matthew. "I don't recognize the car."

Red convertible. Who . . . ? Matthew inhaled sharply as he recognized the figure behind the steering wheel. "Blaze."

"What?"

"No, who."

Blake Hunziker stepped out of the car, shaggy hair sticking

out from under his stocking cap. Blaze lifted one palm as he made for the house, but any friendliness was hidden beneath pressed lips and narrowed eyes.

"Oh my," Izzy said from behind. "I recognize him from the photos on your blog. That's Randi Woodruff's husband . . . pretend husband."

Matthew met Blaze at the top of the porch steps. "Hey, Hunziker. What are you doing here?"

Blaze jabbed a finger at his own chest. "I'll ask the questions, dude."

"Ooo-kay." Blaze angry? This was a first. And it could get . . . interesting.

"And I'll start with this: What is your problem?"

"Excuse me?"

A hand, Izzy's, shot out from behind Matthew. "Hi, I'm Isabelle, Matthew's sister-in-law."

Blaze shook her hand, but his eyes never strayed from Matthew's face. Matthew slid Izzy a glance. She gave a befuddled shrug. "Uh. Obviously you two need to talk, sooo . . ." She let the door close behind her, but then popped her head back out. "Come in for brownies whenever you work out whatever it is you need to work out."

When the door creaked closed, Matthew faced Blaze again. "Shall we try again? What brings you to Minnesota? Did you drive all the way here?"

"Yes, because I couldn't even make it to my flight from North Carolina—your media kin mobbed me. Now tell me, have you been living under a rock or are you just plain stupid? Man, she poured out her heart for you!"

"Miranda?"

"Of course Miranda. And you guys thought I was the dense one. Have you looked at your blog?"

"Why would I? I haven't posted anything new."

Blaze shook his head. "That explains it, I guess. Because if you'd read it and not done anything—"

"Read what?" Matthew spurted, exasperation pummeling his words.

"She let them publish it, man. Your article about her. Not just *let* them, she *asked* them to. They posted it on the blog like a week back, along with an introduction by Rand herself. I called her from the road a couple days ago, and when she told me she hadn't heard from you, I decided to come up here and knock some sense into you."

Matthew couldn't keep up. He was still back on Blaze's first headline: *Today* had published his article? Because . . .

Miranda asked them to. Why would she do it? He'd written it in a weary flurry of irritation and disappointment, outed every secret she worked so hard to protect.

"Blaze, I . . ."

Blaze jerked a thumb behind him. "Get in the car."

"What?"

"I'm taking you to the airport, and you're going to man up and tell that woman—"

Matthew broke into laughter. Unadulterated, bordering on giddy. *Miranda Woodruff, you are something else.* And Blaze . . . "Whoa, buddy, ease up. Give me a chance to digest this. I need to read that article."

"And then you'll do something? You swear? I didn't drive all this way for nothing?"

"Wait a second . . . You drove all this way when you could have just called?"

Blaze rubbed his face. "Yah, well, maybe I was looking for an excuse to put off getting home . . . and I've never been to Minnesota—another checkmark on my bucket list."

They stood awkwardly for a moment, and then Blaze repeated, "So, promise me you'll do something about Randi?"

The breeze set Izzy's wind chimes jingling. From down the street, Matthew heard the rumble of the motorcycle. "Yes. I'll do something."

Blaze backed up. "All right, then. Well, I'll be seeing ya."

"Wait a sec, you come all this way, find me at my brother's house, and . . . Wait a minute, how *did* you find me *here*?"

Blaze hopped down the porch steps. "You can find anything on the Internet."

"But how did you know . . . ? Oh, never mind. Seriously, though, you drive this far out of your way and talk to me for five minutes, and now you're just going to take off?"

"Well, originally I planned to throw a punch, so consider yourself lucky. Hey, I got places to be, man. So, yeah, I'm taking off."

Matthew followed him to his car. "Where to?"

Blaze pulled his car door open. "Home. I've got my own manning up to do."

There was mystery there. But it wasn't enough to pull Matthew's focus. He had an online article to read. A motorcycle to sell. A decision to make.

A plane ticket to buy?

"Oh, one more thing." Blaze turned back to Matthew, leaving his door ajar. "Almost forgot." He bounded back to the porch and held out an envelope. "For you."

"What's this?"

"You talked all the time about your niece. Rand told me about the surgery she needs." He shrugged. "And I don't feel right about keeping the money I got paid to play Randi's housemate. Sooo . . ."

"Blaze—"

"I could still throw that punch, man, so don't argue."

Matthew stared at the envelope. So much emotion . . . all of it good. He clapped one hand on Blaze's shoulder and pulled him into a hug. "You're a good man, Blaze."

Blaze leaned back, smirked. "I know." He was halfway back to his car before he turned one last time. "Make sure to tell Rand her fake guy gives her real one his blessing."

A November chill whipped through Miranda's hair as she balanced on a beam twelve feet in the air. One hand gripped an overhead slanted plank of her would-be ceiling, the other rested on her waist. In the distance, the Smokies rose and fell in rolls of brown and green, a ready bed for the eventual white of winter. Soon.

Which was why she should get to work instead of perching like an eagle atop what would've been the roof of the unfinished half of her house. She took a breath—inhaling pine and cold, exhaling pure pleasure. A bird screeched as it cascaded by, and Miranda could almost taste its freedom. One more deep breath . . . and then she tapped the plank above and lowered to her knees, then her backside, legs dangling over the side of the beam.

"You must have really liked playing on monkey bars when you were a kid."

Miranda's gaze dove down at the sound of the voice, hand gripping her wooden seat. *Oh. Ohhh.* "W-what are you . . ."

"Doing here?" Matthew Knox tipped his head all the way back to look at her. "Ah, well, I came to talk. Was sort of hoping that could happen on the ground, though."

She scooted to where she'd propped a ladder against the finished wall. Seconds later, her feet touched the ground. It shouldn't be so hard to look at him, but it took every speck of resolve in her to meet Matthew's hazel eyes. They danced with flecks of color, like always. And like always, his grin sent butterflies ramming into the sides of her stomach. Her heart did the flip-flopping thing, too. As for the air in her lungs . . .

Wow, love did violent things to one's internal organs.

Wait, love? After only a month?

He took a step closer.

Oh yeah.

"Hi," he finally said.

"Hi." A whisper. And then, "Hi. Um, so, really, what are you doing here?"

He looked good. Hair trimmed, perfect five-o'clock shadow on his cheeks and chin, as usual, and a dark fleece zip-up. Oh great, and she was wearing an old flannel shirt and her holey-est jeans. Lovely.

"Like I said, I hoped we could talk."

"All right." His eyes scanned their surroundings. Was he looking for Blaze? Robbie? "I've got my place back to myself," she offered.

His gaze returned to her. "How's it feel?"

"Strangely quiet."

He moved away, took a few steps around the open-air room, like a surveyor assessing the property. "Decided to get to work on the master suite?"

She stuffed her hands in her back pockets. "Yes and no. I'm actually tearing it out."

That froze him in place. "Say again?"

She shrugged, running a hand along a stud she'd pull down before the day was over. "I realized I like the house just the way it is. It really doesn't need . . . more. And if I do ever decide to add on, I think I'd like to start fresh, with a new floor plan."

His eyes lit up as if she'd handed him a Pulitzer. "But what will you do about the foundation? It's cement."

"You ever used a jackhammer, Knox?" She flashed a sly grin.

"You and your power tools."

Silence draped over them like a canopy. At once, both weighty and light. She'd told herself she wouldn't see Matthew again. That it was best that way. That she'd done what she could to set things right, and that was enough.

Yet the curiosity had refused to stay buried. Did he know she'd called the magazine? Had he read the blog? She gulped. The whole blog?

"I can't stand it anymore. Please tell me what you're doing here." The words burst from her, impatient puffs of white air erupting from her lips.

Another step closer, his voice low and husky. "It's come to my attention, Ms. Woodruff, that you're not actually married. See, I read this blog . . ."

Her heart lurched.

"Actually, I printed it out." He pulled a folded paper from his back pocket and cleared his throat. "This part in italics is a note from Randi Woodruff herself. And I quote . . ."

But he didn't have to read it out loud for her to know what it said. She'd labored over those few short sentences for hours, truth and emotion spilled like twin waterfalls, before sending the article to Greg Dooley.

A girl can learn a lot from a reporter like Matthew Knox: how to ask all the right questions, for instance. How to be a true friend. Even, yes, how to dance. But most of all, she can learn that truth paves the way for love.

"'And it's because I love you,'" Matthew finished, "'my viewers, as well as my crew, my show, and quite possibly a certain reporter, that I've asked *Today* to publish this final article. It's written by Matthew Knox. And it's the truth.'"

Did he see the unstoppable blush taking over her face when his eyes connected with hers? Did he know she'd meant every single word? Should she tell him Lincoln Nash had gone ballistic? That suddenly it looked as if the network was ready to release her from her contract, the chances of a fourth season less likely than ever?

And that she was honestly okay with it?

"You got one thing wrong, Miranda."

She bit her lip. Hadn't expected that.

"You're not just a girl. Nor are you just a tomboy or a television star or a promising dance student—"

"Only promising?"

He touched his finger to her lips. "We'll get back to that. You, Miranda Woodruff, are a beautiful woman. And one I'd very much like to kiss right now."

And then he did. And it was . . . "Perfect," she murmured.

He tipped his head back. "Perfect, huh? Good to know. 'Cause I did come a long way."

"Oh, don't look so smug." She entwined her arms around his waist. "So, other than reading my own words to me and, ahem, kissing me, why else are you here? What next?"

Matthew took her hand and moved beside her. They stood in front of her home, sunbeams showering through the frame of her addition, washing the foundation, the yard, Miranda and Matthew, in glorious light.

"Well," he said, gaze hope-filled and heart melting, "I was thinking you could teach me about building a house. Or maybe in this case, tearing one down."

Her laughter swooped over the yard, through the trees, into the mountains. She squeezed Matthew's hand, leaned into his shoulder. "Pretty sure I can do that."

Acknowledgments

I so desperately want to write something witty and wonderful here. After all, I've spent years dreaming of writing this Acknowledgments page. But all I seem to be capable of are tears and gushing. At least I'm the only one who has to put up with the tears as I write this. As for the gushing, well, my apologies, but here goes. . . .

Love and hugs and all kinds of thanks to:

Mom and Dad—I am so over-the-top blessed to be your daughter. Thank you for always encouraging me, always loving me, always praying for me. I love you so much.

My too-cool siblings, Amy, Nathanael, and Nicole (plus two fun brothers-in-law, Chip and Caleb)—You guys make life fun. And I have a feeling antics from our childhood will make it into many a future story. Love ya.

Grandma and Grandpa—Thank you for encouraging me in so many ways, from reading those hilarious pioneer/orphan stories I wrote as a kid to buying and loaning me books to sending letters to praying for me to . . . the list could go on forever. I love you lots.

Susan May Warren—I don't have words to express how thankful I am for your teaching, support, inspiration, and friendship. I will never stop thanking God for getting me to that first MBT retreat. Life. Changing. You've taught me not just how to craft a good story, but how to live a good story—in a gracious, God-honoring, and fun-loving way—as I walk the writing journey.

Rachel Hauck—One word: JOY! Thanks for showing me oh-so-often what that looks like. And for teaching that symbolism class at the 2010 ACFW Conference that changed my writing.

The My Book Therapy team—Lisa Jordan, Beth Vogt, Alena Tauriainen, Reba Hoffman, Edie Melson, Michelle Lim, Susie, and Rachel. How I admire and love each of you! I'll never forget you praying for me at our South Carolina retreat right after I hit Send.

Lindsay Harrel—Oh, my critique partner and kindred spirit, you've become one of the greatest blessings of this writing journey. Thank you for your constant encouragement and prayers for both my writing and, well, pretty much everything!

My agent, Amanda Luedeke—You are the rock star of agents and a ton of fun. Thank you for your sound advice, savvy career guidance, and friendship. And for not thinking I was crazy for talking about Dr. Quinn the first time we chatted.

My editor, Raela Schoenherr—I kind of want to call you my fairy godmother, except you're too young for that, and

I've never seen you with a wand! Thank you for taking a chance on a newbie and her story. I'm so, so grateful. It's a blast working with you.

The Bethany House Team—Getting to be a part of your "family" is such a dream-come-true. Karen Schurrer, your editing expertise is beyond awesome, and I'm so thankful. To Paul and Dan, thank you for making my very first cover so pretty. To everyone on the sales and marketing teams, I want to give you a great big hug.

The MBT Ponderers—Oh, ladies, I love our community of writers. Thank you for the never-ending stream of inspiration and all the prayers.

And thank you to so many people who have prayed for and encouraged me along the writing journey: like my wonderfully fun and food-loving extended family; the best girlfriends a girl could ask for—Laura, Mel, Maggie, and Ruby; lovely online friends (special shout-out to Gabrielle Meyer!); the sweet ladies of the Central Iowa Christian Writers Group; my local cohorts in fiction—Elizabeth, Heidi, and Sue; Mike and Barb Redig, aka the most amazing youth leaders ever; my oh-so-fun co-workers previously at the *Sioux Center News* and now at Hope Ministries; and my mom's many prayer-warrior friends, including Kim Lee and Deb Thompson, who have sent me such sweet notes of encouragement through the years.

Also, thanks a bunch to that one guy at the hardware store (research!) who didn't laugh at me when I told him I was lost.

Lastly and most importantly, to the ultimate Storyteller. My identity is found in you, Lord. Thank you for reminding me of that over . . . and over . . . and over as you helped me with this book.

Discussion Questions

1. Miranda Woodruff defines herself by her career success. When Matthew Knox looks at himself, all he sees are his past mistakes. Do you identify with either character? Do you find it easy to define yourself by your successes or failures? What do both Miranda and Matthew learn about who they are?

2. Miranda is a celebrity who has attempted to closely guard her private life . . . until she's in danger of losing her show. Now her personal life is on display for all to see. Discuss our culture's fascination with celebrities. Why do you think we're so interested in their lives?

3. When Matthew first agrees to write the serial blog about Miranda, he assumes she's just another celebrity. But the more he gets to know her, the more he sees the woman behind the fame—her hurts, her heart, her compassion. Has your first impression of someone ever been wrong? What changed once you got to know the heart of the person?

4. Miranda finds herself opening up to Matthew like she's never opened up to others. They find an unexpected

friendship in shared vulnerability. Is there a friend in your life who draws you out in ways others don't? Describe your friendship.

5. Miranda spends her free time volunteering at a local shelter for children and helping a family in need. Matthew is determined to help fund his niece's much-needed surgery. What special cause or need is close to your heart?

6. In chapter 11, Matthew asks Miranda why she kept up the charade of her marriage. Why didn't she come out with the truth long ago? Miranda blurts out, "Because I wanted to, all right?" What truth is she facing in that moment? How do you think admitting that out loud affected her? How about Matthew?

7. Also in chapter 11, Miranda reads Psalm 138:8: "The Lord will fulfill his purpose for me; your love, O Lord, endures forever—do not abandon the works of your hands." Have you ever felt abandoned? How have you seen God fulfill His purpose for you?

8. When Matthew learns the truth about Miranda's marriage, he agrees to keep the secret for the time being. Was that the right move? Should he have spilled the truth right away in his blog?

9. In chapter 12, Matthew and Jase talk about the closing of Jase's gallery. Matthew realizes that while his brother let go of one dream, he found a new one. Have you ever had to let go of a dream? Describe that process. Have you found a new dream?

10. When Miranda is on stage at the Giving Heart Awards, her intention was to finally tell the truth about her "marriage" and admit her feelings for Matthew. But, of

course, that doesn't go as planned. What do you think would have happened if it had gone as planned?

11. At the end of *Made to Last*, Miranda learns the network may be willing to give her another shot with a fourth season. But then she risks that chance by allowing Matthew's article to be published. What do you think that sacrifice meant to her? Was it the right move? Could she have tried to save her show and reconnect with Matthew?

12. Although he's one of the goofier characters in the story, it's clear Blake "Blaze" Hunziker has a past of his own. At the end of *Made to Last*, we learn he's now heading home. What do you think is waiting for him there? Have you ever had to face something hard in your past?

Melissa Tagg is a former reporter and total Iowa girl. In addition to her homeless-ministry day job, she is also the marketing/events coordinator for My Book Therapy, a craft-and-coaching community for writers. When she's not writing, she can be found hanging out with the coolest family ever, watching old movies, and daydreaming about her next book. She's passionate about humor, grace, and happy endings. Melissa blogs regularly and loves connecting with readers at www.melissatagg.com.

Looking for Your Next Romantic Read?

Try the Novels of Bestselling Author Becky Wade!

To learn more about Becky and her books, visit beckywade.com.

Meg has never wanted to be known as a "Cole." In the past, the name has brought her nothing but heartache. But when her father dies unexpectedly, she's forced to return home to Texas—and to Whispering Creek Ranch—to take up the reins of his empire. Can the handsome manager of her father's Thoroughbred farm help Meg face her fears and embrace new hopes for the future?

Undeniably Yours

Burned out on work and worn down by dating relationships, Kate Donovan is only too happy to take a break from it all to help restore her grandmother's childhood home. But when Kate encounters the wounded former hockey star hired to do the renovations, she discovers her heart may have other plans....

My Stubborn Heart

BETHANYHOUSE

Stay up-to-date on your favorite books and authors with our *free* e-newsletters. Sign up today at bethanyhouse.com.

Find us on Facebook. facebook.com/bethanyhousepublishers

Free exclusive resources for your book group! bethanyhouse.com/anopenbook